Necromancer's Sorrow

David F. Balog

Books by David F. Balog:

Necromancer's Lament
Necromancer's Sorrow

OWL TALYN PRESS
First published in the United States by Owl Talyn Press in
the United States
www.owltalynpress.com

Copyright © 2023 by Owl Talyn Press
ISBN 979-8-218-24379-1

All rights reserved. No part of this book may be reproduced
in any form on or by electronic means, including
information storage and retrieval systems and artificial
intelligence, without permission in writing from the
publisher, except by a reviewer who may quote brief
passages in a review.

First paperback edition August 2023

Book design by Jasmina Coric
Cover art by Judas Iscariot

To my wife Tammy, who traversed the Greylands and crossed the Bone Gate to stand boldly before the Dark Lady. I will meet you in the Living Library again.

Table of Contents

Incomprehensible

I see your pain.
every emotional, physical, mental,
and psychic wound,
whenever I gaze into your eyes.
I admire your tenacity—
your smile is not a mask,
your joy not a shield—
the scars only visible to me.

Have you enchanted me?
It must be artifice,
for it has created something new.
These feelings are unfamiliar,
untried, unexpected,
unintentionally painful.
Joy blends with sorrow
and I am enthralled.

While my magic is of
flesh and bone,
yours if of the spirit,
beyond my comprehension.
These dusty tomes
provide no resolutions,
only questions unanswered
and unanswerable.

Chapter 1: Homecoming

It was one week after the deaths of Tsukatta and Ial'rafiost at the hands of Cratillus when Glitter and I arrived at her home, hidden in a forest of willow. As I was more accustomed to handling corpses, we went to her tower first so I could assist her in dealing with the body of her mentor, Goldfire, who was attacked only days after my Mistress and I were by wizards working for Cratillus. We rode in relative quiet, as we were both processing our stockpiling losses. I was expecting this to be a traumatizing event for her, so I did not push her to conversation. Neither of us, however, was prepared for her reception.

Goldfire's tower could not be seen at all from outside the circle of three-foot tall mushrooms of various colors, which acted as the border to her property. It was not that her tower was obscured by their size, but a haze of spores emitted by the fungi cloaked it. We dismounted and walked slowly through the gap in the circle, where we were greeted by a dozen faeries of various kinds; some flew up to us on butterfly or dragonfly wings, while others ran or hopped. Normally, a visitor would need to ask permission to enter the grounds of a wizard to avoid the home's guardians, but as I was traveling with the mistress of the house, I was presumed to be innocuous unless Glitter changed her mind about my safety.

Shouts of "Welcome back!" and "Glitter's home!" cascaded over us, while some of the fey eyed me with suspicion. One, a female sporting a dress which looked like a bluebell flower zipped through the air on dragonfly wings towards the house. Now that we were inside the mushroom ring, I could see the two-story structure clearly. It looked haphazardly built, with sections of the second floor hanging precariously over the roof's edge. The whole structure was in something of a crescent shape. Any non-magical engineer would pull his hair out from the impossibility of its imbalance. As we circled through the hedgerows, the house appeared to take on the shape of a kneeling unicorn, then shifted back into its oddly shaped components as we neared the front door, which burst open before a glowing woman ran straight toward us.

"Glitter!" shouted Goldfire, as she raced out to her stunned apprentice. "I thought to never see you again!" she exclaimed, taking her charge in a swinging hug and kissing her on the forehead. "I can't believe you are alive!"

"Nor I you," Glitter managed to push out through a wall of tears. "How?" She hugged back, all her pent-up emotions pouring out in waves of laughter and crying.

I stood by, awkward and silent, so as not to interrupt their reunion.

"Beus and Faldrein got your messages about the attack and teleported here right away. Apparently, my aura kept me at death's door and prevented me from crossing over into the Dark Lady's realm." She pulled Glitter in for another air-expelling hug. "I'm so happy to see you!" In a whisper, which I suppose I was not meant to hear, she added, "Why is *he* here?"

"We have settled our differences and become…friends," Glitter answered with hesitation. "There is much to tell you."

I followed the reunited pair back toward their house, the fey creatures around me gossiping about whether or not Glitter and I were merely friends or if we were closer than she let on. One was a round-faced male with curled horns and the lower body of a light grey cat with a series of black spots, who stood up to my knee. He tugged on my robes and asked with a smile of hope, "Are the two of you to wed?"

"We," I hesitated, "are not at that stage in a relationship. As she said, we are but friends." The half-feline frowned and looked as though he was about to cry. "Should she choose to overlook my faults," *which she has pointed out on numerous occasions*, "I would be honored to be her companion," I added in the hope that it would mollify the creature's disappointment. He thought upon it for a moment, and a smile appeared on his face as he turned to another fey, which was more hummingbird than humanoid, and raised his hands in triumph.

The assembled creatures broke out in applause and whistles around me as my fellow wizards ambled further away. Glitter looked back to see what the ruckus was about, and I merely shrugged as I broke free of the gathered fey and increased my pace to catch up to the ladies.

"I wouldn't spend too much time with them if I were you," warned Glitter.

"They seem friendly enough."

"They are playful and mischievous, and you have exactly all the wrong personality traits to deal with them for long." The hurt must have shown on my face as she continued. "You are thoughtful, deliberate, and staid, all traits the fey enjoy abusing. You take yourself far too seriously, and that will only cause you strife with them. As guardians, they rarely cause any actual harm, but a constant string of pranks and insults, enhanced through enchantments and illusions, can drive an intruder to heartbreak and madness.

"I've gotten to know them, and we like each other, but I still keep an emotional distance from them, lest they take advantage of me. So, what was all the celebrating about?"

I think I told them I wished to marry you. "They seemed genuinely pleased that you have a male friend and are interested in your future."

She glared at me. "Please tell me you didn't say we were getting married."

"No!" I responded, perhaps a bit too quick and loud.

Her face turned sour and her sparkles took on a reddish tone.

"Only that I was happy you seem to like me in spite of our past."

The redness faded back toward gold. "I knew the first time I brought a guest home there would be trouble," she groaned. "The fey seem far too interested in my personal life."

"Speaking of personal lives," chimed in Goldfire as we entered the sitting area, "how did the two of you end up together?" There was more than a bit of venom hiding in her question.

Glitter sat down on a large red cube, which unfolded itself into a soft padded chair to support her as she leaned back into it. Goldfire sat on a similar green one, while I chose a blue seat. The room was designed for comfort, with a large fireplace radiating precisely enough heat, small tables next to each chair with a mug of cold strawberry juice and a plate of honey cakes placed on top, and a hanging light, which glowed a soft pale yellow.

"It started when you teleported me to him in the middle of the woods during the fight," Glitter responded.

Mistress Goldfire looked surprised. "You were supposed to go to Vletraka's. I was hoping she would be able to keep you safe."

"Mistress Vletraka had already been dead four days when Glitter appeared before me. I suppose your spell chose her apprentice as the next best location. Who knows what she would have found had she had appeared there."

"You haven't been home yet?" She asked, sadness and pity evident in her tone.

"We had more immediate concerns. Namely, avenging your deaths." Glitter and I then told Mistress Goldfire of our recent adventures, from Flinjirt and his bandits, to the unfortunate second death of Ormak, to the sacrifice of our friends in killing Cratillus. She only ocassionally interrupted to clarify a statement, but otherwise sat silently as we recited our tale.

"I...I can't believe all you two have been through!" she said with awe, her eyes wet. "This is not what we want our apprentices to deal with. Yes, the world is a dangerous place, and things are going to happen, but we all hope for you to have happy lives."

"That has never been an option for me, nor do I think it ever will be," I sighed in resignation. "A quiet life of study and research would be my ideal of happiness, but there has been far too much to do. Once I return to Mistress Vletraka's tower and take care of her remains, I am responsible for the care of her home. In addition, we have pledged to help clear out the infestation of ruklaa and other undead in and around Ehrghex, and Ormak's tower needs to be secured against pillagers."

Glitter nodded in agreement. "I so badly want to stay. I've missed you so much." She leapt up and hugged her mistress. "But since you are here and alive, we need to leave in the morning for Mithron's tower."

I still could not think of it as *my* tower, though I would have to get used to it.

"I will go with you," Goldfire said with a tone which brooked no argument. "I missed you too and had no idea if you were still alive nor how to find you. For some reason, you were blocked from my spells. Additonally, I need to say goodbye to my friend again." Turning to me, she added, "Beus has already taken care of 'Traka's remains, as well as the two other bodies. I wish we could have saved her."

"I never should have left her—" I began.

Goldfire cut me off. "Don't. The safety of our apprentices is paramount. You know this. Against a foe capable of killing 'Traka, you would have hardly stood a chance."

"I know, but that does not lessen my feelings of guilt. After everything, Cratillus still managed to get—the book!" I nearly shouted while leaping out of my chair.

The two women looked at me with confusion until I continued.

"Mistress Vletraka had cast a spell on *In Between* to hide it from scrying, and I renewed the spell regularly after it wore off. It must have shielded Glitter from your attempts to find her."

"*Mimtrezel*! Of course! I considered it but could not think of a reason she would be casting it upon herself. But if she was in the aura of your spell all this time, then it all makes sense." Mistress Goldfire smiled. "That also explains why you never responded to any of our messages."

Glitter turned to me, her sparkles shifting crimson. "You mean I didn't have to spend the past month mourning her death because you had us hidden from her?" she roared.

I held my hands up in surrender. "I was only trying to keep the book out of Cratillus' hands. I did not know it would hide us as well. Besides, we had no idea anyone other than Cratillus was looking for us."

It took a couple of deep breaths before her sparkles settled back to their normal golden hue. "Of course. You're right," she sighed. "Sorry."

"I would have been upset too," I said, hoping Glitter's lessons in empathy were sinking in. "I never knew for certain Mistress Vletraka had died, and she could have easily been searching for me just as Mistress Goldfire was searching for you; I would have been shielding myself from her as well."

After a minute of silence, Mistress Goldfire spoke up. "We should have some dinner, and then you get some rest. We will leave at first light. Glitter, show our guest to his room, unless the two of you—"

"No!" Glitter interrupted in a shout, her sparkles turning to red and orange. "No way!"

Goldfire grinned at her protégé with mischievousness, while I took a moment to figure out what she was alluding to. Once I did, I was both embarrassed by her implication and hurt by Glitter's vehement denial.

Turning to me, Glitter said in a curt tone, "Come on."

I followed her through her house. The layout was not much different from my own, though it was much more decorated, with flourishes and color which my more somber Mistress would never trifle with. I was about to ask her why her home seemed so normal on the inside when compared to its outer appearance, when I realized the external view was likely a complicated illusion.

"And here is your room," she finished, after the brief tour. Her manner was a little off from her normal cheerfulness.

"Are you feeling alright?" I asked with genuine concern. "I do not wish to be an issue between you and your Mistress, or the fey guardians, if that is what is troubling you."

She gave a slight smile. "You're getting more intuitive. I think I liked you better when you were oblivious."

I frowned in incomprehension.

"What I mean is, you always seem to know what embarrasses me." She noticed my rueful expression and continued, "I'm not angry; I wasn't even thinking about the tournament until this moment. I only mean that…it's just…I mean…you're a boy. In my house."

"And the fey were curious to know if we were more than simply traveling companions," I added. "And then there is Mistress Goldfire's insinuation…"

"Exactly. In spite of who you were when we first met, I've grown to like and respect you." She must have noticed my elation as my vision began to lose color and quickly added, "But it doesn't mean I'm ready for more than that. Getting Goldfire back is all the emotional turmoil I can handle right now. Okay?"

"I understand. Truly, I am pleased we have even become friends. I had no real ones growing up in Split Falls and kept mainly to my own pursuits. You are the first one I have ever felt comfortable actually calling 'friend'." At the last word, my vision once again shifted to grey, and it took a few moments to block out the vision of Glitter's mother's murder.

"You're seeing it again, aren't you?" she asked without anger.

"I suppose it shows." I could not look at her until the images faded.

"I've come to know that expression—you're trying to make the vision go away. It happens every time you are happy or sad."

"Or angry, afraid, joyful; any strong emotion triggers it. Were I not 'thoughtful, deliberate, and staid', I would see the visions continuously. At least I have learned enough control that I no longer feel compelled to narrate them. However, it does mean I need to be careful about what and how I feel. I think you may be right. I should avoid spending too much time with your fey. Who knows what I might see?"

"And if you should embarrass one of them, you have made an enemy for life," Glitter warned. "They are practically immortal and they never forget a slight. I made the mistake of picking Azalea over Sundew when they asked me who was prettier shortly after my apprenticeship started. I should have found a more diplomatic answer and not picked one over the other. Sundew still holds a grudge, even after all of my apologies."

I must have learned from our wiser friends, as I did not mention how long it took Glitter to forgive me over the matter of the tournament; assuming she even had. Instead, I merely nodded.

She must have taken that as the end of the conversation, for she turned and said, "I will call when we are ready to eat," before closing the door on her way out.

'How are you faring?' I asked Thessylia over our mental link. The short-eared owl had been my closest companion ever since we soul-bonded early on in my apprenticeship. She did not like to stay indoors for extended periods, so I had left her outside to stretch her wings.

'The roof is not where it appears to be, so I have found purchase in a maple tree. I nearly ate one of the fey thinking it was a mouse. He is not happy with me.'

'You had best be on guard. Glitter warned me they might take such an attack personally.'

'I will hunt outside the circle then.'

'Good fortune.' I sat down on the exceptionally soft bed and took in my surroundings. The room was austere in comparison to the rest of the house, but as a guest room I suppose it should be open to the sensibilities of the temporary resident. As we were expecting to leave early the next morning, there was no sense in unpacking, aside from freshening my clothes and choosing reading material.

Searching through my extra-dimensional satchel, which had far more space within than would appear on the exterior, I found *In Shadow's Embrace* by Tinnetol Omyuf, which discussed survival techniques for the plane of Shadow, as well as containing spells using material from that plane, and other spells which used a combination of light and darkness.

It took a nudge to my shoulder and Glitter nearly shouting in my ear for her to get my attention, so deep was I in my study. Her yellow-green sparkles displayed her frustration as clearly as her sighs. I murmured my apology, which she dismissed with a knowing laugh as the propensity to get lost in a book is common in wizards, and followed her to the kitchen, where a table was set for dinner. I had thought I appreciated her culinary skills when we were travelling together, but when she had access to a full kitchen, she proved her mastery. She had seasoned a loin of pork with salt, black pepper, and rosemary, and roasted it in a sauce of butter and honey. Alongside, she had prepared a skillet of thinly sliced potatoes and onions baked with cheese and fennel, served with freshly picked peas.

"This," I declared around a mouthful of potatoes, "is the best meal I have ever eaten! It is so tender and full of flavor. How," I looked directly at Glitter, "can you be so talented? I know you learned from your mother, and Nari gave me some advice, but to be able to produce such art *and* be a skilled wizard? You are incredible."

Her sparkles turned a deep pink.

"I will never understand why Mistress Vletraka lets…let me in the kitchen." As I spoke, memories of my fallen teacher came to me in a flood, and it took all of my effort to remain silent and not bawl in front of my hosts.

Distracted as I was, I did not notice at first Goldfire's arm around my shoulder, her warm touch soothing my heartbreak.

"I miss her too. We were friends for most of our lives, and it's hard to imagine life without her. Do you have any family to visit? A touch of home might do you well."

"Not anymore, no," I answered flatly in an attempt to disguise the disdain I carried of the thought. "My father cast me out when I chose a career other than blacksmithing. I have but one home now and I fear my memories will overwhelm me. I apologize in advance for anything I might say to anger or embarrass you; I still do not have a firm control of my Gift."

While training in the art of wizardry, the Weave, the force of magic which unites all things, changes the prospective mage, granting what is referred to as the "Wizard's Gift". The Gift is a magical alteration, often with both positive and negative aspects, which tends to reflect the personality of the wizard.

"Oh? And what did the Weave in all of its glorious wisdom," she said, rolling her eyes, "impart on you?"

"I see the darkest parts of another's memories and souls, particularly under the influence of strong emotions. Until recently, I could not stop myself from describing my visions verbally for all to hear. It first manifested at the tournament under the effects of Glitter's emotion-bending spell."

Goldfire stared at me for a few moments, then turned to Glitter, who nodded at her Mistress. "I always wondered why 'Traka chose such a cruel person for an apprentice. It all makes sense now," she mused, looking through me. "I had no idea you were getting your Gift for the first time. My only thought was to protect Glitter from you."

"It took me a while to realize what had happened as well. I finally began to understand after Glitter and I captured the bandit Flinjirt. I saw a vision of his various evil deeds while I was trying not to kill him for laughing about all the murders he had committed. But it was not until after Glitter pushed me into the Shadow plane while we were researching in Ormak's tower that I connected my emotional state to the visions."

Goldfire looked over to her apprentice. "You still need to control these wild outpourings of magic, I see."

"Sometimes they're useful, though," Glitter said. "I had a lightning bolt turn into an electric unicorn and stomp a vulzaam. It was pretty *pa'qui*!"[1]

Goldfire paused, looking as though about to chide Glitter when her face softened. "Actually, that *does* sound *pa'qui*!" she laughed.

I looked on slightly confused. "You mean… you do not alter your spells on purpose? I thought you discovered different techniques to change them."

"Only to the extent of minor changes in color. It's become something of an imperative for me," Glitter added, her sparkles cascading through the spectrum. "Sometimes, I accidentally add a little extra magic to my magic, and strange things happen." She shrugged with a smile.

"That will save me some trouble, then," I said, mentally picturing her in the act of casting spells which I had seen go awry. "I remember you turning your foot once to turn an *aatokytsrukak's* flames purple."

"Yes. For some reason, that procedure only works on fire and light spells. I have yet to change the coloration of any other type. When we have more time, I will have to experiment further."

"Speaking of which," Goldfire yawned, "I think it is time for us to get some sleep. I would like to leave at first light."

Glitter and I nodded our assent, and we all left the sitting area for our respective rooms.

A small globe of light, about the brightness of a candle, rolled along the ceiling directly over my head, allowing me to easily find my way. A hospitable effect, to

____

[1] 'Pa'qui' is a shortened version of the Zylan phrase 'sellae pa quinost', which roughly translates to 'exceptionally well done', and is used colloquially to describe something positive and remarkable.

be sure, but unnecessary for me, as my eyes had adapted to the darkness from my time with Thessylia; I could see in dim light nearly as well as in daylight.

We left shortly after dawn, nibbling on fresh biscuits made with lime and cinnamon, the sharp citrus flavor balancing the earthiness of the spice. Goldfire's summoned steeds were all blond and orange, reflecting her aura. Since she was dividing the spell into manifesting three horses, it only lasted until mid-afternoon, at which point she allowed me to replace them, seeing as we would only need them for a few hours more, and I was not nearly as powerful. Along the way, I cut off a few hazel branches as we rode beneath them, whittling them down to sharp points without the others noticing.

The journey to Mistress'... no, *my* tower, was uneventful; my traveling companions spent the time gossiping and catching each other up on the events of the past month. Mistress Goldfire even had the foresight to pack small tents and heavy blankets, to make the four-day journey more comfortable.

"I learned a few tricks while we were in Ormak's tower. With a little extra preparation, I can cast a spell without moving," Glitter bragged. "Mithron and I discussed it, and we agree the technique is best used on spells of escape, assuming I'm trapped or bound; the modification requires too much energy to perform unnecessarily."

"I've heard of this, but never delved into it," her mentor responded, eyeing her pupil with pride. "From what I understand, there are also ways to cast without speaking the words aloud, and also for altering the size and shape of some spells. I remember reading once about a wizard who turned all of his round spells into squares, solely because he thought they were more orderly. Can you imagine a *srukakbolmos*[2] filling a cube instead of a sphere?" She laughed.

"Actually, that would be more efficient," I added. "It would fill a greater volume, and enemies would not have the corners as safe zones to evade the blast."

The pair stopped laughing and stared at me, as though they had forgotten I was there.

Glitter looked as though she were about to speak, then paused, contemplated, then spoke. "Will you stop being right all the time?" she asked with a controlled smile.

"Sorry." I shrugged. "I agree the appearance would be odd and I am certain it would require a boost of energy to fill up the extra space. Addtionally, a sphere is a more logical shape for the spell, as it bursts out from a center seed, but a cube is more difficult to dodge."

"This is what you had to put up with the entire time?" Goldfire asked.

"Pretty much," Glitter responded with a light laugh. "Uxadul gets that way too. When you grow up as the smartest one in your village, sometimes you feel the need to keep proving it."

I stared at her, holding my tongue from responding to the verbal attack, before I realized that her summation was, mostly, correct. "It was no great challenge to prove my intellectual superiority growing up in my village." I said with faux haughtiness and a chuckle. "When one is the scrawny son of the village blacksmith, one must find a way

---

[2] For those unfamiliar, *srukakbolmos* manifests as an explosion of flames, which burn quickly and fade away in but a few scant seconds, searing everything within its area.

to use whatever strength one can manifest." I stopped to think more before continuing. "Until I met you and the other wizards, I never had any doubts about where I stood in relation to everyone else around me. All of you, however, are as well learned as me, and our Masters even more so, and I think I need to prove to all of you, and myself, that I belong. To prove I am not simply another untrained village boy. It is also nice to know Uxadul and I have something in common. Perhaps I can use that to help repair our relationship."

"I think you have already proven yourself," Mistress Goldfire smiled. "You two have accomplished more in the past few months than most wizards do in their entire careers. I'm not saying you have to stifle your opinions, but it would serve you better to find a different way of saying them."

"Glitter has been very patient in her tutelage in that regard. The habit, however, is deeply ingrained, and I will have to continue to be diligent."

"You *will* have to be," stressed Goldfire with a note of caution. "Once your house is in order, we will have to hold a wake for 'Traka. Everyone should be invited."

I groaned quietly as I realized how much cleaning would have to be done. A moon's worth of dust will have covered everything, the food stores probably rotted, and all the crawling guardians were likely destroyed by Larzed, as I recalled seeing numerous skeletal hands broken and charred near Mistress Vletraka when I found her a few steps away from the Dark Lady's gate.

At least with winter fast approaching, there would not be any weeds in the garden, though I was late for some of the planting. With luck, some of the vegetables had seeded themselves, and the root vegetables—carrots, onions, kohlrabi, and rutabagas—had not yet gone rancid. The cabbages and cauliflower, I would soon learn, were in decent shape; it takes a lot to really damage a cauliflower, but I was going to have to hurry to get anything in the ground for early spring and hoped we could avoid a deep freeze for the next month to give the plants time to establish themselves.

As we turned onto the side path which led directly to my home, I began to feel the same excitement and trepidation as when I first arrived here with Mistress Vletraka. As with the first time, I was afraid of the unknown future which lay before me. The sense of dread built until my vision darkened, and I had to stop my conjured horse to compose myself.

"Are you alright?" asked Mistress Goldfire as if from a distance, her words drowned out by the sound of my pounding heart.

"Give him a moment," I scarcely heard Glitter say, "he's steeling himself. I was scared to return home too."

Glitter's words and empathy gave me the strength to shake off my panic. "Thank you," I mumbled weakly, the fear still palpable, but no longer overwhelming. "I do not know where I would be without you." As we approached the open gate, I remembered the first time I saw my new abode.

"Welcome to your new home!" Mistress Vletraka beamed, her arms spread open with pride. A small house with an attached outbuilding sat in the center of a clearing marked by a ring of trees grown so closely together they appeared to be a solid wall with but a single path breaking the circle. The trees on either side of the path were marked with what appeared to be the image of an open book carved into the bark, the same image as on the brows of the summoned horses we rode upon.

"Nervous?" she asked. "You are very quiet."

"I mean no disrespect," a phrase I often used with father, "and I remember you said things are not always as depicted in stories, but I expected a wizard's tower to be, well, a tower."

Mistress Vletraka laughed. "I understand your confusion. All wizards' dwellings are referred to as a 'tower', even if that is not what the actual building is. It's more tradition than anything. I hope you are not too disappointed, but actual towers went out of style a century ago, and they are rather expensive to build."

I nodded in understanding. "I am not disappointed, just getting used to having my preconceptions shattered."

"There will be much more of that to come, I'm sure. In fact, that's pretty much the definition of magic. Much of reality is hidden to those who haven't learned to see it, and those who know how to adjust the threads can alter the fabric of the world. It will take a great deal of hard work and study, so don't expect to be casting spells any time soon either."

"That I had expected. I spent my life up until now training to be a blacksmith without ever gaining any mastery of the art. A life of study? That, I believe, I am suited for."

From the gateway, the tower, pond, and general landscape looked exactly as I remembered it, but even a cursory glance over my shoulder proved that first impression to be a lie. Normally, a skitter of bony claws lined each of the trees forming the gate, appearing as large thorns until they moved to attack trespassers. They, and all the other crawling guardians, were gone, no longer rustling through the tall grass, nor mimicking spiky protrusions on trees and the house, nor stacked up like a gothic sculpture until it came time to act. It never occurred to me until now how much they were in the background, ever present, ever ready to defend our home. After my initial shock, I had come to accept them as part of the scenery, and their disappearance was a foreshadowing of what was to come when I entered the house.

Mistress Vletraka's… no, *my* tower was not in as bad a shape as I expected; it was worse. Two of the windows had been shattered, the glass blown out into the flowerbeds, likely, I thought, as a result of my Mistress' final spell. Scorch marks were visible on the windowpanes, and I guessed on the roof as well from my duel with Wosken. With the windows gone, I fretted over what may have flown or crawled inside, not to mention the damage from the rain and wind.

I am not certain how long I stood with my hand on the latch before finally opening the door. My companions stood quietly, understanding my turmoil. Even if my Gift was not complicating the matter, my fear would have been as emphatically crushing, and I made a point to avoid looking at them until I regained control. The murder-suicide of Glitter's parents was always in my thoughts, and I had no interest in learning Mistress Goldfire's darkest memories.

The first thing I noticed upon stepping into the den was the circle of destruction and decay in the center of the room. The rugs were worn and moldy, the furniture tattered, torn, and collapsed, as though neglected for centuries. Even the floorboards and ceiling had rotted away; all within a perfect sphere, as the chestnut beams in the ceiling demonstrated by the curved line between healthy and deteriorated. Hand-shaped piles of dust were visible where they had not been swept away from when Beus and Faldrein had come to remove the bodies.

"They must have had a difficult time of it," I muttered aloud.

"What?" asked Glitter, not catching my words.

"Beus and Faldrein. It must have been problematic for them to remove the bodies, considering the state everything is in. Mistress Vletraka had alluded to having contingencies in place guaranteeing that, if killed, she would not die alone. By all appearances, she caused everything nearby to age rapidly. She and Larzed were probably not much more than dust." A smile cracked through my forced calm; my Mistress never failed to impress and amaze me. "I'll have to repair all this damage before someone falls through the floor or the roof collapses on them." There was not much space between the floor and the ground below, but it would certainly be enough to turn an ankle should anyone step through the floorboards.

"I would offer some food and refreshments, but I do not know if there is still anything viable in the pantry. Obviously, there is no place to sit here. Please, follow me." I led my companions to the kitchen, where at least there was a table and four wooden chairs.

The frost pantry, which was enchanted to stay forever cold, but not quite freezing, and the ice chest, which did keep a temperature below freezing, held a few items which had not gone bad after over a month of neglect. There remained half a small wheel of cheese with but a few spots of mold which could be easily cut away, and a pair of lemons that, though aged, were still edible. The ice chest had a few pounds of beef and two small leather sacks, one with blueberries from Nari, and one of huckleberries from our three trees near the pond. All had a layer of rime but would still be fine once thawed. The dry goods cupboard contained a small sack of oats, some wheat flour, and a number of glass jars filled with pickled items, mostly vegetables and two jars of boiled eggs, and some jam and honey.

I offered my guests the cheese and frozen berries with apologies as I sat with a groan. "I should have stocked supplies for the winter by now. The villages likely have little left to sell at this point, and I am late for winter planting."

"We shall all go in the morning and see what is available. There might be more in Dureltown, but that is a few more days travel, which we don't have time for," said Mistress Goldfire. "Don't worry. We'll help get everything settled."

Thessylia asserted her dominance over a pair of ducks, three finches, and a family of raccoons, all of which had taken up residence within the tower, during the night, which manifested as dreams of hunting and a sense of power for me but interfered with my guests' sleep. When I awoke, I felt energized, and enthusiastically opened my spellbook. I focused my efforts on preparing the spells *bojumak*, to effect repairs, and *mimzelhruk*, to assist with the cleaning. While the elemental entity created by the *mimzelhruk* worked as well as always, the overall damage was far too extensive to be fixed through such simple magicks as *bojumak*, but at least it was enough to restore the windows. I had hoped to have my work done before the ladies awoke, but at some point Glitter snuck into the kitchen and was cooking some of the oats and opening a jar of blackberry jam.

"Did I see pickled eggs in your pantry?" she asked with a disgusted look when the three of us sat down to break our fast.

I smiled. "I felt the same way at first, but they are actually rather good. I am hoping I can get a few more jars from Gayde when we get to Bluestone."

"'Traka offered them to me every time I stopped by," chuckled Goldfire, "but I never had the nerve to try one. When you open a new jar, maybe I'll finally have one in her memory."

"They are an acquired taste," I warned, "so do not give up after only a few bites."

Glitter responded by pushing out her lower lip with her tongue, repulsed at the thought.

After we dined on Glitter's not-burnt oatmeal, the smell of which brought my appetite back and was a sharp contrast to my cooking, we traveled via summoned steeds to Applebrook, the nearest of the local villages.

Foodstuffs were in short supply, but we were able to gather enough to last a while and then found more in the other villages. Gayde only had two jars of eggs left but had plenty of pickled vegetables to get me through the winter.

It was more challenging to find a carpenter who was willing to travel to my home to fix the floor and ceiling. Even though I had been travelling to these villages for three suns, there were still many who feared wizards reflexively, as, I suppose, they should. Magic is a dangerous tool, and I know all too well how it can be used for harm. It took a promise of more gold than I would normally have parted with, but I needed the repairs done quickly, and perhaps word of my generosity, along with the carpenter and his apprentices returning home safely, would improve future relations. I knew where Vletraka kept her money for such things, and I knew she had more gold hidden away; my best guess was in her room, which I had only entered to clean. Hers was much larger than mine, and I suppose I ought to switch rooms at some point. But for now it was more suited to Mistress Goldfire and Glitter.

Two weeks later, with the repairs completed and my pantry fairly stocked, I sent invitations to the other wizards for Mistress Vletraka's wake.

Chapter 2: Eulogy

In one week, I was to host a wake for Mistress Vletraka. Mistress Goldfire and Glitter were already present, and we awaited the arrival of Mistress Nari and Blythad, Master Beus and Faldrein, and Master Tzali and Uxadul. There was still cleaning to do and preparations to be made before the arrival of our guests, but Glitter and I were able to get some planting done in the garden before the first light snow began, while Goldfire transmuted a fallen tree into a podium and a dozen crude chairs.

"I'm no craftsman." She shrugged, while using a group of *mimzelhruk* to carry the items in from the surrounding forest.

Gavis, the carpenter I had hired, said he should have new furniture crafted by early spring.

The morning of the wake, Goldfire and Glitter banished me from the kitchen while they prepared food for our guests, which gave me time to practice my eulogy. Thessylia waited near the entry gate with six amulets, which would allow visitors safe passage to the tower. I had yet to construct new guardians, though I had a few ideas on what they might be. Nonetheless, proper etiquette must be maintained.

Beus and Faldrein were the first to arrive, which soothed my nerves somewhat, as I feared I would have to be alone with Tzali and Uxadul until others arrived. They looked genuinely pleased to see me and confirmed my suspicions about the state of the bodies; there was very little left intact from either. Beus handed me an urn containing all the dust he could gather from Mistress

Vletraka's remains, correctly surmising that her pile of dust was substantially smaller than that of Larzed.

"I tried to contact her spirit," he apologized, "but there was not enough of her left to make the connection."

Shortly after, Tzali and Uxadul, and a creature about the size and shape of a large dog, which looked as though made of black marble, entered. Tzali fumbled over condolences while Uxadul avoided me entirely.

Nari pulled me into a strong hug when she arrived, tears streaming down her face, while Blythad tried to smile, his eyes wet and red.

"We feared you lost!" Nari whimpered into my ear. "And Glitter is here too?"

"In the kitchen with Mistress Goldfire," I whispered back.

She hugged me tighter. "Thank the gods you're alive." She wept and kissed my cheek. After an additional squeeze, she went to seek Glitter.

Blythad remained silent, awkwardly acting as though to speak, but unable to find the words.

I smiled and nodded. "Go ahead." I exhaled, doing my best to not sound exasperated. I expected him to follow his teacher; instead, he wrapped me up in a hug tighter than Nari's, weeping openly. Not knowing how to react, I gently hugged him back until his sobbing subsided. Only then did he drift off to the kitchen.

I stood alone in the sitting area, unsure of what to do next, when Glitter and Goldfire came out with a variety of snacks on trays: sautéed mushrooms and garlic on toasted bread, cubes of three different cheeses, and thin slices of crisp baked squash topped with honeyed cranberries and a leaf of peppermint. Behind them floated a small cauldron of hot tea, along with nine mugs.

The assembled mourners ate and drank, telling stories of their favorite memories of my deceased Mistress. When she was about my age, she wore makeup to create the illusion that her eyes were sunken and her face gaunt and skeletal to accentuate her necromantic studies; her skin had already been pale from her Gift. She also had a habit of summoning swarms of bats and spiders when endangered, earning the nicknames 'Creepy' and 'Spooky' for a time, until she outgrew them. Though I tried to focus on listening to their stories, I kept replaying that last night with her until Mistress Goldfire nudged me toward the podium.

"Thank you all for coming. I wish this gathering was under better circumstances. Nearly two moons ago, Mistress Vletraka gave her life in this very room to save me and to protect the realm from a great evil. She managed to slay her attacker, but did not survive his onslaught.

"When she brought me into her home, I knew next to nothing about magic, except, like most of you, what I had read or heard in stories. I had no experience, no family history, and soon found myself overwhelmed by my new life. As I could not return home, I had to persevere, but the challenge was exhausting me.

"Vletraka sat down with me and we discussed my difficulties. Understanding the formulae and techniques was not the issue, but rather summoning the strength to power the magic. I was still emotionally conflicted by the circumstances of my apprenticeship and had many doubts as to whether I was suited for wizardry. She insisted I had the talent, and I had to have confidence in myself, to believe her until I could believe in me.

"Never in my life had I been treated like I mattered so much." I stopped to collect myself, as tears welled up and color began to vanish. *I cannot lose control now!* "Mistress

Vletraka regarded me as an individual, not as an extension of herself. She respected me for who I was and did not deride me for who I was not. She helped me to become who I could be, rather than force me into a narrow view of who she wanted me to be. She was my teacher, and I loved her like a second mother." *Deep breaths. Control your feelings.*

"Vletraka was a good, strong, and brilliant woman, a friend to all here, though she may not have spent a great deal of time with the apprentices. Four suns ago, Vletraka rescued me from my family and village, opened my eyes to the world of magic, and introduced me to a new family." I smiled, opening my arms to gesture to all in the room.

"As with all families, issues arise, and feelings are wounded. Vletraka warned me when she first took me on as her apprentice that the Weave changes a wizard, granting a Gift which often is also part curse. At the tournament, my Gift manifested for the first time while dueling with Glitter, triggered by her spell of emotional chaos. My Gift is to see the pain and suffering in the souls of others, whether it arises from painful experience or inherent evil, and, until recently, I could not control the compulsion to relate what I was seeing. My Gift comes to the fore during periods of strong emotion, and it is all I can do right now to calm my anxiety and sorrow so as to not have another episode.

"I deeply and sincerely apologize to all of you for the events of that day. I know many, if not all of you, see me as a cruel and hateful person for my actions nearly three moons ago. You have every reason to feel that way, yet I still ask your forgiveness, as Glitter herself has forgiven me. I hope you all will allow me the opportunity to earn your trust."

Everyone looked over at Glitter, who nodded in assent. In spite of that, Uxadul in particular still looked at me with naked suspicion and loathing, which further complicated the next part.

"Though I had hoped never to do so, as Vletraka's sole apprentice, and with the agreement of our Masters, I would not see my and her home abandoned, and therefore claim it as my own. It will be many years before I reach her level of expertise, and I do not in any way place myself on par with her closest friends, but I will maintain and protect my home, seeking and accepting guidance along the way."

In turn, Nari, Beus, and Goldfire nodded, while Tzali abstained, as I had expected. I had spent time with the others, and they had gotten to know me, but Tzali's only frame of reference was the tournament. Uncomfortable as it was, claiming Vletraka's tower as my own was my right, and doing so with the consent of her peers was appropriate. Nonetheless, it put me in the awkward position of being a Master without mastery.

"I don't believe this," grumbled Uxadul aloud. Then directly to me he said, "I hope you don't expect me to call you 'Master Mithron' just because you have your own tower now; one you don't deserve. Even if you have somehow convinced Glitter to forgive you, it doesn't mean I have to."

"Uxadul," began Tzali with a note of warning.

"Let him speak," I interrupted. "He has valid concerns and a lot of anger." I shifted my gaze to Uxadul. "Please continue."

"Stop trying to act nice and diplomatic. I've seen the real you. You're cruel, arrogant, and spiteful, and I want nothing to do with you. I came to pay my respects to Mistress Vletraka, but I will not stay in *your* home."

"You are correct. I *am* cruel, arrogant, and spiteful; aspects of myself which I am working diligently to correct. Believe me, you are not the first to point out these characteristics." I smiled with some bitterness at Glitter. "No, I do not deserve my own tower, nor did I deserve to have Mistress Vletraka taken from me. If I could bring her back, I certainly would, but I have neither the right nor the power to do so. I miss her terribly." My body tightened to forestall my emotional collapse. Shades began to appear around my guests, and I took a moment to clamp down on my sorrow. "This is a situation none of us should be in, but it has happened, and we all have to deal with it the best we can."

Uxadul responded with a huff, crossing his arms and legs and turning away to face no one.

I sniffed and rubbed my eyes with my sleeve. "I do have one more… actually, two more requests from everyone," I continued, attempting to compose myself. "For those who have not heard, the town of Ehrghex was recently blighted by Cratillus, the master of the wizards who killed Mistress Vletraka and nearly killed Mistress Goldfire. Glitter and I, along with some of our friends, managed to put a stop to him, but Ehrghex was left a town full of ruklaa and other undead abominations. We ask for your assistance in putting the dead to rest.

"Glitter and I also discovered Ormak's tower. He had become a jozalk while searching for a way to rescue his… wife, I assume? I never got a direct answer from him about her, nor was he specific in the diaries we discovered. He is gone now." I paused to gather myself once again. "But his tower is largely undefended against looters. We could use your assistance—and will happily share what we find—in securing his century-and-a-half of collected materials and knowledge."

"The Ormak?" asked Beus, shock evident in his voice. "The writer of *Willow, Ash, and Oak* Ormak? The greatest craftsman of wands in the history of wizardry Ormak?"

"The one and the same," I responded. "He was rather genial, for the most part, but he nearly killed the six of us who discovered his lair. Honestly, I do not know why he did not."

"He was laughing and joking when he came out and attacked us," Glitter added. "I think he was entertained by our audacity and spoke of needing the exercise. He didn't take us seriously, until you killed his familiar."

I tried to ignore the glares from around the room; one simply does not target another wizard's familiar except under life-threatening circumstances. "That was an unexpected result. The spell was designed to harry an opponent; it had never exploded like that before. Sooner or later, Ormak's mood would have changed, and he would have attacked in earnest anyway. Vondro almost froze to death, and Brother Ironknuckle had been nearly crushed when we got to him, and those spells were in effect before I destroyed Jarlisk and was able to come to your aid."

"And why did you attack the familiar instead of Ormak himself?" asked Tzali, clearly upset at my breach in etiquette.

"I had temporarily blinded Ormak, hoping I could free my friends from their predicaments before he regained his sight. He surprised me by being able to see through Brildon's eyes in the same manner in which I can with Thessylia. I only meant to distract Brildon, not destroy him."

"And you managed to overcome Ormak?" queried Nari. "A jozalk is no easy foe. Trouble does seem to find you, doesn't it?" She gazed at me with a degree of sorrow. She was there for me after the first time I was forced to kill in self-defense, back before my Gift manifested and I could feel pain and trauma without digging into the past grief of others; she seemed to have taken a special interest in my emotional well-being. Blythad, her apprentice, had a similar expression, combined with awe. Somehow, I always impressed him whenever I did something I regreted having to do.

"We were trying to save him," answered Glitter, nearly in tears. Where I was upset about Ormak's death because I would never have the opportunity to learn from an ancient master, Glitter was concerned that he was never able to find and rescue the woman he loved, and his extended presence in this world had been one of futility.

"I found a spell which forces an undead creature to return to the state it was in before dying," I continued for her, sensing she would not be able to speak further without crying. "It was far beyond my means to cast alone, but with Glitter and Tsukatta's help," I nearly choked on our fallen priestess's name, "we managed to bring him back to life. Not long after, Grustan, an invading wizard which Ormak turned into a yomki servant, killed the newly mortal Ormak.

"He had been following the careers of his students, and their pupils, down the line, including Mistress Vletraka, but was not yet aware of my existence. In addition, he had compiled, collected, and written volumes, filling a large library which will take months to accurately catalog, not to mention the time to break the numerous wards he placed on his more prized possessions. We did not explore his tower in full, as we were pressed for time, and I am certain there are other guardians still within. We should also discuss what to do with his tower once it is secured. I believe we should not abandon it, but we all already have our own homes, unless one of us is ready to graduate?" I asked of our masters, not knowing how far my fellow students have progressed.

"We can discuss that later," answered Beus. "Though, since Glitter was with you in this endeavor, I believe she should be first in line to choose."

"I like the location," Glitter responded softly, "but the tower would need a lot of work to make it habitable. Besides, I don't think I could live there, not after what happened. I would be constantly reminded of Ormak's suffering. Maybe we could keep it as a communal library, taking turns staying in residence."

"That is something to consider," Beus nodded. "Where is the tower?"

"Northwest of Dureltown, about a two-hour ride on horseback," answered Glitter. "There are no guardians on the grounds, unless we missed some, and we warded the entrance, staircase, and the bookcase leading to a hidden passage, but there is no guarantee they weren't bypassed or set off by now."

"I shall have to ward this place before we leave as well," I added, "as all of our defenses were used up against Larzed."

Nari was the first to respond. "We can all help with that. It won't be difficult to set up runes and symbols about the place as a temporary measure until you have time to settle back in."

"Yes," Beus added. "We can prepare the necessary spells in the morning."

"I have designed an area for everyone. Mistress Vletraka kept a few scrolls of *vlimezvemavrim*[3] on hand in case we needed the extra space. I have already divided it into separate rooms, so you can all have your privacy."

Uxadul rolled his eyes at the prospect of having to stay overnight, but expressed nothing more verbal than a sigh.

The next morning, the masters placed summoning sigils on various places on Mistr— *my* property, which would call forth various elementals and other beings to defend the land against intruders, while Glitter and I used the same combination of exploding and life-draining runes on my front door as we had placed on Ormak's tower. All the spells were attuned to the amulets, which are normally passed out to visitors for safe passage, so everyone was safe for as long as they had the amulet on their person. I hoped we would not be gone so long as to need them, but until I had the time to create my own guardians, they would have to do.

To reduce travelling time, Nari cast a *bezyamlialrih*, a circle of teleportation, three yards outside of my garden, to send us all a few minutes north of Dureltown's walls. We made a quick stop in the city for some supplies and left again as soon as possible. Afterward, Beus cast *aaslbokwa* on the assembled group so we could fly through the light

---

[3] *Vlimezvemavrim* creates an extra-dimensional space which lasts for twenty-four hours, large enough to comfortably hold a dozen people. During the casting, the layout and furniture is decided, allowing for customization as needed. Nothing created within this space can be removed, however, but those entering from outside are free to come and go as they please.

snowfall to Ormak's tower. Although I hated having to rely on others, being surrounded by a group of powerful casters definitely had its benefits, even though it also clearly showed how much I had to learn before I could call myself 'Master'. From our vantage point above the trees, Glitter and I had no difficulty in steering the group towards our destination, and with no master or guardians in residence, it was safe to land past the gate.

"The place looks different when it is not raining," I commented.

Glitter replied by dropping her hood, feigning wringing rain out of her hair, and smiling.

"Over there," I pointed to the left of the door, "is where we fought Ormak," I said. "His marker is at the back of the tower. I wish we could have done more for him.

"I do not know what other guardians may still be within. We encountered a wand golem, a creature of Ormak's own creation, guarding a room of mostly mundane treasures: coins, gear, and other items not particularly useful to a wizard. The golem appeared as a collection of wands and staves bound together with platinum wire and cast a variety of low-tier spells. Should you find another one, they are repaired by *ajilek* and other spells of pure magical force but are vulnerable to *yuviiaji* and the like. Otherwise, they are particularly unaffected by magic and are resistant to physical force."

"They can repair themselves too," added Glitter. "We mostly used a combination of alchemical bombs to destroy it, as they don't seem to resist non-magical flames and such. Oh, and they explode," she said as an afterthought. "They glow and shudder for a couple seconds first, so you have time to run. I can show you which book he wrote his notes in; maybe you can find another weakness."

Beus smiled. "A wand golem." He shook his head in bemusement. "Ormak was truly one of the greats. I wish I had met him."

"He was…interesting…to speak with. Full of knowledge and wisdom, but if you forgot for a moment he was a jozalk, it could very well have been your last. I want to remind you again: he warded many of his possessions, so examine any items thoroughly before touching them. The pain ward is excruciating." I shuddered. "His lady love was named 'Suzelle'. It may or may not be the keyword for the wards, if that helps."

Glitter and I walked up to the front door and chanted the syllables to deactivate the wards we had placed there only a few weeks ago. As they had not been triggered, we agreed the rest of the tower was likely undisturbed. After entering, we then did the same for the protective spells on the staircase.

"What happened here?" asked Faldrein from the kitchen door.

I walked over to him to see what he meant. "Jarlisk," I answered, "and his apprentice Grustan. When they invaded the tower, Ormak turned them into yomki to be his servants." I turned to Glitter. "I suppose in our haste to go after Cratillus, we forgot to bury them."

"Even after we came back, we were rushing to get what we needed for Tsukatta. I never even noticed the smell." Glitter shrugged.

Beus and Faldrein looked at each other. "We'll take care of them now." Beus and Tzali lifted the corpses while Faldrein grabbed Grustan's severed head, and they carried the remains outside.

"If you had time to explore and go through the library," sneered Uxadul, "how come you didn't have time to clean up your mess?"

Glitter stepped up to him before I could respond. "We didn't know how to find Cratillus, or even his name, until Grustan came after us. We were searching for clues and anything else which would give us an edge against a foe we didn't even know. Once we had that information, we took off as quickly as possible.

"I know you still think you are 'defending my honor' or some other *zakri*[4], but knock it off. Mithron has apologized numerous times, and I have long since forgiven him. You say you are doing this for my benefit, but it's really about you. He's been nothing but nice to you, so leave him be." As she spoke, I noticed her sparkles brightening in their crimson, and her hair began to rise as if a wind was blowing from below.

I put a gentle hand on her shoulder. "Calm down," I said barely above a whisper. "Don't send him into the Shadow." The last time Glitter had got this upset with me, she had shifted me out of phase with reality, essentially turning me into a living ghost for about an hour. In fact, it had happened directly above where we stood at that point. For all of my issues with emotional control, I sometimes forgot that when Glitter loses her temper, strange magical occurrences often happened.

Her shoulder tensed when I touched her, and for a moment I feared her rage would turn on me. She snapped her head in my direction, opened her mouth to speak, froze for a second, and let out a long exhale. She blinked once and gave a slight nod before turning back to Uxadul. "You

---

[4] *Zakri* is a crude term derived from the zylan words for 'dragon' and 'excrement'.

don't need to protect my feelings. I'm not some feather-headed young girl who dreams of being rescued by a handsome knight and carried away to his castle. Yes, I was upset at the time, and I thank you for standing up for me. But that time has passed, so let it stay there. You don't have to become friends, but you *do* need to apologize for being a jerk." She stomped off, a trail of ruby lights scattering behind her.

Uxadul watched her walk away, then turned to me. "Did you tell her not to send me into the Shadow?"

"It is what she did the last time she yelled at me. The Weave tangles strangely for her."

He turned back to look at Glitter, who was chatting with Blythad and Nari. "Okay. She is officially scarier than you are." He sighed as if dropping a heavy burden, then looked at me with a light smile. "She's right. I have four younger sisters who needed a big brother to protect them from the world, and I've felt guilty about leaving them behind to study wizardry. It's still a habit for me to step up to protect people, and I saw an opportunity to be a big brother again. Obviously, she doesn't need one. My actions have been dishonorable, and I apologize." He stuck out his hand.

I clasped his arm above the wrist, and he did the same back. "You were defending a lady's honor; there is never dishonor in that. Apology accepted." *I am glad that is done with. I feared we would have to duel again.* I leaned to his ear and in a low voice added, "I would sooner stomp a hornet's nest than anger Glitter. You had best apologize to her as well."

He nodded and turned to Glitter.

I held his arm, keeping my voice quiet. "Not yet. Wait about five minutes. Tell her about your sisters and make her laugh." Then continued at a normal volume. "Are you going to introduce me to your... elemental familiar, I take it?" I asked as it crouched down next to him.

"This is Qoga, and you are correct. I summoned it recently, and we are still bonding." He looked down at the stony lupine. "It's never done that before. How long did it take you and Thessylia to fully connect?"

"Only a few days, but our bond continues to grow daily. She is also a creature of flesh. I imagine an earth elemental would be more challenging."

"It is. Qoga obeys my commands, but otherwise just stays at my side. It may look like a wolf, but it doesn't act like one at all. I think what bothers me most is that it never rests; it's always standing, at least until now. I suppose since it's all stone, it doesn't get tired."

"That makes sense. And I am certain the two of you will grow closer in time. The trick is to allow yourself to see their point of view. Thessylia has taught me a great deal about how she thinks, and her advice sometimes makes more sense than human customs." I laughed.

"It seems... contented? Satisfied? Pleased we are at peace. 'Stability' is the feeling I'm getting. Qoga likes stability. I suppose that makes sense, given it is a creature of pure earth ." As Uxadul spoke, the loamy odor he had grew stronger.

"Apparently, emotional stability is as important to it as physical stability," I surmised. "No insult intended, but you smelled more earthy while you were communicating with it."

"My Gift," he smiled. "It appears it makes me more appealing to earth elementals and those strongly connected to the ground, like miners and farmers. Everyone else seems to think less of me, associating me with dirt."

I shook my head. "We shall never understand the workings of the Weave."

"I doubt anyone ever has." He laughed.

"Have you been working on any new spells? Those clay balls you threw at me during the tournament slowed my movements considerably. That spell would do as well to slow a pursuer as to catch quarry."

"Tzali has, repeatedly, insisted I work harder at defending myself, rather than charging into a fight with my staff empowered, so I developed *hysavul*, which makes my skin as strong as steel." He smiled. "The best part is, I can still put *ajiavulhysayt* over it, increasing my protection further."

"That sounds extraordinarily useful, though I hope to avoid being in a position where I can be so easily attacked. I wonder if it would work in combination with *hrukzukladroob*. It makes one's flesh denser, mostly to reduce the effects of arrows and slings, but I don't see why it would not defend against direct attacks as easily."

"From the way you fought me, I thought you preferred face-to-face spell combat."

"Unfortunately, some of my best combat spells require me to be able to touch my opponent. However, those spells *are* good at disabling a foe before they can strike back. Nonetheless, I concede your point. Anything which makes me less vulnerable to excessive steel poisoning is undoubtedly a worthwhile spell to have."

"Care to trade, when we have the time?"

"I would like that very much. First, I think it might be time to make amends with Glitter." We could hear her laughing in the background. "She seems to be in a better mood now. You should do well. You did not offend her nearly as bad as I did, and she forgave me after only a pair of moons."

He glared at me, more out of annoyance than anger. "That is *not* reassuring."

I smiled back and he turned away. I believed he muttered something, but I could not hear what it was.

A few minutes later, Beus and Faldrein came back inside. I stepped up to the pair, stopping the younger wizard as his mentor continued on to speak to Tzali. "My apologies. I should have assisted you in taking care of Grustan. I got distracted by Uxadul."

"What happened this time?" he asked, exasperation in his voice.

"We made amends, I believe."

Faldrein paused in surprise.

"Glitter defended me to him, and it made him reconsider his position. I think we understand each other better now."

He let out his held breath. "That's a relief. All that squabbling was making things uncomfortable. None of us wanted to take sides in the argument, and we saw no way to end it peacefully."

"I am simply glad it did not come to blows. When last we dueled, Uxadul was out for blood. A true fight between us would not end well for either."

"Everyone," Beus raised his voice to get our attention. "Now that the grisly business is done, Mithron, Glitter, would you mind leading us to the library? Show us what you discovered, and what we should be cautious of."

We led the assemblage upstairs and gave them a quick tour of Ormak's extensive library, pointing out books and objects of interest, then led them to the hidden stairwell, where Glitter and I once again removed our protective combined wards.

"Technically, half of the treasure upstairs belongs to Vondro and Brother Ironknuckle, but if you see anything which is of interest to you, feel free. We will subtract it from our share, and there is more than enough for us," said Glitter to the group.

I was somewhat annoyed that she was giving away my portion without asking, but she was right. I had little use for most of the items, and there was enough coin for us to live modestly for the rest of our days. It should have been split six ways, and my vision began to grey as I thought of Ial'rafiost and Tsukatta. Raf had even begun separating everything into neat piles to make certain each of us received their fair share.

"We haven't explored beyond these areas," Glitter continued, "so we don't know what else to expect. There must be hidden chambers and other guards, so be careful."
As the rest of the group moved back to the library, Glitter pulled me aside. "Uxadul apologized to me," she whispered. "I will accept later. He needs to stew about it for a time. I'm glad you two have settled."

I thought back to our conversation after leaving Goldfire's tower and traveled back to mine. *"Uxadul is proud and combative,"* said Glitter without preamble. *"If you give him any opportunity to argue or fight, he will take it. Be kind and sweet to him, and it will leave him flustered.*

Tzali is staid, thoughtful, and will carefully consider all positions before acting. The more positive traits which you can display in his presence, the higher he will regard you."

"Why are you bringing this up?" I asked, genuinely confused.

"They will be at the wake for Mistress Vletraka, and you need to make peace with them. Nari, Beus, Blythad, and Faldrein were concerned at the tournament, but only those two were truly angry with you."

"I had met the others before, so they knew me a little. My first impression with Tzali and Uxadul was at the tournament."

"We have time to practice what you are going to say to them, and how you're going to act around them. You will be ready when the time comes, or else you may never be able to count on them."

I thought about her advice but was still missing something crucial. "Why are you telling me this? Why are you helping me?"

Her face went blank, save for a series of emotions I could not recognize quickly enough, which flashed through her eyes before finally settling on one which seemed like sadness. Or maybe pity.

"Our small band of wizards is all we have. We are a family, and we need to get along. Yes, we will have disagreements from time to time, and we might not even see each other for long stretches, but," she stressed, "we are a family now. You have to make this right.

"I was forced to spend time with you, to find out what kind of person you are, both good and bad, and I accept you. Uxadul will not be in the same position, so you must find a way to convince him that you bear him no ill will. Remember: be nice to him, no matter what he says to or about you. Smile. Listen to his point of view. When you understand how someone else perceives the world, you understand them."

"I owe it all to you and your mentoring." I smiled at her. I felt strangely happy. My breath was light and heavy both at once, and I felt both warm and cold. My vision began to grey, and yet I was still feeling… something.

"Are you okay? You look…"

Before she could continue, I covered my mouth with both hands and ran down the hall to avoid speaking to her, the vision of her near death when Ormak's *srukakbolmos* spell exploded in front of her repeating behind my eyes. *At least it is a different vision, but it is a clear reminder that I have brought more pain into her life.* The vision faded somewhat as the joyful feeling subsided, but re-intensified as the remorse set in.

Chapter 3: Return to Ehrghex

Are you alright?" Glitter asked a few minutes later. I think she had realized I needed to center myself before I would be able to speak with her, so she watched and waited.

My heart shuddered when I turned to look at her, and I had to close my eyes and turn my gaze to avoid regarding her directly. I had no words to describe how I felt about her. I stumbled with a series of noncommittal noises before finally spitting out, "I can't." The memory of the scent of her burning flesh filled my nostrils.

"I thought we had spent enough time together to be past this," she huffed, her sparkles flashing crimson. "You don't have to hide from me every time your Gift gets out of control."

I glanced back at her, only seeing charred flesh instead of the woman before me, and quickly turned away. "Different," I mumbled out, tears streaming down my face.

Her sparkles shifted to indigo as she realized my predicament. She dragged me by the arm further down the hallway near a closed door which had not yet been checked for safety. "What are you feeling? What vision are you having?" she asked, genuine concern in her voice.

"Ormak's *srukakbolmos*," I managed to squeak out between sniffles as I tried desperately to calm myself. "I see you burning away. I smell you cooking." After a couple of deep breaths, I continued, "You nearly died because of me."

Glitter gently grabbed my arms and turned me to face her. "But I didn't. Tsukatta was there to save me. I'm fine."

She smiled, but looked worried. "What brought this on? Why now?"

"I do not know," I sighed. I found my emotions calming while I pondered the situation, but felt them rise again as I looked back at her. I turned away again, pulling myself from her grip. "Perhaps it is from remembering the pain which you endured because I did not consider the ramifications of blinding Ormak. My guilt, my shame at putting you into that predicament," I hedged, fully aware my feelings were deeper and far more complicated than that. "When we were here last, we were acting in haste, and I did not have the time to think about what had happened. Now, I cannot stop myself."

"Go outside and get some fresh air," she suggested. "Clear your head. We'll be fine for a while. After all, what trouble could eight wizards get into in a jozalk's tower?" She laughed. "We can all protect each other, especially with our mast…" She trailed off, suddenly realizing I did not have my master with me. "I'm sorry."

"No, you are correct. You will be, relatively, safe, and I do need to center myself. I am no good to anyone right now." I stepped past her and headed outside.

I wandered the grounds around Ormak's tower, lost in my thoughts, not realizing I had reached the scorched stones where Ormak's explosive fireball nearly killed the woman I was so scared to face. I brushed away the dusting of snow and sat down on the spot where she hovered at the edge of the Dark Lady's Gate, before beginning my breathing exercises, as they often helped center my thoughts.

What is the matter with me? Why can I not manage this? I thought I had gained some mastery over my Gift, and now it is out of control again. I hope my garden does not freeze.

I floated through the twisting corridors of the Mazeworks, the semi-dream construct of my mind. It is strange that I often feel as though I am walking, but I do not touch the floor. The passageway split, and I drifted to the left, where I found myself in a deep forest.

"You like her," Ial'rafiost's voice echoed in my head.

I turned to see him before me, balanced on one hand on a tree branch before dropping to the ground into a roll and sitting before me.

"Your feelings have grown deeper for Glitter."

"I do, and that might be true," I responded, "but I still do not understand."

"Well, you see, when a man and a woman like each other, they have certain…urges…" he smiled and winked.

"Mostly, I feel the urge to vomit," I interrupted.

He closed his eyes and began kissing the back of his hand.

"Oh, you are referring to physical urges. No, you are incorrect. I enjoy being in her presence, but I do not feel the desire for physical contact. When we are together, I feel happy, frightened, hot, cold, excited, and alone. It is all very confusing."

"Oh, that's easy. You're in love."

I stared blankly at him.

He smiled and nodded. "When you see her, does your heart flutter like a moth in the moonlight? Does her voice sound like a melody? Does her smile brighten your day like highsun?"

I paused and gave a slight nod.

Raf grinned in return.

"This cannot be," I responded glumly. "I cannot afford such strong feelings, and I cannot put Glitter in such a position as to have to deal with this. Even if true, I cannot act on it."

"Didn't you want to with that woman with the bandit king, Orla?" Raf asked. "She would have said 'yes' to both of you, you know." He laughed with a wink.

"Orla? She is an attractive woman; strong and in good physical shape. Until her, the only nude bodies I had seen had been withering corpses. I was fascinated by her and her general audacity, but again, there was no physical draw, only curiosity."

Raf stared at me, confusion evident in his eyes.

I sighed, "What is wrong with me now?"

"You have no physical desires?" he asked.

"No. At least, I do not think so. I am still attempting to cope with having emotional desires. This is all too much to deal with right now."

I shook myself out of my reverie. "Well, that cleared up one issue, while raising more," I muttered. "I will clearly have to learn to restrain my emotions even more tightly."

I re-entered Ormak's tower to find a makeshift healer's tent in the den.

"What happened here?" I asked while pulling my herbal kit out of the extra-dimensional pocket within my satchel.

"We had a run-in with a pack of elementals," groaned Tzali.

The left sleeve of his robe had been burned away, and Faldrein was applying a poultice of mortification root over the red and blistered skin.

"I was able to take control of one of the earth elementals and make it fight for us, while Nari banished some of the others," Tzali continued. "The rest we had to fight. They proved to be far more challenging than the demons guarding the entrance to that chamber."

"Demons are easy to banish," said Nari. "They want to go back home rather than be trapped where they can't cause any chaos." Her last word trailed off into a coughing fit, which splattered flecks of blood from her lips.

"I told you to stay still," sighed Beus, as he cleaned her face. "My healing magic has limits, and you have, as far as I can tell, three broken ribs."

I looked over the group and noticed Uxadul was covered in small cuts and was not being attended to. "What got you?" I asked as I stepped quickly over to him.

"Air elemental," he hissed as I carefully removed his robe from his shoulder. The blood had already begun to dry, adhering the cloth to his puncture wounds. "It picked up the pieces of a destroyed earth elemental and flung them at me like a miniature tornado. And here I thought my specialty would protect me against such an attack."

"Considering the depth of your wounds, it could have been much worse. Perhaps you have developed a resistance to physical attacks from your focus on elemental earth after all. It would be nice if I could resist the effects of the undead; perhaps my studies will lead me down that path. Now, hold still, this may hurt." I cast *umakraazt* and placed my hands on his exposed shoulder. The spell does not restore life energy to the recipient, but it does close small wounds, stopping the bleeding and starting the natural healing process, but I did not design the spell to block the pain of the skin rapidly stitching itself together.

Uxadul hissed loudly and glared at me, but relaxed when he saw that some of the wounds had closed.

"There will be scars," I informed him, and he nodded in acceptance. "Where are Glitter and Mistress Goldfire?" I asked, suddenly realizing they were not there.

"They helped to get us out of the chamber, but stayed behind to finish off the remaining elementals," groaned Uxadul, getting back to his feet. "Thanks, now let's see if they need any help."

It took a few steps before his pace quickened to full running speed up the stairs, down a hallway which the tower was not, by outward appearances, large enough to contain its length, and through an opening in the wall which would otherwise be unnoticed when closed. I was about to comment on Ormak's skill and mastery when I recognized Glitter's voice from ahead.

"Well, I'm glad the others aren't here to see me like this," she laughed as Uxadul and I entered the chamber.

The room was filled with boxes and chests, with a number of large items, such as suits of armor, scattered among them. Glitter was soaked head to toe, her pink, violet, silver, and forest green hair matted to her forehead, chest, and shoulders. She turned at the sound of our footsteps on the stone floor and screamed, causing both of us to stop dead in our tracks. She spun away, muttered what I can only assume was either an illusion, an alteration, or an *uvaazrosiit* spell to dry herself off.

"Are you okay?" asked Uxadul.

Glitter sparkled yellow and crimson. "I'm fine," she responded with a heavy sigh. "Goldfire let me fight against a water elemental by myself to practice my battle magicks. I won, but it exploded all over me. I must have looked frightful."

I shrugged. "As much as we have travelled in the rain, I do not see how this would appear any different."

She paused. "You know, you're right. Every time I come here I get soaked. Anyway, I think that was the last of the elementals. How are the others?"

"Beus and Faldrein have them well in hand," answered Uxadul. "Nari has some broken ribs, and Master Tzali got burned pretty badly. Blythad came through without a scratch. He's helping the others."

"That's a relief," sighed Goldfire. "I was sure you were all worse than that when I teleported you away. With only a couple elementals left, I thought it best to get the rest of you to safety. No sense in risking further damage or getting killed."

"As long as you are both safe. It could have gone badly with only the two of you, seeing how the others have fared. You have only recently been reunited, and it would pain me to see one of you lost again," I said.

"No injuries worth noting," commented Goldfire. "A few bumps and bruises."

I nodded, looking around the room. The Weave was tightly warped and knotted around many of the items, and the distortion left me somewhat nauseous. "There is a *lot* of magic in here," I said, while closing my eyes and taking a step backwards. "I can see why Ormak set up so many guardians."

"More stuff to catalog," said Uxadul, rolling his eyes. "We're going to spend so much time here that we'll all be neglecting our studies for months. Let's take a look."

Thankfully, Ormak was fairly well organized, keeping like items together. There were no notes on anything in any of his journals, but it would not be difficult for a wizard of his skill to memorize each item by appearance, assuming he found them useful or interesting at all. Of special note were a dozen staves of varied designs and woods, all locked within a lead-lined cedar armoire. They rested on a purple velvet base and were kept apart with wooden spacers. A staff is bound with different spells which can be released with a single command, but within strict limits. Like a wizard, it can only release so much energy per day, but the spells it contains cannot be changed. Staves can be pushed beyond their limits, but it costs the wizard holding it some of their gathered magical energy. When the time for choosing came, I picked a dark mahogany staff which absorbed, rather than cast, spells, to protect myself from other wizards.

Strangely, there was also a pair of blacksmithing tongs mixed in with the other items. As far as any of us could tell, the tongs were enchanted to never get hot and to improve the smith's skill while using them. Ormak must have misplaced them, as one would have expected them to be in the first room we found, which was full of minor items. It was agreed that I could take them, as I hoped to one day use them as a peace offering to my estranged father.

We spent two days resting, healing, planning, and cataloguing before moving on to Ehrghex by way of another one of Nari's teleportation circles. During that time, we agreed the apprentices would each spend a month here sorting the library and working on independent research. We were expressly forbidden to search the tower for other hidden rooms on our own, and all five apprentices would meet and stay for the first week, once we returned from Ehrghex, to organize a schedule and make the place habitable. Meanwhile, the masters set up a permanent *bezyamlialrih*—to make transportation easier between towers—, placed large quartz spheres in each location for communication, and discussed guardians. For now, it was easiest to set up summoning circles to bring creatures in from other dimensions until permanent guardians could be constructed. As both apprentice and master, I was involved in all aspects, at least as far as my tower was concerned.

During those two days, I also trained under Beus to improve my technique in storing and releasing the positive energy burst which is so effective against the undead horde we were about to face. Beus and Faldrein received their ability to channel this energy from the Dark Lady as part of the exchange for their worship; though I revere her, I am not pious enough to be offered this blessing. They did, however, teach me their meditations for gathering energy and gestures for focusing the release of it. As I had already been practicing the lessons learned from *Accentuating the Positive* by Falleoraeli Zolthliam, the additional insights from the wizard-priests fit in well with what I had already learned, and I found I could more easily hold the extra energy without exhausting myself upon its release.

We all prepared battle magicks and defenses before Nari teleported us inside Ehrghex's walls. The masters caused most of the destruction early on: Tzali transformed into an eighteen-foot-tall giant with a black dragon's head, Nari summoned a swarm of fire elementals, Beus called forth a trio of orbs with five tentacles from the Plane of Infinite Light, and Goldfire conjured a circle of glowing embers which exploded when they made contact with the wandering ruklaa. Once the four masters obliterated the nearby walking corpses, we split off in pairs to search the town and destroy them all. I stayed closer to Tzali and Uxadul but gave them space to fight in their own way.

Tzali would periodically belch forth a stream of acid from his dragon head, but mostly swept the ruklaa away with his elongated quarterstaff. Uxadul followed Tzali's lead, changing into an earth elemental after turning his own staff into iron, while Qoga simply pounced upon and crushed everything in its path. None of the creatures survived their assault. Unless there was a large group suitable for burning with a *srukakbolmos*, I often used *emuvazvul*, which conjured swarms of grubs and maggots which fed on the corpses before dissolving away themselves, and *yuvamimzuklii*, which disrupts the negative energy maintaining an undead creature's existence. Though the latter spell is not nearly as effective, it uses far less energy to cast.

I also found effective targets for the wand I discovered in Ormak's bedchamber. There were few insubstantial undead amongst the undead throngs, but I did find some lurking in deeply shadowed alleyways. Each use of the wand changed the energy type, randomly switching through fire, cold, electrical, acid, and sonic damage and the dragon head image changed color to correspond. The wand causes no damage to anything corporeal, so it is useless on anything fully on the material plane.

Seeing that the battle mages had things well in hand, I felt confident to explore on my own, knowing I could retreat to them at any time I felt in too much danger. I would enter each house we came by to see if there were any undead hiding within, but most were empty, their reanimated occupants already wandering the streets. I had never used my necromancer's sight, the ability to sense living and unliving nearby creatures, for so long a period, and the headache I manifested by midday stopped me from using that ability for the rest of the day.

It was early afternoon, while examining one such building, when I found something unexpected. I heard a thumping noise coming from an upstairs room in one of the larger homes, and carefully picked my way to the second floor. When I opened a bedroom door, I saw a young woman crouched behind a bed with a crossbow pointing at me.

"Don't hurt me," she whimpered.

"You are alive?" I asked dumbstruck. "How did you manage to survive all this time?" I held my hands up in submission and to show I meant no harm. The defensive spells I had cast would likely protect me from her weapon, but there was no point in taking any unnecessary risks. "We are here to destroy the undead infestation, not to ransack the town. I thought Cratillus killed you all."

"I wasn't here when it started. I came to get my family out, but it was too late." She broke into sobbing.

I dared to step forward. "You are safe now. We will protect you. My name is Mithron, what is yours?"

She sniffed. "Therro," was all she could say before tears overwhelmed her.

"Come with me," I pleaded, my hand outstretched. "The crossbow is nearly useless against ruklaa, and my friends will not harm you, so you might want to leave it behind. If you have a blade of any sort, it will hurt them more, but most of the ruklaa nearby have already been destroyed."

"You must be pretty brave or strong to be wandering in here alone."

"Not as much as you, I would wager." I smiled. "You have been here for weeks, while we have only presently arrived."

She took my hand and we crept out of the house.

Four ruklaa were passing by, and I once again cast *emuvazvul*, rapidly decomposing the shambling creatures.

"That's… disturbing," she said with some hesitancy, repulsion apparent in her voice.

"Perhaps," I mused, trying to see it from her viewpoint, "but effective. There are far too many of these abominations roaming about, and I am certain it will take the few of us more than a couple days to…" I stopped short.

We had wandered into a market district where hundreds of ruklaa had gathered, as if it were a normal day to shop. The nearest ones saw us, leaned forward, and emitted a guttural hiss. I responded by casting *srukakyelk*, which brought forth a sheet of flames scarcely long enough to seal the street.

Ruklaa have neither fear nor understanding of fire and were drawn to it. Most of them turned to ash as they passed through the flames, and piles of scorched bones began to accumulate on our side of the wall.

"We had better move away," I warned Therro. "That spell will not last long." *At least it will destroy a good number of them.*

Therro grabbed my hand as we ran from the market and guided me through the streets littered with destroyed ruklaa. After some time, I began to recognize the area and I brought her to where we had first appeared. Looking about, I could hear the occasional burst of energy from my fellow wizards and determined the area would likely be safe. She did not want to be left alone, so I stayed to keep her company, vowing to protect her against anything that might meander our way.

We had been chatting for a while, Therro telling me tales about Ehrghex before Cratillus turned it into the charnel house it had become. She grew restless as the day progressed, and we walked around the city streets;

fortunately, we didn't run into any patrols of undead. She was interesting and charming, and I wished I had either Raf's talent for remembering stories or a stack of paper and ink to write them all down. She was so distracting that I had not noticed the sun had set, and we were alone in a small alley.

She looked over her shoulder to the reddening sky, then turned back to me with a wicked smile. "Finally," she cooed, her eyes turning the color of the sunset, "I've been waiting for another taste of you." Her mouth stretched open beyond normal for a human, her teeth elongating and sharpening. With the speed of a cracking whip, she sunk her teeth into my shoulder, while her dagger-like fingernails dug into my arms.

The maraika pulled away after only two seconds, her eyes beginning to glaze over. "What? What is wrong with your blood?" she slurred.

"Well, *Verria*," I sneered, suppressing the pain while revealing her real name, "I suspected we would meet again, so I prepared myself, and my companions, just in case. I drank a tonic of birthwort, garlic, mullein, and torem[5] before coming here, and I also brought this," I crowed as I pulled out the sharpened hazel branch which I had the priests of Lephix—the sun god—in Dureltown bless when we stopped for supplies, and stabbed it into the creature's

---

[5] Torem, also known as 'blood ivy' or 'lover's end', grows best at the edge of forests, the dark brown-green stem climbing up the nearest tree to gather sunlight, and small purple flowers bloom for about three days before winter. When the wide, red-veined leaves are steeped in clear alcohol, along with the other herbs, it makes one resistant to blood-borne diseases, and also makes the blood toxic to creatures which consume it. Were it less rare, it would serve as the perfect bane against the mosquitos living around my pond.

heart. She stiffened, unable to move so long as the branch stayed in place.

Maraika are difficult to actually destroy. When we first met, Vondro chopped off her head while she was feeding off of me, which caused her body to discorporate into mist. When that happens, they return to a safe place to regenerate, typically until the next evening. Even if "killed" during the day, they spontaneously reanimate once the sun dips below the horizon. In order to stop them, the body must be destroyed utterly, through fire, positive energy, or other means. Theoretically, if they can be trapped while in their misty form and exposed to daylight, this will also burn them away, but I had neither the spells nor the inclination to test that hypothesis.

It is an odd quirk in magic that spells sometimes only manifest in particular ways, whether the creator of the spell wishes it or not. In the case of *uvaazkaekdmuuvad*, the intent of the spell is to put the dead to rest, so the magic focuses on the caster's lips, forcing a 'kiss goodbye'. I grabbed her in the same way in which Orla grabbed me, pulling her close so I could kiss her on the lips. It was a peculiar sensation, as she was literally as cold as the grave, and smelled the same; so very different than she was before sunset. There was no emotion behind the kiss, aside from revulsion of both the act and her existence as a maraika, and, perhaps, a touch of pity, for someone had to have created her into this state. Whether true or not, I blamed Cratillus. As the positive energy poured out into her, it also healed the wounds which she had caused. Within seconds, she disintegrated into dust, along with the hazel wand.

As planned, we met up in the noble district shortly before night completely pushed the day aside. A pair of oversized suits of armor, built for creatures standing about ten feet in height, lay broken on the ground in front of the Byrrel estate, where Cratillus had set up his home base during the desolation of Ehrghex.

"Look who we found," waved Goldfire, who was escorting an armored man, their arms locked together.

A raven-haired woman in similar armor followed. Glitter's bright golden sparkles denoted her joy before I could see her features.

"Captain Vondelos!" I exclaimed as he neared. "How are you? How is Vondro?"

Vondelos' expression turned grim. "Vondro is… not doing well, I'm afraid. I thought bringing him here would help him to deal with his grief, but he has proven to be reckless and foolhardy in our skirmishes against Ehrghex's infestation. Yesterday, I was forced to relieve him of his duty, for I feared he would get himself and his squad killed."

Glitter's sparkles turned blue, almost disappearing in the darkening sky. "Poor Vondro. Is he still nearby? Can we speak with him?" she asked.

"He's still at the base camp outside the eastern wall. We find it safest to lock the town gates from the outside at night, and not worry about taking territory. Mara will take you to him."

The woman nodded.

"Thank you, sir," I responded. *I wish Raf were here. He was always good at cheering people up. I only hope we do not make things worse.*

Glitter and I turned toward the others. We were always in haste back when we were last here a little over a moon ago and never took the time to gather more information than was necessary.

"We don't know what Cratillus may have left behind," Glitter reminded everyone as they prepared to enter the mansion. "We fought off a ryelt, which is probably still on the floor upstairs, gathered Mithron's books, and left." She turned to me and said, "We should get better about burying the bodies. I'm only now realizing how much damage we've left behind us."

"Agreed. At least now we are not under so many time constraints. Let us see if we can help Vondro; they should be fine without us for a while."

Mara led us through the streets of Ehrghex, past numerous remains of ruklaa and other undead creatures. We occasionally noticed a few ruklaa, never more than three at a time, and easily dispatched them with simple *yuvaminzuklii* myzlings and Mara's sword.

"How long have you been here?" I asked.

"Just over two weeks," Mara replied as she beheaded a lurching rukla. "When Captain Vondelos informed us that the entire city had become these things, I thought he was exaggerating. It's good they are not organized, or they could have easily overrun us by now. Thus far, our best strategy is to make quick attacks and retreat. They are awfully slow, but deadly if they get hold of you. Occasionally, we encounter a group led by something more powerful, and I have lost many good soldiers to those squads. The wandering groups are easily handled so long as they don't surround us. We should have conscripted more priests, but I suppose some need to stay in Dureltown to see to the needs of the city folk. Some of the Sun's Daughters[6]

---

[6] The clergy of Lephix have been given many nicknames by the laity, including the Children of the Sun and Lightbringers. Few refer to the male priests as the Sun's Sons in their presence.

are still helping the few who escaped this doomed place resettle."

"Were you able to cure them?" Glitter asked.

"It took some doing from what I've heard. Apparently, there was some sort of curse on them which protected the refugees from their disease whilst still allowing them to act as carriers so they could spread it further. Her Luminescence, Lephix's High Priestess herself had to call the sun's blessings to heal them."

"I am glad they are better, they were decent folk. I think with our help, perhaps this," I waved my hand at Ehrghex, "will not take too much longer. Our magicks can destroy large groups all at once, and our masters know spells far more powerful than we do," I said, trying to not sound boastful. "Still, this town had thousands of residents, and it will take time to destroy all the creatures they have become."

"Perhaps not. I've seen some of the devastation you have caused. With that kind of magic combined with the full force of our troops, we should be able to cut a swath from one end of town to the other. Afterwards, it would simply be a matter of sending out small squads to clean up the stragglers."

"What happens to the town then?" asked Glitter. "Once the bodies have been buried, this will be a walled city with no residents."

"I suppose that's up to King Alferen to decide," answered Mara. "Best guess is he grants the land to a lesser noble, who will then have to convince people to move to this accursed place. Here we are."

She stopped outside a moderately-sized tent, large enough to hold a dozen soldiers uncomfortably,

Dureltown's red flag with a golden bear's paw flying from the central pole.

"Vondro, report."

A sunken version of Vondro shifted through the tent flap. He was gaunt, as if he had not eaten since we last saw him over a moon ago; his eyes showing as much sleep in that time. Joy and anger fought for dominance on his face when he saw us, but his voice settled on apathy. "Why are you two here?"

Glitter's sparkles dimmed as he spoke, her gold and silver motes dulling to yellow and grey.

"Originally, we came to free this town," I said, "but now we are here to see you. You do not look well."

That earned me a glare from Glitter, but Vondro answered before she could say anything. "That doesn't matter. What have I to live for? I would rather join Tsukatta in the Greylands than to keep going without her."

"I know," sniffed Glitter, taking his hand. "We miss her too, but she wouldn't want you to give up your life for her. There is still so much good you can do here, and she would want you to keep fighting in her name."

I added, "And we both understand."

Vondro attempted to protest.

I cut him off, continuing, "For we have all lost those important to us. My Mistress is dead, Ial'rafiost is lost to us, and my family turned their backs on me when I became a wizard. Glitter has had her own losses. True, I have never lost, nor even loved someone as close as Tsukatta was to you, but we have recovered from our losses, and, perhaps, are stronger for them. You are strong, my friend, and I have seen your spirit as you fought to protect us all. Now, you must fight for yourself."

"You can't understand," he shouted, tears streaming unbidden over his cheeks. "I was nothing before I met her, and now I'm nothing again. I can't let her go."

"You have always been good, and strong, and noble," said Mara, "all the makings of a great leader. You should not forget her, but fight in her memory, for her honor. Yes, she helped you become a better man." She pushed him back, keeping her hands on his shoulders and looking him straight in the eyes. "Now you must continue to *be* that better man. We need you. Your father needs you. Your friends need you. You need to work through your sorrow, not wallow in it."

Vondro stared at Mara for a good half-a-minute, every feeling cascading through his features before the tears overwhelmed him and he collapsed into her arms. After Glitter moved to embrace him from behind, I stepped up to put a hand on his shoulder while he sobbed.

"She must have been a very good woman for you to have loved her so much," said Mara gently as she held her commander's son. "Let that love guide you."

We stayed with him for a while until he cried himself out and went to sleep.

Mara thanked us and shooed us off, demanding we get some rest as well. "Have your leader report to Captain Vondelos in the morning, so we can coordinate our efforts. It is time we finished here."

We passed her order to our masters, and they elected Tzali to take command, due to his knowledge of military history and tactics.

In the morning, Glitter and I sought out Vondro, finding him in full armor outside his tent.

"It is good to see you both," he said, first kissing Glitter's hand, and then clasping my forearm. "You're becoming a better leader."

"No, it is simply that I understand pain and loss," I replied. "Ask Glitter. I am clueless on every other subject concerning other people."

She laughed but could not help nodding in agreement.

A slight smile cracked through Vondro's pain. "Thank you both. I've missed our time together, and I'm glad you two have found each other."

"We have been travelling together ever since. There was much to take care of before we could return here."

Glitter blushed, her sparkles matching her cheeks. She clutched my arm and whispered into my ear "That's not what he means." Then she gave me a light kiss on the cheek.

The world instantly turned grey, and my ears filled with the dull roar of the ocean crashing on a beach. Actually, it was the dull roar of a *srukakbolmos* repeatedly exploding on Glitter. I pulled away and stumbled off, clenching my fists and breathing rapidly, hissing through my teeth as my jaw clenched. *No, no, no. She cannot have feelings for me. I am fine with our friendship, but I can only hurt her more if we get closer.* I made the mistake of glancing over to Vondro, only to see a desiccated Tsukatta in his arms.

"I think you broke him." I heard Vondro's voice as if from a distance.

"He'll be fine in a moment," replied Glitter from even further away. "But, yes, I didn't think it would hit him this hard."

Unfortunately, Glitter's compassion only bolstered my feelings for her, making it more difficult to control my emotions. I took a deep breath, holding it for as long as I could while screeching like a corlitene[7] in my head. Afterwards, I noticed my throat had clogged from tear-produced phlegm, and I went into a fit of coughing. My companions stood quietly by, waiting for me to compose myself, the concern on their faces obvious even to me.

"I'll give you two a minute," muttered Vondro as he returned to his tent.

Glitter stepped up to me and clasped my hand. "I'm sorry. I didn't know you felt this strongly."

I gave a wan smile, "Neither did I." I took a deep, ragged breath, coughed, and sighed. "Our time together has deepened my feelings for you. Before, I was purely afraid of hurting you again; now I fear you might feel the same bond that I do. Raf would say I am in love with you, but to be honest, I do not know what that means."

She pulled me into a tight hug, which was oddly comforting. "I've grown fond of you too. It took a while to even like you, but you were always kind, except when your Gift kicked in." She tightened her grip. "This… this has got to be torture for you."

I squeezed her back and nodded, unable to speak.

"We're smart. We'll figure this out."

---

[7] Corlitenes are ghost-like creatures born of sadness and regret. Their wailing and crying cause others to wallow in the same emotional morass as the corlitene, slowly stripping the will to live from their victims. Those committing suicide due to the corlitene's keening are trapped with them, forming a chorus, and can only be freed when the corlitene is destroyed. Though more pitiable than malicious, they are still exceptionally dangerous.

I sighed again, still concerned, but soothed by her embrace.

Chapter 4: Experimentation

Once we cleaned Ormak's tower and made reed mats and straw mattresses for sleeping, we began redesigning the library. We first listed categories, such as magickal theory, planes and dimensions, spellbooks, mystical beasts, and biographies, then later devised subcategories as we delved into the collection. During this time, we also made a scheduled rotation for us each to spend a moon organizing the library.

Naturally, to properly catalogue each volume, it needed to be studied, drastically slowing our progress as we got lost in each text. Though it proved mostly unnecessary, every volume was checked for protective runes to avoid mystical traps. Only Ormak's personal spellbooks were safeguarded, and after our efforts failed, often painfully so, we contacted Nari to dispel his wards.

As expected, Ormak's spellbooks proved to be a treasure trove, not only due to the quantity of spells, including ones he had devised himself, but also owing to his notes describing his processes, failures, successes, and his insights into techniques, reagents, and general spellcraft were invaluable. Many spells were still too complex for any of us junior wizards, but we were all intrigued and little else was accomplished until we all had the chance to peruse his works. Those books alone were worth a sun of lessons, and our combined efforts improved all our arcane abilities.

A particular favorite of mine was *mevzemlialavulhysayt*, which twists the space around the caster, preventing anything from touching him and shunting it to a random nearby location. This is predominantly used against weapons, so that the blade vanishes before piercing flesh and appears somewhere around the wizard, preferably behind the attacker so that they stab themselves in the back. Unfortunately, there is no way to control where the attack is shifted, but so long as I avoid getting hurt, it does not matter. Care must be taken, however, to stay some distance away from allies so they are not harmed.

Glitter and I opted not to inform our friends of our relationship. Her opinion was that it would put additional pressure on us, and it would be prudent to establish our bond in private before it became influenced by others. To that end, we avoided being alone together and separated ourselves on the schedule. Instead, we would visit each other during our shifts, leaving for our towers before the moon renewed when Blythad would take Glitter's place and Uxadul would follow me.

It took some time to find a balance when together. We would spend hours in conversation, assist each other in cataloguing, practice her techniques for altering spells, and inuring me to the anguishing aspect of my Gift while with her. At first, we were so focused on learning about each other that little work was getting done and we would rush to make headway on the library. Over time it became easier to be with her and my emotions were less intense as I learned to relax.

"I want to try something if you're up for it," Glitter said when I visited on her second shift. It was a mild autumn day, so we were walking on the grounds followed by a phantasmal unicorn, one of Glitter's tower guardians. Thessylia rested in a tree a few feet outside the fence, as there were few places to perch within.

Much of the grounds had grown desolate while under the purview of the previous undead master, and greenery was slowly returning to the area. Everything we planted died within days for the first six months, forcing us to stock provisions and travel to Rabbit's Den, Silver Pines, and other local villages for fresh produce. Though Dureltown was closer, the larger population made getting through the market more troublesome. Goods were also less expensive in the villages, though money was no longer an issue, and we thought it prudent to add to the local economy.

"What do you have in mind?" I asked, not detecting any mischief.

"There's a spell that triggers a single emotion for a time. Essentially the opposite of the one I hit you with back at the tournament. I want to cast it on you and help you with your Gift. It will sustain the emotion—don't worry, I'll make you happy—," she said, "so you won't be able to just shut it down."

"Thus, forcing me to confront my feelings and the images associated," I concluded.

"Precisely. Maybe if you are pushed to stay with your Gift for an extended period, you can control it better."

"That seems reasonable. As we both already know what I see during my episodes, there should not be any surprises or additional harm."

"Do you want to do it here, or wait until we're inside?"

"Here should suffice. I have enough control that I can handle walking while seeing your pain."

"It still feels weird hearing you say things like that." She smiled ruefully. "And you say it so matter-of-factly. Maybe it isn't such a burden for you anymore."

"No, it still is. I have stopped fighting it and accepted that it is part of me now. Faldrein has informed me about stoicism, a philosophy that, in part, requires a tamping down of emotions. There is more to it, but the emotional control is what I require. The tricky part is allowing myself to feel but pull away from those feelings when the world begins to grey. I do not wish to stop feeling at all, but to gain enough control to avoid seeing everyone's pain."

"I think that's a good start," she nodded, "but I think avoiding your Gift is making it harder for you to control it. That's why I want to push you towards it. If you can control it better, you won't have to shun it. Maybe you will finally find the positive in it."

"What could be beneficial about seeing others' anguish?" I asked, exasperation seeping through despite my claims of acceptance.

"You can be more empathetic, for one," she responded with more hope than I felt. "Like you told Vondro when we met up with him, you 'understand pain and loss'. If you can understand people's pain, then you can understand their actions better and maybe even help them through it."

"I believe you are giving me more credit for comprehending others than I am due."

"You don't give yourself enough credit," Glitter countered. "You may not always know the right thing to say or do, but your heart is, usually, in the right place. Considering what you told me of your upbringing, you could have turned out a whole lot worse."

"I could say the same for you. How are you so genial and cheerful? My family situation was bad, but you had a terrible childhood."

"I've suffered, but I also found good people to care for me afterwards. Molissa and Rhimos, the zyla who owned the Verdant Sunrise, gave me a home, taught me some

Zylan, and encouraged my interests in cooking. They were very proud when Goldfire took me as an apprentice."

"I am glad you had so much support. Perhaps a bit jealous too, I admit. Maybe your sparkles grow from your jovial nature. Aside from always glowing, I do not see a downside to yours."

"Everyone knows how I feel if they're paying attention," she said. "I know you have figured out my moods and my colors. I've learned to dim them, but I can't hide them."

"I had not looked at it from that perspective."

"You've learned to dim your Gift too, but you've never used it outwardly or to see past the darkness."

I took a slow, deep breath to steel myself. "Very well. Let us try."

Glitter cast *umslyktresree,* and I made no effort to resist her magick. The feeling was unusual for me, as I had rarely had cause to feel such joy, and I was immediately overwhelmed.

"Tell me," Glitter prodded.

"I see your parents," I responded, giddy despite the gruesome scene.

"More."

"You are hiding under a table. Your father seems intoxicated. He is yelling and crying, accusing your mother of stealing his masculinity by running the business." I laughed. "She is trying to console him, that he works hard to keep the place in good repair and handles the bar, but that makes him angrier. He punches her in the face, knocking her down. Her nose is bleeding. You come out of hiding, but your voice catches. He kneels over her and continues to hit her, and you hear bones break."

Glitter was sobbing. "More," she squeaked.

I wanted to stop but could not. Instead, I hugged her while continuing to describe the scene, smiling the whole time. "Weary, he stands, his hands and shirt bloody. He turns to see you standing there. He reaches out to you, pleading for forgiveness, but you still cannot speak. He cries, grabs a knife, and plunges it into his chest."

"Deeper," she sniffed. My shoulder was damp with her tears.

I focused my attention on her. "You are afraid. He… he had hit you before. You thought that he would kill you too, so you froze." The new scene overlayed the original, distinct, yet separate. "He overheard you telling a friend that your mother ran the inn and did most of the work. Later that night, he scolded you and knocked you to the floor. You never spoke about him again until after his death. You blame yourself for his actions, that he acted because of what you said." I squeezed her tighter as the spell wore off and I could pull the visions back. "Are you… can I…?" I fumbled, not knowing how to properly comfort her.

"Just…" she began and held me. We stood there for a few minutes, unmoving, while she cried into my shoulder. "This…um…this was harder than I thought." She coughed, then sniffed. "Maybe we should do this sitting down next time."

"Are you sure you want to try this again?"

"No, but yes." She stepped back, her hands taking mine. "I hadn't realized that about my father, that I didn't talk about him anymore." Her chin quavered.

"I can understand why. I am certain there are things I stopped doing after mine hit me. Did it happen often?"

"Not that I recall. He was good to us most of the time. I can't think of another instance, but maybe you will see it."

"I hope not. I have already seen more than I wish."

"I know, and I'm sorry. But you were able to go beyond seeing the instance and saw the situation from a wider perspective. That's good."

"I suppose. It does not make me feel any better about it."

"Maybe in time. We'll practice again tomorrow. We should do some work while our emotions settle," she suggested.

I nodded. "It is not your fault," I said gently.

She nodded in response, but her yellow and blue sparkles belied her affirmation.

We held hands as we returned to the tower, stopping for a few minutes to check on the garden. Though sickly, some of the herbs had managed to survive for two weeks. We pulled the dead ones up and added them to the composting pile. The survivors would not be useful for magic, healing, or consuming, but served as an indicator that life was slowly returning to the grounds.

"I wonder if Faldrein could heal these?" I mused. "Perhaps adding more life energy will improve and accelerate their growth."

"Could you do it?" Glitter asked.

"Possibly. I have only ever used my energy to harm undead, not to heal." I focused my life energy outward to cascade over a section around me to no apparent effect.

Glitter took a handful of stones and marked out a circle. "That's about where your energy burst reached. Let's see if this area grows better. If so, we have a new project for you and Faldrein."

I looked around the great swath of land bordered by Ormak's fence. "It will take far more than we have to heal all of this. I would be happy if we could get the garden to grow. We shall see about the rest in time. Grab some more stones." I moved over eight paces and released another pulse of energy, slightly overlapping the first, to see if an area with two bursts would have a greater improvement.

We went back inside to prepare lunch. Glitter had me peel, core, and cut two kohlrabies into thin wedges while she started a fire in the brick oven. When finished, I placed them in a shallow pan. She drizzled pressed oil over them and sprinkled the sliced vegetables with crushed salt and powdered chilies, then put them into the oven. When tender within and lightly browned and crisped, she added shredded sharp cheese and chopped parsley to the vegetables.

"Here, I wrote it down for you," she said, handing me a page with ingredients and instructions. "It's simple enough, so long as you don't over season them. Too much salt or chili will make them inedible."

"Thank you. I usually boil root vegetables that are best when not raw. Assuming I cook at all."

"That's why I'm going to teach you." She smiled, popping a wedge into her mouth then breathing heavily around the hot kohlrabi. "You need to eat better," she said after drinking a sip of water to cool her mouth.

"I eat," I protested.

"I've seen how and what you eat. Honestly, I'm surprised that you don't show signs of famine. I won't give you anything fancy or tricky, but I do want you to start cooking for yourself."

"Yes, m'lady."

She threw a kohlrabi slice at me. "Don't you 'm'lady' me," she cackled. "I am Glitter, the Shining Star, Wizard of Amrawood," She exclaimed with as much pomposity as she could muster before bursting out in laughter.

I joined in her merriment to my limits, for I had seen enough of her pain today. "So, you have a title now?"

"Yep. You should too by now, especially since you are your own master."

"I had not given it much thought. Vletraka was 'the Alabaster Moon, Necromancer of Cuyokale, and Wizard of the Ivory Tome'. I suppose I could adopt the Cuyokale part at least. The rest will come in time."

"Well then, Mithron, Necromancer of Cuyokale, shall we work on the library, or do you want to practice with your Gift more?"

I held up my hands. "The library, please. Tomorrow we can work on prismatic control of your spells."

"Deal."

We each chose a random volume off the stacks we had removed from the shelves. They had been emptied so that we would not lose track of which books had been catalogued and to avoid leaving tomes in the wrong category. Glitter had picked up *Abominations: Creating New Creatures from Old* by Pumliov, while I chose *Skin Twisting: A Study of Distortion Through Flesh Manipulation of the Self and Others* by Cogrist Ojo. Both works were easily categorized by their titles, so it took little time to leaf through them for verification. I made a point to study my volume later, while Glitter made several sounds of disgust as she paged through hers.

"I can't... that's awful." She slammed the book shut.

"Dare I ask?"

"You don't... actually, you might find it interesting. There's a ritual in here that creates hybrids of two different animals. They must be alive when they are merged into a single, larger creature with features of both. It sounds painful. Those poor creatures."

"That does sound unpleasant. Is it reversable?"

"Umm..." She paused, flipping through the book. "Not that I can tell, but I'd have to read deeper to be sure."

"As troubling as it is, it is still worth studying."

Glitter gave me a cold stare.

"I obviously did not study necromancy to create undead, but to destroy them. Learning from a tome like this might give us insights on how to repair the damage caused through that ritual."

"'There is nothing inherently evil in the Weave. That is the purview of those that manipulate it to their own ends'," Glitter quoted.[8] "Yes, I know. But this... this is horrific."

"I agree. That is why we need to learn it. Many wizards have done horrible things, this is part of the reason we have such a bad reputation with those unfamiliar with our ways. I used to think all necromancers were hideous monsters until I met Vletraka. We must learn the terrible things so that we do not repeat them and, if possible, undo them."

"Fair enough, but not today. I can't handle this one any longer." She wrote the name and placement in the logbook after shelving it with the five other volumes of magickal beasts we had found thus far.

We continued reading well into the night. I was deep into *In Pieces and In Whole* by Brosqua, a treatise on animating amputated sections of creatures, when Glitter

---

[8] *A Philosophy of Magic*—Revance, pg. 83.

poked my shoulder to make me stop and eat. The book included the technique for creating klaatoo. I had aided Vletraka in creating skitters of the crawling hands before, and this tome had other procedures to try so that I might improve them. Glitter had to poke me again to remind me to sleep.

Glitter had conjured a soft mattress on the floor—Ormak's ancient bedframe collapsed when we tried using it during the first week that we were all here—which was larger than the straw-filled ones we had sewn ourselves. I had begun to lay on a reed mat when Glitter stopped me. "We can share this one. I made it big enough for two."

"Thank you," I said, my eyes bleary.

"Is this comfortable for you?" she asked after I joined her.

"It is softer than I am used to, but manageable," I responded.

"No, I meant, being here with me."

"I am enjoying our time together. I like you."

She smiled. "I like you too. I meant are you comfortable on the mattress with me."

"Oh. I think so. I have never slept next to anyone else aside from being on the floor with my brothers, so I have no way to judge. Is there a protocol for this? Should I face you or turn away? Do we stay close or keep a distance?"

"I… I'm not sure. I never thought about it. I think since we're a couple, any way is fine."

"Okay then. Pleasant dreams."

The room brightened after I closed my eyes. I opened them to see Glitter in a nimbus of orange sparkles.

"Don't you want to kiss me?" she asked.

"Oh, sorry. I did not know that I should." I leaned over and she pulled away.

"What do you mean 'you should'? Don't you want to?" Her sparkles began to redden.

"I do. Am I just supposed to kiss you before we sleep? When are other appropriate times? I know we decided not to do so in front of the others. What are the rules for this?"

"We, um, we…" She laughed nervously. "I really don't know either. I guess whenever we feel like it, unless the other doesn't want to? And before you ask, I don't know how to tell either. I've also never done this before. I should probably ask Goldfire, but I don't want her to know about us yet."

"What about Orla? Does her profession not have something to do with this?"

"No!" She bolted upright. "She… she has a different specialty." Glitter blushed.

"Oh. I thought that kissing was something she would learn before becoming skilled at sex."

"I don't think it works that way. Let's just go to sleep. We can figure it out when we're not so tired." She laid back down, shifted over to kiss me, then rolled to her other side.

The next morning, she left to run errands after making a batch of sweet breads with chopped nuts and lemon zest. They were light and tangy, with a cake-like texture. She did not leave a recipe for them, so I assumed they required a greater skill set than they would seem.

While she was gone, I cleaned the kitchen before returning to the library. I wanted to study further Ojo's volume on *Skin Twisting*, but instead decided that I would borrow it until it was time for my shift.

I picked up a green leather-bound tome entitled *Secondaries: A Guide to the Handmaidens and Generals of the Gods* written by Yasky Huftici. Yasky spent far too much of the treatise on her credentials and research process before delving into her topic, and there was less information than I hoped for. In general, however, it was useful data, as I was not aware of many of the names and duties of these high-ranked underlings.

After logging Yasky's work, I began skimming Fotroc's *The Wizard's Cudgel: Creating Staves for Combat and Mystic Supplementation*. Vletraka had taught me the basics of creating such items and left it up to me as to whether to pursue the subject further. This work proved to be complex, yet written in a prosaic style which made the process feel more of an art form than an undertaking. It also gave me a better understanding of the magic-negating staff I had chosen from the treasure room.

"Uxadul and Tzali should read this one," I said to myself and wrote a note to give Uxadul when I saw him next. I had nearly completed my perusal when Glitter returned.

"I'm back," she shouted from the tower door.

"I will be down in a moment," I returned. I marked my page, making a conscious effort to stop reading. As I stood, my stomach grumbled, and I wondered how late it had gotten. "I really should develop a spell to mark the hours," I mumbled as I descended from the library toward the kitchen.

Glitter was putting sacks inside the ice chest when I entered. Two long loaves of bread sat on the counter, and I ripped off a piece.

"Do you need any help?" I asked as I bit into the bread. It had a sour tanginess to it with a hint of oregano.

"Can you put the cheeses in the frost pantry for me?"

"Of course. This is a lot of food. Did you go to Durcltown?"

"Yeah. I wanted to stock up on things before Blythad comes next week." Once she had finished loading the ice chest, she turned to face me.

"You colored your face," I commented.

"Do you like it?" she asked, leaning against the ice chest.

I stepped closer to her. "The orange on your eyelids sets off nicely against your copper eyes." I paused. "You have streaks of silver radiating in your eyes. Has that happened before? They are usually just one color, or have I never looked this closely before?"

"I don't know. I guess you'll have to pay more attention." She grabbed my robe and pulled me closer.

I sniffed. "Are cherries in season? Is that why your lips are darker?"

"You tell me." She tugged my collar and kissed me. There was an unusual warmth in her kiss.

"Cherry wine?"

"A little. Do I look pretty?"

"You always do."

"Prettier than normal?" she prodded.

"The colors do accentuate your features. They are colors I would use to paint you."

"You paint? How come you never told me?"

"We have been busy. It is something I should spend more time doing, but there are so many books to read."

"There's more to life than books." She stared deeply into my eyes.

"Obvio-" I began before she kissed me again. This one was longer than any before and her sparkles flashed orange and pink, with the occasional yellow mixed in. I expected to lose color, but something seemed off with her.

"Is this too much for you?" she asked. "You aren't kissing me back as much."

"This seems… aggressive? It does not feel quite right."

She pouted then kissed me again, softer this time, cupping my face in her hands. "Better?"

"Yes, but—"

"But what?" She pushed me back a pace. "You don't like kissing me anymore?" Her eyes began to glisten.

"You…it feels…it feels like you…" I shook my head. "When we kissed before, it felt relaxed and comfortable. This feels different. Are you alright?"

Glitter responded by pushing me away and running to the bedroom.

I spent a few minutes deciding whether to follow her, during which time I finished the piece of bread and pulled a pair of strawberries out of the ice chest to quieten my protesting stomach.

Glitter lay on a reed mat on the floor in a sea of yellow sparkles sobbing when I opened the door; the fluffy mattress had long since vanished.

"Did I do something wrong?" I asked.

Glitter sniffed and wiped her nose on her sleeve, smearing the artificial color from her lips. "I don't know what I'm supposed to do," she cried. "It's your fault. She said she'd make me pretty and to take control and be innocent if that didn't work and… and…" Her tears flowed harder.

"Who? Why? I do not understand."

"Orla. You told me to ask Orla, and I did. Now you hate me."

"You said that asking Orla would not be wise."

"And I was right," she yelled, red motes interspersing with the yellow. "It's all messed up now."

"No, it is not," I said quietly. Her sadness was infectious, and it took a couple breaths to keep the world at grey. "What did Orla tell you?"

"She said that all men like painted faces, that it makes us prettier."

"I think you are beautiful either way."

"Thanks." She almost smiled as she sat up. "She said that I needed to 'take charge' and 'be in command' because powerful men like that sort of thing, and if that didn't work then play shy and innocent, because men like that too. I spent much of the day with her as she showed me how to act. A lot of people stared at me at the market, and I felt confident until I got home. I guess I did it wrong."

I knelt next to her. "You did not have to act in any way except as yourself. I like you being you. I only thought of Orla because we cannot go to our friends or the few adults in our lives, and she seems to understand relations with others. I have no idea how to do this right. I only know that play-acting feels wrong to me and that my parents represent a bad example of doing so."

She laughed and cried together. "This was stupid. I should have trusted my instincts and not done this, but I don't know what else to do."

"As you said, 'we're smart and we'll figure this out'. Neither of us has any frame of reference, so why do we not just do what we feel is right and make our own rules?"

"That is the most sensible thing I've heard all day." She laughed and kissed my cheek. "First rule: stop listening to adults. I'm going to wash up, then we're going to make meat pies. You didn't eat lunch, did you?"

"I had some of the bread you brought home."

"I thought so. Come on."

Making the crusts for the pies reminded me of the kuluba root, due to the repetitive process in making it edible. Glitter mixed the flour, egg, salt, and butter then rolled it into a ball and chilled it. She then added more butter, beat it with a wooden roller, folded it, and repeated the process until she determined that it was ready. The filling was essentially a thick stew which even I could make. I have tried to repeat her dough-making, but it always comes out tough and chewy—where hers was light and flaky—and never seals in the juices.

With dinner, she poured out a small glass for me and a larger one for her. "I know that you don't like alcohol, but at least taste it," she said, sniffing her own. I gave her a skeptical look. "Trust me." I took a tiny sip.

"This is quite good. I taste grapefruit and hibiscus."

"It's mead. There are a few mazers in Dureltown, and this one has the best flavors."

"It is like tea, but stronger. I should not be drinking this."

"Small portions will not harm you or cause you to lose control. I understand your concern—I may have had too much wine earlier. Just have a little for the flavor, but not enough to feel odd."

We elected to sleep next to each other while holding hands. Somehow, I was on a reed mat when I awoke instead of the mattress. Glitter had splayed herself over the mattress and had the blanket twisted around her legs and waist. She mostly sparkles a deep, peaceful blue while sleeping, and I have noted color flashes in response to her eye movements. On the rare occasion I see flashes of yellow or red, I gently and carefully woke her, if necessary, as those colors often indicated fear and anger and I did not wish her to have nightmares. She was usually grouchy the next day if her sleep was disturbed, and sometimes a simple nudge would change her dreams without waking her.

That day we focused on her magic. I watched her repeat a basic *juut* myzling, paying close attention to her feet, then hands, to see if the light shifted in color if she moved or gesticulated differently. At first, it was the same yellow-white light, but her hand motions got sloppy after repeating the spell so often and the spell reduced in brightness. I suggested different motions and we discovered a few tricks.

We knew that rotating her right foot outward created a purple light and used that as a baseline. Turning her foot out less caused a blue shift and the colors followed a rainbow pattern with the base color set at not moving, and rotating her foot inward led toward red. This did not hold with fire spells other than *aatokytsrukak*, however, but by then she was too tired to experiment further.

Glitter and I settled on a routine of working on the library every afternoon while using the mornings to work on our magic. The time passed too quickly, and Blythad was soon due to arrive.

"I need to go if we are to keep this a secret," I said standing at the edge of the *bezyamlialrih* for the third time between kisses.

"I know, but I don't want you to. It's been…comfortable being with you. A year ago, I wanted you dead, and now I want to keep you at my side."

"I will be replacing Blythad in a moon. You can visit me then. We can practice what we learned and work on other projects meanwhile. I would suggest coming to my tower…"

"But Goldfire would catch on. I won't be able to stay long with you unless she's really busy. I can tell her I'm running errands, but she'll expect me back before long."

"You could tell her," I suggested.

"I...I might have to. It's so much easier for you, you..." She trailed off, remembering why I no longer had a Mistress. "I didn't mean..."

"I understand." The *bezyamlialrih* began to glow. "Blythad's coming," I said with concern.

"*Mimzeldroob*!" she nearly shouted, slapping my shoulder as I stepped away from the engraved circle.

"Hi. I wasn't expecting you to greet me." Blythad laughed, looking startled.

"I was...um...checking on the *bezyamlialrih* to make sure it wasn't damaged."

"Oh, I don't think we'll have to worry about that. Nari and the others put a lot of energy into this." He tapped the edge of the teleportation circle with his foot.

"Well, then I guess it's fine." Glitter smiled, her sparkles yellow and green.

"Is everything okay? Nothing happened to the library, did it?"

"No, everything's fine. Just...just a bit distracted, I guess. Let's get you settled in." She waved Blythad toward Ormak's tower and fell in behind him.

She glanced back toward me and mouthed "I love you", then followed Blythad through the gate.

'I am glad her spell concealed us both. An owl hovering in midair would surely have given us away.'

'I still do not understand the need to keep your mating a secret,' said Thessylia.

'We are not "mating". We are simply trying to establish our relationship on our own terms without anyone else's judgement.'

'Do you fear how they would feel about it?'

'No. From what Glitter said, others will offer their opinions which could influence who we are as a couple. It makes sense, though I do not fully comprehend it either. She understands people better than I, so I will trust her.'

Thessylia ruffled her feathers. *'Human customs. She should just come to your nest and be done with it.'*

'And owls do not have ritual displays?' I asked, knowing full well that all birds did.

'Yes, but that involves calling, dancing, displaying, and bringing food, all perfectly normal actions. Humans become different when together.'

'So long as it is for the better, I do not see a problem with that. They are inside. We can go home now.'

Chapter 5: Yoffa's Call

It was two summers after the events in Ehrghex, where our combined forces put to rest all of the unliving residents of the town, when I had an unexpected visitor. Upon returning home, I focused on creating new guardians to protect my property, both as a defensive necessity and a distraction. As useful and disturbing as Vletraka's skitters of klaatoo were, I felt I had to create something new and different, though I did make a few skitters to have a baseline of defense until I was ready. I returned a number of times to Ehrghex to collect the rotting heads of the ruklaa we had destroyed, making sure to choose ones decayed enough to be unrecognizable as the people who they once were, preferably ones with the skull showing through the remaining flesh. Through further study of *In Pieces and In Whole* by Brosqua, I discovered how to animate them and imbue them with rudimentary flight.

Like the skitters of animated hands, my mookali, mookal in the singular, were manufactured in groups. Each congress of mookali could be modified further by adding different spells to them during their creation; some had a burning gaze, while others breathe ice, scream, have acid in their bite, an electric aura, or explode when destroyed. One problem I have yet to solve is that they constantly chitter and babble incoherently to themselves and each other, sounding something like haunted cicadas as the whispering rises and falls. While at rest, they pile themselves in small pyramids, appearing as misshapen stones until something catches their attention.

During this period, I had begun study of the *Ivory Tome* in earnest. Vletraka had shown it to me when she had taken me on as her apprentice, and it was part of her title, but at the time of her death I was not fully prepared for the lessons housed within. That is not a statement of humility—the *Ivory Tome* would not open for me until eight moons ago.

Contained within its dragon-bone covers, carved from the sternum over the dragon's heart, was the collected wisdom of previous vitae necromancers, those dedicated to destroying undead and strengthening life, and the spells they had created for that purpose. Most of the spells were still beyond my ability to cast, requiring more power than I could gather, though some, such as *juutaatok,* which manifests a blade of light, I discovered a variant of on my own. Vletraka had added to the volume, and I learned a final lesson from her; I could temporarily sustain a shell of life energy around me to deflect and repel the negative energy which animates the undead. With practice, I have slowly expanded this aura so, theoretically, I can protect another person standing nearby.

The paired trees which marked the only path to my home now bore my sigil, an upturned crescent moon over a curved dagger, rather than Vletraka's open book symbol. I did nothing to change it; in fact, I never intended to, but, at some point, I had noticed it had altered itself all the same. I eventually learned it is part of the same enchantment which signals the arrival of visitors, allowing the voices of those who call out for invitation to be heard clearly within the tower and on the grounds, should the wizard be outdoors. The symbol itself had evolved, adding in the nine stars, representing compassion and selflessness, aspects I need to strengthen, which formed the constellation when Troj's sword vanished during my vision suns ago. It was on a particularly hot day, the kind when Vletraka and I would have avoided each other due to irritability, that I heard a call from my past.

"Um, hi. I, um, I'm here to see…wait, she wrote it down. 'I am Verond, here to visit the Master of the tower.'"

I looked up from *Tongue of Stone* by a scholar named Urvanu, a primer on the dialect of the denizens of the elemental plane of Earth, which has distinct variations from the common language of the elemental realms and wondered if I had heard correctly.

What is my brother Verond doing here? 'Thessylia, we have a guest,' I thought to my constant companion. She had no need to answer, and I trusted her to snag one of the amulets hanging from a rod on the roof and bring it to our visitor.

Meanwhile, I marked the page, grabbed the cooling cylinder I had created after last sun's heat wave, and headed for the front door. The cooling cylinder works on the same principle as the frost pantry, chilling a small area around it, and is portable, so it can be carried from room to room. I have also attached a small ceramic bowl to it, as it condenses the moisture in the area as well. There is still a round stain on the library table from before I added the latter feature.

I opened the door to see a tall, muscular young man carefully picking his way down the winding path to the tower. Even from here, I could see his trepidation as he eyed the stacks of mookali and klaatoo, trying to determine the true nature of the odd sculptures which would leave him unmolested so long as he carried the amulet with him. When he saw me, he waved and began to make a direct line to the house.

"Stay on the path." I shouted. Not that he was in any danger from the guardians, but the footing was treacherous in that area, full of large, loose stones which I had moved out of the garden and was piling up for another klaatoo nest. He quickly backpedaled and walked with increased speed down the path and all but bolted to the door. I feared he might tackle me when instead he lifted me up in a powerful hug which caused my ribs to pulse in discomfort.

"Brother, you've shrunk!" Verond laughed as he set me back down.

"Actually, I have grown a bit, but you," I said, marveling at the thirteen-year-old boy who had travelled quite far from home, "you are already nearly as tall as father." As I spoke, Thessylia landed on my shoulder and I scratched her head absently.

"You have a pet owl? I thought necromancers had skeletons and spiders and stuff. When I saw him…"

"Her," I corrected.

"Sorry, her drop the necklace in my hands, I didn't realize she was your pet."

"She is much more than that. Many, but not all, wizards bond with a companion. There is a day-long ritual to call them, and we do not know what will answer the call until the ritual is complete, though spiders and such are not unheard of. Thessylia is as much a part of me as my arm, or, more aptly, my heart, and she has saved my life on more than one occasion. Come in," I insisted as Thessylia flew off to her favorite shade tree.

"It's a lot colder in here than outside," Verond commented as we walked through the seating area to the kitchen.

I handed him the cooling cylinder. "Only because of this. Walk away from it, and it is unbearably stifling in here, even with the windows open. Vletraka loved the heat, but it is far too much for my tastes."

"That reminds me, Yoffa apologizes for not coming for the funeral. It's just too far for her to travel."

"I thought so and expected as much. I knew they were close and merely wanted her to know," I said as I set a kettle in the fireplace and cast *uvaazsrukak* to ignite the wood.

He was staring at me when I turned around. It took a moment for me to realize that he had never seen magic being used, at least by me.

"That's amazing." He beamed. "What else can you do?"

"I have learned quite a bit, now that I think on it. Most of the spells I know are for combat, but when at home, I mostly prepare for general utilitarian purposes. Once the tea is ready, I will use another spell to chill our drinks, as I am sure you do not want a hot beverage after your travels. Are you hungry?"

"Famished," he said in a loud sigh, smiling as he did so.

I gathered a small wheel of mild cheese, a loaf of dark bread, a knife, and a pouch of huckleberries, and placed them on the table. As I did, the kettle began to whistle, so I moved it off the fire and tossed in a handful of mint leaves. When I turned back around, half the cheese was already gone. I smiled and grabbed another wheel, this one a bit sharper in flavor.

"So, what brings you all the way out here? And how did you find me?"

"Yoffa," he mumbled around a mouthful of bread. "Mmm, this is good." He swallowed. "She's sick, and sent me to bring you home."

I froze. Yes, Yoffa was old. Six suns older since I saw her last, so it should not surprise me. Yet she was always so strong and healthy, it was not fantasy to think she might be immortal. In my line of work, however, I should know better.

"What is wrong with her?"

"She coughs a lot and has gotten very weak. I suppose she's been taking her herbs, since she knows more about healing sick people than anyone, but it's not enough anymore. I think she misses you and relied on you more than you think."

"Then, by all means, we should leave at first light. Did you walk all the way here? It takes days on horseback."

"I caught rides on a couple of wagons bringing goods toward Dureltown, then switched to one returning from there to Huntingford. It was hard to find someone willing to give directions from there."

"Wizards are generally treated with suspicion, at best," I said with a heavy sigh. "No matter how well we treat others. Rightfully, they fear our magic, but we are just as human… actually, not all wizards are human, but we are the same as any other member of our species. We simply know things which the average person does not."

"Maybe they don't fear your magic, but fear other humans. Magic just makes it worse."

I mulled Verond's statement over for a while before deciding that he had an argument which I could not refute. I had met my share of humans with no understanding of the Weave who were dangerous enough without magic.

"I suppose I will have to continue to prove that I am not a bad person and hope someday they will see me for an individual, not purely as a potential threat.

"So, tell me, what else is happening in Split Falls? I have had no news in six suns. I assume Larshon has gotten married and moved off."

"Yes, about four years ago. He moved to Turtlebog with Ivette."

"He married Ivette? I thought he was going to marry Milique."

"Milique died shortly after you left. She was found lying on the shore under the Falls. It looked like she slipped and her head landed on a rock."

"That is too bad," I said flatly. I did not know Milique well, but she seemed pleasant enough, and seemed to moderate Larshon's more aggressive tendencies. In actuality, I did not know most of the villagers well. I grew up with them and had plenty of opportunity, but I only had a passing interest in the things which entertained their lives. I know how arrogant that sounds, but there was little commonality between the rest of Split Falls and myself.

"How is Mother?" I had to assume she was in good health since Verond had not spoken of her yet.

"She worries about you. You know how she feels about magic, and now she has a son who's a wizard. She prays a lot, but never mentions you in front of Father."

"I had not expected him to have changed his mind about me. Mother always had good reason to fear him. I will speak with her when we return. Mayhap I can make her understand that I have not been possessed by demons, or whatever awful thing she has imagined."

"If I were you, I'd avoid Father altogether. Who knows how he'll react."

"I had hoped to put our past behind us, but you are likely correct," I answered without trying to disguise my anger at the man who had disowned me. "Still, if our paths cross, I, at least, will make the attempt."

Verond continued to regale me with stories from home, about people I barcly knew and new techniques he has learned at the forge. I feigned interest, but Verond did not appear to notice. Instead, I contemplated the possible causes of Yoffa's illness and considered which books to bring along with me. After Verond yawned a few times, I became aware of how much energy his travels had taken from him. I showed him to my old room; I had since moved into Vletraka's larger room. He plopped onto the too-small bed.

I ambled over to the library and perused the shelves holding books on herbalism. There was probably little here which Yoffa did not already know about and try, but I had to check. I grabbed four volumes which focused on healing properties and put them on one of the tables. Without actually examining her, there was no way for me to find a cure, but I could take some time to familiarize myself with some possibilities. Eventually, I realized I needed to sleep as well. But first, I wrote a short note and called to Thessylia as I stepped outside. I tied the note to her leg, cast an enhancing spell to speed her journey for the first half-day, and she flew off.

When we are separated, there is a noticeable absence of… something. It is not the same as losing a sense, like being deafened or blinded, but more akin to the loss of color when my Gift manifests, but in a more spiritual sense. Without her, I am alone, regardless of who else might be with me. A painful experience to be sure, but at times such as these, it is a necessary one. There are spells to send messages, but they are limited in scope. For a longer message, it is better to send it in this fashion than as a series of short missives. At least the receiver in this case is another wizard. Those who do not use or understand magic tend to brush off the mystical communications as random thoughts and pay little heed to the messages.

I awoke to the sound of shattering pottery. I began to bolt toward the alchemical laboratory for fear of Verond blowing himself up, but then heard mild swearing from the kitchen. It was not yet dawn, so I had only been asleep for a few hours, having gotten out of the sleep schedule of working the forge. Verond would have taken over all of the apprenticeship duties of sweeping out ash, starting up the coals, and organizing our father's tools before he came to work, bringing a bowl of gruel, or a stack of Mother's hearty wheat cakes to break the night's fast. When all three sons were there, either Verond or I ran back to the house for food. Since he would not be able to leave the forge unattended, for that is when fires happen, he would have to rely on father.

Now, however, it appeared he was attempting to forage for himself, and dropped a jar of raspberry jam, which sent globs of red, sticky goo and fired clay flying across the floor, cabinets, and furniture. Verond had grabbed a towel in order to scoop up the shards, cutting himself in the process, drops of blood mixing with the jam.

"Why do you always seem to hurt yourself whenever you are around me?" I asked after surveying the damage, my head shaking in disbelief. When I last saw him, he was recovering from a severe burn and a hornet's sting.

"Just lucky, I guess," he chuckled, wrapping the pottery-and-jam covered towel around his hand.

I grabbed a clean towel. "Do not use that one. You do not want jelly in the wound." I pulled his towel away, revealing a deep gash in the palm of his hand, the pooling blood covering the scars from his burn. I jammed the clean towel onto the wound, the white towel quickly turning red. "Hold this with your other hand," I commanded. "Press hard and sit there. I'll be back in a couple minutes." I opened the small closet next to the kitchen door and grabbed a sickle.

"You're not going to cut it off, are you?" He blanched.

"And have you bleed even more all over my kitchen?" I managed to ask with a straight face before sputtering with laughter. "I am going to harvest something for that wound." I stepped out into the garden and lopped off the blooms from five great mulleins, the large yellow flowers had begun opening in the pre-dawn twilight. Upon returning, I grabbed a wooden bowl and the marble mortar to crush the flowers before adding a little wine to the mashed petals to thin the paste. I have never tasted the wine, but I have been told it is of good quality and prefer using it as an antiseptic.

I wiped off the sickle and returned it to its proper place, then grabbed the healing kit off of the shelf. The kit contained clean strips of cloth, a small bottle of distilled grain alcohol, a hooked needle, fine silk thread, a small knife, and a jar of herb-infused waxy balm. I splashed some of the alcohol onto my hands and wiped them off on a clean towel before gently pulling away the one Verond was using to staunch the wound. He hissed in pain as he saw the deep cut in his palm, which began to slowly fill with blood. I grabbed another cloth and pushed it onto the wound.

"Hold this tight for another minute. We need to stop the bleeding." While we waited, I stirred the mullein paste, which had absorbed the wine and was smoothing out well, and then threaded the needle.

I removed the towel, and saw the bleeding had, for the most part, stopped. "I need you to hold still. This is going to hurt." I used the hook-shaped needle to pierce the skin on either side of the gash and pulled a length of thread through his flesh. He gritted his teeth, moaning deeply as tears swam out of his eyes. It took eight passes of the needle to close the wound. After cutting the thread, I dabbed the mullein paste over it, folded a cloth over the stitches, and tightly wrapped his hand in yet another cloth strip.

"I'm sorry to keep causing you so much trouble," Verond cried.

"Do not fret over it. Things happen. I can do more healing with magic later, after some preparations. This will keep your blood inside until then." I smiled. "Now, let me prepare a meal. I want you to sit still until afterwards. Fair?"

"Fair," he answered, a smile growing on his face. After a particularly cruel teasing from Larshon when Verond was little, I promised him I would never lie to him, so that he would always trust me. 'Fair' became our code word to ensure honesty.

"I must warn you, I have never learned to cook well. Magical and alchemical recipes come to me more easily than culinary ones." I have gotten used to bland and over-spiced food, with few meals flavored between those extremes. I find bland to be better and eat more because my body requires sustenance than for pleasure, except when visiting with Glitter or Blythad, for their skills have proven exceptional. Glitter's lessons have helped, and my diet has a greater variety than before, but my talents are still limited in this regard.

I whipped up batter for dark wheat griddle breads and opened a clay jug of hickory syrup. As a good host, I gave Verond the less-burnt breads, which he ate with relish, along with most of the syrup. Fortunately, I did not require large quantities of food to sustain me, so two of the breads were more than enough. Also fortunately, I did not have to feed Verond on a regular basis and began to wonder how much our father must have sold and traded to keep enough food available, as Mother could only grow so much in her garden.

Afterwards, I showed him the library, pointing out a few books which I thought might interest him and were not too deep on an esoteric level, to keep him occupied while I prepared the spells which would be useful for travelling and gathered the necessary equipment for which magic was wholly unnecessary, such as blankets, a pot, and a sack of vegetables. I could conjure the items needed, except the food, but the energy needed would likely be more useful to ward off an attacker. Though Verond had grown quite large, he was still only thirteen, and I did not expect him to fight if we were threatened, even with the iron hammer he wore on his belt. His size was intimidating, but I doubted his skills are anywhere near Vondro's.

After dragging our supplies to the door, I went back to collect my brother, who was intently paging through *A History of Enchanted Weapons and the Warriors Who Wielded Them* by Voorsha "Songhammer" Thurssif, a vycru woman famed as much for her knowledge of military history as her martial skills. Vycru are a serpentine humanoid race, with fine scales in a variety of colorful patterns; they are highly toxic, swift and deadly in battle, yet charming otherwise.

"Give me your hand," I commanded gently.

He slid his arm across the table, never taking his eyes off the book.

I sighed. "The injured one." I smiled, slightly annoyed but more amused. *Thank you, Mother, for teaching us the value of reading.*

He switched arms, unsuccessfully repressing a wide grin.

I unwrapped the bandages to see the stitching and salve were holding up well. I intoned a few words while running my index finger along the gash, causing the skin to knit itself together.

"You made my hand fall asleep," Verond commented.

"A minor side effect. I am not a healer. The spell used to be more painful, but I have improved it."

"Will there be a scar?"

"Probably, but there are enough lines in the palm that it likely will not be noticed. When you develop callouses like father, your hands might never get injured again."

"At the rate he works me, that shouldn't take long," he chuckled, flexing his fingers. "That really does feel better. Thanks, *big* brother!"

Although I am five suns Verond's senior, I had ceased to be his *big* brother years ago.

"It must be difficult for him to handle the forge alone while you sought me out," I said without sympathy, though I gave a fleeting thought for Mother, should our father's solitude grow to anger. "Yet, he managed before we were born, so I suppose he is fine."

We carried the travelling gear outside, setting it down on the path leading out. "Do not be frightened," I warned Verond before shouting, *"hyhyidovcaz!"* and patting the door. A skitter of klaatoo leapt off of their perch and scrabbled to the front door, building themselves over it like a web of bones, while triplets of mookali floated to perch on the windowsills.

Verond stared at the animated remains, his mouth hanging open in fear and astonishment.

"They serve to protect my home," I said softly in an attempt to reassure him. "As long as you are under my aegis, they will not harm you."

"Th-those," he stammered, "are heads. And hands." His gaze looked over the yard, resting on the unusual sculptures with the sudden realization of what they were comprised of. "Are they human?"

"Not for some time and not all of them, no." Before he could speak again, I continued, "I did not kill them, or pull them from their graves, if that is what you are thinking. Another wizard had turned them into ruklaa. I took the parts I needed after we destroyed the monsters they had become."

"But… they were once *people*. How can you cover your house in *people*?" His look of disgust reminded me once again how much he looked like our father.

"I am a necromancer. We study the edges between life and death, blurring them when necessary. There is no life to these bones, no soul fragments attached to any of them. This door is made of wood, your clothing of leather. You are *wearing* dead things. You *eat* dead things. It is all part of the cycle. I merely use the leftover pieces in the same way you wear that cow's hide."

"A cow is not the same as a human!" he cried, tears rolling from his eyes.

"No, but bones are bones. I repeat, there is nothing left of the person they once were. Just bones."

"But how can the souls rest if they aren't buried? What about their families?"

"Burial is not necessary for a soul to pass gently into the Dark Lady's realm, but a convenience for the living. Bodies rot and can become infectious if not handled properly. Putting a corpse into the ground avoids having to smell it as it decays and prevents scavengers and vermin from consuming it. The rites performed for the deceased are for the living, to reassure them and protect their sensibilities at a time of emotional trauma; it has nothing to do with the soul of the deceased. The families of these constructs," I added, pointing to the heads and hands, "were all murdered at the same time and all turned into monsters. My colleagues and I released their souls from their bondage to their animated bodies. These are only dead bones."

Verond continued to stare at me, his eyes red with tears, and I could tell he was not completely convinced. Facts rarely change deeply held beliefs, no matter how ridiculous they are. Though, to be fair, I had not visited the Dark Lady's realm myself, nor had I interviewed Her about the state of souls and the process of separation, so I suppose I was merely espousing my own theories based on my education without first-hand knowledge. Tsukatta claimed to have personal contact with her deity, but I think even that was suspect, as I wonder how one can know if a goddess would take a particular interest in one mortal or another.

Taken to its logical conclusion, can anyone trust any belief or even their own senses, as they can be easily fooled? Or is such an extreme the gateway to madness? I have suffered from delusions instilled by disease, hunger, and sleeplessness, which led me to believe all my fears and guilt had become manifest in those I thought friends. There is fluidity to reality, filtered by our senses and minds, so everyone perceives it in their own fashion. The greatest philosophers of all ages have debated these questions and more, with little consensus, and my observations are no more or less valid than theirs. I wonder if even the gods themselves know.

"We need to go," I said flatly. "You can believe what you wish, but at least consider my words. I am not a villain."

We had been traveling for over an hour before he spoke. "Does it have to be bones? Or even people?"

"What?" I asked, as I could barely hear his raspy whispers over the clopping of the horses.

"Couldn't you use something else besides people parts?" Verond asked louder, sadness evident in his voice.

"If they were available, yes, I suppose I could. When Ehrghex was decimated, there was an abundance of materials to use. Using human heads and hands creates a demoralizing effect and instills fear, which are equally as important as the physical threat to deter intruders. Animal skulls would not have the same effect, unless I hunted down all of the large predators in the area, which would throw off the natural balance. Though adding a few sharp-toothed puma skulls might not be a bad idea.

"I am sorry to have put you at unease. My guardians are meant to ward off intruders, not to frighten friends and family. Please do not tell Mother; she would not even try to understand."

Verond nodded but did not speak again for some time.

He thinks me a scoundrel now. I had no idea he would be so repulsed by them; by me. I should have waited until he was outside the gate, but I had *to try to impress him. Now, he is likely to fear magic just as Mother does.*

Our journey to Split Falls was generally uneventful. Verond kept his silence for much of the first day but became more talkative by nightfall. Perhaps my explanations allayed his fears or he had the same forgiving nature as Mother; I could not know for certain. Glitter knows spells which would be able to probe his mind for answers, but such magicks have never interested me. When my training began, my obsessive focus on destroying the undead kept me from pursuing those types of spells, as they are generally useless against such creatures.

Actually, Glitter would have discerned Verond's thoughts without resorting to magic. I often found myself missing her company and insights. As uncomfortable as I was with her, with most people, I was sometimes more distressed being apart from her for extended periods. For a while, we were meeting monthly to reduce my Gift's reaction to her, under the theory that regular exposure might begin to inure me to the more dramatic effects of my feelings for her. It has helped somewhat, as I am no longer completely debilitated in her presence. I have learned to live with the images of her near death.

I adjusted the ring she had given me. It was Ormak's. We had kept the magical items which he wore and set them aside, both to honor him and for fear that they might be protected like many of his other personal items. Glitter felt enough time had passed and had taken to wearing his necklace with the snowflake pendant. The ring was gold set with onyx and conjured a phantasmal hand which flew short distances; it not only sapped the strength of those it touched but could carry spells which normally required physical contact so I could stay further away from close combat.

Our most recent communications have been through letters left at Ormak's tower, mostly detailing and updating recent findings. We still visited during each other's shifts, but not for the full moon as we had earlier to lessen the distractions. Glitter has been adding easy recipes to her letters, however, so I could prepare a wider variety of foods rather than relying on whatever might be handy at the time, generally raw vegetables when I stepped away from studying or experimenting. It was only for guests, like my brother, that I made more of an effort.

Verond was thrilled every time I had to cast the *hivliuose* spell to conjure another pair of horses, so at least I had not frightened him off of magic altogether. *I suppose that as long as I avoid animating anything, perhaps he will be all right.* I am hardly one to use magic frivolously, but I found myself periodically casting *uvaazrosiit* to entertain my little brother, creating small lights, objects, sounds, and smells to make him more comfortable with magic. He was still young, and I discovered he was most amused by scatological humor, so many of the noises and odors were reminiscent of flatulence.

I asked Verond to tell me as many stories of our village as he could and tried to pay attention so I would not be caught by surprise or say something embarrassing. Unfortunately, I could not remember meeting most of the people whom he talked about, though I was certain I met everyone in Split Falls; their lives did not matter to me then, and I have no connection to them now. *It is probably best if I appear as a stranger than the outcast smith's son.*

I told Verond not to tell anyone who I was, to see if anyone recognized me and let him think it was a trick the two of us were playing on the village. The game played out well, and no one had any idea who I was, and likely did not know me then, either. *I may as well have never lived here. Aside from Yoffa, I made no impression at all.* To this day, I cannot say whether or not that insight bothered me.

Verond left for home as we neared Yoffa's cabin. Her garden had become poorly tended, with a few weeds and dead or dying plants interspersed with the unusually crooked rows of herbs and vegetables.

A loud hacking coughing greeted me before I could knock on her door, and I rapped lightly before opening it without waiting for a response. "Mistress Yoffa?" I called from the doorway.

Lying on her straw bed, she turned her rheumy eyes toward me. "Smith's son?" she croaked. "It's good to see you again." As she tried to sit up, she broke into another coughing fit.

"Easy, Mistress," I said, rushing to her side and clasping her ancient hand.

Her grip was still strong as she squeezed my hand in return.

"How are you? How can I assist?"

"To be honest, I'm dying. No tears now, I've lived a good, long life, and I'll be nestled in Ioddenri's bosom shortly. There's nothing you can do but keep me company."

Even though I was prepared for this possibility, her words still came as a shock. My vision shifted before I could stop it, but rather than the usual scenes of pain and darkness, I only saw a massive gate of bone and iron chained shut. *Strange, she must have some defense against my Gift. That is fine—I do not wish to have my memories clouded by knowing her sorrows.* I squeezed her hand tighter.

"Can I at least try? Or perhaps ease your pain? I do not know what ails you or what you have done thus far."

"I've been drinking a tea of comfrey and adder's tongue. It soothes the coughing and seems to have stopped the bleeding from it," she said between light coughs. Her breath was raspy and there was a slight gurgle when she inhaled.

"Then I will make you more tea. Is this ailment truly beyond your curing?" I asked, hoping for more information.

"Thank you, lad. There is no cure for old age, I fear. Even if there were, I am happy with my life, and don't wish to prolong it unnaturally. You studied under 'Traka, so I know what you're thinking, boy. No magic."

I smiled wanly. "I would never go against your wishes. Besides, those spells are too advanced for me still."

This caused her to chuckle and cough.

"I had better make that tea."

We… mostly I, talked through the rest of the day, and into the night, interspersed with periods of Yoffa drifting off to sleep for no more than an hour at a time. On occasion, I would hear a light tapping from villagers dropping off baskets of food at her door, of which she ate very little.

"You should visit your family," she coaxed on numerous occasions, to which I reminded her that I had no family here besides her. Nevertheless, I left early the next morning to visit with the people I had grown up with.

In spite of my misgivings, I decided to ignore Verond's advice and make an effort to mend my relationship with our father. I freely admit to being frightened of the situation, as we had not parted on friendly terms, and I found I was still cross with him. The cart-wide dirt path which led to the forge and our… their… house had changed little over the past six suns, though I was certain the wheel-ruts must have gotten a little deeper.

The staccato rhythm of hammer on iron was evident long before the forge came into view, a steady beat for a few seconds at a time before the iron was placed back in the forge to reheat while another was removed to be worked on. *"Always keep at least two or three on the fire, so you aren't wasting time waiting for just one to heat up, but don't forget what each iron is being made for. Best if they're all the same, if you can help it. And don't leave 'em too long neither, lest they melt."* Say what you will, the man was both practical and efficient.

Had I done a painting of the man who was once my father and the forge before leaving six suns ago, they would have looked the same as now. It was a small shack of thick wood and fired brick, solid and strong like the man within. The mallow I had cultivated had grown uncontrolled, with many of the central plants stunted or dead from overgrowth, while the edges of the semicircle flourished. I was surprised he had not torn them all out after I left but as he was aware that the sap within was useful for healing burns, his pragmatism probably won out over his malice. Either that, or he clearly could not be bothered.

My former father looked much the same as well, perhaps a bit grayer in the temples and beard. He did not seem so tall and imposing, though his frame was still muscular beyond reasoning for a man of his age, but I had grown a little taller in the intervening years. Nonetheless, his presence was still intimidating, and I had to steady my breathing to push back the memories of the last time we spoke. It would not do for me to lose my composure and relay the darkness within his soul, for I expect there was more than I was already aware of.

Beyond the forge stood our small shack of a house. It was a good thing I no longer live there. I could not believe the house is large enough to fit even the three of them as it is. Though the tower was not luxurious, it is certainly spacious, particularly since I lived there alone now.

I do not *want to do this,* I thought. *But it is necessary for me to find a way to close out this chapter. Remember Glitter's advice: "Be nice to him, no matter what he says to or about you. Smile. Listen to his point of view. When you understand how someone else perceives the world, you understand them."*

"Greetings," I avoided stammering as I walked up to the shop.

"What can I do for you?" he asked, never looking away from the hot iron, hammering out a sharp point before placing it back on the fire. When he finally bothered to look up, he showed no recognition of me. When I did not respond, he continued, "I'm a busy man. If you don't know what you want, then leave me to my work."

"My apologies, you looked familiar," I blurted. "I was hoping you could make a pair of items for me." I handed him a sketch of my personal symbol. "About two feet tall, and nearly as wide."

"That's different. It'll be nice to work on something creative instead of just tools and such. What is it?"

I hesitated. "It is my family crest. It symbolizes hope over conflict, but the strength to use force when necessary."

"Hmm. What family?"

"Cuyokale," I lied, remembering Vletraka's title. I despise lying, but I could not bring myself to confront the man.

"Never heard of 'em, but I know of the region. Five gold drakes, and I'll have 'em ready by sundown."

I pulled the coins out and placed them on the table where he had a number of tools for sale.

"Thank you," I breathed before turning and walking away. *Either he has become very adept at disguising his feelings, or he has no idea who I am. Granted, it has been six suns, and I was only a boy when I left, but am I so different? After he is finished,* I lied to myself, *then I will tell him who I am.* I also had the sudden realization I would need to hire a cart to transport the crests home.

Chapter 6: A Flowered Grave

I wandered around Split Falls for some time before returning to Yoffa's shack. Little had changed in my home village, but I honestly did not recognize most of the people, as I had generally paid little attention to the adults when I lived here, and all of the children had grown up. After failing to confront my father, I could not muster the courage to visit Mother either. I told myself it would seem odd that a stranger would walk up to their house, and would rather not rouse my father's anger; if I also lost my temper, the consequences could be disastrous.

With care and caution, I snuck into Yoffa's home, and I was pleased to find her asleep. I prepared another pot of tea, adding globs of honey to soothe her wracked throat. Afterwards, I slipped back outside to weed her untended garden, a more prominent sign of her failing health than even her coughing, for on the rare occasions when she had been ill in my youth, she had still managed to take care of her duties. The grasses were easy enough to identify and remove, but her herbs were grown in clumps and clusters, and I had to take the time to identify each young plant before deciding whether or not to remove it.

As focused as I was on the task at hand, I was still aware that my efforts were not going unnoticed. I was nearly finished clearing the area around a patch of bell peppers when someone finally dared to approach. For once, I detected their presence without relying on Thessylia to warn me, as she had not yet returned; it was almost as if I could feel the person before I heard them carefully walking up behind me.

"Is there something I can do for you?" I asked without stopping my weeding.

"You, um, you're in Yoffa's garden," came a soft feminine voice.

"Yes. As you well know, she is not feeling well, and cannot do this herself."

"Indeed. What I mean is, who are you?"

"I am an old friend. I recently received word of her condition and came to help." I took a moment to turn to see with whom I was conversing.

She was about my age, wearing the same simple clothes as any other villager. Her long dark brown hair was held in a pair of braids, reaching almost to her small waist.

"Would you like to help?"

She looked over her shoulder at three other young women standing by Yoffa's house. They looked concerned, and ready to run for help if necessary. I took a deep breath and let my eyes relax. Both Blythad and Faldrein had been allowing me to practice using my Gift in order to gain better control. I often still had trouble when my emotions are heightened, but I could now, with some concentration, determine whether someone meant me harm without peering into their pain; basically, I can see a "surface" darkness in their intent.

"I mean no harm to you or this village, any more than you wish to hurt me," I tried to reassure her.

"Um, all right." She moved over to a patch of garlic, making sure she stayed well out of my reach. Her friends stepped a little closer but kept their distance. As she began weeding, she said softly, "Yoffa must really be ill to have let so many weeds grow."

"She is. Do you know how long she has been this way? I only found out about a week ago. As her garden is so ill-kept, I assume she has not found a new apprentice. If you have any information on her sickness or what herbs she was taking, it will help me greatly."

"Yoffa helped my sister birth her son three moons ago, and she seemed ill then. She coughed a lot, and looked a little pale, but told us she was fine," she answered while her practiced hands cleared out the weeds.

I was certain some of the weeds were young herbs that encroached on the garlic, but I saw no need to quibble about it.

"I figured she'd be better by now."

"She should have been. As far as I can tell, she should have either recovered or died a while ago. She was always a strong woman, but something about this seems wrong." I stood up, causing her and her friends to flinch. "Thank you for your assistance. I should check on Yoffa again." As I strode toward the house, her friends circled away, watching me the entire time. I nodded to them before entering Yoffa's cabin, looking away before they could respond.

The light was much dimmer inside, but even if my sight had not improved from my time with Thessylia, I would be able to find my way around despite all these years gone by. Still, a number of items were out of place and the cabin could do with a deep cleaning. I would have to do the organizing on my own, but summoning a *mimzelhruk* to remove the excessive dust and cobwebs would at least improve the atmosphere. While the *mimzelhruk* worked, carefully wiping the dust without kicking it up, I washed the dirt off of my hands and warmed the tea kettle.

Yoffa's loud gasping for air drew my attention and I hurried over to her. I sat her up and gently rubbed her back with an ointment of aloe, henbane, and adder's tongue. This relaxed her and eased her breathing somewhat, and soon she was taking slow, shallow breaths.

"Tea?" I asked, my voice barely above a whisper.

"Thank you, no," she answered between inhalations. She reached up and pulled my head close to hers. "You've always been a good boy." She kissed my cheek then relaxed back down to her bed, her last breath escaping as she did so.

A chill ran over me, as though her spirit had passed through my bones on her way to the Greylands. I had never felt that before, and I allowed my intellectual curiosity to buffer my sorrow over losing such a dear friend and teacher. However, I could not stave off my feelings for long, and I took advantage of my solitude in her cabin to mourn for her without having to worry about my Gift.

The next morning, I walked over to the house of Paz Hoken, the village's leader and king's representative of Split Falls. With Yoffa's passing, I believed he was now the eldest member of our or, rather, their village. We discussed her death, her burial spot, a gathering for her remembrance, and the future of her home and property. According to the paz's records, she had wished to be buried under a particular rowan tree at the forest's edge, following the rites of Ioddenri. The cabin and land would be passed to her daughter, if she could be found, as she had left some thirty suns ago. Should Onafa not be found, or if it revealed that she was also deceased, then they would seek out her last apprentice.

Yoffa had a daughter? *I suppose it makes sense that she would have family, but she never spoke of anyone to me. Perhaps they had a falling out, or mayhap Yoffa merely focused on the present and did not concern herself with those who had moved on. But when she grew ill, she sent for me, not Onafa. Of course, she knew where I reside, and may not have known where her daughter lives. I hope she is found; I cannot handle caring for yet another piece of property, and I especially do not wish to keep returning here.*

"Did you know Onafa? Do you have any idea where she might be found?" I asked the paz.

He leaned back in his padded chair and let out a grunting sigh. "I knew of her, but didn't really know her. She was a good ten suns my junior. I remember she was a pretty thing, but always dirty from working in Yoffa's garden, poking around in the woods, and fighting." He leaned forward so that all four of the chair's legs rested on the floor and chuckled. "The fighting… I don't think there was a boy she couldn't beat. I'd forgotten about that. As I recall, she left around her twentieth year to seek her fortunes elsewhere."

"Do you have any idea where, or what she might be doing?" I pressed. "I can aid in your search."

The paz stared at me for a moment, wizened eyes narrowing. "Why are you so interested in Onafa? Who was Yoffa to you? Who are you, anyway?"

"I knew Yoffa when I was younger; she was friends with my Mistress. I knew her to be a good woman, she was always kind to me, and I only wish to honor her passing." I took a deep breath and held it as color began to fade.

"And where is your mistress?"

"She," I paused to steady myself, "she was killed two autumns ago."

"Oh, I'm sorry. Well, as to Onafa, I would start in Dureltown. It wouldn't surprise me if she had joined the city guard or some such. I'll send couriers to the local villages to see if anyone knows anything about her in the meantime. For all I know, she is kingdoms away. We'll also try to find her last apprentice, just in case," he finished with a shrug.

I had no inclination of informing him of the ease of the latter search, but instead stood and nodded. "I have friends in Dureltown and had planned on stopping there anyway. I will see what information I can find once Yoffa has been laid to rest. Thank you for your time."

I pulled four silver talons out of my pouch to pay for the grave diggers, and a gold drake for the cleric to perform the rite of burial. I would donate more later, but I saw no reason to give over too much money to the paz. I easily could have used magic to dig the grave myself, for there are numerous spells which can move earth around to one degree or another, but I thought it best not to advertise my abilities and instead add to the local economy.

After the meeting with the paz, I walked over to the Twin Falls Inn. After my time spent at the Inn of the Weeping Rose in Dureltown, the Twin Falls was bound to be a disappointment. After all, Dureltown is a large city with travelers regularly passing through, while Split Falls is merely some place people sometimes end up as the sun sets, while journeying on to somewhere else. Regardless, it was well kept and clean, if small, as though the owner had little else to do except maintain the building. Both rooms were available, and I took the one with a window facing the rear of the building so that I could see Yoffa's cabin. I also hired a cart to pick up the crests from the smithy with explicit direction to leave them at the property's entrance. Although I tried to convince myself it was because they were too heavy and bulky to carry and were not worth the energy to transport using magic, I knew I truly did not wish to see my father again.

I awoke early so I could go out into the fields and dig up an orange rhopalo, a patch of small vines with sticky orange flowers which attract butterflies—Yoffa's favorite was a purple and white variety with large wings—and placed it in a small clay pot. While searching for the right plant, I could see figures moving about in the woods, and incorrectly assumed they were other villagers also looking for something to honor Yoffa with; I shifted my sight to be certain they were not vulzuu. By the time I reached the rowan tree where Yoffa was to be buried, a small crowd had already gathered, weeping and sharing stories. It had not occurred to me to what degree Yoffa had touched every life in Split Falls, but seeing as how she had been midwife to all but the oldest residents, it was clear that she had literally touched the lives of everyone in the village.

The celebration of her life ran from dawn, symbolizing birth, until dusk, representing death, while the Ioddenrian cleric stopped at certain points of the day to pray over Yoffa, the assemblage, and to praise her goddess. Ferai, the priestess, was a round-faced woman, ample both in size and kindness. She made time to talk with everyone, adding her own stories of Yoffa to those of the villagers. Her skill at making one feel at ease reminded me of Ial'rafiost, and I began to mourn him anew along with my mistress. A number of times I had to separate from the crowd, as I got glimpses of the shadows residing within everyone, particularly when I heard my parents' voices.

Yoffa was buried in the late afternoon. As dusk approached, during the final rite, we planted our flowers on her grave, or as near as we could, as there were more flowers than the space would allow. With the planting, we described the plant of choice, and why we thought it was appropriate to the deceased. Through their choices, Yoffa's grave would bloom all sun long, as one flower or another would blossom at various times. There were so many mourners that it was nearly dark when my turn came. Shortly before I could place my rhopalo at Yoffa's feet, a howling, hissing noise emanated from the forest.

The crowd startled into quiet as a band of raquoli crashed out of the trees and interrupted the funeral. Raquoli are small humanoid creatures, standing roughly three feet in height, resembling dogs or jackals but with differently-hued scales instead of fur, with rough, sharp talons on both hands and feet. A few of them carried wooden shields and spears, while others had primitive stone axes or hammers. The human crowd fled, pushing each other over to get away from the raquoli before the creatures could get close enough to attack.

Where the rest of the village was afraid, not without reason, I was furious. Images of dead humans and zylii mixed into the landscape as the world turned grey.

"How DARE you attack while we honor our fallen elder?" I shouted in Draconic, which, after suns of studying magic, I spoke as easily as common Umani, while adding the syllables to call forth a *bezyamhysa*.

Raquoli believe themselves to be descended from dragons, and though no dragon would admit it, there is a possibility that their legends may be correct. Internally, raquoli are similar to most humanoids, but some are hatched with vestigial wings, and even fewer are found to have an organ similar to the one which allows a dragon to breathe powerful energy, such as fire or lightning, or matter like streams of acid or clouds of poison. No one, not even the dragons themselves, fully understand how or why these organs work, only that it has something to do with their inherently magickal nature.

"Humans weak. We take," shouted a raquol immediately before launching his spear at me. It deflected off of the mystic shield and I burned him and three of his fellows with an *aatokytsrukak*, turning my foot in the way Glitter showed me to turn the fan of flames a deep purple. This gave the raquoli warriors pause, but the sorcerer in their midst hissed in laughter and cast *liskakhuuma* in the hope of paralyzing me. I cannot say whether it was my training, willpower, or my rage which allowed me to shrug off his spell, but there was no doubt that he was the most dangerous foe.

The reddish hue of his scales hinted at the possibility that he might carry a fraction of red dragon in his blood, so I ruled out using fire on him to be safe. Instead, I opted for conjuring *avularihbolmos*, which summons a mass of small iron spheres which explode out from a central point, above his head to tear through him and all the nearby raquoli. As the central sphere burst into smaller ones, a raquol flew awkwardly, twisting heel-over-head, into the blast zone. Glancing over, I saw my father, a trunk-like leg still raised from kicking the poor creature into certain doom. Two remaining raquoli were outside the blast of my spell and fled before their fellows had hit the ground. In my rage, I had not taken into account the damage that my spells would do to the plants and rowan tree at Yoffa's gravesite.

I dropped to my knees, sobbing on the fresh earth. "At least you're still working with iron," said a gruff voice. "An impressive trick. Who knew you were so talented?"

My whole body tensed up and I forgot to breathe for a few moments. I was in no condition to have this conversation at this time. When I answered with silence, he continued, "Tore the place up a bit; not as much as those little devils would have, though."

"What do you want?" I growled through clenched teeth. Even though I kept my back to him, I saw fleeting images of various faces and large fists.

"I overreacted all those summers ago," he said awkwardly, the weight of six years heavy in his voice. "You were just a kid, and you decided to leave us without any discussion. I could see that you were breaking your mother's heart, both for leaving and for using magic, and I couldn't let my own son treat his mother that way. I got angry." He then muttered, "I always get angry."

"And how many fights have you had over the suns?" I asked, finally turning to face him. A red pool of blood had formed on his torn pants. "How many have you beaten? Your children? How often did you hit Mother?" I barked, incessant tears cascading over my cheeks.

It was his turn to look away. "Too many times."

We were silent for a while.

As I glared at the back of my father, the images shifted. Rather than being beaten by him, his victims were latching onto him, climbing on top of him, and trying to wrestle him down. I saw myself in that crowd, and the image startled me out of my vision.

"All that guilt is going to kill you, you know," I said, getting to my feet while wiping my nose on a sleeve. "When did you recognize me?"

"I thought it was you at the shop, you look so much like your mother, but since you didn't say anything, I figured I was mistaken. People were talking about the stranger at Yoffa's, then seeing you here confirmed it. You really did learn magic." He shook his head.

"Yes. A woman taught me," I sneered, "just as a woman taught me herbalism." I turned back to look at the disaster of Yoffa's grave. If Thessylia were here, she would have warned me. Corpses littered the area, and the rowan tree had a few limbs sheared off and was filled with pock marks from my spell. I took a long, slow breath and turned back again. "You taught me anger, but you also taught me discipline," I said without emotion. "I do not know where your rage stems from, but I carry it too, and I have also hurt people with it. We need to do better."

Of all the things I have seen in my long existence, the one which surprised me most was watching my Father cry. We had a few minutes to sit quietly together before some of the villagers, led by Ferai, returned, armed with various farming implements, cudgels, and axes.

Father stood to compose himself and I proclaimed loud enough for the coming group to hear that the priestess would see to his wound, in case someone noticed his tears.

The gathering muttered. They had expected to run into the lizard-dog creatures within the village proper, and not to see over a dozen corpses littering the forest's edge.

"I apologize for the damage done," I bowed to the crowd. "I feared the destruction would have been worse if I had not stopped them here." Turning to Ferai I added, "We will have to replant on Yoffa's grave. Is there anything you can do to heal this tree?"

She smiled, nodded, and placed her large hands on its trunk. She spoke a few words which I did not understand, and the holes created by my spell sealed up, leaving small scars in the bark. Meanwhile, the crowd dispersed to switch out their weapons for shovels. If anyone deserved to have two funerals, it was Yoffa. The entire village turned out again for a second day to once again honor her memory, this time without any interruptions.

That evening, minutes after I entered my room, I had a sensation of exhilaration, of a joy I had nearly forgotten I had ever felt. Thessylia was nearby. It was not until I thought about it later that I realized my Gift did not manifest at the time. There was no loss of color, no fear that I would see the darkness and pain in the world, even though I was alone at the time. For a single moment, I felt pure bliss.

I bolted to the window to open it, though I knew she was still nearly a mile away. No communication was necessary, as I could sense she felt the same way. A few minutes later, she streaked through the window, nearly stopped in mid-air, and landed gently on my shoulder. We sat in silence, rubbing heads and reconnecting for some time.

'Thank you, and welcome back.' I kissed her on the head, scratching under her cloud-like feathers with my nose.

There was a gentle knock on my door.

"Come in, Faldrein."

"Mithron," he beamed as he entered, breathing heavily. "Thessylia disappeared on me as we entered the village; I had to run to not lose her entirely. It is good to see you again, though I wish the circumstances were better."

"As do I. Unfortunately, Yoffa has already died."

His face dropped.

"I think she had been ill for months, and perhaps my being here helped her to let go. Yet, I am troubled by her lingering. To be sure, she was a strong woman, even at her advanced age, but, by my reckoning, she should not have survived so long. I could use your insights."

"Of course."

I detailed as much of Yoffa's condition to Faldrein as I was able, from her symptoms to the herbs on her table.

"It sounds like a basic case of raven's cough to me," he said after some contemplation. "It does tend to linger in the elderly, though one usually either recovers from the croaking and wheezing or perishes within two weeks. That she had it for months is unheard of."

"My thoughts exactly," I responded. "Perhaps it was something else altogether, but few understood herbal remedies like Yoffa, and I do not think she would have made such a serious mistake. I wish she had informed me earlier, so I might have been of assistance." The room began to grey, but I pulled myself back before I could see anything from my friend.

"You seem to be getting better at controlling that, especially considering the circumstances."

"Your assistance has been immeasurable. Thank you again for allowing me to work on my Gift with you. This stoic philosophy seems the best way to control it while others are around, and I can let my emotions go when I am alone."

"Just be careful you do not shut down your heart entirely," he warned. "Eventually, it will all come crashing down on you at once."

"I know; thank you for the reminder. I understand the pain that a hardened heart can cause." I paused, thinking about the night I left Split Falls. "I do not wish to hurt anyone else in that fashion."

Faldrein and I talked into the night, mostly discussing philosophy and magickal theory before settling in to sleep. I promised to take him to Yoffa's cabin, but first had some final personal business to take care of in the morning.

The next day, later than I intended, I finally went to visit Mother. I first went to the forge, as it is easier to follow the path than to tramp through the fields, where I saw Father and Verond.

My brother smiled, then frowned, then looked nervous. "How may I help you, stranger?" he asked with perhaps a little too much volume.

"Hello, son," said Father between hammer beats.

Verond paled and looked at each of us in turn.

"I suppose you're here to see your mother. She's inside, weaving."

"You… how… when?" stammered Verond.

"We talked at Yoffa's funeral. The first one," I clarified.

He released a held breath. "Oh, thank the gods. I'm glad that's settled, and you didn't kill each other."

I am precisely as surprised. Although I cannot forgive him for his violence, I do understand him more. "We have had six years to reflect, and are both better people for it," I told him without getting into details. "What are you working on?"

He pulled a wedge of iron out of the forge. "Axe heads," he beamed, turning over the red iron held in his tongs. "The hard part is punching the hole through the metal and stretching it out so you can slide the handle through."

"That does seem like a lot of work. It is a good thing you have gotten strong enough to do it," I smiled. "Have fun. I am off to see Mother."

Verond waved as he returned the iron to the fire.

I had never thought I would walk down the path of my childhood again, and I began to remember some of the better parts of my youth; drawing in the dirt with a piece of scrap metal, reading in the grass, gazing at the stars after a hard day at the forge until I fell asleep, following a butterfly from flower to flower while trying to sketch it. If only it were as easy to forget the pain as it was the good.

When I got to the door, I was momentarily conflicted. I almost walked straight in, but since I no longer lived there, that seemed like an intrusion. However, this was my family's home, and so I should be able to come and go as I please. Before I could decide, the door opened, and Mother clasped me in her willowy arms.

"My boy," she cried into my shoulder.

When did she get so much shorter?

"My boy is finally home!"

I could not answer her aside from returning her embrace. All the anger, resentment, and fear I carried melted away in that moment; there is perhaps no better medicine than a mother's love. Of course, in that hug was all of her pain, fear, and suffering as well, though I blocked out as much as I could.

She grabbed my hand, pulled me inside the small cabin, and sat in her chair while I took my place on the floor. "So, tell me about the man you've become. Do you work? What kind of trouble have you gotten into that you can share with your old mother? Girlfriend?" she asked, a wicked grin growing on her face with the last question.

Mother knows I left to become a wizard, and I know she fears magic. I had no wish to lie to her, yet, telling the truth would only terrify her. "I spend most of my time studying and researching. My friends and I recently came into possession of an ancient library when the original caretaker died, so we have been cataloguing and reading the collection. Yes, one of them is a girl that I am fond of, but our relationship is… complicated."

She smiled. "All of them are. When you love somebody, you find a way to make it work. Tell me about her. Is she pretty?"

"Classically so. Sculptors would chisel statues of goddesses based on her. Glitter is brilliant, talented, and charismatic. It is a pleasure to watch her work, whether with m..." *I nearly said magic.* "making food, she seems to have an intuitive understanding of flavors, or organizing the library. She charms everyone she meets and has taught me to be a better man. It is perhaps because of this that I am frightened to be with her. She has suffered a great deal of pain in her life, and I fear causing her more."

"Such a thoughtful boy," she leaned down and kissed my forehead. "If only more men were like you." She glanced at the door. "Why do you think that you'll hurt her? If she wants to be with you too, why not let her make the choice?"

"Because it is all I can think about when I am with her," I exclaimed, throwing my hands in the air. "You know how when you are knitting a pattern, and you can see it in your mind before you pick up your needles?"

She nodded.

"I am like that with people, except I can only see the loose threads, knots, tears, and thin parts of the yarn. She deserves to be with someone who can be as ebullient in life as she is."

"Maybe you're looking at the pattern wrong. Sure, there are always flaws in the stitching and thread, but if you step away from the fabric, you can't see them as clearly. People aren't perfect. Try as you may, you aren't either," she smiled knowingly. "Don't be so hard on yourself. Let yourself have some fun, and maybe you won't feel so nervous around this girl."

"I... cannot. I wish I could explain it to you."

"It's a magic thing, isn't it? Did somebody curse you? I tried to stop that woman from taking you away." Mother's eyes began to fill with tears.

"No, Mother, nothing like that, not exactly. Studying magic changes a person; I see people more clearly than they see themselves. It is simply more than I wish to see."

"What," she lowered her voice, swallowed, then continued, "what do you see when you look at me?"

"Pain and fear. I saw Father's rage, and how much of it fell on you, more than I had witnessed with my own eyes. Why did you never flee him and this place? You could have taken us with you, and we all would have been better off."

"You don't understand. Your father works hard to keep the village running. Without him, there would be no tools for the farmers or other craftsmen. It's a lot of responsibility, and it weighs heavily on him sometimes. Sure, he lashes out once in a while, but a kettle needs to let out steam or it will explode."

I jumped to my feet. "He is not a kettle, Mother, he is a man." I was beginning to get angry, but I held enough control to not look too deep into her. "You do not have to put up with him anymore. I have means and friends in Dureltown. I can find you a place there, or even a nearby village if you would rather. Verond can continue his training, or even find another profession should he so choose. I can protect you now."

A series of emotions crossed her face too rapidly for me to fully follow. I recognized hope, fear, and consideration before panic set in. She stood up and shouted, "No. I can't," she cried. "Don't you realize what that would do to him?"

"What about what he is doing to you?" I interrupted.

She released an exasperated sigh. "Without me, he would give in completely to his anger. *I* keep him stable. *I'm* the one who keeps him from hurting anyone else."

"*You* were supposed to bring lunch," my father interjected from the doorway, his face red and seething. He turned to me. "*You* should have stayed away." For a large man, he can move quickly when he wishes to, faster than I at least, and his punch caught me squarely in my sternum, knocking me flat. *That man is as strong as a rukla.*

"Please! Stop!" Mother cried, grabbing his arm.

He glared at her and she quailed back, but her distraction gave me enough time to cast *ajiavulhysayt* to protect myself against the stomp to my midsection. His foot slammed onto the magical force, bowing it to less than an inch from my skin.

"Do not make me hurt you," I growled, threatening him while flat on my back. "You have seen what I can do."

He responded by kicking me again.

The mystical armor cushioned the blow though the impact rolled me against the wall. I cast *uvazvriijuut* to momentarily blind him.

Mother screamed. At me. She then began to pray to Lephix, the sun god, to protect her from the evil invading her home.

As my father blinked out the spots in his eyes, I repeated my spell, stood up, and glared at my mother as I stormed out. When he roared to chase me down, I cast it again. "I can do this all day. Do not make me use something lethal to stop you."

"Do you think I'm frightened of you?" he snarled, getting faster at shaking off the *uvasvriijuut*.

"As a matter of fact, I do." I raised my shoulders and cast *treyuf*[9].

He immediately stepped back, tripping over his own feet, and ran away.

I could now see my mother standing in the doorway, bawling and praying, and I knew I had ended any chance of taking her from here. I wanted to explain to her what I had done and why, but the spell would wear off in about a minute, and father would return angrier than before I scared him away, so instead I turned and started walking back toward the inn. As I passed Verond at the forge, I called out, "When you have had enough of this, you know where to find me."

When I got to the Twin Falls Inn, I saw Faldrein sitting at one of the outdoor tables which were set up for visitors to drink on pleasant days. He had a pot of honeysuckle tea and two cups. Thessylia was perched on the Inn's peak, watching for mice.

'This is why fledglings destroy the nest, so they cannot return.'

I stopped and stared up at her. She returned my gaze with her head turned upside down. *'Why is it you constantly point out that my life would be better if I were an owl?'*

'Because it would be,' she answered without judgment. *'Human society is designed to conflict with your natural instincts. This is the cause of many of your problems.'*

---

[9] In general, spells which affect emotions fall under the school of enchantment and are more Glitter's prevue than mine. Fear, however, ties more closely to necromancy than enchantment, and is more useful for buying time or reducing numbers of foes than causing actual harm, though more powerful versions can frighten someone to death.

'Without the rules of society, we would destroy each other more rapidly than we already do.' We both paused.

'Fair enough. I am having difficulty seeing the problem with your logic right now. We shall continue when I am in a better frame of mind.'

I sat across from Faldrein and poured myself a cup of tea. "I shall be leaving at first light," I said without preamble. "Though part of me wants to go upstairs, dig out a scroll of *bezyamlial*, and teleport home now. I *should* save it for an emergency, and it might prove necessary regardless."

"I take it your 'personal business' did not go well," he said with eyebrows raised, sipping from his own cup. "If you're in trouble, I can help."

"Thank you. I hope it does not come to that. I had prepared for this eventuality, and I have come to realize how few spells I know which are not designed to kill. I have no compunction about hurting the man, but even doing that would complicate matters even further. I am surprised that he has not found me yet."

"Dare I ask what you have gotten yourself into?"

I released a long-held sigh. "I attempted to reconcile with my family. At first, it seemed as though we were making progress, but it all came crashing down. Every option I can envision only causes more strife down the line; the only choice left is to leave." I refilled my cup. "I will take you to Yoffa's once we finish this pot."

On our way, we passed the four young women from Yoffa's garden before she died. The one I had spoken with came up to me, the others standing a few paces behind her.

"Did you attack the blacksmith?" she asked, keeping her voice hushed. "He's really angry and storming about the village asking about a wizard."

"He attacked me. I only damaged his pride. Thank you for the warning. Let me know if he hurts anyone; we are on our way to Yoffa's cabin, and then staying at the inn for tonight."

"Are you really a wizard?" Her fear was palpable, along with a degree of fascination.

"Yes. Yes, I am, but you have nothing to fear from me, or my friend."

Faldrein bowed his head.

"Well, if Yoffa trusted you, then I can too." She gave a quick slap to her heart, and ambled on, her friends in tow.

Faldrein turned his head to watch them walk away, catching up to me a few steps later. "Don't worry, I won't tell Glitter."

I looked over to him, not comprehending. "About what?"

"About your pretty village girl."

It took a moment for me to understand his insinuation. "There is no relationship between us. She saw me at Yoffa's, and we talked for a while. I have not seen her again until now. Have you forgotten your lesson of the tournament already? You must stop becoming so distracted by outward appearances," I warned.

Faldrein dropped his head. "You're right. They are pretty, though."

When we got to Yoffa's cabin, there was a woman in her garden pulling weeds as I did when I first arrived here. She looked much like Yoffa, only decades younger. "Onafa?" I asked cautiously.

"Flatterer," she smiled, "calling me my daughter's name. Acting as though I'm younger will not gain you any favor, smith's son."

"Y-Yoffa?" I stammered. "How? What are you doing here?"

"Whatever do you mean? This is my home. This is my garden. Where else would I be?"

"You died five days ago. We buried you under the rowan tree you specified, and the whole village planted tributes on and around your grave."

"She's only a spirit," whispered Faldrein. "Though from what you told me, there's no reason she should haunt this place."

"I do remember being ill," Yoffa commented as if searching for a lost memory. "Yes. You made me tea. And," her face fell and she began to age, "then the pain stopped. I did die, didn't I?"

"Yes, Mistress, you did."

"Was there something you left unfinished?" asked Faldrein. "We would be happy to help you."

"A woman always has regrets. My garden is a mess. You mentioned Onafa; I would have liked to see her again. But no, nothing pressing."

"Have any dragonflies come up to you?" Faldrein pressed.

"Dragonflies? Oh, you mean the kazkulim? No, none of the Dark Lady's messengers have come to lead me to the Greylands."

Faldrein and I looked at one another in shock.

"That's not possible," said Faldrein in a hoarse whisper. "The kazkulim always come. Only a few can refuse them, and they become ghosts and the like."

"But to have them not show at all," I continued, "is unheard of. If souls are not being guided, and people die every day, then there must be hundreds of souls haunting the living right now waiting to move on to the spiritual realms."

"What can we do?" asked Faldrein.

Yoffa seemed to have forgotten us. She was younger again and had gone back to her weeding. Though she could not physically remove the unwanted plants, the essence she managed to extract was enough to kill them in seconds.

"Can we summon one?"

"Not a bad idea." Faldrein beamed. "I've called on their help in the past. They may look like dragonflies, but they transform into something truly frightening for combat. Stand over there and help me draw Codrian's Circle[10]."

Even the most basic of summoning circles can be complex, so it can be time-consuming to ensure there are no mistakes. Circles can hold a creature indefinitely, so long as they are not broken, but should not be used as a prison except under the direst of circumstances, for, once the circle is broken, the imprisoned creature will most certainly seek vengeance upon its captor. For this reason, such circles are typically engraved into stone, and filled with strong metal enhanced with gems to ensure permanence. The circle we were drawing was of pure magical light, and only intended to last a few minutes.

As Faldrein had had dealings with kazkulim before, he took the lead on our cooperative spell while I focused on maintaining the circle's integrity. When he had finished, a large dragonfly, about the length of my hand, appeared within the circle. Its head and thorax were bone-white, its

---

[10] A common summoning circle comprised of two rings with various symbols etched in between them to bind whatever creature is to be held. It is most often used when the wizard expects a peaceful transaction, as opposed to Vorvon's Circle, for example, which punishes the creature until it complies.

back darkening to an iron grey at its long tail and its wings translucent. It looked like a normal insect, were it not for the yellow pinpoints of light that replaced its eyes—that and the telepathy.

"What? No. There is no time for this. No, no. Too much to do," the kazkul buzzed in every language I understood.

"We are sorry to trouble you," Faldrein kneeled, "but we need your assistance."

The extraplanar dragonfly flew three circuits around the circle. "Not for harm," it commented, "not for battle. Be quick. No time to waste."

"Our friend over there died five days ago yet has not been guided across. Can you help her?"

The kazkul hovered and stared at Yoffa. "Yes, yes, she is on my list. Much further down, I'm afraid. So far behind."

Faldrein and I stared at each other in confusion.

"Has there been so much death that you cannot guide all the souls? What of the raquoli that recently attacked? Will they haunt her grave?" I asked.

"No, no. Too few of us free. Raquoli live short lives and have kazkulim assigned specifically for them. Our Lady has slowed the dying as much as she can, but this causes suffering. The Bone Gate has been sealed, and souls are milling about. Let me go, and I will take her now. I must get back on schedule."

We nodded and I dropped the circle. The kazkul flew into Yoffa's heart and they vanished.

"Too few of us free?" we repeated in unison. "Who or what could capture the kazkulim, and why?" I asked.

"And why has the Bone Gate been sealed?" added Faldrein.

"And is there anything we can do about it?" I finished. "Wait… is that what that meant?"

Faldrein looked at me in confusion.

"When I was with Yoffa, instead of seeing her pain, I saw a pair of massive doors chained shut. I thought she had a way of blocking my Gift, but her suffering was due to her inability to die."

"We should ask Beus," offered Faldrein. "He is more attuned to the workings of the Dark Lady than I. I will send him an *ikaaskiil* to let him know what we've learned. Perhaps he can find out something before we get there."

"There you are," a voice growled. "I thought I might find you here."

I sighed, rolled my eyes at Faldrein, then turned to face my father. "Let it go. I am leaving at first light, and you will never see me again. Unless, that is, I learn you have harmed my mother or brother. Go focus your rage on your precious iron and make something useful instead of rampaging through the village like a brez. Your childish tantrums have become an annoyance." I turned my back on him, watching Faldrein's eyes for signs my father was charging to attack. It only took as long as it did for me to cast *zuuvdaama*.

"I should have shut you up suns ago," he bellowed.

As expected, he swung for my jaw, and I crouched under his anvil fist, placing my hand on his belly; it felt like patting a cave wall. I would have preferred to use Ormak's ring to cast the spell from a distance, but he was too quick. *The man is as solid as Brother Ironknuckle.* He doubled his fists to bring them down on my head and froze in place.

I shifted away from him and stood, looking him in the eyes. "You shall never attack in rage again," I commanded. "Should you do so, you will find yourself as paralyzed and helpless as you are now. You *may* fight to defend yourself and others, but only if they are physically threatened or harmed, or in the cause of justice for those so harmed. The paralysis will wear off once you have calmed down.

"I have a friend who can teach you how to control your anger, if you are willing. You may find me at the inn until the morrow, should you wish to talk like an adult. Goodbye, father." I looked to Faldrein, then turned to walk to the inn.

Chapter 7: Spirits of Friendship

I can't believe you cursed your own father," Faldrein said in astonishment as we walked to the inn.

I released a long breath before answering. "I could think of no better option. I do not wish to harm him, but he needs to stop hurting others, and it is obvious he has not been punished for his crimes. He will only be defenseless if he instigates violence and, even then, he may fight under righteous cause. The curse is merely a restraint."

"That… that sounds reasonable, I suppose. I just don't think it's the right use of magic."

"I have talked to the man. We had even made peace for a couple days. He cannot provide for the family or the village in prison, and I do not have the means to remove his aggression from his heart. Brother Ironknuckle deals with a similar rage but has learned how to control and channel it. Perhaps he could teach my father to do the same.

"Until then, he needs to be held in check before he kills someone, especially now that he can no longer hurt me. My mother and brother are the next likely substitutes, and I will not have them harmed, even if mother hates me too."

Faldrein kept his own council until we returned to our room.

Before he could speak, I cut off his argument. "I have been playing this out for six suns, considering various scenarios. I know you do not agree with the means, but this really is the best option."

"You are probably right. Any other alternative I can think of is a far worse fate. My only concern is if his curse becomes common knowledge. His rivals may instigate a fight, only to have him at their mercy."

"I allowed for self-defense," I countered. "The spell will allow him to protect himself if attacked, and to retaliate if in danger. He will not be able to be the aggressor, nor will he be able to hit someone without cause. Preventing that was my primary motivation. He is right about one thing though. I do like working with iron."

"Then you need to spend more time with Uxadul. That seems to be his specialty over stone," Faldrein opined.

"I was thinking the same thing. Now on to important matters: what do we do about the kazkulim? 'Too few of us free' it said. How are the others being held, and why?"

"And where?" Faldrein added. "The Dark Lady's work is sacred and necessary to keep the world in balance. Why would She seal the Gate, so that even those who die cannot enter Her realm for judgement and assignment?"

"My first guess is that it would have something to do with Coruld."

Faldrein blanched at the name of the god of the undead.

"Cratillus was trying to destroy all life in this world so it could be made into undead. Perhaps the Dread Lord has other agents working toward that same cause. But of course, I cannot speak for the gods or their actions, and anything right now is merely supposition."

"Let me send that message off to Beus; he is bound to have more insight into this than us." Faldrein cast *ikaaskiil*, scratching his finger in the air while mouthing his missive. "With any luck, he'll have some information for us by the time we get home. We should stock up on provisions before leaving; it's a long journey."

"Do you know the *lialaasl* spell?"

"That would be nice," he mused. "A long-lasting flight spell would be so much faster than horses, and more direct too. *Uvaazaasl* doesn't last long enough to make a difference, unless we need to cross a ravine or something. If you're in a rush, we can use your *bezyamlial* scroll."

"Though haste is important, I was mostly hoping to avoid spending nearly half-a-moon on horseback," I grimaced, drawing a laugh from my companion.

'There is a person standing at the door.'

I stepped over to the door and opened it, revealing the same village girl from before. "How long have you been standing here?" I asked without accusation.

"Umm… a couple minutes? I was afraid to bother you. How did you know I was… oh, yeah, magic," she stuttered.

"I have already dealt with the blacksmith. What brings you to my door?"

"My father's ill, has been for a long time. Yoffa was helping him, but she's gone now, and he doesn't have any more medicine. Can you help?" Tears of sorrow and fear mixed on her cheeks.

"Did Yoffa say what she was giving him?"

She shook her head.

"May we see him?"

She nodded, failing at an attempted smile.

"Please, lead on."

We followed her through a field of squash and melons to a small cottage. The sun had nearly set, but there was enough twilight to avoid tripping or crushing any of the fruits, at least for me. Faldrein stumbled a few times but avoided hurting himself or the crops. While we walked,

Ezme—I finally learned her name—informed us of her father's symptoms.

"He's got a bulge on the side of his stomach. He sometimes can't eat, and what he does don't always stay down. Yoffa's herbs eased his pain and helped him eat."

She led us inside where her family was finishing a dinner of squash and peppers.

"Who are these two boys now, Ezme? You can't bring home everyone you meet, girl."

She blushed. "That was one time, momma, and I really liked him."

"He was no good, and you knew it. You were blinded by his pretty face." She turned to us. "What's your story then? Chasing after my eldest daughter?"

"My apologies for interrupting. Ezme told us of your husband's illness, and we only wished to see if we could help." I bowed my head.

"What are you then, travelling potion vendors? None of that garbage ever works."

"No, ma'am," answered Faldrein. "Travelers, yes, but not here to sell." He glanced over to Ezme's father, who was slumped, barely conscious, on a wooden chair. "He has a knot in his bowels, and an obstruction as well. Mithron," he turned to me, "can you get…"

"Chamomile for tea, and jinzibar steeped in apple vinegar. I shall return shortly." I turned to Ezme. "Once Faldrein says he is ready, feed your father as much ripe melon as he can handle. It will help to clear his bowels and bring up his health."

I rushed over to Yoffa's cabin, pleased that my father was no longer frozen in her garden.

I dug up a jinzibar root—its warm, spicy odor filled my nostrils—broke off about a thumb's worth, and replanted it. There is something comforting in the taste of jinzibar, whether as a spice or partially dried to a thick, chewy candy, and I have been accused of adding too much on the rare occasions I've cooked for guests. It was Vletraka's favorite, and she often said it was the only thing which made her feel warm, even more so than the fiery peppers which she would eat raw out of the garden. Those burned my mouth and gave me hiccoughs, but when crushed into a paste, they are soothing on sore muscles.

With a small blade, I scraped the olive skin off of the jinzibar, then thinly sliced the ivory root and placed the pieces in a clay jar. I then filled it with vinegar made from old cider and sealed the top with wax. Next, I filled a small bag with dried chamomile flowers to take back to Ezme.

Before leaving, I scratched out a note and a map and tied it to Thessylia's leg. *'I hate to send you away again so soon, but there is too much information to convey with a simple spell.'*

When I returned to Ezme's home, Faldrein was sharing a cantaloupe with Ezme's father, two of her sisters fawning over them both. My friend appeared in quite the good mood. "It went well, I take it," I said aloud to no one in particular.

"Yorzme had a torn muscle, which his innards were trying to escape through," Faldrein said around a bit of melon. "I managed to fix the tear, but it will take time to heal on its own." He turned to Yorzme. "Remember, stay off your feet, and don't pick up anything heavier than a fork for the next moon, or you could hurt yourself again. Even then, be careful and build your strength back."

"But my farm…" Yorzme began.

"Will be fine," Faldrein interrupted. "Let your family handle the burden for a time, and hire some hands if need be." He set a handful of copper and silver coins on the table.

"This," I handed the bag to Ezme, "is for tea. Make sure he drinks a cup at every meal. And this is a tonic. Shake the jug before opening it tomorrow to mix the flavors. He should take a spoonful with each meal also. The taste can be off-putting, but a bite of bread will cleanse his tongue."

Tears welled in her ice-blue eyes. "Thank you both so much. How can we repay you?"

"We are leaving on the morrow, and I think a pair of ripe melons will make the journey more pleasant," I smiled. Were this any other village, I could have felt more content. This is what Yoffa trained me for, to help and heal others. Herbs alone would not have helped, and I was glad to have Faldrein's magic to repair Yorzme's injury. Would I have instead followed Ioddenri's teachings and learned nature magic had Vletraka not discovered me and taught me an arcane path? There is no way to know, and no use regretting my choice. One way or another, I was destined for magic.

We had traveled northward for four days when the landscape began to look vaguely familiar. "I could be wrong," I mused aloud, "but I believe we are near Mistress Goldfire's tower."

"We are," Faldrein responded. "I'm not used to coming from this direction, but it should be about a few miles to the east. Beus visits periodically," he said in reaction to my quizzical look.

"I believe it is Blythad's shift at Ormak's, so Glitter should be home. Perhaps she would like to travel with us."

Faldrein looked over at me with a grin. "You don't have to make excuses to visit your girlfriend. You know exactly where we are."

I reddened. "I did not think my motives were so obvious. Yes, I do want to see her. If our timing is correct, we should be meeting an old friend there as well."

"Really? Who?"

My heart leapt. "That depends on the answer Thessylia carries." She was near, and I felt whole again. A few minutes later, she landed softly on my outstretched arm, hopped up to my shoulder, and rubbed her head against mine while I scratched under her neck feathers.

Faldrein watched us for a time with an expression of wry amusement. When I looked a dagger at him, he said, "I don't think I've ever seen you this happy. Usually by now, your Gift has made you pull back."

"This happened at the inn also," I responded, rubbing Thessylia between her shoulders, causing her wings to flex. "It seems our reconnecting temporarily overwhelms my Gift. While she is gone, it takes conscious effort to avoid depression."

"You have been rather sullen recently," he commented. "I thought it had to do with your father."

"Have you ever lost your necklace?" Some wizards bond with a companion, like I had with Thessylia, while others instill part of their essence in an object. Generally, a bond such as Faldrein's stores magickal energy, allowing the wizard to cast spells unprepared within the limits of the object's capacity. As the wizard gains power, so does the item in question. I do not deny the usefulness of such a bond, but I would not trade Thessylia for anything. The downside of creating any bond is that it can be taken away or lost.

When I send Thessylia away, a piece of my soul is missing. I have a vague notion of how distant and which direction, but nothing else. While I was captured by Cratillus, our bond was somehow hidden or suppressed, making his tortures all the more brutal without her support.

"I've never removed it since the bonding ceremony," said Faldrein, grasping at the gold-wrapped rose quartz charm.

"Is the necklace part of the bond, or only the crystal?"

"Why are you asking," he eyed me with suspicion.

"Merely curiosity. Necklaces break easily, and the talisman can be lost. If the necklace is linked, then your magic should reduce its fragility."

"They are of a piece," he assented. "I don't know how I would react if it went missing. It's not alive like your owl, but it's still a part of me. My aunt gave it to me when I was younger; said it would bring me luck and love. I feel fortunate I got to become a wizard, but it hasn't brought me love."

"You have friends. I have been told it begins there. I do love Glitter, at least as far as I understand the concept, but she deserves to find someone better suited for her than I. With Thessylia, our love is unconditional. We simply are a single soul. My Gift does not make me a suitable lifelong companion for anyone else."

"I thought the two of you were working on that. Has it not been going well?" Faldrein asked with genuine concern.

"To a degree. The visions are less intense than when my feelings for her first developed, but they are always there." I shook my head and sighed. "I can never fully connect with her, nor anyone for that matter. After seeing what Ormak went through, it is probably best it never progresses further."

"Is that what you want?"

"No, of course not. I want to be everything she needs, but I cannot. It would be best for her to give up on me." I slumped in my saddle then threw my head back and sighed to the clouds. "It is her choice, I suppose. She knows who and what I am. If she can love me in spite of that, who am I to deny her?"

After a pause, Faldrein responded, "You should give yourself more credit. She *does* love you. Do you think she would if you weren't worthy of her? I know first-hand how charming she is, even without magic." He cast a minor illusion draping himself in purple mist. I could not help but crack a smile. "After everything that happened, she still fell in love with you. So, accept your incredible fortune and don't sabotage it."

"Thank you," I said and wiped a tear off my cheek. I pulled back as the world began to grey, for, in spite of his words, I had already seen his jealousy.

"So, who is our mystery guest?" he asked.

I had been so pleased with Thessylia's return that I had forgotten about her mission. With care, I untied the missive bound to her leg. My excitement grew until I was forced to calm myself again. "We are to have *two* guests. Both Vondro and Brother Ironknuckle are on their way to meet us at Mistress Goldfire's tower."

"You told me about them. They were part of the Cratillus situation, right? Vondro is the guardsman, and Brother Ironknuckle, the monk? I suppose having some muscle on our side would be beneficial."

"Agreed, that is part of why I invited Vondro. I had no idea Brother Ironknuckle was back in Dureltown. The last I saw him, he had decided to return home to settle some personal matters." Brother Ironknuckle had killed a man, then fled, eventually to be taken in by a monastery and taught how to channel his inner rage. It was not my affair to discuss with Faldrein, so I kept the details private. "I gave them a map and instructions for entering Mistress Goldfire's tower, should they get there first."

They had not, which afforded us more time to talk before the group got larger. Mistress Goldfire's guardians had become aware of the relationship between Glitter and I, and I was forced to fend off numerous inquiries about kissing, weddings, and children while maintaining civility and avoiding disappointment and lying. Should any of them decide to leave Goldfire's employ, they would make fantastic barristers in any court of law.

Glitter waited at the door, taking rude pleasure at our discomfort. When I finally reached her, I scarcely got past the formality of "I am Mithron, Necromancer of Cuyokale, Wizard of the Ivory Tome, here to see the Mistress of the tower," before she jumped out and hugged me, to great applause from the fey. I returned her embrace, pushing the shadows of her near-incineration to the back of my mind.

Now that I was no longer an apprentice, I needed to develop a title. Vletraka was 'of the Alabaster Moon', based not only on her exceedingly pale skin, but the symbolism of the moon as a light in the darkness. As I can perceive the darkness in others, perhaps a similar moniker would befit me, but that was something to contemplate in due time.

"Come in. What a nice surprise. What brings you two here?" Glitter asked while escorting us to the sitting area where Mistress Goldfire lounged on her green chair with an embroidery hoop; various colors and thicknesses of thread were lined up on the table next to her. She looked at us, smiled, and went back to her work mouthing words while doing so.

"Don't mind her, she's very focused on her stitching," Glitter explained.

We watched Goldfire for a few moments. Her movements were slow and precise, and every fifth word was an audible whisper.

"What is it?" asked Faldrein gently breaking the silence.

"It's sort of like a silk scroll," whispered Glitter. "It won't burn up like a normal one. The spell she's stitching will teleport us to a safe spot and fill the house with traps and illusions should we get attacked again."

"Were you attacked recently or is this in response to Cratillus's people? I forgot their names," I asked.

"Forzo and Yurtha. No one else since then, but it's best to be prepared. Let's leave her to her work."

We followed Glitter through her home to the library. As we sat, she remained standing.

"Where are my manners? Did you need anything to eat or drink first?"

Faldrein shook his head. "We stopped for lunch a while ago. I'm fine."

I waved my hand in the negative. "We are on our way to see Beus to see if he can help us," I said, then explained the situation with the kazkul. "We wanted to see if you wished to join us. Vondro and Brother Ironknuckle are on their way here as well."

"Really? I miss them. We should meet them outside when they arrive." She gave me a wicked grin. "I'm afraid of the fey prodding them for information. Have you asked Blythad to see if he's noticed anything at Ormak's?"

"No," answered Faldrein, "but I was just thinking about that. I should send a message to Uxadul as well, in case he might come across anything of interest."

We talked for a few hours, catching each other up on current affairs. Glitter had finished cataloguing Ormak's biographies during her last shift at his tower, and Faldrein was still working on the items which we had found in the second treasure room. I had been organizing Ormak's collection of tomes relating to other planes, sectioning off the elemental planes from the dimensions of the gods.

I also told them about my latest congress of mookali. "They moan in disharmony, causing fear and panic," I said with pride.

"It's things like this which make me glad you're a friend and not an enemy." Faldrein laughed. "Simply hearing you describe them makes me *seeduyufoz*[11]. I pity any who enter uninvited."

"'A wizard must maintain his mystique, so that he is feared by lesser men'[12]," I quoted Revance, receiving synchronized eyerolls in response. I grinned. His writings paraphrase this statement a number of times. At first, it gets the point across, but, after the fifth iteration, becomes repetitive.

Glitter's head suddenly shot up. "They're here. Mithron, go meet them at the gate while Faldrein and I pack up some provisions."

I nodded and left, receiving only a humming grunt from Mistress Goldfire as I passed her. When the fey came to accost me again, I pulled out a bag of honey drops which

---

[11] From Draconic; *seeduyufoz* literally translates to "shiver with fear".
[12] *A Philosophy of Magic* page 46.

I took from Yoffa's cabin and set them down on a flat stone.

"I hope there is enough for everyone. Please share." I would learn later that my act of giving began a series of unexpected complications as the fey have strict rules about presents and debts. However, at this time, the rest of my walk to the gate went in peace.

Vondro and Brother Ironknuckle stood outside, anxiously looking for the carrier of the tokens of entry. When they saw me, Vondro started forward and I waved him back before he was noticed. We clasped arms, though my hands hardly came close to encircling either of their forearms.

"It is good to see you both again." I beamed before pulling back both physically and emotionally. "Glitter and Faldrein will be out presently. Were you caught in a fire?" I asked Brother Ironknuckle, noticing the scars on his face and lack of beard.

"Somethin' ta that effect," he said, his voice sullen, "but everything's fine now."

"Glad to hear it," I smiled, avoiding the pain he was hiding. "How have you fared?" I asked, turning to Vondro.

"I've been promoted to Plovas," he stated with pride. When he realized we did not fully comprehend, he added, "it's the rank above Bresom, the basic foot soldier. It should have happened earlier, but I had to be certain that I earned it without my father's influence."

"Then, congratulations." Brother Ironknuckle and I said in unison.

It was not long later when Glitter and Faldrein joined us, each carrying a large pack. Glitter hugged our friends while I introduced Faldrein. A few minutes later, we were on our way.

Having real horses sped our journey, though they required care and feeding, unlike summoned ones.

We had been riding for three days since leaving Mistress Goldfire's tower when we heard the sounds of conflict. As we began to rush forward, I noticed a pair of spirits drifting through the trees, with more accumulating as we neared the battle.

A few yards off the road were an ulim warrior astride a semi-transparent wolf, a copper-haired woman casting spells and laughing, another woman with short black hair dancing and throwing daggers, and a green-skinned half-zyla whom I recognized. Ulima are smaller humanoids, standing about half as tall as humans, with close ties to the animal kingdom. It is not uncommon for them to display characteristics of one beast or another, leading to the stereotype that all of their members are feral. This one in particular had wolf-like ears and sharp teeth.

The four of them were fighting a giant blue and yellow flightless bird, taller than us on horseback, with wicked talons and a black trunk instead of a beak, its face speckled with blood. The ghost of a young boy drifted up to me mouthing soundless words.

"Capture or kill?" shouted Vondro to the other party.

"Kill," the ulim cried. "Can't you see the carnage in its wake?"

Vondro's distraction proved costly as the creature wrapped its thick trunk around the warrior's neck.As they fought to avoid the fangs at the end of its trunk, the creature picked them off of the wolf, leapt straight up into the air, kicked its talons out, and nearly disemboweled the small wolf-rider. Faldrein immediately rushed over while I cast *yuvjuutmroozik*, creating a cone of deep shadow from my outstretched palm. The spell is not designed to kill but weakens and disorients a foe, so it is less likely to cause harm. The phantom child smiled at me.

Glitter aimed a *vezivhilsk* at the creature, but the bolt of lightning sank into the ground before reaching its target. It did, however, get the bird's attention, and it turned to charge at her, the bony protrusions on its wings set to pierce her like twin lances. As it moved, the lightning emerged from the earth, electrocuting and stunning the bird. Tree limbs reached down to batter it while Vondro charged ahead, his sword opening a wide gash at the shoulder. Brother Ironknuckle pummeled its abdomen and tumbled away.

It spun to return the favor to Vondro, but stepped on a large rock and lost its balance long enough for Vondro to ride away. The red-haired woman continued to laugh, and I could feel something of the Weave in her cackling while the dancer continued to leap and spin, releasing a fusillade of daggers. Two missed completely, while one lodged in the wound made by Vondro, and another entered the base of its neck.

Aggressive in spite of its numerous wounds, it began to race after Vondro, stopping dead after my *bezyamdulaaseedu* spell shattered its bones. The ghost boy jumped in joy and faded from sight, though I could sense he was still there. Everyone gathered around the fallen warrior, who was groaning in pain. The red-haired woman added her own healing to Faldrein's, sealing the ulim's innards back in.

"It's a miracle ye survived that attack," said Brother Ironknuckle, holding out his hand to the ulim, who accepted the assistance to stand.

"The kazkulim seem to have forgotten this place," intoned the copper-haired woman in a sort of drifting melody. "I'm surprised the big birdy died."

"Judging from its wounds, it should have been nearly dead before we arrived," I said, looking over the fallen creature. "Wait. Was that a miskarn?" My curiosity pulled me away from the group, toward the bird. Now that I had time for a better look, I was certain of its nature. I had thought them to be creatures of myth and legend, and never expected to see one in person. During my cursory examination, I saw locks of red hair extend out, pluck some undamaged feathers, and retreat back to the woman who seemed not to notice her new decorations.

"That's what I thought too," said the dancer, drawing my attention. "I couldn't believe my eyes. I would have liked to learn more, but it wasn't very friendly. I'm Farandi, by the way. That's Hyxi," she said, pointing to the ulim, "their wolf Waltheri, Gwenaz," she added, turning to the red-haired woman whose locks were rearranging the feathers into a floral shape, "and…"

"Effay'ost'kao," I finished. "You are a long way from the woods where we last met."

She popped up and hugged me. "You got me in trouble, human wizard," she laughed. "Master Dawnthistle became even more strict in my training afterward. Recently, he insisted on my traveling and following my instincts to where I'm most needed."

"Well, we are glad to meet you all. This is Glitter," I gestured.

Glitter looked upset for some reason.

"Vondro, Faldrein, and Brother Ironknuckle."

Greetings were exchanged all around.

"So, how did you come across a miskarn?"

"We followed the trail of spirits," answered Gwenaz, who was looking past me. A small fox poked its face through the flowing locks at her shoulder. I glanced over to see the young boy playing with two other children.

"She can see things most others can't," added Hyxi. "We've learned to trust her in these matters. It seems the creature was holding the souls of those it killed."

"They are still here, though," I responded glumly. Turning my gaze back to Gwenaz, I added, "The kazkulim have not forgotten, they have been captured."

"That's not possible." exclaimed Farandi.

"It's true," said Faldrein. "We asked one about the slow deaths and lingering spirits. Apparently, there are only a few free to do their duty."

"We're off to speak with someone who might be able to help," Glitter said, taking my hand and giving it a hard squeeze. "Would you like to join us?"

They took a moment to confer before Hyxi answered for their group in the affirmative. As our new allies were travelling on foot, except occasionally for Hyxi, we offered to share our horses. Effay chose to ride with me, while Gwenaz joined Glitter, and Farandi rode with Faldrein—Hyxi remained on Waltheri. Brother Ironknuckle and Vondro split and repacked the extra traveling gear. Having extra passengers slowed our progress so as to avoid exhausting our mounts, but we still travelled faster than we would without them.

"I see you no longer use summoned horses," Effay teased.

"I see you no longer speak in rhyme," I returned.

"That was out of boredom; Dawnthistle was no fun, and now I'm free to go run." She laughed. "I have new friends and a new life, and I've never been happier. I will always be thankful for Dawnthistle's teachings, but now I can be Ioddenri's instrument in my own manner." She opened her palm, and a purple flower grew there which she tucked over my left ear. "So, what other trouble have you gotten into?"

"We stopped a madman from killing everyone and animating them as undead two suns ago. Now, we are trying to figure out why no one is dying properly."

Effay gave me a playful slap. "Don't tease."

I turned and looked her in the eyes.

"Oh, you were serious. There are actually people like that?"

"He followed the Dread Lord equally as fervently as you follow Ioddenri. It cost the lives of two friends, plus thousands of others, before we could stop him."

"How horrible. I can't imagine what kind of pain someone must be in to follow that kind of life."

Effay's insights were much kinder than mine. "He lived without love—I think he feared it, even. Malice was all he had left, and he turned it out against the world." I glanced over at Glitter. *If I denied my feelings, would I become like him? Cratillus claimed I was on the same path as he, but that was simply manipulation, was it not? But if I surrender to my emotions, there can be only sorrow for us both.*

"That's so sad."

Is she reading my thoughts?

"There's always hope for love. You can't turn away from everything just because it hurts sometimes. Life should be fun." There was exasperation in her voice. "You shouldn't hurt others because you're in pain. I'm glad you stopped him. It sounds like he could have thrown everything out of balance."

"Still, he caused a lot of damage." *More than I would care to confess at this stage; I still have nightmares about my time as his prisoner.* "Tell me about your friends," I said to change the subject.

"Gwenaz is a witch. She can manipulate luck, cast spells, talks to her fox Stella a lot, and her hair has a mind of its own. Hyxi lost their squad in a brez raid and is a bit over-protective. Waltheri's spirit is bound to them. Farandi is a dancer, singer, historian, and the cutest thing I ever met," she sighed, then giggled. "Every time I think about what Dawnthistle would say about me falling in love with a human, let alone an ulim and a sonchia, it makes me laugh."

"Gwenaz is a fox-person? I would not have guessed, though now that I know it does seem apparent." As I glanced over, a lock of Gwenaz's hair shot up, speared a pear, and brought it down into Glitter's hand. When she looked back at the witch riding behind her, she saw that Gwenaz was asleep.

Sonchias are generally considered to be playful and free-spirited, their society comprised of loose clans with close family ties. Children are encouraged to find their passions early, and many gather a list of rudimentary skills before settling on a craft or profession. They have three forms, which they can transition between at will: humanoid, fox, and a hybrid which blends the characteristics of the two extremes. This innate shapeshifting leads many toward magic, whether arcane or divine, though the majority, like most other peoples, follow more mundane paths.

My earliest thoughts on witches were molded by my father, as he often referred to Yoffa derisively. I loved Yoffa like a grandmother, and anyone father disliked deserved greater scrutiny in my eyes. Revance referred to witches as "third-rate arcanists at best", as their magic comes from a near-divine power rather than "proper study of the esoteric mystic arts".[13] The prospective witch will make a compact with a powerful entity, typically not deity-level but near enough from mortal perspective, which grants the witch access to arcane abilities. The patron's reasons for doing so are inscrutable, but it is thought they desire mortal agents to increase their standing among their peers, though many believe darker motives are to be ascribed.

"So, tell me a little about your friends."

"Both Glitter and Faldrein are wizards. Glitter is playful and enchanting, but her magic sometimes runs wild when she is stressed. Faldrein follows the Dark Lady in addition to his studies, combining both arcane and divine magic. Vondro is warrior born, and protective like Hyxi. Brother Ironknuckle is as wise as he is strong. They are some of the few people I call friends, and they accept me in spite of the anguish I've caused them."

She leaned in against my shoulder. "What did you do?"

"I can see the pain within the hearts of others, and sometimes I cannot help but express what I see aloud. It must be difficult for them to travel with someone who cannot keep your secrets."

She hugged me. "It must be hard. You seem so nice. What do you see in me?"

"Nothing now. It mostly happens when my emotions are heightened. In any case, I do not wish to know, though I warn you that it could happen at any time, and I will

---

[13] *A Philosophy of* Magic pages 133-135. Revance refused to give witches more than a passing reference.

embarrass you and your friends." I released a long sigh. "It is inevitable."

She squeezed me tighter. "Poor human wizard."

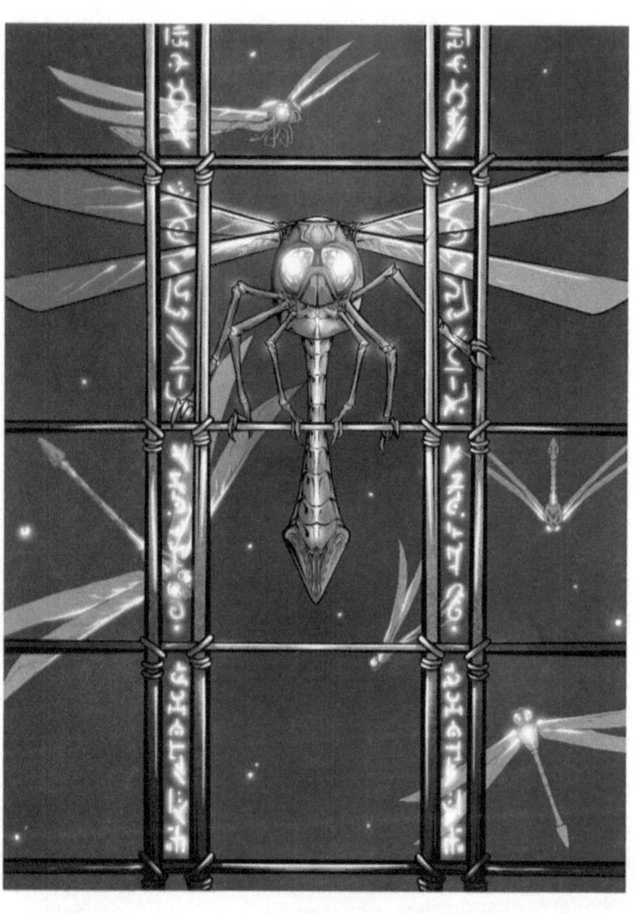

Chapter 8: Boxes

Thessylia flew ahead to find a clearing large enough for our growing band to rest for the night. The small patch of land was not ideal, but it did have room for the tents and a small fire. Effay saved us some time by churning a ring of stones from the ground with her magic.

"How did you know that serving your deity was the path for you?" I asked both Effay and Faldrein while we sat at the fire. "I was taught herbalism before I learned magic, so I have some connection to both Ioddenri and the Dark Lady. I suppose what I am asking is where is the line between honor and devotion?"

"I was raised with Ioddenri's teachings," answered Effay first. "I can't remember a time when She wasn't in my life and I can't imagine myself any other way."

"It wasn't until Beus discovered me at my father's beehives that I began to understand the Dark Lady's place in my life," said Faldrein. "I understood Her place in keeping the world in balance, but not how She maintains the spiritual world. I devote myself to Her because Her work is important, and I wish to help in whatever way I can."

"Yes, they are both important, all the deities are, but how do you pick one over the others? Effay, what if you followed Mamoel or Lephix? The moon and sun are also part of nature. Faldrein, would you feel the same if Beus was an adherent to Farvost the Traveler or Acclin the Crafter? I am not questioning either of your faiths. I am simply trying to understand."

They both began to answer at once before Faldrein stopped for Effay.

"Of course, I honor the Mother and Father, the Moon and the Sun, for there would be no Green without them. They are above, while Ioddenri is here." She picked up a handful of dirt. "And here." She pointed to the trees. "And there." She gestured to the rabbits over the fire. "She is here with me, with us. I can touch Her, feel Her—through Her works and through the Green. That is how we are all connected to this world."

"You were a smith, and now you are a crafter of magic," spoke Faldrein, "so you must honor Acclin as well, correct?"

I nodded.

"We honor the gods each in our own fashion. I *devote* myself to the Dark Lady because Her cause is most closely aligned with my spirit. Through my devotion, I receive Her blessings."

"I think I understand. My 'devotion' is to the Weave itself. Ormak was convinced that it does not possess any consciousness or will, but I am not so certain. There are times when it seems the Weave has patterns beyond our scope, and the threads of magic and fate are one and the same."

"Perhaps that is why there are individuals who can see into the future," Faldrein opined. "Maybe they can see those patterns. Why did you bring up the subject in the first place?"

"Curiosity," I said, shrugging, "and perhaps to understand myself better. There have been many paths I could have taken, and I suppose I am reflecting on those choices. I do not expect to comprehend how and why the gods choose to gift some worshippers and not others, but I am intrigued how each of you shapes the Weave based on the source of your magic. There is always more to learn."

"I like this one," said Gwenaz to Effay. She stood behind me with her hands atop my head. "Your aura is dark, but softly so, like butter or velvet. A velvet shade. Farandi's ready."

Effay grabbed and shook my arm, pointed to Farandi, and rested her head on her hands which she placed on my shoulder. Gwenaz leaned back, her hair supporting her, while Hyxi shushed the others. Then, when Farandi was certain of everyone's attention, she began to sing:

I was lost in the darkness,
Blinded by fear,
Clouds swam above me.
The moon disappeared.
I called to the heavens,
"Please guide me from here.
I'm lost." How I pleaded,
And then they appeared—

A circle of owls!
What a sight I should see!
Flying in rings up above.
A circle of owls
Shared their secret with me—
My strength and my power is love.

Then off to the forest
The owls did fly.
I chased through the darkness
Not really sure why.
Then the moon showned unhidden

And brightened the sky.
A dove cooed above me
I let out a sigh.

A circle of hazel trees,
The song of the dove,
Mending my heart, which was torn.
A circle of hazel trees
Protecting my love.
The grove where spirit is born.

I cried, as though wounded,
My heart was laid bare,
My feelings of sorrow
Had so long impaired
My judgment and reason,
But now I can care,
For the moon granted me with
This gift I now share—

A circle of silver
So pale and fair
Yet solid of beauty and love.
A circle of silver
And diamonds I wear.
Eternal—my promise to love.

I gazed at the moon for
The rest of the night.
Remembering the heartaches
That brought on my plight.
Then as the dawn broke
I gained this insight:

I'm as the sun is, for
I too am light!

And a circle of butterflies
Surround me in love.
They spread their wings, so do I.
A circle of butterflies
Crowning my love.
Now I know that I too can fly—
I know that I too can fly.

We applauded, then Hyxi, Gwenaz, and Effay enveloped her, hugging and praising Farandi. She responded by kissing her friends in turn. Glitter walked off toward the tents. I would have assumed she was merely fatigued, but her scarlet motes told a different story.

She is clearly upset about something. As I began to go after her, a low rumble and a flash of light hinted at a more immediate concern.

The two tents which our new friends were travelling with were not large enough for the nine of us, but as the rains grew harder with the addition of hail, we made do. We separated into our familiar groups at first, but Glitter left after the hail stopped. Both her crimson sparkles and the angry look she gave me before leaving had me baffled.

"What did you do this time?" asked Vondro echoing my thoughts.

"I have no idea. She has not spoken to me since this morning."

"What were ye talking about then?" Brother Ironknuckle asked.

"She had noticed her electrical spells have been acting more strangely than normal as of late and we were attempting to deduce the problem. I do not think I did or said anything to hurt her feelings."

"Maybe it was the way you said something," Faldrein suggested. "You can be a little…"

"Haughty," said Vondro.

"Superior," Brother Ironknuckle added.

"I was going to say 'condescending', but yeah," finished Faldrein.

I narrowed my eyes at my friends, relaxing as I considered the truth of their statements. "It is possible, though I certainly did not intend it."

"Women," said Faldrein in exasperation.

"What do you mean?" I asked

"Umm…it's just something my father used to say about mom. You know, 'Lephix gave men intellect and Mamoel gave women feelings.' I think he meant that women are mysterious and hard to understand."

Vondro threw his hands up. "I'm staying out of this one."

"I find everyone mysterious and hard to understand," I responded to my wizard friend.

"Well, women more so," he said without conviction.

"In what way?" I prodded.

"Well… they think differently… with their emotions…" He trailed off.

I looked to my other companions. Vondro tucked deeper into his sleeping sack while Brother Ironknuckle shrugged. To Faldrein I responded, "While I believe your father had difficulty understanding women, your mother in particular, I feel that was a failing of his, and not of women in general."

Vondro snickered.

Faldrein sighed. "You may be right. Maybe I don't understand either."

"You get along with Glitter, yeah?" asked Brother Ironknuckle. "She's a woman. Do ye think of her as a woman or as a person?"

"As a person, of course." Faldrein's voice rose. After a minute of silence he continued, "I... I think I used to think of her as a girl. She beat me so easily at the tournament. I was embarrassed to lose to her, and blamed it on her beauty. She outsmarted me. I've gotten to know her over the past few years and I... think differently about her now. Glitter's a friend, not just a woman."

"So ye don't judge people on how they look?"

"I... no? Maybe? Mithron, help me."

"Everyone is different. What they look like, how they were born, seems less important than how they act. It takes me a while to figure it out because people do not always act the same all the time. I do know I cannot assume that any particular category of people can be treated as if they were identical. There are far too many variables."

Faldrein sighed. "I didn't mean to denigrate Glitter or anyone else."

"We all pick up bad habits from our elders," Vondro said. "Once we realize they're wrong, that's when we can be better." He rolled over to face us. "Dad doesn't think non-humans are as good as humans in general. They have 'certain specialties' that, he believes, defines them, but humans are more than capable of surpassing them. I've learned there are unique styles which others employ, but I've never thought I was better than anyone else because I'm human. How many times have you beaten me?" he asked Brother Ironknuckle with a chuckle.

"Ye've given me some great workouts, lad, and ye hold yer own."

Faldrein yawned. "I will have to think more on what I say. I don't want to be a *uuaarih*."[14]

"And I shall let Glitter calm down," I dropped into my sleeping sack with a yawn of my own, "and will speak with her in the morning."

The stone corridor split up ahead. Many of the arched doorways were bricked up, the doors I already knew were locked. I was in the Mazeworks again, the dimension between dreams where I often find myself when my mind refuses to settle. In the past I would regularly find answers, but since my tortures at the hands of Cratillus, nightmares have been more common. I no longer look forward to the Mazeworks.

Doors are not doors here, nor solid walls barriers. One journeys down a path until another way is found, either via a portal opening or the path leading directly into a dream. Once within a dream, it is easy to be caught into the temporary reality and forget that one is dreaming, though they are easier to remember upon awakening whether I wish it or not.

After an unnecessary deliberation, I chose the left path. At some point, I noticed the stone corridor had changed to wood, though there was no obvious transition. The ceiling tapered away to open skies, the walls faded to brambles then ever more distant trees, and the floor was covered with leaves, dirt, and twigs.

---

[14] From Draconic: "ball of dung".

I stopped when I was grabbed from behind.

"Human wizard!" squealed a voice in my ear.

I turned my head to see Effay'ost'kao beaming at me.

Her face distorted into that of Cratillus and once again said "human wizard", but with his arrogance and disdain. I was no longer being hugged by zylan arms, but rather restrained by red vines, one of which had wrapped around my throat. I turned away and struggled to get free, but the vines held me tight and rough bark scratched my bare back. Out of the darkening woods, the parade of images began with the sound of sobbing which lasted throughout the dream.

"You realize of course that we don't need or want you here," said Farandi dancing into my vision through the moonbeams. She pulled a pair of daggers from her belt as she spun against me, her eyes inches from mine. The blades scratched their way down my arms to rest against my wrists. I gritted my teeth to prepare for the expected stabbing, but she laughed and whirled away.

"Aww, helpless as a little baby." Gwenaz floated down from the branches above, her hair slicing a path through the leaves. "He can't even do magic." She made an exaggerated frown then began laughing, vanishing into the darkness.

"You almost got me killed," growled Hyxi, intestines swinging at their knees.

"We were fine until you came along." Waltheri rushed out through the moonbeams and leapt for my throat.

I woke with a gargled scream.

Faldrein looked around without focus and fell back to sleep.

"Another nightmare?" whispered Vondro.

I nodded in the darkness before realizing that he probably could not see me. "Yes."

He stood up and moved to the tent flap. "Me too."

I followed him out of the tent into the misty pre-twilight. Thessylia shook out her feathers above us then settled into an alert stance.

"Tsukatta?" I asked, knowing full well her death still plagued him.

"Yeah. Cratillus?"

"Yes." Glitter slept next to the dying embers, shivering and wet. I cast *uvaazrosiit* to dry her and her bedroll. Vondro and I walked a short distance away but close enough that I could still see our camp. "I am sorry I got us involved in that. It is all my fault."

"It would have been worse if you hadn't. We would have all died fighting hordes of kuldaa and ruklaa if we weren't there to stop it before it started. I never would have met Tsukatta if it weren't for you. I mourn her every day," he sobbed.

Glitter or Effay would have hugged him without hesitation, whereas I merely stood helpless and took a deep breath. "I am sorry," I repeated. "You know I would bring her back if I could, but even Mamoel's priestesses could not. I miss her as well and cannot imagine how much it must hurt for you."

He sniffed, nodded, and pulled me into a tight embrace. Not knowing how else to react, I hugged him back. After a time, he released his hold and pushed me to arm's length.

"Was yours the same dream as always?" he asked.

"Nearly. This time it was our new allies abusing me instead of you. I fear I am only going to cause them anguish just like I did for all of you. Anything causing trouble in the Greylands is not something we will walk away from unscathed."

"Yet, here we are," he smiled, but not with his eyes, "ready to face unknown dangers to make the world a better place. Our fates uncertain, our cause honorable."

My smile was a little more genuine. "That sounds like something your father would say to rally the troops."

Vondro's eyes brightened, and he slapped both of my shoulders. "That is *exactly* what my father said right before we entered Ehrghex. Here I thought I could be clever for a change," he laughed.

"Even if the words are not originally yours, they are still inspiring. We will all need your bravery in the time to come—it is why I asked you to join us. Your strength of character may prove even more important than your physical strength. We…*I*…need you."

"Thank you." He patted my shoulders. "Since we're awake, we might as well get the fire restarted." Vondro picked up a few fallen branches. They would be easy enough to dry with a simple *uvaazrosiit* myzling, but he would have to use flint and steel to start the fire. Glitter usually prepares the spell for that, so I rarely bother when we are together.

I wished I knew what was bothering her. For the first few months which we knew each other, I had gotten accustomed to her being upset with me, and for good reason. I had known her for scarcely a day, and I divulged her most painful memory to our entire wizard community when my Wizard's Gift manifested for the first time. We grew closer over the past two suns, and, in spite of both our better judgements, are in a relationship of sorts. I cannot explain how it happened or even how to describe it, as I have never loved before.

Knowing better than to wake her, I sat far enough away from the fire to avoid wandering cinders while still receiving some of its warmth and studied my spellbook while Vondro cared for the horses. I focused on divinations, as we were mostly seeking information, but still prepared a few combat spells as one is never safe in the wilds. Afterwards, I walked over to Vondro. I had not noticed Hyxi had awakened as they sat quietly by the fire with him.

"I am going into the woods," I whispered, pointing toward the hollow tree which Thessylia had found for me. "I will be casting a spell which requires my full concentration and might be dangerous. If I have not returned within the hour, or if it sounds as if I am in trouble, please come looking for me."

"Do you need a guard?" asked Hyxi.

"I do not think so. Thank you. Thessylia will come for you should something come sniffing around me while I am entranced." I paused to reconsider. "However, if you wish to watch over me, do not get too close—I do not want you to get caught up in the spell."

"What kind of spell are you casting?" Vondro asked.

"I am going to seek information from a powerful source so that we have a better understanding of the situation. I will not be physically harmed, but the strain may leave me addled for a time. Tell the others to prepare additional combat magicks on the chance that I will not be able to in case of danger."

"Are you sure you want to do this?" Vondro shook his head. "Let's wait until we hear from your friends. Maybe they already have that information."

"The sooner it is done, the sooner I will recover. We do not know whether or if they have, or even will, find anything. I must try."

They both nodded slowly.

The hollowed tree was not necessary for the spell, but I thought it would be best to have shelter from wandering predators while in the midst of the spell. It was more cramped than I would have liked, but it served its purpose. Thessylia perched at the top of the rotted maple, turned and bobbed her head, and clacked her beak.

'There are no large predators nearby,' my familiar confirmed.

'Thank you. If any should threaten, try to drive them away or fly to get help from the others, but do not fight them. I do not want you harmed.'

'Would they not disrupt your spell?'

'Then the spell is lost, and I can try again another time. I cannot replace you.' Technically, I could summon a new familiar should Thessylia die, but I wished to avoid that situation altogether whenever possible. For her safety, I placed an *ajiavulhysayt* spell on her. The mystical armor would protect her from most harm.

I began the ritual that would send my mind through the veil which separates our plane of existence from the Greylands, where the dead go before moving on to their final residence. The kazkul whom Faldrein and I talked to said the others had been captured. If so, the easiest place to catch them would be in the Greylands. That being the case, the entity I sought would likely be trapped with the kazkulim—Sylckhis, the Chief Soul-Gatherer.

According to the description of *mbikvlidyk*, the spell should lead me directly to the entity or source of my choosing. It may not be the Greylands after all, but it seemed the logical assumption. Of course, contacting higher powers without warning or consent can be dangerous and one needs to be careful of how obsequious one can act depending on the entity contacted. Most deities prefer mortals to grovel and fawn, whereas others might see submissiveness as weakness and be insulted by a sycophantic parishioner. Little is known about Sylekhis aside from being first among equals.

The ritual also limits the questions one can ask. Most of the magic is used to get the caster's mind to the right place and hold it there for a short time. The shorter the questions and answers, the more information I might potentially receive, so I needed to be direct and not waste too much time on platitudes.

I chanted the *mbikvlidyk* ritual, emptied my mind of everything save the name Sylekhis, and at the final syllable, my body fell limp as my mind raced to its destination. Colors flashed through my vision: a long stretch of brown, then grey, black, blue-white, grey, turquoise, and more grey. Without warning, I found myself floating before a large cage covered in runes which I wished I had more time to translate, but the predominate one was *wulmiiv*.[15] Buzzing within the cage were thousands of dragonflies.

"Sylekhis!" I called.

One dragonfly, much larger than the others and bone-white from head to tail emerged at the front of the swarm. "What do you want, mortal?"

---

[15] Wulmiiv loosely translates to "block" or "stop" and is often used in barriers and summoning circles intended to contain the creature summoned.

"To help. My time is short. Are we in the Greylands?"

"What is your interest?" Sylekhis sounded displeased with my very presence.

"The world is out of balance. Please. Are we in the Greylands?" The droning of wings was making me uncomfortable.

"Yes."

"Where? We will try to release you."

If a dragonfly could narrow its eyes, I believe Sylekhis would have. "Atop the Twilight Terrace, trapped in our own home." Anger filled his tone, and my mind began to hurt.

"Why has the Dark Lady not freed you?"

"I wish I knew. I have not seen Her since I was pulled into this box."

"Who put you here?"

"Mortal wizards."

No. It could not be. "Did you see their leader? What was his name?" I could feel the Weave begin to tear around me.

"Yes. He called…"

The colors rushed back through in reverse order as my mind snapped back to my body. My head spun and I leaned forward to vomit. Afterward, I began to laugh.

And laugh.

I looked at the hollow cavity which I had been sitting in and stared at the flat shelf-like mushrooms growing within. "Squishy," I chuckled as I poked them.

'What happened?'

'Hi, Thess. I talked to a big dragonfly.'

Thessylia blinked and turned her head upside-down, making me laugh. She blinked again and turned her head. *'I will get help.'*

As she flew off, I waved and shouted, "Bye birdie." I could not explain it, but something about the world seemed brighter and more distinct: colors were pure, sounds crisp, and even the air smelled strong, each individual scent clearly defined from the others. A beetle climbed up the tree, black and green, like crushed onyx and emeralds, and it became my whole world.

"Mithron?" called a strong voice which reminded me of gravel.

"Shh. You might scare it," I said in a harsh whisper, waving the speaker away. The beetle scuttled around the tree, so I walked around to follow it. It found a hole in the bark and burrowed into the tree.

"Are ye alright, lad?" the same voice asked.

It sounded familiar. I turned to see a grommold with burn scars on his face. He looked at me as if he thought I was someone else. "Brother," I shouted, throwing my arms wide. I ran up to hug him but tripped on a root and fell flat on my face.

He pulled me up by the shoulders. "Are ye alright?" he asked again.

I laughed until my stomach hurt, and I had to sit down in the dirt. I hiccoughed and laughed some more.

"Is he drunk?" asked a small child with dog ears.

I sputtered in dismissal. "Me? No. Never in my life, li'l pup."

"He warned me the spell might damage his mind," said a tall man covered in silver, "but I wasn't expecting this."

"What did you do?" asked a pretty voice.

It sounded upset. I turned to look and got lost in her eyes, orange like a sunset.

"Mithron?"

"You're pretty," I pointed. She turned to look at the other people and I noticed little flashes of yellow and orange light around her. "Sparkles." I shouted and clapped.

"What happened?" asked the sparkly one.

"When?" I asked. Something about her made me happy.

"You cast a spell. You said you were looking for information." She looked right at me and I fell into her eyes again. Her sparkles switched between red and yellow.

"There were lots of colors, and I talked to a dragonfly in a box."

"I've never talked to a dragonfly before," said another voice.

She spoke like she was singing. She had a lot of hair, and it was bright orange like the other one's eyes. No, it was more like copper.

"What did the dragonfly say?"

"It said that wizards put it in a box with the others, and it was waiting for a dark woman to find it."

"The Dark Lady?" asked another voice. He was grey and boring and seemed nervous.

I snapped my fingers and pointed at him. "Yes." I snapped my fingers again purely to hear the sound. It amused me. I did it a few more times before the person with a lot of hair put her hand over mine.

"Are you thirsty?" she asked.

"Yes." I said with a large breath, as if I had been waiting for someone to ask me that.

She handed me a hard, brown object with a hole in the top. I drank from it. The liquid felt warm as it went down but tasted like rotten grapes.

"Blech," I handed the thing back to her. "It tastes like vinegar. Grape vinegar." I began to wipe off my tongue with my fingers until she held my hands. I put my head on her hair. "You're comfy."

"His aura is shifting. Scintillating," she said, but not to me.

"Faldrein?" said the pretty eyes woman.

"It's as though part of his mind is in a chest. He's not injured or broken. I think he's protecting himself. I've never seen anything like it before," said the grey man. He looked at the pretty-eyed woman a lot when she wasn't looking at him.

"Can you help him?" asked a pile of green leaves which looked like a skinny girl.

"I wish I could. Beus might be able to. We're still a couple days away from his tower."

"Then we should make haste," the dark and silver man said.

"Would you like to ride a horse?" asked the big-hair woman.

"Horsey!" I shouted with excitement. *What is wrong with me?*

"Come, let's get you on a horse."

"Yay!" I clapped. My head spun as I leapt to my feet and I giggled.

"I should ride with him," said the sparkly one as she moved towards my horse.

The puppy girl stepped in front of her. "Let Gwenaz take care of him. If anyone can handle someone whose mind has snapped, it's her."

The woman with sunset eyes looked upset, sparkling red and purple, and went to another horse. The big-hair woman got on my horse behind me. "Do you like horses?"

"Uh-huh." I nodded and shook the straps.

"Gently," she breathed, and I felt relaxed. "That's better. Always be nice to animals."

"Okay." We began to travel on one, two, three, four, five horses and the doggy girl was on a bigger dog. I laughed, sputtering at how strange everything looked.

"Tell me about the dragonfly," asked a pile of hair behind me. There was a person face and a dog face in the hair. I don't know which one asked the question, so I answered the dog.

"It was big, and white, and had big round eyes like moons," I made a circle with my hands, "and long wings," I stretched my arms out. "It didn't seem happy to see me."

"Dragonflies…" the human face began.

"They were all in a big box." I interrupted. "But not a real box." I fluttered my lips. "I mean, you wouldn't be able to see them in a real box. It was a pretend box like the quiet clowns do, but with squiggles."

"Squiggles?" the hair asked.

"Floating squiggles," I clarified, waggling my finger around.

"Runes?" asked the pretty eyes.

Why can I not recall her name? I snapped my fingers. "Yes, Runes. Magic squiggles." I nodded with vehemence and began to slip off the horse before the hair grabbed me.

The hair turned to look at the sparkles. "Who could trap the kazkulim in a mystic field, and why?"

Sparkle-pretty-eyes stuck out her lower lip.

I chuckled.

"I don't know," she said. "But whoever it is must be powerful. We definitely need help."

I leaned back into the hair and it wrapped around me like a warm blanket. The sparkly one turned purple again. The person in the hair began to hum and I fell asleep.

When I awoke, we were in front of a large tower.

I have been here before.

A golden sphere with five long tentacles hovered before me, gentle warmth radiating from the tips. I tried to shift away but the copper-haired lady, Gwinn…Glim…something like that, hushed me and reassured me it was only here to help. I forced myself to hold still while it touched my forehead, wrists, and knees, and the creature's soft heat calmed my anxiety.

Other people were standing nearby. I recognized their faces, but had trouble remembering their names. I felt safe with them yet worried they might harm me in some fashion. The one with the pale yellow and green sparkles around her in particular made my chest ache. An older man was directing the orb and the tentacles shifted along my spine. My breathing grew heavy when it touched the base of my skull.

Colors cascaded through my vision, browns, greys, and blues, all wrapped in unyielding darkness.

"No," I croaked as futility and despair began to collapse my protective bubble like an avalanche over an open grave. "Stop!" I screamed, and the orb backed away. I was not aware of my sobbing until I realized I could not breathe through my nose.

There were arms all around me and bodies pressed against mine as I wailed in misery, my despondency turning everything to a flat grey so I could scarcely make out the faces of those around me. Their pain only added to my own but was still overwhelmed by the wretched distress of the dragonflies, and I could no longer hold their suffering at bay. I felt every anguished soul, from the fatally wounded to the diseased to the infirm, unable to find release in death, trapped either in bodies they could not discard or as spirits tormented to linger in the physical plane, as they called for peace which would not come. My mournful keening continued until I could no longer process it all and collapsed into the arms of my friends.

It was dark when I next opened my eyes, the only light coming from a sliver of moon and the nearly invisible indigo sparkles from Glitter sleeping in a chair next to me. The straw-filled mattress was poking my lower back and I sat up slowly so as not to wake her. As I did, I felt the recurring waves of despair once again and had to steady myself to avoid falling. I was not aware of Glitter moving until her arms were around me, squeezing me tight.

"It's okay. You're back. We're all here," she whispered while rocking me gently.

All I could do in response was cry.

A second pair of arms joined in as the sky brightened to twilight. I did not know Effay well enough then, but she always wakes up exactly one hour before dawn like a flower preparing for the sun. "Poor human wizard."

I turned to Glitter as the sun broke the horizon. "May I…?" I began, barely able to rasp out the words, then put my finger to my throat.

"Water?" she asked.

I nodded in response.

She handed me her waterskin, and I sipped slowly to avoid choking from bouts of sobbing.

Effay never let go.

As the others awoke, they either joined in the embrace or stood nearby. Brother Ironknuckle sat on the floor before me and chuckled.

"What's so funny?" asked Vondro, his voice a combination of irritation and confusion.

"Just thinkin' about Raf and his reaction to seein' Mithron getting all this attention," Brother Ironknuckle smiled.

Vondro looked at me and could not stifle a laugh. For a moment the oppressive sadness lifted. But only a moment.

I thought of my friend's sacrifice in ridding this world of Cratillus and began to mourn him all over again. And Tsukatta. And the town of Ehrghex. And all the souls crying out for release in the present.

"It is all too much," I stammered out between sobs. "We have to free the kazkulim or this will never end."

"You're in no state to do that right now," chided Beus, handing me a goblet. Faldrein stood by his side, his eyes bloodshot.

I gave the drink a skeptical look before Beus confirmed that it was a potion and not alcohol. Small bubbles gathered along the interior of the goblet, occasionally breaking free and floating to the surface of the indigo liquid. It smelled of pine and cinnamon, and I lowered it to my lap.

"Drink," he commanded, stern but gentle. "All at once would be best."

I wish I had Brother Ironknuckle's ability to pour liquids down my throat without seeming to actually swallow so I could avoid tasting concoctions such as this. I gagged about two-thirds of the way through but managed to finish it all at once.

"Why could you not," I said, pausing to burp, "find a way to make this taste better?" I burped again, took a deep breath, and slowly exhaled.

Beus smiled. "Sometimes we need to go through something awful to get to a better place. Feeling calmer?"

I took another slow deep breath. "Yes. Thank you."

"It should help for a few hours at least. Enough to quell the pain so you can begin processing it. So, tell me what happened."

I explained to the gathering—there were far too many people in the room for comfort—the images I saw and my conversation with Sylekhis.

"That is why one shouldn't cast spells like that without precautions," he reprimanded. "Your zeal nearly cost you your sanity."

"Fair. But the situation becomes more dire by the day. I thought it worth the risk." My stomach churned in revolt and I closed my eyes to stop the world from drifting. "Your potion is not settling well."

"Slow breaths," Beus said, placing a hand on my shoulder.

I stared into his calming eyes and followed his instruction, holding my breath on occasion as my stomach continued its attempted revolt. Tears flowed freely down my cheeks, but I was no longer certain if it was from the despair or the concoction.

"We have to go to the Greylands. Do you know where the Twilight Terrace is? How would we even get there?" I asked. "The kazkulim are scared."

"The Twilight Terrace is part of the Grand Mausoleum, the Dark Lady's residence," answered Beus, his voice strangely flat. "Only the kazkulim can bring people directly there—the Dark Lady has closed her realm to spells creating temporary gateways. Blythad sent me a note and may have found something in Ormak's journals. You should all rest here today while Mithron recovers," he announced. "I will open the *bezyamlialrih* tomorrow and teleport you all to Ormak's directly."

Faldrein took us to the third floor of the tower which had a number of small chambers for guests; I learned I had been in his bed. They were far from opulent, but not uncomfortable for one or two people. As I was settling in, my friends would stop in to check on me every few minutes until I began to lose my temper. Unfortunately, this occurred on Glitter's second interruption, and even *I* knew I owed her an apology.

Chapter 9: Recovery

Sleep came in short bursts through the hot, late-summer day. I was physically and emotionally exhausted, but when I slept, I was plagued with dreams of watching others suffer while I was either tied to a tree, paralyzed by a vulzu, or locked in a windowless room; it did not take a diviner to understand my feelings of helplessness. Tears came at random intervals, but not with the same vehemence as earlier.

After my outburst at Glitter, I was left alone until mid-afternoon. At some point, a plate of soft rosemary bread and berries, along with a cup of cold peppermint tea, appeared on the table next to the bed. Though I had no appetite, the bread did help to neutralize the lingering taste of Beus' potion. Out of habit, I sought my spellbook, but found it difficult to concentrate on gathering the energy for more than the simplest of spells. I kept glancing at the door, hoping Glitter would come in so I could apologize to her, yet was glad to avoid further confrontation. Finally, I got up and shuffled out the door.

Beus' tower is ringed with small rooms on the third floor, with gaps allowing access to the two windows. Mine was near the spiral staircase which led to all four floors, and I had no idea which room anyone else was in, or even if the rooms were occupied. Hoping Glitter was nearby, I went to the first door on my left and heard a rhythmic tapping, like boots on stone but not walking. When I knocked, Farandi answered the door. She had a light sheen of sweat, which matted down her black hair.

"You're up," she said with mild surprise. "How are you feeling?"

"Better, thank you." I got lost for a moment in her deep brown eyes. "My mind still drifts about, and the sadness comes and goes, but, overall, I am feeling much better. How are you? You seem out of breath."

"Just dancing," she answered with a smile. "I don't do well sitting for too long, but I could take a breather. Come in." Her room appeared much like mine, except all the furniture had been pushed against the walls, leaving as much open space as possible. She spun about a few times before flopping on the bed. I strode over to the chair and sat.

"How are you… how is everybody? I am sorry for being such a burden on everyone."

Too late, I turned away from her, after watching her parents physically eject her from their home after she confessed to being in love with another woman. Farandi's mother was as skilled with a broom as Vondro was with a sword.

"We're all fine," she answered, oblivious to my Gift. "We had joked about going on a grand adventure and becoming heroes before meeting you lot. Now, we're going to have to make good on it." She laughed. "Fay-Fay said that you saved the world a couple years ago. Is this a regular thing for you?"

It took a moment for me to realize she meant Effay'ost'kao.

"We stopped a lunatic from raising an army of kuldaa after turning the town of Ehrghex into undead soldiers. I do not know if we 'saved the world' but things could have been dire had we not been there. And had he not attacked us first, we never would have been aware of his machinations in the first place. Faldrein and I stumbled upon the situation when a former teacher died..." I paused to steady myself, but could not prevent the tears from streaming down my face.

After a deep shuddering breath, I continued. "Yoffa's spirit lingered in her garden, and her death took far too long from the illness she suffered. We talked to a kazkul and learned that only a few were retrieving souls rather than the swarms which should be in the world. Shortly thereafter, we met you and the spirits haunting the miskarn, which confirmed the kazkul's tale."

"So you decided to seek out the chief kazkul and ask him directly?"

"The idea seemed prudent at the time. So, where was your 'grand adventure' taking you?"

"Pretty much wherever Gwenny wanted to go," she replied. "We all met up in Willow's Walk and were immediately drawn to each other." Farandi closed her eyes and smiled. She let out a long breath and gave a little shudder as she flushed. "I had never been so happy in my life. But then a band of raquoli charged in, tearing through the market and attacking the villagers. We rushed out and found that we worked well as a combat team too. We tracked the little lizard-dogs to their base camp and drove them off. After that, we decided to explore the area to see what else might threaten the villages and stop it before it could cause any harm.

"You met us after we caught up with the miskarn. It had decimated a logging camp near Birchtown, killing the workers and their families. According to legend, they only appear every twenty-five suns to gorge themselves on fresh meat and mate. There was likely another one nearby, which we failed to find before getting caught up with this larger situation."

"If there was, hopefully someone else is around to stop it. I am sorry to have pulled you away."

"Like I said, we've learned to follow Gwenny's instincts. If following you is more important, than that's the way we go. It's almost like someone is whispering in her ear."

"Stella?" I asked.

Farandi responded with a laugh. "Probably. I'd wager heavy money that little fox is smarter than anyone would guess. Gwenny isn't mad, you know, she merely has a greater awareness of things than most and it makes her seem odd to those who don't know her."

A wave of dizziness passed through me.

"Maybe you should return to bed," she suggested.

I did not recall her standing nor pulling me to my feet.

"No." I tugged my arm away. "I need to find Glitter."

"What for?" she scoffed. "I'm sure you have history, but she's been nothing but cold and dismissive to us ever since we met."

I blinked in confusion before another dizzy spell came over me and found myself sitting on my bed before I could respond. *How did I get here?*

"That is odd. Glitter makes friends with everyone, even me, and I gave her plenty of reason not to."

When I next opened my eyes, it was evening. My stomach turned over when I smelled a spicy-foresty odor which I had no desire to be familiar with. Against my wishes, I downed the potion and leaned against the wall while sitting on the bed. I had hoped the stones would be cooler than they were to counter the rising heat from my stomach.

While I was concentrating on keeping Beus' tonic down there was a light rapping on my door before it swung open.

"How are you doing?" Faldrein asked from the doorway.

"I could use some bread to get the taste of your potion out of my mouth," I answered with a grim smile. "Otherwise, better? Definitely less melancholic. Have you seen Glitter around? I wish to speak with her."

"I've been in the lab most of the day, but I'll see if I can find her. The tower isn't so big that she could hide for long," he joked. "You do look better—more… integrated." There is a visible shift in Faldrein's eyes when he uses his Gift, as though they become like glass for a time.

I wonder what the downside is to his healer's sight.

"Do you think you'll be okay to travel tomorrow?"

"I believe so. I cannot see how teleporting to Ormak's would cause me any harm. Perhaps after more rest I will actually be able to concentrate for more than a few minutes."

"Great. I know we have more important things to do, but I'm hoping to get in a game of Gargoyles against Blythad. I have a four-game winning streak and I want to expand my lead." He smiled. "Do you play?"

"I know of the game," I answered, "but have not played. Mayhap when the kazkulim situation is resolved, you can teach me."

"I'd love to. I need more opponents other than Blythad and Glitter. I'm surprised she hasn't taught you."

"That would be a fun activity. We spend a lot of our limited time together controlling my Gift. I should really do something more for her." My yawn was loud and unbidden.

"You should get more rest now. I'll bring you some food."

"Thank you," I managed to say as I slumped back down and fell into another sudden sleep.

 "I tried to warn you about this, my boy," came a hollow voice from the darkness. I turned to see two orange lights, like round candle flames, floating toward me. As they neared, the mostly skeletal face of Ormak came into view. "She's in your heart now—it will be your downfall."

"It does not have to be that way," I responded, shaking my head. "Why is it so bad to finally be loved?"

"That's exactly the problem. You don't know what love is. Come, sit by me." The jozalk gestured to a bare wooden chair next to him, the padding long since rotted away.

I eyed the seat suspiciously before accepting his request. He continued to stand as soft music played from somewhere in the room. I could not place the tune at first.

"Love is a noose, designed to strangle you until it takes your life away. Your mind, heart, even your very identity choked out of you, leaving you a dried husk in the wind. Look at you, asking around for Glitter when you should be taking care of yourself. She's draining you like a maraika and you don't even realize it."

"No. We are there for each other. She has been helping me control my Gift and I have been helping her figure out her color shifts and surges of power. We make each other better."

"Truly, you believe this?" His hollow laugh made my jaw clench. "Two years of practice, and you still see nothing but her anguish. She is nothing but misery for you. Are you so desperate for companionship that you are willing to subject yourself to constant agony just to have her nearby? She has done *nothing* for you." He poked my abdomen to emphasise his point.

A supernatural chill flowed through my center until he pulled back.

"I am corrected. She has done one thing for you. You are eating better." He laughed again but this time with mirth. "But where has she been while you have been convalescing? Sitting by your side nursing you back to health? Helping Faldrein make potions? No? The moment you came back with your mind tattered, she was more than happy to hand you over to that sonchia woman. She doesn't want or need you. She doesn't care for you. You're solely a burden which she finally foisted off."

I opened my mouth to respond but he cut me off.

"Don't bother trying to deny it. You know this to be true. Men like us are not meant to love. Our destiny is greater than our personal wishes and subjecting ourselves to the whims of the heart will only cause endless suffering."

The song was Lixia's *The Eternal Heart* from Suzelle's music box.

"Simply because you suffered does not mean it will be the same for me," I countered. "You must remember the joy as well as the sorrow. Yes, there is a risk of pain—it is the same with all friendships. I stopped trying after I was betrayed as a child by Kived and never sought to make friends again. Yet here I am surrounded by those who care for me. I have even made friends of rivals if only because I wanted peace. I may get hurt again, in fact I am certain it will happen, but it is worth some pain to feel greater joy."

His glowing eyes dimmed as he shook his head, bone scraped on bone in his neck.

"The young always think they know better. Even if I do not persuade you now, remember our conversations. Your joy will turn to eternal pain."

Ormak shattered like glass.

When I looked at his remains on the floor, I saw a melding of his face and mine reflected in the shards.

I jolted awake, nearly falling off the bed. The room was completely dark, save for a soft purple glow next to the bed. Between that and my enhanced vision from Thessylia, I could make out Glitter's face as she slowly woke.

"How long have you been here?" I whispered.

She yawned. "I don't know. A few hours maybe? You need your rest, so I didn't want to wake you." Her motes slowly brightened.

"You should have. I have been worried about you."

This made her chuckle. "*You* have been worried about *me*? After what you put me through?" Her sparkles shifted to red as her voiced rose. "Why did you do that without asking for help? You could have lost yourself forever."

"I thought it would help and it did. You would have talked me out of it."

"You're damn right I would have talked you out of it. There are precautions to take, ingredients to use. You should have waited at least until we got here. Beus knows more about these things."

"I cannot rely on others all the time, and the longer we spend seeking a resolution, the more everybody suffers. I am sorry I did not include you in this decision, but I did what I thought was right."

"Yes, and you're always right, aren't you? We've talked about this too many times. You don't know everything."

"No, I do not, that is why I had to use the *mbikvlidyk* ritual, to learn more. And I did. It was worth the risk."

She crossed her arms and the room brightened in crimson. "We are supposed to be partners. You shouldn't do something like that without telling me." Tears began to form in her eyes. "I nearly lost you."

"I am sorry to have worried you, but I am fine."

"No, you're not. Maybe you're better now, but you're not fine. That you can't see that is either hubris or proof that your mind is still disjointed." Purple and blue motes began to mix with the deep red ones as she stood. "I... I have to go."

"Please stay. I need you."

"You don't need me, you want me. You're afraid of being alone so you keep dragging me in while pushing me away. I can't do this anymore. I'll still help with freeing the kazkulim—that's more important than us—but we can't be... this... anymore," she murmured, leaving blue and red sparkles in her wake.

I sat in the darkness alone, wanting to cry, but unable to after days of unrelenting tears. I had expected and made peace with our inevitable separation long ago. *Glitter is intelligent, caring, and beautiful. She should have no trouble finding someone more suited to her than I.*

After casting *juut* on the ceiling directly over the bed for light, I pulled out my spellbook to prepare for the day. Even with my enhanced vision, reading is still difficult in darkness, and I had slept so much in the past few days that I could not fall back asleep. Over the past two suns, we had cleared Ormak's tower of his traps and guardians, and Beus was going to teleport us there through the *bezyamlialrih*, so there was no need to ready any combat spells. Instead, I focused on divinations and enhancements to increase my perception, memory, and mental acuity in order to find and assimilate more information. Afterwards, my stomach complained about my lack of attention of late, so I sought out the kitchen.

After putting a cauldron of water on for tea—our large group would need a lot of water—I rummaged through the frost pantry and came away with a loaf of bread and a pear. As I tore a hunk off the loaf, Hyxi walked in and grabbed my pear.

"Good to see you up and around again. Your eggs less scrambled now?" they asked.

"Yes, I believe so," I answered, digging out another pear for myself. "You are awake early."

"I don't handle being boxed in well. I should have slept under the stars," they said, stretching their arms up and back. "But Effay got snuggly, and I didn't want to disturb her. She should be up soon anyway."

"I appreciate you, all of you, for tolerating my… fracture. I do not appear to make good first impressions."

"Magic does funny things to folk. I've spent enough time with it to understand. So, we're supposed to go see another wizard next?"

"Yes, Blythad. Ormak had a large library which might tell us how to get to the Greylands. Travel to the tower is but an eyeblink. How do you feel about going to another plane of existence?"

"I do like seeing new places and meeting new people. This'll certainly be a new experience." They finished the pear, core and all. "I'm going for a run. Care to join me?"

I smiled and shook my head. "I would never keep up with you, nor would I last long. I think I will read instead."

"Nope." They grabbed my arm and pulled. "You need some exercise and fresh air. I'm not asking you to keep up, Spirits know I've been running since I could stand, but you won't get better without trying."

Before I could protest further, we were out the door. Hyxi started with a slow jog to get me moving, slowly increasing their pace until I was too winded to continue. "Get your breath and keep moving. Pick up again when I circle back." they called as they disappeared into the pre-dawn darkness.

"Make sure you stay within the grounds," I called back. The area around Beus' tower is a flat, grassy garden-scape with the odd golem standing around appearing as sculpture. Even the topiaries are not as they seem and can kill an intruder with their venomous brambles. Hyxi had no trouble running through the darkness lit only by stars and a rising waning crescent moon; her senses are as keen as mine.

'This is new. Your thoughts are more coherent, but I have never known you to run without cause,' commented Thessylia.

'Hyxi had me running before I could pull away. Considering how far and fast they can move I cannot argue with their assessment. I do spend a great deal of time sitting, but one cannot read while running.'

'No, but you should strengthen your body. What good is your mind without it?'

'Perhaps, but my time is better spent on learning and studying.'

'You are not an apprentice anymore,' she chided. *'You do not have to impress Vletraka or anyone else. Take time for other things in life. When is the last time you painted?'*

'Winter? Yes, there was a freezing rain which perfectly captured a spiderweb in ice.'

'Hyxi is returning.'

I began to jog as they neared, slowing their pace to match mine.

They pointed ahead. "See that statue of the spearman?" Hyxi asked.

"The one near the fence line? Yes." I chose not to correct them on the nature of the object.

"You are not to stop until we get to it."

"I cannot run that far," I began.

Hyxi interrupted. "You can. We will pace ourselves so that you will," they said slowing to a jog. For someone nearly half my height, Hyxi can easily outpace me. As they said, they have been active all their life, but I would have expected someone the size of a human child to move much slower.

With Hyxi's encouragement, I did manage to reach the spearman golem and dropped to my knees at its feet, gasping for breath. My legs and chest burned, and I could feel my racing heart in my ears.

"I knew you could do it. How do you feel?"

I wheezed in response.

"Here. Sip." They handed me a waterskin.

The water was cold and refreshing, and it helped relax my breathing. "Do you do this every morning?" I asked between rasping breaths.

"When I can. This is a safe environment, so I don't have to guard my girls. It feels good to run free."

"Do you fear they would not be safe without you? From what I have seen, they are capable of protecting themselves."

"They are. I don't doubt that in the least. But if something were to happen and I wasn't there…" They trailed off.

"I understand. Plus, should you be off running and got into trouble alone, they might not be able to arrive in time to assist you either."

"Well, since no one is dying, it does take some pressure off." Hyxi gave a half-smile.

"If only it were without cost." I stood, having recaptured my breath. "Thank you for this. Running is not for me, but you got me out of my thoughts for a little while. Would you mind, when this has been settled, if I did your portrait? It has been pointed out to me that I have been neglecting my creativity."

"That might be nice, but won't I have to sit still for it?" she asked with some trepidation.

"At least at first. Once I have the basic structure done, I can do the rest from memory, though I might ask you to sit again for detail."

"Okay. Race you back?" They laughed, already moving towards the tower.

"I will catch up eventually," I called back. Though my heart had settled from my run, it reminded me of another pain once I was alone again. *She is better off without me,* became my mantra, though, to be honest, I knew I was better with her.

Thessylia was perched in a tree halfway back to the tower; I did not remember passing it while running, but I was more focused on not collapsing at the time.

'You should be more active. A healthy body lives longer.'

'I know. I promised myself I would do some of Vondro's exercises and I have not done those either. All my exercise comes from carrying books.'

'Very well, I shall remind you every morning until it becomes a habit for you.'

The tree shook and began to shrink, causing Thessylia to fly to my shoulder. Within a few seconds it had become Effay.

"Good morning." She stretched, the remaining bark and leaves melding into her skin. "Feeling better?"

"Yes, thank you. I was not aware you could transform yourself like that."

"I usually do it a couple times a moon. It helps me recharge my energies to root myself for a while. This is the safest place we've been in a while, so I wanted to take advantage of the situation." She held out her hand and Thessylia flew to her. She then let out a series of barks and trills to which my owl responded in kind before fluttering back to me. "She's a lot smarter than the average owl, probably even more than Stella, and that little fox knows more than she should."

"Farandi was telling me the same thing… yesterday? I have lost track of the days. I have learned much from Thessylia as her viewpoint widens my perspective."

Hyxi and Vondro ran past, each attempting to outpace the other.

"It looks like Hyxi found a better partner than I," I commented. Brother Ironknuckle followed the pair, running on his large hands, smiling broadly. I could not help but shake my head and smile as his physical prowess always impresses.

"He is not at all what I expected."

I gave Effay a confused look.

"The grommold. Brother Ironknuckle. He seems happy, playful, and thoughtful. I always had the impression… actually, that's Dawnthistle's thinking—I'd never met a grommold before. Why do we learn the bad stuff from our teachers too?"

"Until we gain first-hand experience, we only have the opinions of our elders to guide us. If their thoughts are misguided, then their ideas carry on to the next generation until we learn otherwise. As you said, Dawnthistle was upset you fell for a human due to his selective viewpoint. I was ejected from my family for not following my father's profession. I expect you are aware of Farandi's story."

"She told you? She never talks about it."

"My Gift. I saw her pain before I could turn away. She is not aware that I know, and I do not intend to share her secret."

"I guess we all have our burdens. 'If life were easy, there would be no growth,' as Dawnthistle used to say. Animals kill to eat, trees burn to create space for new plants, environments change to accommodate new inhabitants. Stagnation is death."

"And now death is stagnant. I hope Blythad has found some information for us. As much as I enjoy researching, there is no time for distractions. We need to fix this."

"Why does it have to be us?" asked Farandi, hugging Effay from behind and kissing her neck. "Don't get me wrong, I'm all in for doing this, but why us in particular?"

"Because we are aware of the situation and have some leads on how to make it right. If there are others working toward a solution or can solve it first, that would please me. I do not care who restores the balance, only that it happens," I answered. "I would prefer to return to my studies in peace, though to be honest, the thought of travelling to another plane does intrigue me."

"We should start getting ready then. Someone put on a pot for tea, and Glitter and Gwenaz are making griddle cakes," Farandi announced as the trio of runners circled back to us. Vondro and Hyxi skidded to a halt and reversed direction back to the tower while Brother Ironknuckle cartwheeled to his feet while changing directions.

Farandi laughed. "I guess they are really having a race now. We better hurry before the food is gone."

We need not have worried, for the pair had cooked up platefuls of round flat breads, some plain while others had small pieces of peach, strawberry, or blueberry mixed within. Brother Ironknuckle grabbed the plate of strawberry cakes for himself until Vondro slammed a dagger into the table. The two warriors laughed and each speared four for their own plate.

"No fighting. There's plenty, and more can be made," Gwenaz sang while setting a warm jug of walnut and birch syrup on the table.

A loud crash came from the kitchen, followed by Glitter cursing in Zylan and a fruit-and-batter covered fox rushing through the doorway. Stella ran up Gwenaz's leg, was caught by a loop of hair before she could get any further, and then placed back on the floor.

"I'll be right back," grimaced Gwenaz, seemingly oblivious to Stella's condition. "What happened?" she asked from the kitchen.

"Your familiar was on the table eating berries before sticking her snout in the batter. Next I knew, she and the bowls had tumbled off to the floor. Teach her some manners or keep her out of the kitchen," Glitter shrieked.

"Stella has the right to eat too," mewed Gwenaz.

"Then pay attention and give Stella her own bowl instead of letting her get everywhere. *Uvaazrosiit*."

I assumed she was using the spell to clean up the mess on the floor.

"It's nothing to shed tears over."

"Get out!" Glitter screamed.

Gwenaz flew out of the kitchen carried by a flock of orange starlings before the door slammed shut with enough force to rattle the dishes on the table. Farandi grabbed Gwenaz out of the air as the birds vanished while Hyxi slammed their hands on the table. As they stood, both Brother Ironknuckle and I got to our feet.

"Sit and calm down," he said to Hyxi before turning to me saying simply, "No." He opened the door, caught a pan flying toward his head, and closed the door behind him.

"That's it," snarled Farandi. "I have had enough of that one." She stormed out, dragging Gwenaz behind her.

"Wait," Effay called out before chasing after them.

"This is your fault, isn't it?" Vondro asked me.

I glared back.

"Well, it usually is," he shrugged.

"What's going on here?" asked Beus, striding into the room with Faldrein in tow. "I could hear the shouting from outside."

"Your Sparkles attacked my Gwenny," growled Hyxi.

"Only after Stella made a mess," I countered. "And she did not harm Gwenaz. Trust me, it could have gone much worse."

"Of *course* you defend her."

"Had Glitter been in the wrong I would say so. Yes, she overreacted, but no one was hurt. I trust Brother Ironknuckle to settle her down."

"I should—" began Faldrein.

Beus put a hand on his shoulder. "Too many voices will overwhelm her right now. Go see to the others."

Faldrein nodded and followed after Farandi. After he left, we heard sobbing from the kitchen.

"So… um… Ormak's tower again?" asked Vondro a little too loud. "I hope we don't have to stay there as long as last time."

"I am certain we eliminated all of the guardians of the tower," I said, looking at the kitchen door instead of my friend, "but we found something which should keep your interest. Hyxi, I think you will enjoy it as well." From the corner of my eye, I could see them glaring at me, arms crossed. I began to rise from my seat toward the door.

Beus shook his head. "You said Brother Ironknuckle would calm her down."

"Yes, but, I should—"

"Sit and stay out of it," Beus finished for me. "Eat."

I placed a bite of strawberry griddle cake in my mouth. It tasted like ashes and sorrow.

When the pair walked out of the kitchen, Brother Ironknuckle had his large hand on the center of Glitter's back. Her eyes were red and there were drops on her cheek and chin.

Hyxi leapt out of the chair and stood in front of her, a low growl emanating from them.

"I… I need to apologize to Gwenaz," Glitter said to the ulim, new tears adding to her face.

Hyxi visibly calmed and walked through the dining hall with Glitter in tow. She never even glanced in my direction.

Once they were gone, Brother Ironknuckle reclaimed his seat, speared a few more breads, and drenched them with syrup. "Ye've stepped into it deep this time," he said to me around a mouthful of griddle cake.

"I knew this was your fault," Vondro pointed with a scowl.

"Glitter is upset because I hurt myself acting without her consent. She may be correct that I could have found a safer way, but the spell saved us time and gave us much-needed information. Given the circumstances, my life means little compared to everyone else."

"It seems yer life means more ta her than it does ta ye."

"That is not the case," I protested. "This situation needs to be resolved expediently. There are many who are suffering, and we need to help. I have no wish to die or harm myself, but I am willing to accept that risk. This was *my* choice."

"Maybe so, and though I respect your sacrifice for the benefit of others, if you and Glitter are to be in a relationship, then you need to take her ideas and feelings into consideration," Beus countered. "Your actions also affected your friends. You cannot act alone when you are part of a group when the potential consequences are this high. You did well finding this information, but you should have found a better, safer way to do so."

"I was counting on the others to aid me," I responded, "and would not have done this alone. I was fully cognizant of the dangers and told Vondro and Hyxi I would likely need help afterwards."

"But you didn't say what kind of help or that it was going to be that bad," said Vondro with a frown. "You should have told us."

"Honestly, I did not expect it to be that bad. There was nothing else you could have done."

"But we could have," said Glitter from the doorway, fresh tears of anger welling in her lavender eyes. "Both Gwenaz and I could have bolstered you and strengthened the tether between your mind and body. We could have prevented or at least lessened the damage you sustained. But you went off on your own. Why won't you let anyone help you when you need it?"

Her disappointment hit like one of Brother Ironknuckle's punches, and I had to turn away before my Gift manifested. She left before I could compose myself.

I am so sorry, I screamed in my mind, but could not find the strength to say it aloud.

Chapter 10: Here and There

Once we had gathered our gear, Beus directed us to the *bezyamrialrih*. The wide circle was etched into a slab of stone, the runes specifically connecting to similar ones at Ormak's tower. The teleportation circle at the other end was more complicated and could bring others to any of our towers, a few yards outside the gates. Leaving an open portal within the grounds was an invitation for trouble, as our guardians would either attack everyone teleporting in on sight or allow free access.

We had considered setting them up so we could travel easily to each others' towers, but the energetic patterns of multiple pathways could create interference, causing the network to malfunction. Should that happen, the best outcome is appearing elsewhere and merely being lost. More likely, however, someone would be shifted into the Shadow or even appear within the earth below and be petrified. The risk was not worth it and there are other magicks which are as effective though require additional effort. If needed, one could use the Ormak circle as a midpoint, then teleport again to the required destination. Though a standard *bezyamlial* would be more efficient and direct, it uses more energy than the permanent *bezyamrialrih*.

Teleportation can be disorienting until one gets used to the process, as there is no obvious transition—first you are in one place, then another. It is generally useful to close one's eyes to avoid witnessing the incongruity of the two scenes, assuming one is expecting to appear in a safe locale. There are spells and wizardly talents which allow for short jumps through space which might be done in combat, either to gain a tactical advantage or to escape a dangerous situation. In these instances, one *must* grow accustomed to the sudden change in perspective to avoid a potentially fatal delayed reaction. I have witnessed Uxadul use this tactic—teleporting behind a foe, tripping it with his staff, and shifting out again to attack another. Due to his experience, it is far more confusing for his foes than for him.

All but Glitter, Faldrein, and I staggered out of the circle outside of Ormak's tower, as we three had done this many times; I nearly vomited from dizziness after my first trip through the *bezyamrialrih*. We took a few moments for everyone to regain their balance—Farandi compared it to the transition from a long sea voyage and stepping back on land—and we walked up to the rusted gate.

"We have come to visit the tower," Faldrein called.

We had to alter the typical protocol as the tower currently had no master. After a few minutes passed, a whirlwind carrying six amulets wound its way to us, vanishing in a puff of soil and dust. We wizards did not need them. Technically, our companions would be safe travelling with us, but only for as long as they are within our company, and it was wiser to announce our presence and demonstrate to our companions how best to enter a wizard's territory.

They donned their protective symbols and we strode through the courtyard, passing by a pile of stones—which were actually a congress of mookali at rest—, an iron statue of a burly warrior which would animate to attack while the earth around it turned to silt, a number of sigils carved into the stones which summoned elementals or other extraplanar denizens when activated, and a herd of phantasmal unicorns which would become all too real should someone enter these grounds uninvited. I patted my animated heads as we strode by, which caused the volume of their muttering to increase. One in particular always follows me while I am on the grounds for reasons all its own.

Effay began to inquire about them before Glitter warned her off with a head shake. "You don't want to know."

"Ye've spruced the place up since I was here last," said Brother Ironknuckle with approval.

"And knowing you, it's all lethal," Vondro added to me.

"We wizards do prefer our privacy," I responded. "It was not only me, though; this was a group project. We all share the tower and its storehouse of knowledge, so we all worked together to protect it."

A ghostly unicorn silently trotted up to Glitter and nuzzled her.

"Our masters all devised plans to guard their towers," said Glitter, before kissing her illusion on the nose, "so it became incumbent that we all shared the responsibility since we share our time here."

A number of the runes glowed violet.

"These are mine," said Faldrein with pride. "Since some of them are keyed to kazkulim, I don't want them to trigger unnecessarily. I assume whatever power has them caged would block any summonings and the runes would pull in the few still doing their duties."

"Perhaps we should disable those for now then," I suggested. "There are enough guardians available that we can avoid the risk."

"You're probably right. Care to help?"

"Of course."

"I'll take the rest to *esnir Ormakissom*, then," offered Glitter.

"*Van alif Zylan?*" Effay asked with a smile.

"*Han. Oa kinowip ge Molissa ud Rhimos zum oa ujez i ylawinakki.*"[16]

Effay paused. "*Ylawinakki?* I don't think you have the right word there." She laughed nervously.

"*Ylawinakki*—servant girl," Glitter said, doubt evident in her voice.

"Actually… it means 'garbage child'."

Glitter turned away and ran off toward her illusory unicorn herd trailing dull yellow and blue sparkles. Effay called out to her and followed.

When I turned to join them, Brother Ironknuckle waved me off. "Let them sort it out. I'll lead this lot while ye take care of tha magic." He led the rest of the group to the tower.

Faldrein and I sought out the runes specific to kazkulim.

"What was that about with Glitter?" Faldrein asked.

"When her parents died, she worked for a zylan couple in their inn. It sounds like they were not as nice to her as she thought."

Faldrein grunted in anger and sympathy while wiping away the first rune. "I can't imagine how much that must hurt, to find out those you thought cared about you were actually mistreating you. It makes you wonder how much of our childhoods are different than we remember."

---

[16] Translations from Zylan: Ormak's tower. "You speak Zylan?" "Yes. I learned from Molissa and Rhimos when I was a (servant girl)."

"It does not matter, I suppose. Whether there were good or bad pieces which we have forgotten or misunderstood, the effects on our current state will not change. We are who we are."

"But what if bad feelings stem from misunderstanding? Those relationships can be redeemed. Say, for instance, your father's anger. What if it was caused by someone else?"

"He took his anger out on me and my family," I said cutting off his argument. "It does not matter why he was angry or how justifiable the cause, it matters what he did with it. He did provide for us and was not always the brute you saw. There is much to admire about the man. However, that does not absolve him. Glitter has had her illusions dispelled; her good memories inverted."

"And what about you?"

"My good memories lie with Yoffa. At home, there are bad memories and not-bad ones. Is this the last one?" I asked, indicating the runes to change the subject.

"Yes, just the four for the kazkulim. There are still four others to summon zyegri, so I'm still contributing."

"Very good." I turned toward the tower. I could not remember at that moment what a zyegra was and I felt foolish asking, especially when I had seen one recently: the five-tentacled creature which helped to heal me at Beus' tower. They are comprised of pure positive energy and are naturally adept at healing. Zyegri can also disrupt and overload a living creature's system with the same energy, eventually causing them to explode. Needless to say, undead are particularly susceptible to a zyegra's touch. Even healing can be too much of a good thing.

Effay and Glitter reached the tower door moments before Faldrein and I. "Are you… how are you?" I fumbled.

Glitter sniffled. "I'm okay," she said, wiping a tear from her azure eyes. "Let's get caught up."

I nodded and we entered the tower.

Ormak had required no light to get around, and I suspect he rarely came downstairs. Now that living beings were here consistently, *juut* spells were placed regularly to bring light inside and the rotted furniture had been replaced. Finding craftsmen to make the furniture had not been a problem, but it was difficult to find teams willing to transport the items to the tower, and none were willing to go past the gate. Instead, they unloaded their carts at the fence line and teams of *mimzelhruk* were conjured—they are not very strong individually—to carry things in and arrange them. There are certainly stronger creatures which could have been summoned, but those are typically used for combat and are more difficult to direct for mundane tasks.

The front sitting area now had room for a dozen people, plus several extra cushions which can be placed on the floor. The kitchen had not been used in over a century and required days of cleaning and pest removal, even with magical assistance. Killing the rats and other vermin was easy with *huuhbabyil*, as the ochre toxic fog devastates everything within its confines but clearing out all the bodies took time and effort. Enchanting a frost pantry and ice chest for food reservation became a necessity, as Ormak had neither luxury.

Mostly to please Blythad, I commissioned a down-filled mattress for the main bedroom. The tower is filled with coins, gems, and other valuable objects, more so than actual living space, so we allowed ourselves some extravagance, and converted one of the smaller treasure rooms into a guest chamber, which we mostly used if two of us were staying at the tower at the same time. The library and alchemical laboratory were well stocked with blank books, loose papers, ink, quills, reagents, and other supplies, so there was little we needed to add aside from extra chairs.

"Oh, good, everybody's here," said Blythad with obvious excitement. "Effay'ost'kao! I haven't seen you in some time. I assume you graduated from Dawnthistle's care."

"Yes. It's good to see you again. You didn't come out into the woods often." Effay turned to Hyxi. "He was always easy to track."

"You were following me?"

"Only at first when I was learning to trail creatures and practice stealth. After the first few times you weren't a challenge, so I merely kept note of where you were in case you needed help."

"Well, it's nice to know someone was watching out for me. We wizards do seem to attract trouble." Blythad laughed, looking at me.

I thought back to when we first met, and both my heart and leg ached with the memory.

"Since we don't usually have this many people, I set up a *vlimezvemavrim* with rooms for everybody. The entrance is on the side of this bookcase," he said while tapping it twice. "Simply say your name, or the name of whoever you want to visit if they're already in the extradimensional space, and the portal will open directly to that room. You can come and go as you please, and I will renew it every morning while you're here."

"Can we move to other rooms while inside?" asked Gwenaz.

"Yes. Just step to the exit and call the name of the other person. With their permission you can go to their room. If I can figure out how to make this spell permanent, I could run an inn on a horse cart." Blythad laughed.

Vondro tapped the bookcase and called his name. "In that case I'm going to put my armor away. You did say the tower was safe now, right?"

"Yes, but if you need some exercise, I found someplace you might find interesting," said Glitter.

"The Wax Room?" Faldrein asked.

Glitter nodded.

"The Wax Room?" Hyxi and Brother Ironknuckle repeated.

"Let me show you," said Glitter and led the warriors down the hall.

Ormak's tower has more room within than apparent from outside due to manipulations of extradimensional space. The Wax Room, as we have dubbed it, is a small hemispheric demi-plane, approximately one hundred yards in diameter with the apex of the dome nearly half that. Every surface is made of a waxy substance which shapes itself according to the desires of the room's occupants. According to Ormak's notes, the chamber was designed as a safe practice space to test new spells.

I later overheard Vondro, Hyxi, and Brother Ironknuckle discussing the fun they had in there. Considering how bored Vondro was last time he was here I was happy there was something interesting for him to do. They could make the room form warriors and creatures to battle until they were exhausted. The figures created are not fully detailed by design, according to Ormak's writings. A human or dragon would have the body shape and the essence of features, for example, but could not pass as a real creature should it somehow leave the room. Considering the challenges we have had with a shape-shifting ryelt, I am grateful for his foresight.

"I finished the ledger this week," Blythad announced proudly as the rest of our group wound through the bookcases. "Ledger," he called out and was answered by a light chirping song.

When we came to the center of the library, a purple-breasted budgie sat on a large leatherbound tome, bobbing its head and whistling. Thessylia began rocking on my shoulder.

"The ledger will stay around here, but should it get moved, or likely covered in papers, calling out to it will summon this little guy."

The budgie chirped happily then vanished.

"My book budgies only stick around for about a minute, but you can always call for them again if you need to. *Buried Secrets*," he called out again with his hand on the ledger.

A new budgie, this one yellow with a green breast, appeared above the ledger and flew to the shelves, chirping the whole way. Thessylia watched with interest, and I could feel her desire to chase the conjured bird.

"We did a good job organizing all of this, though there was some debate over a few volumes which could easily fit into multiple categories. Also, we sometimes forget where we found a book or forget to put it away, so these little birds make sure nothing gets lost."

One we had argued over was *The Trials of Nuviellu* by Troskin, which details the, possibly mythical and certainly exaggerated, voyages of the great sea captain and her adventures. Blythad insisted that it should be categorized under historical fiction, but the details given suggested it could be filed with maps or even general lore, where it eventually landed.

When we turned the corner, the budgie was perched atop *Buried Secrets: A Compendium of Fabled Artifacts and their Disappearance from History* by Rujin Steeplish, singing happily until it vanished a few seconds later.

Faldrein pulled the heavy tome, which was bound between planks of cedar wood, off the shelf with both hands.

"I'm hoping some lost item in that book found its way into the Greylands and it will give us a clue. I put together a list which might lead us in the right direction. Is everyone ready to do some research?" Blythad asked with a wide smile.

"Master Beus said you had already found something?" asked Faldrein.

"Oh, yes. Ormak wrote in his journals that there are three trials to pass before reaching the gate. Unfortunately, he didn't say where the gate is." Blythad moved some papers covering the journal. "'Once the Atrium of Stories is found, those seeking passage to the Greylands must face the Darkness of the Grave, the Cold of the Grave, and the Silence of the Grave'," he read to us.

"Those don't sound too ominous," quipped Faldrein.

"Ormak continues at length, and it's probably better if everyone reads it on their own rather than have me blather on for pages," Blythad continued. "But the gist of it is: the darkness is a walk of faith, the cold has some frozen guardian, and the silence tests one's endurance and willingness to continue. The gate itself he described as 'a ring of turquoise' where 'one must ask for permission before entering'."

"It's something to work with, at least," shrugged Farandi.

"We may not know how to get there, but now we know what to expect. Sort of," added Gwenaz.

"'There's always more research to be done and more knowledge to gain', as Nari always says," Blythad responded. "I wish Ormak gave us more, but it's more than we had. Now we only have to find the path. I'll call for some books and you can follow the birds."

"Are any of them written in Zylan?" Effay asked. "I never learned to read Umani."

"Some of it, but Uxadul found a translating glass," I answered. "You place it over the page and the words appear in whichever language you understand best. When I have been doing a lot of spell research, which requires a lot of focus on Draconic, the glass shifts between that and Umani."

"Uxadul is another wizard, I take it," said Farandi.

"He's the fifth of our group," said Faldrein as he shifted the weight of the tome. "He's at his home tower looking through Tzali's library. I need to put this down." He moved past the group back toward the center of the library, and a few moments later we heard the cracking thud of cedar on oak. Blythad and I assisted the others in finding books which might be both useful and interesting.

Shortly after Glitter returned from dropping her charges off in the Wax Room, I announced that I was going to head back to my tower. "We have enough people here, and our masters are searching through their libraries. No one is in mine."

"Do you want some help?" Farandi asked. "As you said, there are enough people here."

"If you wish. Vletraka's study of necromancy likely has some useful information, and an extra pair of eyes will not hurt. I can bring you back here any time you want."

"Okay." Farandi waved to Gwenaz and Effay. "Let Hyxi know where I've gone. Have fun."

"You too." Effay waved back.

Gwenaz was already deep into a tome, but her hair flicked as if shooing Farandi away.

We walked back through the tower and out to the *bezyamrialrih*. "Are you sure you can handle two teleportations so soon?" I asked.

"I know a spell which lets me dance as if I were in two places, so I'm used to the disorientation, though for that I'm merely looking at the same thing from different angles. This is a little different."

I called for my tower and we appeared outside my gate.

"You will remain safe as long as you are with me," I told her once she had steadied herself. Meanwhile, Thessylia had flown off to fetch an amulet. When my owl returned, I passed on the protective necklace. "Should you decide to step outside alone, make certain you are wearing this." As we neared the tower, the guardians which had covered the doors and windows moved away to their normal resting positions on the grounds.

"That's more than a little creepy," she shuddered. "But that's probably the point."

I nodded. "Fear can be a much better motivator than violence, though they are certainly capable of both. 'A demoralized foe has already lost'."[17]

---

[17] *In Shadow's Embrace* by Tinnetol Omyuf, page 8.

"What are they? I've seen the crawling hands before, but not the floating heads. I can't understand what they're saying."

"The mookali do that. I have yet to understand why or how to stop them, though I find their susurrations comforting now. It is the sound of home. Each congress has different abilities, and as a team they can combine their efforts into devastating attacks." I summoned a spider nearly the size of a horse and commanded the nearest congress to attack. A dozen heads floated above it and unleashed spurts of acid, causing the spider to pop back out of existence in seconds.

"You wizards really do like your privacy," she said, half whispering.

"We do. In addition, we tend to collect a lot of information that could be dangerous if used by the wrong person. Some knowledge is best hidden away."

"Do all wizards keep their personal lives as private?"

"I cannot speak for all wizards, but that is likely the case. Why do you ask?"

"It's Glitter. Her emotions are easy enough to read, given her sparkles, but I can't figure out why she hates us."

"I have never known Glitter to hate anyone but me," I responded. Colors began to fade as I thought about her and I had to take a moment to calm myself.

"She hurt you?"

"She did what I had not the courage to do and freed herself." I could not prevent the tears from escaping and turned away from Farandi.

"It's okay to cry. You don't have to hide your feelings."

"I am not hiding the tears. I have no wish to see you beaten by your mother again."

She was silent for a few seconds before asking with steel in her voice, "What do you mean 'again'?"

"I first saw it when I stumbled into your room in Beus' tower. My father did something similar when I left to become a wizard. We all get a Gift when we learn magic. Glitter has her sparkles, Faldrein can gauge the health of others, and I see people's greatest pain."

She stared at me, her chin quivering, though from sadness or anger I could not determine.

"I told no one, if that helps. The visions come unbidden, and I cannot always stop them."

"That doesn't sound like much of a gift," she said, sniffing and wiping away a tear.

"It has its uses, but overall, no, it is not." I showed her around my home, including my old bedroom, should she decide to stay overnight.

As we entered the library, she asked, "Earlier you said Glitter 'freed herself'. So you two were a couple and she ended it? Were you trying to leave her first?"

"Because of the nature of my Gift, I cannot love her the way she deserves. I want her in my life, but she is better off finding another. Perhaps she finally realized that."

Farandi grew quiet, as if in contemplation, so I took the opportunity to begin a list of likely sources of research materials. After setting down a binder and a pile of loose maps, she came up to me.

"I understand her now."

"Hmm?"

"Glitter. I know why she has been so angry with us. When we met, you rode with Fay-Fay instead of her. Then Gwenny looked after you when your spell went wrong. She's jealous."

"I… I do not understand. I have shown no interest in anyone but her outside of friendship. Had I not already known Effay—"

"But that's not how she sees it. You have been giving and receiving more attention from us than from her. She thinks either we are trying to take you from her or you want to leave her for one of us."

"That is not true," I protested, confused by the argument. "I love *her*. Why would she doubt it?" I dropped into a chair. "It no longer matters, I suppose. She has made her decision, and I think it is the best one for her, though her rationale is flawed."

"You aren't going to try to win her back?"

"She deserves better. Now, we have research to attend to," I stated with finality, as I no longer wished to discuss my failings as a friend.

To her credit, Farandi left me in peace the rest of the day. Once she started reading, she fell into it the same as any wizard and only stopped when she needed to get food.

I poured over Vletraka's maps, looking for any sign of an entrance to the Greylands, and made note of anything which looked interesting, such as the Gray Caves, Valley of Skulls, Lake Mortia, the Dead Plains, and the Bay of Broken Bones; death-related place names are far too common. I then researched the history of those places for further connections.

"I'm going to bed, coming?" Farandi announced while I was deep into the history of Dead Man's Ridge in the Southern Spine. There are a number of stories of travelers resorting to cannibalism in that area due to the inclement weather trapping them.

I glanced up to see her leaning against the open bookcase doorway completely naked. "I will probably stop in a few hours and then take a nap. Pleasant dreams." I had only returned to my reading for less than a minute before her hand came down and covered the page.

"Stop reading and come with me," she said in a heavy whisper which reminded me of Orla.

Does being naked change one's voice?

"You need to have some fun."

"This is what I enjoy," I said sliding her hand off the page.

She grabbed my hand and placed it on her breast.

It was about the size I would surmise her heart to be, though much softer.

"Don't you enjoy this?"

"It is only flesh." After a moment of contemplation I stated, "But this is something you find pleasurable, and you want my assistance."

Farandi blinked rapidly then stared at me. "Have you and Glitter never done this? Or you with anyone?"

"Done what?"

She stepped away, laughing without mirth. "How long have you two been together?"

"Approximately two suns."

"And you've never…"

I waited for her to finish her statement.

"But… she's *gorgeous*. Honestly, if she hadn't been so angry all the time, I would be with her right now. You have never had sex with her?" Farandi's voice was incredulous.

"No. Is that what this is about?"

She closed her eyes and shook her head.

"Are you angry with me?"

"No, merely confused. I don't understand why you two haven't… why you're not even interested…" She sat down on the table next to my book.

"It is not something I ever thought about. I love her mind and spirit, not her body."

"And she never tried to do anything?"

"She understands my Gift and the pain it brings. We embrace often. She likes to kiss me and hold my hand. I think Glitter knows anything more intimate is something I cannot risk, though she may not be aware that I have no interest in that regard. Were she to seek physical companionship elsewhere, I would understand. What about you, though? What about Effay and the others?"

"I told them before I left to come here. They like you. Actually, Gwenny is fascinated by you. Something about your aura and twilight fuzziness or something. I love her to death, but I don't always understand her," she laughed. "So, you don't want to have sex with me?"

"Not really, no. I do not wish to hurt your feelings."

"That's okay. I'm more surprised than anything, but I'm not going to force or coerce you. If it's not fun or pleasurable for both of us, then it's not worth doing." She kissed my forehead. "Does this bother you?" she asked, waving her hand over her nude frame.

"Not at all. You are much healthier than the bodies I am accustomed to working with."

"If I didn't know you're a necromancer, I would find that disturbing." She laughed. "Make sure you get some rest."

"I will. Thank you. Pleasant dreams." I poured through the documents for a few hours more then headed off to bed.

Thessylia roused me at dawn each morning to keep me on a schedule, otherwise I easily slid from diurnal to nocturnal and back, which causes me to lose track of the days. Sunrise always feels like a good time to take care of my garden, and that routine also helped. I had used very little magic yesterday, so I had not needed to spend more than a few minutes to recharge the stored energy.

I was in the process of shifting the slugs back to the tomato plants which I had designated for them—they have as much right to survive as anything else but are impossible to train—when Farandi came outside.

She still had not bothered to get dressed.

"The strawberries are perfectly ripe," I pointed while plucking off the last slug.

"Ooh, yummy." She skipped and twirled through the garden, lithely stepping over and around the plants.

It occurred to me that if I gave her spiked shoes, she could till the soil while dancing.

"You have a huge garden for one person."

"Many of the herbs are useful in spellcraft and in medicine. Glitter is trying to teach me how to cook with them. I've learned how to pickle some vegetables and turn the fruits into jams for storage. The freezer chest and cold pantry help as well. Two suns ago, I was away for a time and my garden died without harvesting. I managed to gather barely enough stores for the winter and vowed not to let it happen again. If there is *far* too much—like last year's zucchini—I take it to the nearby villages and give it away."

"Why don't you sell it and make a little extra money?" she asked while popping a whole strawberry in her mouth.

"I do not need it, nor do I have the time to add 'produce vendor' to my list of chores. It serves me better to gain the goodwill of the villagers than to add a few scales and talons to my pocket. Feel free to take anything you want."

"We should gather a basket for the others. I'm sure they would like something fresh."

"That sounds like a good idea. The soil at Ormak's is still corrupted, and the few things we can harvest are mediocre at best. We will continue our research today and return to the others at sundown. Then we can collaborate on our findings thus far," I suggested.

"Great. Let's break our fast now then get back to work. I will stop later and do a quick harvest before we leave."

"Thessylia, alert me a few hours before sunset."

'*Certainly. Will you flush out the mice hiding in the rosemary?*'

'*Done.*' I hopped over to the rosemary bushes and shook them. Three mice fled in different directions, one into a more open space for Thessylia who was already gliding in. The mouse was so afraid of me, it never noticed her before she had it in her talons.

It was late afternoon when I received a missive from Beus. Farandi had gone out to gather fruits and vegetables while I was deep into *Harkin's Journey: The Quest for Love Lost* since his tale involves seeking a path to see the Dark Lady and get his family back. The tale is apocryphal and full of inconsistencies from centuries of retellings and the fact is no one ever saw him again after travelling north into the Salted Sands. I packed the book and the limited maps of that desert, the area has not been well documented, and went out to get Farandi. She had not bothered to dress all day.

"Beus has some information," I called out to her. "I will finish harvesting while you get ready. He will meet us at Ormak's tower."

She wiped off a twinned carrot and placed it into the basket. "Okay. I'll be right back."

She had a good selection of vegetables already, so I moved to pick more strawberries, along with blue-, black-, and raspberries, which I placed in a smaller basket to prevent them from getting crushed by the heavier vegetables. I was still working on the blackberries when she returned.

"I'm ready."

"Excellent. Let me clean these. *Uvaazrosiit*," I said, casting perhaps the most useful spell in any wizard's book; the dirt vanished off our freshly picked foods.

"This has been the most comfortable day I've ever had," Farandi grinned as we ambled to the gate. "I've never felt so free and safe. You can't walk around anywhere nude without being harassed or judged, and the wilds are too dangerous to really feel relaxed. Thank you." She hugged me.

"I am happy you found some pleasure here after all, in spite of my non-companionship."

"That was never really the goal. You looked like you needed cheering up. My methods are different from yours, but I think you are happier all the same."

I nodded to her and activated the *bezyamrialrih* to take us back to Ormak's. Thessylia flew ahead to fetch her an amulet as we entered the grounds. The green-eyed mookal was resting a few feet inside the gate and followed us to the door, its electrical aura periodically crackling.

"Is that the same one as before?" asked Farandi.

"Yes. I have no idea why it behaves this way, and only this one. One would expect the entire congress to act the same as they were all created together."

"What's his name?"

"Why would I name them?" I asked.

"Lintner, then. There was a stray dog in our neighborhood in Arquel by that name. Somehow this one reminds me of him. Probably the smell, like the cheese."

I shrugged. "Lintner it is."

We turned at a flash of light behind us to see Beus step out of the teleportation circle. Thessylia perched on Lintner while we waited for him to catch up. The mookal focused its electrical field into its mouth to avoid harming my owl. I have witnessed them doing that to cause more damage while biting an opponent, but never in response to avoid hurting another.

"Hello, my boy. Feeling better?"

"Yes, Master Beus. Thank you for all your assistance."

"You can stop calling me 'master' at this point. You're practically one yourself. And how are you, young lady?"

"Fine, sir, thank you. Snack?" she asked, proffering the basket.

He grabbed a tomato and took a large bite, chuckling as juice ran over his chin.

We continued to the door, Thessylia transferring to my shoulder as we went.

The library was a haven of quiet study when we arrived upstairs, and it was difficult to see everyone hidden behind stacks of books.

"I would wager Vondro and the others are still in the Wax Room," I whispered.

"I'll get them," Farandi responded and danced down the hall.

Beus snuck up on Faldrein, causing him to jump out of his chair. The startled scream garnered everyone's attention.

"I may have found something useful," Beus announced, delaying until the whole group was gathered. "There are a number of tales about those seeking out a path to the Grand Mausoleum to reunite with lost loved ones."

"I came across one of those as well," added Glitter, "but they were looking for ancient treasures."

"Those are all pretty much the same," Farandi shrugged. "I'm quite sure any differences in those stories are from so many retellings."

"Perhaps," agreed Beus, "but all of the stories lead through the Salted Sands and into caves beneath a lake. It has been called different things: The Hidden Sea, Dead Waters, The Inland Sea, Lake Morsia—"

"I found a map with a Lake Mortia. It is probably the same sea," I interrupted, reaching into my magical satchel. Over time I came to realize that if I concentrated on a particular item, I would always find it first. Otherwise, I would pull objects out at random. I rolled out the map showing Lake Mortia in the northwest section of the Salted Sands. No legend was given as a scale, and the only other thing of note was a ridge of flat mountains known as The Giant's Teeth.

"That should be enough to start with," Beus said triumphantly. "Faldrein, Glitter, help me with the preparations to scry the area. Everyone else begin preparations for traversing a desert and delving into the caves below."

Chapter 11: The Salted Sea

While much of the group began readying gear for travel in the sitting room, I took some time to reallocate the energy for the spells I had prepared for the day. I had planned to do more research, and the small bit of magic I had expended was used to improve my memory and reading speed. But travel to the unknown would likely require a more combative approach.

Still, 'knowledge is our weapon' as Vletraka would say, and one must be prepared for all circumstances, so I left some spells untouched while shifting the rest. I would have preferred to rest the night first, but I imagined the situation was continually deteriorating, so we wanted to waste as little time as possible.

I had never been to a desert before, having lived my whole life in the forests of the kingdom of Loerendoch, and I had only spent one day in a cave. In addition, the goal was to travel to another plane of existence, one with which brief contact had nearly shattered my mind. This time, however, we would be prepared, and I knew where I was going and why. Nearly nothing is written that I am aware of about the Greylands beyond their existence. Aside from the tales we had read, those who travel there do not return, and any discussion of the Greylands beyond the Grand Mausoleum is scant.

"I guess we should have filled another basket," I heard Farandi say as I came out of my meditative state. "At least it's better than travel rations."

"That should still get us through the night," Vondro responded. "I wonder how far we will have to go. Nothing on Mithron's map gives a distance, only direction, and even that is approximate."

"If Beus is scrying the area, he might be able to teleport us close," I offered. "Personally, I have no wish to roam through the desert any longer than necessary."

"Once you acclimate yourself, there's nothing wrong with deserts," Effay said, hugging both Farandi and Vondro from behind. "Dawnthistle and I travelled to regions all over these lands in order for me to experience the variety of climates on the globe. We spent a moon in each area, though he never said where they were. 'What they are called has no bearing on what they are. Experience it, don't name it'," she quoted her teacher.

"Since yer tha expert, we'll be relyin' on yer advice then," said Brother Ironknuckle. "What precautions should we take? Is tha hunting good? What kind of beasties could we be facing?"

"Soft loose clothing to block out the sun and allow perspiration, preferably light colors. Travel at night is preferable and shelter during the day. Plenty of water, which I can conjure as needed," Effay began. "There are lots of lizards, snakes, and insects to eat, and cacti are good sources of water too. Some of the cacti are aggressive, as are the animals, you know, you hunt them, they hunt you… normal natural stuff.

"There's a cactus which grows a single large purple flower with orange veins—it is one to avoid. The spines are venomous and cause your mind to go numb. Its pollen is hypnotic, and it will try to implant seeds in your water-filled corpses to grow new ones."

"That sounds interesting. I would not mind examining one to understand its toxic properties," I said, receiving many glares in response. "For knowledge."

"You've had enough mind-numbing, don't you think?" asked Vondro.

"Fair point," I acceded.

"You might want to wear lighter armor, if any at all," Effay suggested to our warriors. "The heat would likely kill you faster than any creature."

"I don't like that idea, but I'll take your word on it. Hyxi, do you mind helping? I'll get yours also," offered Vondro. "I'll keep the leather jerkin on at least. I know how hot it gets in here on warm days, and if this place is as hot as you are suggesting, wearing all this metal would be brutal."

"We should all keep our heads covered as well to protect from Lephix's light. He shines more brightly in the desert. I have a spell which will protect us from the heat, but it's better to also take mundane precautions," Effay advised.

"Soft cloths are easy to conjure also," I added. "They should last for a couple days at least and do not require ornate craftsmanship. Harder materials do not last as long."

"We have tents and other traveling gear which should still work there," said Hyxi. "As long as we have enough food, I think we'll be okay."

Once we had decided what we needed for the journey, we only had to wait for Beus to get us to our destination. I took the time to once again reallocate some mystic energy to prepare the *buvliboj* spell to create the soft cloth. It appeared in piles of grey fabric which we cut apart to suit everyone, and I then used *uvaazrosiit* to change the color to suit the wearer. More fabric was needed than I expected, which reduced the amount of time it would exist to little more than a day. I could have made it permanent, but the energy cost was not worth the effort. Afterwards, I took the opportunity to nap like the rest of my comrades so we would be in better condition for nighttime travel.

When Beus, Faldrein, and Glitter returned, their expressions read for ill news.

"The Dark Lady prefers Her privacy," Beus announced. "We managed to find Lake Morsia, but not the caves below. I can get you in the area, but from there you will have to explore on your own."

Glitter and Faldrein began to hand out small silver tokens.

"These will bring us back here," said Glitter, "so we won't have to find our way back through the desert. Hold it in your hand and say 'home' and it will teleport you back outside the gate. There's one for each of us, though each one can carry three people should some get lost or ruined."

"They won't work from the Greylands, so you will have to return to this plane first," Beus continued. "I will stay here and continue to research with Blythad. If I discover anything useful, I will send a message. Is everyone ready?"

We turned and nodded to each other.

"As much as we'll ever be," Brother Ironknuckle spoke for the group.

"Good luck. Give the Dark Lady my regards," he said, turning a common threat into a sincere declaration of gratitude, and sent us away with a *bezyamlial* spell.

The heat hit us like father's forge and the overwhelming smell of salt nearly caused me to disgorge my last meal. As warm as the summer evening was when we left Loerendoch, by comparison it may have been early winter there.

Brother Ironknuckle, Effay, and I adjusted quickly due to our experiences, but the others reeled from the salt and sudden temperature and location changes. Gwenaz fainted. Her hair shot straight into the rocky soil around her and kept her upright until Brother Ironknuckle and Effay could support her and lay her down gently.

Vondro looked over to Effay. "This is worse than you let on. Thank Yaltin[18] you had me remove my armor. I already can't imagine how much hotter it would be at high-sun."

"Can everyone gather around and hold hands?" asked Effay. "Hands," she repeated, smiling at Hyxi whose hand rested on Effay's posterior. Effay chanted a few words in her mystic language and the heat became less oppressive.

I noticed some time ago that divine magic used its own language, precisely as arcane uses Draconic. Effay's was different still. When asked, she said it was the language of nature itself, granted to her from Ioddenri. I have inquired about it from her and other druids, but they refuse to teach any who have not taken the nature goddess's oath.

"Couldn't you have done that before we left?" asked Farandi, still woozy but recovering.

"Sorry, but I have to be in the right environment to make the spell effective."

---

[18] The goddess of strategy, tactics, and puzzles. She is often in conflict with her twin Pliedorn, god of strength and battle, though most warriors, soldiers in particular, revere both.

"Let's get our bearings then," I suggested. Thessylia flew up and I closed my eyes to share her vision. "There is a lake that way," I pointed, "we are perhaps a couple miles from shore. I cannot see the opposing shore from this height. The coastline is longer than I can see. I have no idea how long it would take to circle it, let alone explore searching for cave entrances." I pulled my vision back from my familiar.

"We need something more, then," said Glitter. "We don't have time to look everywhere ourselves. If the entrance were but a hole in the ground, it would have been filled by dirt and sand by now, so it must be in the side of a hill or rock formation."

'Higher,' I commanded and rode my owl's vision again.

Thessylia climbed, straining wings not meant for such heights. At some point she merely soared, resting on currents of warm air, circling slowly.

"I can see the opposite shoreline, though barely. The lake curves toward the other side that way," I pointed, "but continues beyond sight that way," I pointed in the opposing direction. "There are a number of rock formations scattered about and an island near the center of the lake."

"Who wants to bet it's on the island?" joked Faldrein.

'Can you get a closer look of the island?'

'I will glide that way. My wings are tired.'

'I know. Be safe.' "Thessylia is heading that way now."

"I didn't think we would need a boat," Hyxi grumbled.

"That's okay. I can give us all fins," responded Effay.

"Really? That sounds like fun." Faldrein said. "I worry about how salty the water is though."

"Oh, you can't breathe underwater? No, of course not. That's silly. I can share," offered Gwenaz.

"What do you mean?" asked Faldrein.

"I can help you all breathe underwater, at least for a while."

"Gwenny has all kinds of tricks," Farandi smiled, hugging her friend.

"Well, that helps then. How's Thessylia doing?" asked Vondro.

"Still over the water. The island is… quite far. It was not visible until she flew higher. I do not think we can swim that far unless Effay's fins also increase our speed and endurance. I have no way to accurately gauge the distance," I said.

"Shall we start walking that way, at least?" Vondro suggested. "No matter what, we do need to get closer to the lake."

"As long as someone guides me," I said. "I can only see through one set of eyes at a time."

A familiar hand grabbed mine. "I have you."

"Thank you, Glitter."

We, that is to say, I stumbled over the rocks, dirt, and sand as we moved toward the inland sea. While most of my companions did not see well under starlight, at this time I could not see at all. As we ambled, I heard Glitter whisper *drasedmuu*.

"Did you have fun with Farandi?" she asked through the spell, which connected our speech so only we could hear each other. Her hand squeezed mine tighter, almost painfully.

"We found the maps and did research. She showed herself to be very studious," I answered.

Her hand gripped with more force. "Not a day after we end our relationship you run off with another woman. Do you care about me at all?" Her anger and sadness were evident even to me.

"Of course I do. You decided we were no longer a couple, but I have no interest in forming that kind of relationship with anyone else."

"So, it was just for sex then?"

"No. Nothing like that at all. You know me better than that."

"I overheard her telling her friends that she was naked the whole time and that you had fun together." She sniffed. I believed she was crying.

"Not the whole time. She said she wanted me to have fun with her, but I declined. Actually, she said she would have preferred you, but was put off by your unwarranted jealousy."

"I'm not jealous, I'm angry. You do whatever you want and don't care at all how it affects me." She broke our connection, but still held my hand to guide me.

When I tried to speak aloud, she crushed my hand to silence me.

"Faldrein, you may have been right," I said after nearly half-an-hour. "There are carvings around an entrance which look like it may have been a temple at some point." *'Thank you. Come back for your reward.'*

I could feel Thessylia's elation until I pulled my vision back. If we are connected while she flies away, I can maintain it for some time, but once broken I can no longer feel her until she returns. After some experimentation, I found a way to preserve skinned and deboned voles, her favorite, for her so she would not have to regurgitate a pellet after digesting the meat.

Though we had travelled closer to the lake, the scenery had hardly changed from what I had last seen, and despite Effay's spell, the heat was palpable and it was not yet sunrise.

"I've never seen anywhere so desolate. How does anything survive out here?" asked Vondro to no one in particular.

"We wait for meat," snarled a voice like an angry child. A pragun, a humanoid about the size of a human toddler with a bulbous head and long gnashing teeth, stepped out from behind a rock. He held a long bone chipped down to a serrated edge and one of his teeth pointed out toward us. We heard rustling and the sound of rocks falling on each other as two dozen more pulled themselves from the ground in a wide circle around us.

"Ye'll not find us easy prey," said Brother Ironknuckle, rubbing his fist into the other hand. His battle-grin grew in anticipation.

Hyxi, Farandi, and Vondro pulled their weapons while the others considered which spells to use.

"I cannot decide," I announced loud enough for the praguns to hear. "Do I create a barrier and hope they leave, or should I simply kill them all?"

A few of the creatures looked at each other uncertain of their fate when the leader spoke. "Skinny meat. Can't kill tribe. Longfang and tribe eat." As he raised his primitive sword to goad on his fellows, a wave of sand and rock gathered a third of the praguns and carried them away.

"Longfang, we've discussed this. No humanoid meat. Anything else you can catch is yours," spoke a zyla riding on a giant scorpion covered with plates of dried leather and an unusual saddle designed for the arachnid.

"Fah. Longfang tired of you. Leave praguns to eat."

The zyla raised his hand, swiped it away, and another five praguns were carried away by a second wave.

Longfang looked around to see nearly half of his forces gone. "We get you another time. Praguns crunch your skinny bones!" he cried before turning and walking away. The remaining praguns scattered and disappeared into the desert.

"Kaldril," Effay squealed and ran up to the scorpion and its rider. "And, yes, I remember you too, Shenkhar," she mewed, grabbing the scorpion's massive claw and kissing it.

Shenkhar lowered himself for Kaldril to dismount.

"Effay'ost'kao. What are you doing back in this wasteland? Who are your friends?"

After she made introductions, Effay continued, "How long have you been following us?"

"I saw you appear in the Sands. I wanted to see what you were doing before acting, but Longfang forced my hand," Kaldril said. "Those little ones will eat anything despite our truce. I'm guessing you're not here to visit."

"We're looking for the entrance to the Greylands. I'm sure you've noticed that nothing is dying as it should," said Effay.

Kaldril lowered his head. "I wish you had asked about anything else but that. Our Order is here to guard the site from intrusion. Can't you find another way?"

"It's the only one we've found. Things are out of balance, and the longer we wait, the worse things get. I understand your oath to your Order, but our Oath to the Balance must come first. Please, can you help us?"

Kaldril stared at Effay, his face twisting with conflicted thoughts. "Shenkhar, what do you think?"

The massive scorpion arched its tail and pointed toward the lake.

"I agree, the Balance must come first." He patted Shenkhar's back. "Along the shoreline, about four miles north, there is a boat hidden in a tiny cove," he said, turning back to us. "It's probably too small for all of you, but I trust you will find a way to make it work. There is an island in the center of the Salt Sea, but I see you have already figured that out," he smiled. "Be wary of the salt serpents along the shore, and of Chelixar on the island, guarding the entrance. According to lore—I've never actually seen it—it's a huge scorpion which outsizes Shenkhar here." He clambered back into the scorpion's saddle.

"That... bigger than this one?" stumbled Hyxi. "Ancestors protect us."

"You're the best." Effay smiled. She climbed aboard Shenkhar to kiss Kaldril. "I know, 'we never saw you', and 'we found our way on our own'."

"Thank you," he returned her kiss and helped her back to the ground. "Ioddenri guide you all."

Shenkhar stepped backwards, and both vanished into the background as their colors shifted to blend with the rocks and soil.

"I hadn't expected them to be so big." said Faldrein. "I brought antivenoms in case we had trouble with scorpions, spiders, and snakes, but I don't know if they will be strong enough to help against things that size."

"Anything helps. Could ye make an antidote here if someone gets poisoned?" asked Brother Ironknuckle.

"I brought some basic equipment for that, but it takes time. That much poison might kill someone before I could make a remedy, but, of course, I'll try."

As we neared the lake, the soil turned black. Salt crystals, mostly small grains but some as large as me, were evident against the dark backdrop. Though we had gotten used to the smell, it was even stronger here, with a coppery hint added to it.

"Mithron, Gwenaz, your noses are bleeding," Faldrein said before turning around with a cloth in his hand.

I knew he could sense the state of health in others but did not know he had refined his Gift to diagnose someone without looking.

"That explains why I smelled blood," I said as he wiped my nose.

"It's this dry air," Hyxi responded. "I can feel my skin starting to crack."

"You'd think it would be more humid this close to the lake. Oh." Gwenaz pointed. "That's why."

We turned to see a pair of serpents behind us, at least twenty feet long and the same hue as the dirt beneath. They were not smooth like living snakes, however, with random jagged edges of white and grey crystals jutting out in all directions. The closer they got, the drier the air became, making it difficult to even breathe.

"Left one first," Brother Ironknuckle tried to yell, but his voice was a harsh whisper.

Vondro and Hyxi charged behind the grommold, Waltheri manifesting beneath the ulim as they ran. Farandi moved closer, throwing daggers as she spun and twisted while staying out of reach. I managed to cast *avularihbolmos* with some effort as my tongue dried out while pronouncing the required syllables before our warriors could get any closer. The explosion of iron pellets cracked through both creatures while Glitter's *srukakbolmos* partially melted and fused their salt structures at the same time.

Without warning, a gentle rain began to fall, relieving our dehydrating bodies. Effay chanted at the cloud, adding energy to it. The rain sounded like hail as it hit the salt serpents. Cracks began forming on their surfaces, as their crystalline structures snapped and popped, making it easier for our warriors to penetrate their rocky exterior.

"More water," I called, my voice still dry but improving as I caught raindrops in my mouth. "They cannot handle too much at once."

Both Gwenaz and Faldrein took this cue to cast *akthilskvlok*, their twin jets of water ramming into the leftmost serpent, dissolving deep divots and forcing it back. A final blow from Brother Ironknuckle shattered it. The second one dug into the earth and escaped.

"Aww, and I barely got my cloud charged with lightning," Effay pouted.

"When Kaldril said 'salt serpents', I wasn't expecting them to actually be made of salt," said Faldrein, wiping the lessening shower off his face. "Good idea with the rain."

"I was only trying to keep us from drying out," Effay shrugged. "I didn't know it would hurt them."

"Let's hope the other one stays away and there aren't any more," said Glitter as our warriors returned.

"All yer magic makes fightin' a bit less fun," Brother Ironknuckle joked, wagging his finger at us. "But ta be honest, I could feel the beast sucking the juices out o' me with each punch. It would'a drained me dry afore long."

"Being close to it was dangerous," Hyxi added. "I could feel it too."

"I could barely see, my eyes were so dry," said Vondro. "Thanks for the rain."

Effay bowed, her emerald hair brushing the ground.

Hyxi grabbed Effay's head and kissed her before she straightened. "You softened them up good. It was like trying to stab iron until your rain made them crack."

Effay blushed and hugged her friend.

"Let's get to that boat," urged Faldrein glancing across at the sun rising over the horizon. "I wonder how small it is. Effay, you said you could give some of us fins?"

She nodded.

"I can fly," Gwenaz offered. "That will save room."

"I have a spell for that too," said Glitter. "I think we have enough options. As long as we can get on course and don't take too much time, we should be fine."

Aside from a few small lizards which watched us with unexpected intelligence, we encountered no other signs of life as we marched along the shoreline toward the boat.

"I want to eat the yellow one," Gwenaz pointed, licking her lips.

"I think they're poisonous," cautioned Faldrein.

Perhaps the heat was affecting me, but I swear the lizard smiled at him.

'Can you give us an aerial view? The boat should be visible from above if not from the ground.'

'Certainly. And I think Faldrein is correct about the lizards. My instincts are to avoid them.'

I informed Faldrein of Thessylia's opinion as I put a hand on his shoulder. "I need you to guide me for a while," I said as I shifted my vision to share my familiar's. "We are not far. There is a small wall of rocks bordering a trench cut into the shore. Perhaps four or five of us will fit comfortably."

"Flying it is, then," said Glitter. "I can take two others with me."

"If Vondro and Brother Ironknuckle take the oars, I think I can have the water push us," offered Effay.

"Waltheri can run on water, so we'll be fine," Hyxi said.

"Then I guess no one needs to swim," said Farandi. "Keep your spell handy in case the boat isn't as safe as we hope."

"As long as it isn't too bad, I can do some minor repairs," Glitter said.

The boat was in passable condition, but obviously had not been maintained. The dry, salty air made the wood brittle, and it cracked when Brother Ironknuckle grabbed it. Glitter's *uvaazumak* spell repaired that break and a few others on the bottom and she also used it to strengthen the oars.

"Not the best, but it should get us there," said Vondro after examining Glitter's efforts. Brother Ironknuckle got in first so he and Vondro could help Effay and Farandi before Vondro settled in.

As they pushed off into the lake, Effay used her magic to make small waves, which rose behind them and they gained speed. Hyxi called Waltheri, and the phantom wolf appeared beneath them and ran off alongside the others. Gwenaz floated up and followed as Glitter cast *aaslbokviwa* on Faldrein, herself, and I, allowing us to fly with Gwenaz.

Once we were all moving, Gwenaz flew straight up to get our bearings. "A little to the left," she called down to us and we relayed the message to the boat. "Ooh, that *is* pretty far away. You're on course." Even with Effay's waves pushing the rowboat, it took nearly two hours to reach the island; it would have taken twice as long without her.

Lake Morsia is vast. I later calculated it to be nearly thirty miles from shore to shore along the narrow points and over eighty miles long. The mountains to the northwest are most likely the water's source, flowing through an underground river which drops into the desert valley near the lake's edge. There is no outflowing river, as the water is either absorbed into the ground or evaporates. The change in the ground around the shore indicates that the lake was once larger and may have been part of a longer water system at one time; some have theorized that the Salted Sands were once an inland ocean. As it shrinks, the salinity concentrates further, ensuring that few, if any, living things could ever survive in its depths.

The island was bordered by cliff faces over two hundred feet high, the sole shore being a section of collapsed stone on the southeastern edge, and nearly a quarter mile across. Were it not in the middle of a lake, it would resemble the stone towers visible in random places throughout the Salted Sands. Vondro and Brother Ironknuckle carried the boat onto the rocks to prevent it drifting away then stared up the broken cliffside.

"A little help?" shouted Vondro to those of us flying near the top of the island.

Brother Ironknuckle began climbing, but it was easy to tell even he was tired from rowing. Glitter and Faldrein grabbed him by the shoulders and hoisted him to the top while Gwenaz and I carried Vondro. Effay had transformed into a large vine and wrapped around Farandi and Hyxi while she climbed. Once the heavier warriors were dropped off, we returned for the others. Afterwards, we stopped to rest and gather our strength.

The top of the island tower was smooth and weather-worn if not entirely flat, and we consciously moved further from the edge to avoid the down-curving slope. Large boulders were scattered about as were small hard clumps of sharp grass—life always finds a way. Once we regained our breath and ate, we sheltered until nightfall then moved toward the center of the island and the possible temple—Thessylia had not gotten close enough for more details.

I have never seen so much sky. Though the area is open around my tower, the trees still block the horizon. Here, in the middle of a desert on a pillar of stone taller than any tree I know, the stars felt close enough to touch and the horizon extended for miles beyond anything I had ever seen. When I returned years later, I spent a full sun making observations of the sky from this open vantagepoint. Mountains are certainly higher, but the horizon is filled with the rest of the range rather than this vast openness.

Mamoel offered us some of her light to guide us, but the half-moon was nearing the end of her journey by the time we began our trek inwards.

"Everyone keep an eye out for that giant scorpion," Vondro warned.

"Trust me, none of us have forgotten." Faldrein responded, his voice shaking.

"We should be close," I said, attempting to gauge our location compared to what I had seen via Thessylia. I shifted to my necromancer's sight in order to detect Chelixar, should it be hidden.

"That looks intriguing," said Gwenaz, pointing to a set of paired upright slabs of stone with lintels atop. There were seven sets, all next to each other, which got progressively smaller as if they had been hammered down into the pillar.

"Stop," I commanded. "There is something there, but it does not make sense. It feels like it is undead, but also teeming with life. It sits atop the first lintel."

"Let's get a better look at it then," said Effay calling for Ioddenri's blessing.

An orange light emanated from atop the stone slabs in the shape of a scorpion. It scrabbled down the twenty-foot-tall stones, the body from claw to tail the same length, glowing from her spell. A series of expletives were uttered by my friends.

I cast *looskjejleemyt*, summoning thick black tendrils from the ground which grabbed the massive arachnid, while Glitter aimed a *vezivhilsk* at it, the bolt of lightning forking to both the massive creature's claws. The electrical arcs tore through the outer shell and hundreds of small scorpions poured out through the cracks. Vondro, Hyxi, and Brother Ironknuckle stepped back to avoid the shower of arachnids which collected themselves and advanced like a tiny army.

"Hit and move on the main body." Vondro commanded. "Casters, clear the swarms." He then raced around the small creatures, ducked below a broken snapping claw, and slashed at one leg causing more scorpions to crawl out.

Chelixar's stinger lashed out at him, missing with the tip but knocking him down with the tail. A fan of flames burned through the arachnids closing in on him from Gwenaz's *aatokytsrukak*.

Meanwhile, Brother Ironknuckle and Hyxi moved to Chelixar's other side, hoping to distract and confuse the creature, but to little avail. With each attack, more scorpions were released, forcing them to retreat. A brilliant grey-white light pulsed from Faldrein's outstretched palm, coalescing into a beam which tore through Chelixar's shell and frying the scorpions within.

The gigantic scorpion began to tear away from the tentacles I had summoned, the tendrils evaporating into smoke and shadow with each break. Most of my strongest evocations were likely to catch one of our warriors in the blast, so I settled for casting *srukakalsk* at the swarms, the three lines of fire burning through a long stretch of scorpions.

A great claw grabbed Hyxi off of Waltheri and pulled them high above the ground. As they struggled, more scorpions scrabbled out of the damaged claw and onto the pinned ulim. Hyxi cursed as they were stung repeatedly. Brother Ironknuckle leapt onto the opposing claw and used it to springboard onto the one holding Hyxi. He punched down at the joint, nearly severing it from the main body and causing it to drop Hyxi. As the ulim fell away, the stinger arched over and stabbed Brother Ironknuckle in the thigh.

"Pull away," Glitter shouted, as the swarm pooled around the host shell.

Gwenaz lashed out to the grommold with what I thought was a rope or whip at first, but it was made completely out of centipedes. The string of bugs grabbed him and dragged him away as Glitter surrounded Chelixar with a *srukakyelk*, containing it within a curtain of green flames. Chelixar screamed and hissed, claws and tail reaching for us through the fire and pulling immediately back.

"Run!" screamed Farandi as she lobbed a small orange orb through the flames. We bolted past the titanic creature and nearly fell forward as an explosion erupted behind us.

I looked back while regaining my balance to see bits of Chelixar scattered throughout the area, including a few leg and thorax parts near us. Smaller scorpions gathered up the pieces and carried them to the center of the blast.

"They are going to reassemble it," I said in an astonished whisper. "We need to be gone before they finish."

We scrambled through the stone arches, the ground sloping into a long downward spiral. Once we were past the entrance, Glitter clutched Ormak's necklace and sealed the passage with a block of ice.

Brother Ironknuckle kept pace until then, even while limping from his wound, and slowly sank to the ground. "Now would be a good time fer tha' antivenom, lad, but see to the wolf-rider first."

Hyxi had grown large purple welts on their face and arms.

Faldrein pulled the vials from his satchel, tossing one to Farandi who quickly administered it to her friend.

"Drink these three first," he commanded the grommold, "while I extract some of the poison." He pulled out his medicine kit and stabbed Brother Ironknuckle's wound with a steel cone which tapered to a hollow needle at the end. The cone filled with blood and a green-black oily substance.

Meanwhile, Glitter and I had separated the ingredients from the medicine kit so Faldrein could get right to work.

He poured the blood into a glass vial, sealed the top with a cork, laid it down on a flat disk with a clamp to hold the vial in place, and spun it as rapidly as possible to force the venom to separate from the blood. He siphoned off the venom and placed drops into an array of powders and chemicals until he got the results he was seeking, a white powder which turned bright purple when the venom came into contact with it. Faldrein mixed the powder into a tincture, sliced open Brother Ironknuckle's leg, and poured the mixture into the wound.

Brother Ironknuckle's veins had taken on a dark, greenish hue by this time, all the way down the leg with the wound and past the knee of the other. His breathing was shallow, his eyes glazed.

"Hold on, you tough old bastard," Vondro said, the fear of losing another friend evident in his voice.

Hyxi, their wounds reduced to swollen bumps which were regaining their normal color, crawled over to him. "I will not have another companion sacrifice themself for me. You have to live. I cannot carry another ghost."

"Don't none o' ye worry," Brother Ironknuckle wheezed. "Acclin carved my ancestors from granite. We don't die tha' easy." His body spasmed and he stretched out on the stone floor. Then he began to laugh. "I just remembered, none o' us can die." He slapped his hands on the ground in a five-beat pattern and began chanting. After nearly a minute the venom began to leak out of his wounded thigh and his normal color returned.

"I think it's under control," said Faldrein, his voice and gaze distant. "Your stamina is remarkable."

"As I said, 'made from stone'," Brother Ironknuckle began to laugh then groaned. "If ye don't mind, I think I'll stay here a bit."

"That stuff you put in his wound really worked well," said Effay. "Which herbs were in that powder?"

"Web wort and penberry, mixed with ground limestone for binding," Faldrein answered. "Still, it shouldn't have pulled it out of him that quickly."

"Brother Josten taught me ta control my body as well as my anger," Brother Ironknuckle rasped. "Given the chance, I can speed up the healin' process fer a bit. Thanks lad." He coughed.

"That ice won't last very long," Glitter warned. "The outside heat will wear it away faster than usual, magically created or not. If you're up to it, we should get a little further away from that scorpion in case it has reassembled already."

"I've got him," said Farandi. She placed a hand on his shoulder and cast *bojaaslska*, which caused Brother Ironknuckle to float up three feet off the ground. She then grabbed his foot and pulled him down the spiraling tunnel.

"This is undignified," Brother Ironknuckle grumbled, "but it works better than a stretcher."

"And since we don't have one of those, nor the materials to make one," stated Vondro, "this is faster than dragging you."

"I think enough of the poison has been expelled," Faldrein said. He placed his palm on Brother Ironknuckle's wounded thigh and said a prayer to the Dark Lady.

As we watched, the skin and muscle knitted back together, leaving a grey puckered scar.

"Tha's much better. Thanks again," Brother Ironknuckle said, stretching the freshly healed leg. "I think I can walk now. Ye can put me down, lass."

"Nope," Farandi smiled. "The spell is still working, so you will just keep floating until it wears off and we can't have you bobbing around in mid-air. You were willing to sacrifice yourself for my Fuzzy Ears, so you rest while Faldrein heals you. We're going to rely on you as we get deeper, but for now you let us take care of you."

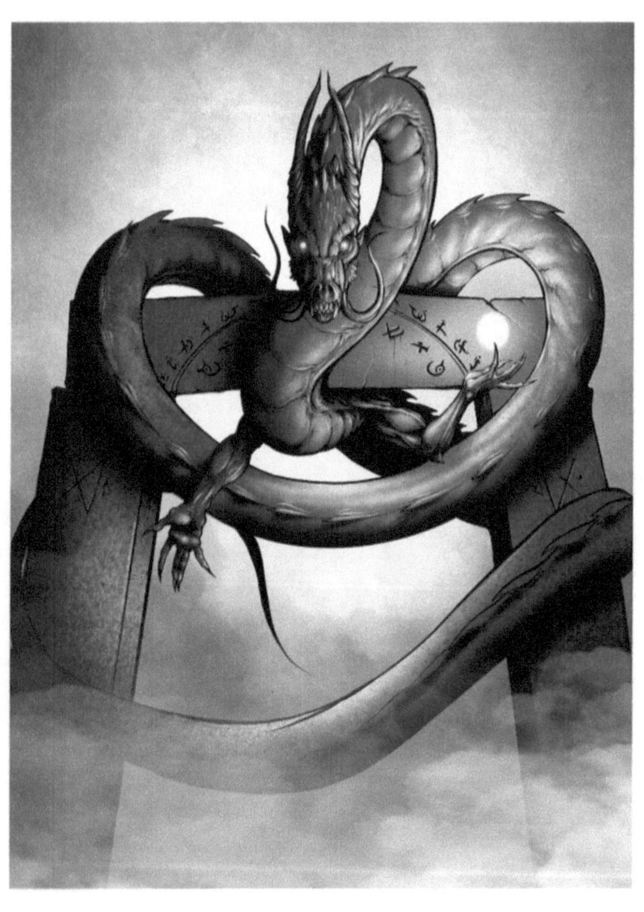

Chapter 12: Depth of Darkness

We travelled deeper into the tunnel, our way lit mostly by Glitter, though Brother Ironknuckle did not require any light. Many grommoldi live their entire lives underground and have adapted to absolute darkness; the trait is still held those who dwell on the surface. The walls were moist and covered with green-grey lichen and brown mold. Small flies flitted from mold patch to mold patch, while beetles scuttled away from the light into crevasses and under the lichen. Fortunately, the path was large enough for us to walk upright most of the time, though sections of harder stone had forced the tunnel to narrow to mere feet across, causing us to squeeze through on knees and elbows as we spiralled down deep below the lake.

"Stop," called Brother Ironknuckle from the front of the line. There was a clanging of steel and stone. "Right. It's a short climb down ta the next landing. Looks like the path continues on from there."

I think Brother Ironknuckle forgets that most of us are not nearly as physically adept as he, as his "short climb" was probably forty feet. At least the rope was knotted, making it easier to hold onto as I took care not to fall. Gwenaz merely floated down like a feather on a breeze.

We spent the better part of a day, as far as I can tell, pushing through the twisting passages beneath Lake Morsia before the path opened into a large cavern. A slow rhythmic dripping echoed from within. Brother Ironknuckle continued to lead until we found a semicircle of stalagmites, three of which were fully connected to the stalactites above into thin stalagnates. The floor was hard, with thin ridges and whorls from where water once flowed.

"This is as defensible a place as we'll find," Brother Ironknuckle said in a harsh whisper. "We rest here but stay on guard. I'm sure there are many things down here which would love a fresh meal. Keep light and sound ta a minimum."

We found spaces within the barrier to roll out our sacks. Glitter moved away from me to the other side of the group, her sparkles a dull crimson as she walked away. Once she settled, I cast *drasedmuu* to communicate with her through whispers which only we could hear. "I am sorry I failed to consult you. Please, you have barely spoken to me in days."

"I don't want to talk to you," she responded with finality.

"Why? Did I do something else to hurt you? You have to tell me what is wrong."

"It's not only because you didn't include me."

"I should have, though," I interrupted. "I have already apologized for not discussing with you when I cast *mbikvlidyk* and, you are right, I should have taken your counsel in the matter," I stated calmly, which seemed to aggravate her further. "I promise to do better. What else is bothering you?"

"I spent a lot of time and energy getting to know you and forgiving you. I thought maybe you were worth the time, that it wasn't all your fault. I thought the last two suns we spent together, and letters left, meant we were a couple. Obviously, I was stupid to believe that."

True, it would be better for her in the long run if we were not emotionally linked, but that was not the case.

"What makes you believe you were wrong? My feelings for you are still the same."

"Then why did you, who has trouble making friends with anybody, get so close so fast with that crazy witch or the pretty green zyla girl? Why did you run off with the dancer? Why do you love *her*?"

"I do not. I love *you*. Gwenaz understood how to handle my mental collapse. You know I was not in control of myself. Farandi was helping me research and thought I needed cheering up. And I knew Effay before you and I even met—maybe that is why the others accepted me so readily. Have you not noticed she has befriended everybody? It simply is in her nature."

"You keep hugging her," Glitter pouted.

"She keeps hugging me," I corrected, "and everyone else. I thought it would be rude to not hug back. Effay has a tactile disposition. I can see how you interpreted my actions, but you misunderstood. I will refrain from her embraces if you want, though she may think I am upset with her then. You taught me how to be nicer to people. Am I doing it wrong?"

There was an extended pause. I shifted my vision to examine the Weave to ensure the spell was still active. "No," she finally responded.

"I did not see how taking Farandi to assist in research would be an issue as there were enough of us at Ormak's. Her actions were unexpected."

"Surely you must see how it looks from my perspective."

"I do now, yes, but you know things are not always as they appear," I countered. "You made an assumption which has proven to be false, though you know me well enough to know it could not possibly be true. Do you honestly think I could start a new relationship when I am still trying to understand ours?" Glitter did not answer. "Is this because we have not been physically intimate? Farandi informed me that such things are important to some."

"No. Maybe? You have never tried to be physical or even complimented me that way. I thought maybe you didn't think I was pretty enough. Gods, that sounds vain."

"You are beautiful, but that is not what makes me love you. You are brilliant, talented, and charming. I have not expressed any physicality because I do not desire physicality. That has nothing to do with you. It is who I am. I never meant to deny you—I did not know it was an issue."

"I thought… I don't know what to think. Just… just come here."

I shifted out of my sack and carried it over to her.

"Finally," I heard Vondro mutter as I passed him.

I set my things down next to Glitter and she hugged me tight as I sat next to her. I squeezed back as she cried softly onto my shoulder and whispered, "I'm sorry."

"As am I."

When I realized I no longer felt her burning away I began to relax. Until it was replaced with her fear, jealousy, anxiety, and heartbreak.

"Something's here," called Hyxi, their voice echoing off the stone.

"Where?" asked Vondro pulling his sword.

"It smells of rot and iron," said Gwenaz, her sing-song voice reminding me of my mother.

"More light," called Brother Ironknuckle. "Look up and around."

Up? I cast *juut* on the tip of the nearest stalactite. The glow should have reached in a sphere, but there was a darkness pushing against it. "Behind the wall!" I exclaimed, as blackness oozed through the cones and columns of stone.

"Umbrhiz!" cursed Brother Ironknuckle. "Its touch eats away at anything other than stone." He threw a heavy rock at the black blob, causing it to ripple.

"*Aatokytsrukak*," Glitter and I cast in synchronicity, her purple flames overlapping my yellow-green ones. I have tried to match her color, but either cannot seem to twist my foot to the correct angle or my timing is off. The umbrhiz backed away, acrid smoke trailing in its wake.

"Here," shouted both Vondro and Hyxi.

The creature had stretched around, attacking both warriors from either end of our useless barrier. They had each managed to block an attacking pseudopod with their shields which sizzled and bubbled at the creature's corrosive touch.

A ball of lightning alighted on the umbrhiz from Gwenaz, while a jet of water cast by Effay pushed the creature back, the two spells interacting to trace the electricity further into the monster. Faldrein cast *klivevuzul*; the shard of ice bit through the creature's skin and exploded, freezing a section of it, which dropped off and shattered.

The umbrhiz pulled back into the darkness.

We stood at the ready, not knowing if it would renew its attack. With so many spellcasters, we were able to circle ourselves with light spells to warn if it returned. We forgot to look up.

The umbrhiz landed with a thudding splat, completely engulfing Brother Ironknuckle, Vondro, Farandi, and Effay, while shoving the rest of us aside. I cast *zumulalsk*. The bolt of black energy easily hit the massive blob and drained off a portion of its vitality. Both Glitter and Faldrein released *vezivihilsk*, the bolts of lightning intermingling within the umbrhiz and scattering throughout the creature, lighting it so we could see our four comrades prone beneath its bulk. The umbrhiz bubbled and expanded before exploding in a shower of acidic goo.

The four on the ground gasped for air before releasing screams of agony while the rest of us merely yelped from the corrosive remains splattered over our bodies. Faldrein released a burst of healing energy to stave off further damage, allowing Effay enough reprieve to create an underground cloudburst to wash us clean. In spite of their efforts, we were all covered with bright red splotches to some degree.

Faldrein looked around, scrutinizing each of us. "No one is critically injured. No disease or poison," he announced as if from afar. He then stepped up to each of those caught under the umbrhiz to heal them individually, turning a different shade of red as he approached Farandi. "Your, um, clothes have…"

"Your butt is showing," giggled Effay, who twisted around in worried realization. As she did so, the left shoulder strap of her brambled armor snapped.

Farandi reached back to find her skirts had indeed been eaten away. She rolled her eyes and shamelessly walked over to her pack to look for a replacement. Hyxi helped Vondro check over his armor, finding the metal was thinner in some sections but still defensible. Gwenaz cast *uvaazumak* to repair Effay's broken strap.

"We should be safe now," Brother Ironknuckle announced. He had broken off a piece of a stalagmite and was stomping on it, crushing it into smaller pieces. "All of ye, pat a little of this on yer burns, but don't rub it," he said demonstrating his technique. "It'll help clear any lingering acid."

Had I been in my alchemy lab, I would have suggested something similar. That he can powder stone, albeit a softer one, with the heels of his feet is nothing short of amazing.

"What if there's another one?" asked Hyxi. "Or something else. We haven't been quiet like you suggested."

"Umbrhizzes are apex predators," Brother Ironknuckle responded. "Tha' one likely ate anything else nearby tha' could pose a danger. We should still keep a watch ta be safe."

"Was this the darkness test?" asked Vondro.

"I don't think so," answered Faldrein. "There should be a marker of some sort to show the path. I think this was us walking into a creature's lair."

After sleeping for an undeterminable time, we continued traveling through the cavern which, as Brother Ironknuckle had surmised, had been stripped bare of nearly all life. We found the source of the dripping sound—a trio of stalactites leaked water into a small pool, which had a few small crustaceans swimming around within. The water tasted of dissolved stone and, I presume, would have reacted to the umbrhiz's acid. It was not so alkaline, however, that it would not slake our thirst.

We traveled for uncounted hours through another series of tunnels until we encountered a large carved-out chamber, at least sixty feet square and thirty feet high. One wall was carved to resemble a giant mausoleum, complete with a solid stone door. The other walls were adorned with writings and pictographs detailing the ancient mythology of the Dark Lady.

She was among the first, for even gods may die, springing into existence along with Lephix, the sun, and

Mamoel. Lephix and Mamoel created the world and all the creatures which roam upon it, while the Dark Lady gave them spirits, then set Her own realm aside to prepare for when those creatures left the physical world behind.

She had met a mortal soul who espoused an eternal love for Her. They grew close and She elevated him to godhood. But time proved he loved not Her, but Her station, and sought to usurp Her power. Unable to strip him of his divinity, She instead cast him out. His name has been removed from the carvings, but we know him as Coruld.

Tales of those brave enough to venture upon this path have been painted on the walls. It appears few have returned and, of those, none with the prize they sought. Most, attempted to bring back a loved one, whether spouse, child, or otherwise, while others thought to find lost riches. Only the heartbroken ones ever returned, if at all. As I examined the paintings, I watched as our images appeared upon the stone.

"We are part of the Dark Lady's legend now," I announced pointing to our likenesses.

"Are we successful?" asked Vondro, scratching at his acid burns.

Faldrein slapped his hand away. "You'll tear the new skin."

"But…"

"I know, but you have to leave it alone," interrupted Faldrein, his voice stern.

"The paintings only show us within this chamber. It is the same as all the others begin," I answered Vondro.

"These must depict the challenges," Farandi indicated three symbols at the beginning of each story. The first was a black square, second a white hexagon, and third a plain circle—not all of the questors made it past these points.

"And this fourth one," she pointed to what looked like a coiled serpent, "must be the gateway."

"I suppose the first step is through the door," Gwenaz said to no one in particular as she rapped thrice upon the stone.

"Why do you seek Death?" asked a voice which sounded of bones scraping against each other. We looked around the chamber, but there was no apparent source.

"People are not dying as they should," I answered, turning slowly and forcing my voice to remain steady. "The kazkulim are being captured and we want to restore the balance."

"Why do you believe you are worthy?"

My back teeth began to ache at the voice's tones.

"We don't," answered Faldrein. "We aren't worthy to stand before Her, but there is something wrong within Her realm and we are here to offer assistance."

"If you pass through, you might never return," the voice warned.

My spine began to twist.

"If it means the world will return to its natural course, then I am willing to take that risk," Effay quavered.

"Aye," said Brother Ironknuckle.

The rest of us echoed their sentiment.

The stone door ground open, the grating vibrations rumbling through my bones. Brother Ironknuckle again took the lead down the lightless passage. Glitter grabbed my hand and shone with pink and yellow light, allowing the rest of us to see. The hallway was completely bare, with no signs of insects, moss, or anything else alive, yet it smelled faintly of decay.

"Halt," commanded Brother Ironknuckle softly. "I can't see past here." He stuck his hand out and it disappeared into darkness.

"The first challenge," nodded Hyxi. "The Darkness of the Grave."

Glitter stepped forward and focused her sparkles into the darkness. They vanished the moment they contacted the edge. "I didn't expect it to be that easy," she shrugged.

"We have to make sure we stick together," warned Vondro. "No telling how far this goes or what might be hidden in there."

Effay chanted a few words and extended her fingers. Vines grew out from her, gently wrapping around each of us. "There, now no one will get lost," she smiled.

I shifted my vision to see the auras of the living and unliving. "With luck, I will still see all of you in there, even if nothing else is visible. Faldrein?"

"Everyone is generally healthy, though the umbrhiz has left raw marks on everyone. I'll keep tabs on everybody if I can."

"Anyone else have any ideas?" Farandi asked, to no positive response.

"All right then," Vondro stepped forward and vanished, as though stepping through an ink waterfall.

The darkness was absolute.

'I can see nothing,' fretted Thessylia. *'I cannot even see my own wings. I hear nothing besides us, so I do not believe we are being hunted.'*

There was a sudden tug on the vines connecting us and a yelp. I could not see Effay's aura, but the faint life energy in the vine holding her was pointed down.

"Hold on," grunted Hyxi as she tugged on the vine.

Vondro moved over to help pull her up.

"Good thing I attached us all," Effay laughed without much humor.

"Okay everyone, slow down and watch your steps," commanded Vondro. Before I could remind him none of us *could* watch our steps, he amended, "You know what I mean."

We inched our way through the darkness, the floor dropping off at intervals as the path wound around. There were several near falls, particularly when the path narrowed to only about as wide as my two feet together. I could not calculate how deep the drop was when listening for loose stones to hit the bottom, but Thessylia's amazing hearing gauged it to be more than three tall pines.

After an indeterminable amount of time, I heard Brother Ironknuckle cheer, "We made it."

Still moving with care, we followed his celebrating when Glitter lit up the tunnel.

"I thought you said we were free," said Gwenaz, her voice quavering. "It's still dark."

"No, honey, we made it." Farandi hugged her.

"But then... why can't I... no. No," she cried. Her eyes were completely black, as were her tears. Gwenaz's hair reached out in all directions, whipping about and keeping the rest of us at bay while Farandi held her.

"Shh, shh, I've got you," Farandi said, kissing her cheeks. "Please. We can figure this out."

Hyxi and Effay tightened around the pair. Gwenaz's hair grabbed them, felt along their faces and bodies, and released them.

"Let me try to help you," said Faldrein, stepping back from her lashing hair.

"Yes, you're a healer. Okay," Gwenaz sniffed, her hair beginning to settle.

Faldrein recited his prayer to the Dark Lady while gently pressing his hands over Gwenaz's eyes. Nothing happened. He repeated to the same results.

"I don't understand. She did not answer." He cast a minor healing spell on Gwenaz which caused her remaining acid burns to fade.

"It is the Dark Lady's challenge. Perhaps She will not allow us to circumvent it so easily," I opined.

"No, no, no, no…." Gwenaz repeated, dropping to the floor and hugging her knees.

"We'll figure this out," Farandi repeated, continuing to hold her. "If the Dark Lady won't heal you, maybe a priest from another god will."

Gwenaz sniffed. "Do you think so?"

"I have friends all over Loerendoch. I'm sure I can find the right one," Farandi said.

"I'm going back to Beus. I'm useless now." Gwenaz fumbled with her pouch until she found Beus's token.

"You're not useless." Farandi looked to the rest of us, tears streaming down her face. "I'm going with you. I'm not leaving you alone." She kissed Gwenaz on the cheek before they both vanished.

"Isn't there anything else you could have done?" asked Hyxi, her voice filled with anger and frustration.

"I wish there was," Faldrein answered. "I don't know if anyone else will be able to heal her either. The gods tend not to interfere with each other's works. If this had been caused by anything else, I'm sure I could have healed her. I'm sorry."

"This is not your fault," I said, putting a hand on his shoulder. "As you said, you serve at the Dark Lady's whim. She has placed these challenges to keep interlopers out of her realm. It is conceivable that none of us will succeed, but we must press on. There is no guarantee anyone else is actively trying to solve this, so we cannot rely on them."

"You're right," Effay sniffed while wiping away her tears. "Balance needs to be restored. There are too many lost spirits already."

Brother Ironknuckle pulled his heavy wool coat, boots, hat, and gloves out of his pack, reminding us of the next challenge.

We all put on our winter gear in preparation for the Cold of the Grave.

In retrospect, it would have been better to wait until we were closer before putting on the extra clothes, for we were all overheated traipsing through the tunnel for another half hour or so before the temperature dropped dramatically. Nothing in the description of the challenges had mentioned the distance between them. When it got cold, Effay gathered us in a circle to cast a spell to further insulate us from frigid temperatures, but not magickal cold.

The tunnel opened into a small, flooded cavern, though large enough that we could not see the other side, with a central thick stalagnate in the center. Chunks of ice floated in the water and the walls of the chamber were covered in rime.

Vondro stuck his sword into the water, which only came halfway up the blade. "It's not too deep, at least at the edge," he whispered. "I didn't expect us to need another boat."

"Let's see if this works," said Glitter. She grasped the snowflake necklace which was once Ormak's and stretched out her other hand. A long plane of ice at least a half-foot thick formed from the water's edge and stretched to the stalagnate. The edges of the bridge curled up to prevent us from sliding off and was wide enough for two of us to walk side-by-side comfortably.

"Well, that's a good start, at least," commented Hyxi. They stepped onto the ice bridge taking care to keep their footing. "It's even colder on here, but it seems stable."

Brother Ironknuckle joined Hyxi and knocked on the ice. "Strong. It should easily hold us all." He pushed forward and slid to the center of the bridge, slowly making a half-turn as he stopped. "Come along."

We stepped onto the bridge and I had to put a hand on Vondro's shoulder to keep from falling.

He glared at Glitter. "That thing nearly killed me." When fighting Ormak, he was trapped under a dome of ice which nearly froze him.

"And now it's helping," Glitter responded with unusual haughtiness. "Remember, magic isn't good or bad…"

"It's how it's used," Vondro finished. "Yes, I remember."

"I think I see an exit," called Brother Ironknuckle in a low voice which still echoed off the walls. As he pointed to our left, a blue-white cone of freezing cold caught Hyxi, Effay, and Faldrein from above, while Brother Ironknuckle instinctively slid to the stalagnate. The thick winter clothing protected their skin from direct contact, but the intense cold dropped the trio to their knees. Once again, we had failed to look up.

To be fair, even if dwe had, the blue-white hexagonal creature was well camouflaged against the ice-covered and shadowed ceiling, and it was not until it shifted to a position above Vondro, Glitter, and I that I could see enough of its form to identify it.

"That looks like a cryogalt," I announced as Glitter began casting *srukakalsk*. I nudged her, throwing off her aim so the three lines of fire missed their target. "They feed off of heat," I announced still staring at the creature and ignoring her glare. "*Skialoskhilsk.*" I threw open my arms, releasing a wave of acid, searing a line along a corner, and removing two of the cryogalt's twelve legs.

I felt the warmth of Faldrein's healing burst as two arrows from Vondro hit the creature, one barely penetrating the icy crust and the other snapping on contact; Hyxi's sling stones proved to be entirely as ineffectual. A spear of solid ice formed near the cryogalt's center and launched directly at me. It was Glitter's turn to shove me, so the giant icicle only tore through my side and thigh instead of my heart. The pain was momentary as I went numb from the intense cold. I collapsed on the bridge, staring up at the creature as it scuttled directly above me for another assault.

Fortunately, I had friends ready to protect me. Glitter knelt down and cast *ajiavulhysayt,* covering my vitals in mystic armor, Vondro stepped over me, holding his corroded shield over his head, and Effay made the air swirl around above us all, causing the next icicle to veer away and crash into the bridge. Deep cracks formed in the ice, but it held together.

"Gotcha," bellowed Brother Ironknuckle, whose legs were wrapped around one of the cryogalt's own legs and was hammering on its body with his powerful fists before squirming between the creature and the ceiling to attack it where it could not retaliate. He had a rope around his waist, which trailed to a pair of pitons driven into the roof of the cavern. He told us later he swung from the stalagnate to a nearby stalactite for support before setting the second spike in place.

Finding their stones ineffective, Hyxi summoned Waltheri and strapped themself onto the phantom wolf. Waltheri ran up the stalagnate and then along the ceiling, leaving Hyxi disoriented as they fought from an upside-down position. Waltheri continued to circle the cryogalt, avoiding its piercing legs, while Hyxi attacked the limbs. The cryogalt sprayed an icy mist around it to hide from their attacks, but to no avail. Soon, it fell into the water, leaving Brother Ironknuckle dangling.

The water froze around the cryogalt as it plunged, flailing its three remaining limbs. Waltheri rushed back to the stalagnate and ran down to the bridge. Hyxi shook their head to reorient their bearings.

"I didn't know you could do that." Vondro beamed at Hyxi.

"As long as she keeps running, and only for a short time," Hyxi patted the phantom wolf. "Sooner or later, gravity remembers her."

The bridge jumped.

"It's not dead?" cried Effay'ost'kao as she backpedaled to the stalagnate. She yelped when she saw the faces of previous seekers frozen against the stalagnate. The center of the bridge cracked, and a pair of large spider-like legs poked through.

Vondro and Hyxi charged the cryogalt from each side and hacked at the limbs before the middle of the bridge shattered, forcing the warriors back.

It floated on the water, new limbs growing from its corners.

"It's using the water to repair itself," growled Glitter as she cast *uuomtiimu*. The thunderous roar echoed off the cavern walls and broke away more of the bridge, but the magic was focused on the cryogalt.

A series of cracks formed throughout the creature's body and the still forming legs broke off. Then a plummeting grommold crashed through the center of the creature, spraying us with ice and frigid water.

As pieces of the cryogalt dispersed along Brother Ironknuckle's ripples, a gloved hand tried to grasp the edge of the shattered bridge, but kept slipping off.

Vondro reached down to pull up the soaked monk.

"The drink's a bit weak fer my tastes, but it's refreshing." Brother Ironknuckle laughed as he clambered out of the freezing water.

I cast *uvaazrosiit* to dry and warm his clothes as though they had been back in the desert rather than this arctic chamber.

"Thanks, lad, but it looks like we'll have ta swim out of here anyway." He took off his gloves and rubbed his bluing hands together.

"I thought…" I paused, remembering Effay's spell specifically would not help against magical cold. "Do you need healing, or just a small fire?"

"A few moments to warm my hands, I think. Even through the gloves, tha' creature chilled my bones with each hit. My feet are frozen too."

"You need to stop getting yourself hurt," said Faldrein sardonically, "I can only heal so much." He covered Brother Ironknuckle's hands with his own and called to the Dark Lady to once again repair the grommold's injuries.

I looked over to Glitter and tapped my chest under my throat.

She shook her head. "I thought the same thing, but it only works once each day," she said grasping her necklace.

Hyxi whispered into Waltheri's ear, and the pair ran off along the water's surface without even a splash into the darkness. A minute later, Waltheri returned, leapt onto the remains of the bridge and stared at Effay.

"Are you sure?" she asked the wolf, who continued to stand still. "Okay," she sighed and mounted Waltheri with trepidation. Waltheri ran off again as Effay's squeaks of fear and laughter trailed off into the dark.

Waltheri returned for each of us and kept us all dry and safe. It is difficult to describe the sensation of the phantom. She is not quite solid, but enough so we could ride her and grasp her fur. Her texture is akin to old gelatin; springy but not squishy. When she desires it, or on Hyxi's command, she can become completely insubstantial, ignoring solid objects like a true ghost.

In spite of this, she is not undead, which of course was a primary concern when we first met. Rather, her spirit is linked to Hyxi in the same fashion as Thessylia is to me, and strong enough that Waltheri continues to exist beyond her physical death.

Once she had gathered us all to the exit tunnel, she nuzzled Hyxi and vanished.

Hyxi placed a hand over their heart and said, "Thank you. Rest now."

We moved away from the frozen chamber until we no longer felt the cold. Once the tunnel was warmer, we took the opportunity to remove the insulated clothing and take a few minutes to rest.

"Two down," said Vondro, examining his sword for damage. Finding none, as it had been mystically enhanced, he slid it back into its scabbard. "Any thoughts on what to expect next?"

"The Silence of the Grave," Faldrein said, his chin resting on his palms, his elbows on his knees. "The only thing I'm certain of is we won't be able to cast any spells there."

I looked at Glitter next to me.

She winked, "I've got a couple I can use; I think. But without knowing what kind of situation we're facing, I simply don't know if they'll be helpful."

"I thought that technique was only for casting without gesticulation," I commented.

"The first book taught me that. I found a similar volume in Ormak's collection called *Without a Whisper*, also by Geimoll Ovicht. I thought if we were going to be silenced in some fashion, then I should prepare some spells which I can cast without speaking."

"Brilliant, as always." I smiled.

Glitter's sparkles flashed brighter before she kissed me.

My control must be improving, I thought, as I only got a whiff of her burning.

"They're so cute," giggled Effay, who snuggled against Hyxi.

Vondro looked sour. "All right, time to move."

We had not traveled far before I felt a light breeze against the back of my neck.

"Does anyone else feel the wind?" asked Hyxi before I could.

"I was just going ta ask that," said Brother Ironknuckle. "Odd place fer a breeze." A few steps further, the wind gained strength. He planted his feet and leaned backward against the ever-increasing gust.

"Help," screamed Effay as she skimmed along the ground, her toes scraping along the floor.

Brother Ironknuckle turned to catch her as she tripped over Hyxi, who had dropped to the floor on hands and knees to maintain their position.

The airstream continued to blow harder, forcing us all to the ground; even Brother Ironknuckle could not withstand the assault for long. We were pushed and rolled along the wide passage, bouncing along the floor and against the walls as the gale rose to a deafening roar.

Then, without warning, it stopped. We all laid on the ground crumpled like abused toys along with four other bodies that had been perfectly preserved. I groaned in pain but did not hear my voice. I looked around to see Brother Ironknuckle and Vondro getting to their feet. Each had a hand over their mouths, and Vondro was pinching his nose. When I tried to ask what they were doing, I felt a sudden pressure on my chest, as though a weight had been placed upon it.

Everything became clear when I found that I could not inhale.

Brother Ironknuckle grabbed Effay and Faldrein and began to drag them forward, moving deliberately but swiftly. Glitter grabbed my hand and put the other on Vondro. The Weave began to warp around her before becoming still. Her sparkles all winked out at once. Disappointment and panic filled her eyes, and she began to run.

Hyxi waved their hands at Glitter in a sign to slow down, but Glitter had already expended too much energy and, unable to breathe, passed out on the floor. Vondro and I picked her up, putting her arms over our shoulders and began to drag her, but I am not designed for strenuous activity, and it was not long before the world filled with dark red spots then faded to black.

I came to with a sharp gasp, a series of blood-tasting coughs, and a trail of ectoplasm on my cheek.

Waltheri stood over me, blinked once, and stepped over to Effay.

"Welcome back, lad," Brother Ironknuckle wheezed. Trails of blood stemmed from his eyes, ears, and mouth while he sat against the wall.

"Where is Glitter?" I tried to ask, finding I had lost most of my voice. My chest felt as though Brother Ironknuckle had been punching it for exercise. It took a conscious effort to take more than short gasping breaths.

"Relax," commanded Vondro in a harsh gargle. He shared the same bloodstains as the grommold. "Everyone's alive."

I nodded, saw Hyxi crawling to Effay, and laid back on the ground. Over the next few minutes, the others awoke, each receiving the same advice I had.

After Gwenaz had been left blind from the Darkness of the Grave, I thought perhaps at least one of us would be struck deaf or mute from the Silence. We were all damaged to be sure, but none of us permanently, as far as I could tell. Were it not for the strong constitutions of Brother Ironknuckle and Vondro, along with Waltheri, who does not breathe, we all would have suffocated in the vacuum. I know a spell which has a similar effect on a single target, but since this experience I am loath to use it.

I fumbled with my belt pouch; my fingers were not working as well as they should have been as I searched for a small blue vial. Crawling over to Faldrein took more effort than I expected—he was only a few feet away—and I nearly collapsed when I got to him.

He took the vial in shaking hands and carefully swallowed the contents.

"Thanks," he croaked. "I needed that." With each word, his voice became clearer as the healing potion took effect. He prayed to the Dark Lady to heal our wounds suffered from passing Her tests and was granted a surge of energy.

Though it was not enough to repair all of the damage, it did ease our pain.

"Whatever is going on in the Land of the Dead, at least She's still answering prayers," Faldrein said with a grim tone. "I'm exhausted." He barely managed to say as much before laying back down and passing out.

Vondro looked over to Brother Ironknuckle and Hyxi then shrugged. "We're as safe as we're gonna be. Let's rest."

I dislike sleeping on stone. It is even worse without a roll or sack to sleep in, but I was too physically drained to care. Glitter's foot was barely within reach, so I gave it a squeeze to let her know I was near shortly before passing out again.

None of us slept well, but what rest we got was therapeutic. My muscles had stopped twitching and I found my voice again by the time I woke. Still, it was difficult to concentrate on my spellbook as my mind was bleary. Glitter was obviously affected too. She usually enjoys creating meals for everyone, but settled for a mixture of crushed oats, honey, dried fruit, and simple spices rolled into balls to break our fast. Delicious, but far simpler than her usual fare.

"How are you?" I asked her as she struggled to mix the ingredients. "What happened in the Silence?"

"Everything hurts," she answered with a rueful smile. Her breaths were short and shallow. "I tried to cast…a short-range teleportation to get us…out of there, but there wasn't…enough of the Weave…to finish the spell."

I have noticed changes in the wind on the occasions when the Weave has torn during Glitter's tantrums, but never experienced a sustained hole in the warp and weft of magic itself.

"So, where's the gate?" asked Vondro, stretching his back.

I gave him a quizzical look.

"We've passed the challenges. Isn't the gate supposed to be here?"

"It must be further in." I shrugged with effort. Vondro's stretching looked comforting, so I mimicked him. There was a slight crack and my mind felt clearer.

"Onward then." Hyxi pointed ahead without enthusiasm.

We all struggled to get on our feet and ready our packs; all save Brother Ironknuckle that is. He remained strong and solid, despite the life-draining vacuum. Whether this was due to his training, innate fortitude, or an unwillingness to appear weakened, I could not say. I also could not be certain whether his pace was slowed by injury or a conscious effort to allow the rest of us to keep up.

We pulled ourselves through the tunnels for over an hour before entering a damp cavern. A streambed had carved deep into the rock to a slow waterfall. We climbed the steep incline alongside the pouring water and followed the stream to a shallow pool. Sheets of flowstone created a curtain of wet rock and crystal and as we rounded the corner, we nearly walked into the face of a sleeping dragon. With slow and careful steps, we reversed our path back around the corner before turning and walking away. About five minutes later we reached the waterfall.

Faldrein stopped and pointed back. "THAT was not in the books. There was nothing about facing a dragon."

"'One must ask for permission before entering'," Glitter quoted. "I thought we would just state our intent at the gate." Her breath was rapid and her sparkles a pale yellow-grey.

"The symbol for the gate was a serpent," added Effay. "Back where the paintings appeared."

I looked at my assembled friends and could not help but see all of their manifest fear. After all we had faced thus far, we could not let the fear of death stop us now, particularly considering where we were going. "I will talk to it. You stay here."

"You can't be serious." Glitter glared. "I remember when you went in alone to speak with Ormak, and I relented to your arguments then. But this," she pointed down the riverbed where we spotted the dragon before rapidly retreating, "is insane. You *cannot* face a dragon alone."

"One of us must," I responded, "else it will seem like a show of force. I, for one, do not wish it to feel as though we are here to cause it harm. Would you rather do it?"

Her frightened expression was all the answer I needed.

I grabbed her hands and held them tight. "If this goes badly, get the others to safety, and find another way to stop the chaos."

She nodded, her eyes becoming wet with unformed tears.

I crept back down the dank path to where we spotted the dragon. Columns of attached and separated stalactites and stalagmites were interspersed throughout, along with small puddles of brackish water. Life always seems to find a way, and the caves were full of creatures adapted to this limited environment. Blind shrimp scuttled around in the puddles, while albino centipedes vied for prey against the grey and brown spiders which blended in with the stone. With all the care and courage I could muster, I maneuvered my way to stand before the dragon.

He was massive. At least sixty feet long from head to tail, his serpentine body was at least three feet taller than me, even lying down, and I could not even begin to calculate his weight. His scales were generally of a turquoise hue, with mixes of blues and greens throughout, and were rather small, about the size of my hand, but they fit together in a manner which left no opening for a blade to pierce. His face was long, more like a greyhound than a lizard, and his fore and rear legs only about as long as I am tall, more for utilitarian purposes than combat. Naturally, I was overawed by his mere presence.

"Welcome," he yawned in the Draconic tongue, his bulk stretching to the roof of the cavern, looking down upon me as an owl on a mouse. "It has been far too long since I have had a visitor. What is your name?"

I was unable to answer right away, as my voice had fled when I beheld the great dragon. He stared patiently until I was able to squeak out, "Mithron." Clearing my throat, I continued, my voice gaining strength as I spoke. "Mithron of the Velvet Shade, Necromancer of Cuyokale, Wizard of the Ivory Tome."

"And what is your purpose here, Mithron of the Velvet Shade, Necromancer of Cuyokale, Wizard of the Ivory Tome?" he interrupted before I could ask his name.

Responding in his language, I said, "I seek entrance to the Dark Lady's realm. People, animals, creatures are not dying as they should, and I believe there is trouble in Her realm."

The dragon stared at me, as if weighing my words. "Mortals are not supposed to wish to visit Her realm. Why do you want people to die?"

"It is not that I wish for needless death, but only for death where it is necessary. The elderly, the diseased, the gravely injured are all suffering long, lingering deaths; some are not dying at all. There has also been a great increase in the number of haunts and other lingering spirits, ones who should have passed on to the realms of the gods. We spoke to a kazkul, and it said that many of its kind had been captured.

"Some time ago, I was held captive by an agent of Coruld, who boasted of his plans to aid the Dread King in his attempt to take over the Dark Lady's realm. I believe those plans are seeing fruition."

The dragon's eyes, large and yellow, like lightning trapped in glass globes, looked down on me with an intensity which made me feel as though he were peering directly into my soul. "Your words are honest, at least as far as you believe. Are your friends as honest as you?"

Of course, he would sense the others. He probably knew we were here before we spotted him.

"Yes," I answered, my throat still dry, intimidated by his mere presence, "we all share the same purpose. May I ask your name, so I may introduce you properly?"

The great dragon smiled at me, kindness in his eyes belying the baring of fangs. "Aerioma'sadae'iot." He relaxed somewhat, lowering his head to slightly above mine.

I called my friends over and made the proper introductions, being especially careful to pronounce his name correctly, as any error or perceived insult could be disastrous.

He asked each of them in turn why they wished to visit the Dark Lady's realm, pausing when he got to Hyxi. "You carry a spirit with you." The dragon said, somewhere between a question and an accusation.

Hyxi addressed the dragon without a whiff of fear or trepidation, unlike the rest of our band. "Waltheri has been my constant companion since long before her death. She still protects and battles along with me. Our souls are intertwined."

"Ah, yes, I see that now," the turquoise dragon responded. "I have heard tell of those like you but had yet to encounter one. You may pass, and I shall allow Waltheri to return, should she so choose." Aerioma'sadae'iot unfurled his massive bulk, arching over and circling a portal of dark grey smoke.

"Be warned. Everything you see beyond the threshold is real, and an illusion. The Greylands are filled with those who refuse to pass the Gates of Acceptance, and many of them have been twisted by fear, resentment, or other negative emotions. Distance is relative there; the greater your acceptance of your own mortality, the faster you will find your way to the Grand Mausoleum. The longer you remain, the more difficult it will be to leave, as you begin to lose your sense of self. The portal is ready. You may enter if that is still your desire."

"Thank you," I bowed my head. I turned to the others, giving them one final chance to recuse themselves. "Shall we?"

"For Life!" exclaimed Brother Ironknuckle, raising his fist over his head.

I smiled. "For Life!" we shouted in unison, mimicking his gesture.

Chapter 13: Greylands

Travel through the Greylands is, perhaps, more difficult mentally than physically. There are no terrain features to speak of; merely a flat expanse and grey dust, which eventually coats everything you wear, and finds its way into and onto every item you carry, so that, in time, everything is camouflaged by and within the landscape. The horizon, if there even is one, is the same dull shade, and the only way to know you have travelled anywhere is by the footprints you leave behind. The Greylands abhor change, however, and all signs of passing disappear within an hour, or to be more accurate, the nearest approximation of an hour. There is something to be said about watching your footprints vanish back into smooth dust as you sit and rest.

There are places to find in this dreary expanse and coming upon them is more an event of chance than intent. There is no sign of anyone or anything on the horizon, no clue you are nearing a village or structure; you are nowhere, then you are there. Hyxi, Faldrein, and I found the journey easy, as if we were only a fraction of our weight and full of energy. Thessylia too was alert, if confused, and she looked around often for any signs of movement; the interminable stillness had her on edge.

The others dragged their feet and plodded along as if through a bog. Effay appeared to be ill and only moved when prodded by Faldrein or Hyxi. Though she is fully attuned to the cycles of nature, Effay carries a love for life even greater than Glitter, and the Greylands are not fit for someone such as her. Perhaps had we come during winter, she might have fared better, but it would not have been prudent to wait for the seasons to pass.

The Greylands have no ecosystem to speak of. In a normal desert, life can still be found—scrub grass, snakes, and scorpions for example. Sometimes it is difficult to find, but it exists nonetheless. Here, there is nothing aside from the spirits of what used to be. There is no weather, no precipitation. Even the air is still, disturbed only by our passing. The sky above is as devoid as the land, boasting neither sun, nor moon, nor stars. It is neither hot nor cold nor temperate, yet the air is stifling, as though it were too thick to breathe properly.

Time is as completely subjective as distance, and there was no way to know how far we travelled or for how long; it might have been days or a week. No shadows are seen in the twilight haze, as there is no direct source of light, yet the world is neither bright nor dark. The ever-present dust muffled our footsteps, adding to the quietude of the bleak landscape.

"I need green," mumbled Effay. She stopped dead in her tracks and shouted, "I NEED GREEN."

We turned to her and saw a tree behind her, a well some twenty feet to her right, and a group of small buildings surrounding us. Though she had demanded green, there was little of it slipping through the grey dust covering the leaves and trunk of the tree.

"There ye go, lass," pointed Brother Ironknuckle, "as ye demanded."

She turned and sighed. "Even the trees don't feel right, but at least it's something." The soft tones of a harp floated over to us from the largest building, and we turned to each other.

"An inn?" shrugged Vondro.

"Always a good place to find answers about a town," answered Faldrein with a half-smile.

We ambled toward the source of the music, anxious about what we might encounter in this odd land. Surprisingly, it was a tavern like any other, full of boisterous patrons talking, laughing, and drinking, and we were pleased, and wary, that there happened to be a single table free surrounded by seven chairs.

"Welcome to the Solemn Vulture," announced the serving wench. "I'm Ashleth. What can I get for you weary travelers?"

"Ales all around," Vondro ordered for us. "And a hearty meal."

She bent down between Vondro and Glitter, keeping her voice low. "Ale's decent enough, but I'd avoid the duck if I were you. Our new cook can handle vegetables, but canna seem to tell when a bird's fully cooked."

Glitter smiled at her. "Do you mind if I go into the kitchen and help?"

Ashleth looked around.

I nodded to her. "Trust me. One evening under Glitter's tutelage and your cook's food will vastly improve."

"All right." She nodded back. "Follow me, and I'll introduce you. I'll have your ales in a shade," Ashleth added as Glitter stood.

"Well, this is not anything I expected to find," Brother Ironknuckle said with a grin. "I thought maybe a lost soul or some deathly creature. But a small town, with drink and... excuse me." He got up and ambled over to the bar, straight for another grommold. The other turned and smiled; his face sported burns similar to Brother Ironknuckle's. As they stepped up to each other, they clasped each other's shoulders, butted heads, and roared in laughter.

"Well, he makes friends fast, doesn't he?" chuckled Faldrein.

"Best part of taverns is meeting new people. And ale, of course," joked Vondro. "I met Mithron in a similar place. We almost killed each other right off."

Faldrein looked over at me.

I shrugged. "You know me, always bringing out the best in people."

Vondro laughed. It was good to see him relaxing and smiling again. It was odd it had to happen in the Land of the Dead, but maybe this was the only place where he could move on from Tsukatta.

"You do tend to make terrible first impressions," said Faldrein, shaking his head. "When we met, you started an argument with both of our Masters."

"To be fair, I had just used magic to kill for the first time, and I was having difficulty dealing with it emotionally. That was shortly after I first met Effay."

She looked lost, surrounded by so many people, not to mention pale and gaunt.

I never should have brought her here. This place is draining the life out of her.

"I liked him," spoke Effay'ost'kao, her voice hoarse. "Of course, Master Dawnthistle didn't approve of me talking with a human. He chided me for days after and made me practice being quiet and stealthy for a whole moon." As she spoke, life returned to her eyes and her skin became a little less grey.

Hyxi noticed Effay's change as well. "Remember these things. Our memories, our lives, both joys and sorrows. The dragon said this place would strip these things away from us, and we would be lost here." They leaned over and took Effay's hand. "I refuse to lose another companion. None of us belong here, but you have to keep yourself alive."

"I know, but it's all so depressing here. Even in winter, even in the harshest deserts, there is still life. This whole world is empty. Even that grand tree in the center of town makes me feel squirmy."

"Let's explore the town a little then," Hyxi suggested. "I don't do well with crowds either."

As they stood, Ashleth arrived with our drinks.

"Leaving so soon?" she asked.

"We want to see your town," Hyxi responded. "We'll be back for those in a bit." They placed two silver coins on the table before walking off with Effay.

Vondro paid for the rest of the drinks while I turned mine into grapefruit hibiscus tea. I have rarely partaken in alcohol aside from a few sips on occasion if the flavors are interesting, such as the meads that Glitter introduced me to; I have seen enough times how it affects people, and never to the positive. Revance, a great arcane philosopher, warned against its use, as spellcasting under its effects often proves dangerous. Plus, I do not usually care for the smell of it. I have always preferred tea, and lately I have been drawn to floral, rather than leaf teas.

"Have you made your peace with the Dark Lady?" queried a voice behind us. We turned to see a tall man in grey robes, the same shade as the rest of this land. His face was painted white and black, resembling a skull.

Faldrein stood. "Of course. Like you, I am Her devotee." He bowed.

The stranger nodded in return.

"I am Faldrein. These are my companions Mithron and Vondro."

"Zonos," he answered, his makeup causing his smile to feel unsettling. "Have you been to the Temple yet?"

Of course She would have temples here. There is no reason for Her priests to hide in the Greylands.

"A full temple?" asked Faldrein excitedly. "Please, show me." He left with Zonos without a goodbye, leaving Vondro and I alone at the table.

"Have we been travelling so long that everyone needs to find new people to be with?" Vondro asked, his voice becoming sullen.

"Usually they are merely fleeing my company." I smiled, attempting to lighten his mood. As usual, my attempt failed.

"Honestly, I'd rather be alone anyway. And at a table filled with drink, no less."

I pushed a few of the drinks to the other side of the table from him. "Please do not over-indulge. It is not healthy."

He stared at me with a combination of anger and sadness.

"We all loved her, if not as deeply as you, and we all miss her. I suspect you shall mourn her all your life, but you must continue living. If you surrender here, you might not be able to return."

"Would that be so bad?" he murmured. "At least we can be together here."

"Possibly. She is likely with Kimitsu already, and not to be found here, while I surmise Yaltin would call you to Her realm. You must hold onto life. Trust me, I am a necromancer." I smiled, knowing full well the irony of my statement.

Vondro grinned despite himself and took a long draught of his ale.

"Excuse me," came another voice at my side.

I turned to see an old tillal woman. She was a dull yellow, with a crown of muted lavender hair, which stood out from her head before twisting down in tight curls.

"You are new here, yes? Would you mind if I painted you? There are so few new faces," she said with a piccolo staccato.

I turned to Vondro, who waved me off. "I would be honored," I said to her.

"Excellent, excellent," she hopped. "Outside, before the tree? The light is better and there is more room."

I looked over to Vondro again. He was sliding another mug toward himself. I tapped the bottom of the table five times, leaving the flavor of the ale while removing the alcohol in the remaining mugs. I stood and followed the painter out into the courtyard. Her easel was already set up.

"Please, please. Pick a pose. But be comfortable," she commanded. "I will do a rough sketch first. A full painting takes time."

I mimed the gestures for casting *avularihbolmos* without intoning the runes, as I did not want to kill the old woman, stopping at a point which seemed dramatic.

"So, from where do you hail?"

"I was born in a small village called Split Falls in the kingdom of Loerendoch. Currently, I reside in the Cuyokale region. How about yourself?"

"Obkel, the 'Bronze Hill', in Uljan," she answered without looking away from her sketch.

I could hear the charcoal scratching with enough speed to tear the page.

"Have you been to the Sea of Salted Sands? It's been too long. Nothing invigorates like the desert heat."

Before I could respond, she took the pad from the easel and showed it to me. Her sketch was not of me, but the tree, with some frightening differences. The tree was depicted with several bodies hanging from its branches, an open maw at the top of the trunk, and seven long, vertical eyes peering menacingly through the bark. At the top of the page, she wrote "RUN!". As I turned my gaze back to her, a deep crimson vine appeared over her shoulder, wrapped around her neck, and yanked her away, both her and the vine vanishing into mist.

I turned with dread, for I knew without a doubt her depiction would prove accurate. The tree was far more hideous than expected. Its eyes were bright red, practically glowing against the dull grey of this dimension, phosphorescent orange ichor oozed over the craggy bark from the gnashing teeth. Vines lashed out from its branches, one whipping through an upstairs window of the inn and dragging out a naked Brother Ironknuckle. Strangely, he was not struggling, but rather seemed in a state of bliss. Both Vondro and Faldrein calmly walked toward the tree and were similarly ensnared.

My first impulse, besides following the tillal's advice and fleeing, was to cast the spell I was posing with, but with my friends within the blast radius, I had to consider other options. I cast *zumulalsk* to weaken it, but the black bolt of energy dissipated on contact with the bark. Meanwhile, the vine holding Brother Ironknuckle slowly shifted toward the nightmarish creature's open maw.

Before I could cast another spell, Waltheri raced up the tree, her ghostly paws stepping on two of the eyes, leapt over the rasping wooden teeth, and snapped the vine holding the grommold in her jaws. Her momentum carried them to another branch, which bent and twisted attempting to push them into the maw, but she was too quick and agile and escaped back to the ground with Brother Ironknuckle in tow.

Uncertain as to whether the creature was resistant to the negative energy from my spell or magic altogether, I tried *srukaklek*, aiming each of the twin jets of flame toward the vines and branches hanging my other two friends. The fire worked, though not as well as one would expect against a tree, but was still enough to free them.

As they fell, a large, thick vine slammed into the trunk, cracking off some of the bark. The vine withered shortly afterward and retreated, transforming into a pale and dazed Effay.

Glitter rushed out of the inn, skidded to a halt, and exclaimed, "What in Revance's massive ego is that?"

"Something more dangerous than we might have expected," I answered. "The trunk seems to be resistant to magic and may be toxic."

Seeing Glitter gave me an idea, one which she would be furious with me later. In Ormak's tower, she had discovered a tome which taught her how to cast spells without using gestures. This led me to consider other weaknesses which we wizards have, and I created a spell which protects the caster's neck to avoid being choked. It is not one I normally would prepare, but I did write it on a scroll.

A wizard can never have too many spells at his disposal, but he can only contain so much magic at a time. Though this increases with experience, there are still limits. Scrolls can aid in surpassing those limits but are each written with expensive inks and quills which are designed specifically for one spell. Once the magic is released, the scroll disintegrates. This makes them best suited for special purpose spells which one does not expect to need, such as *mrikyelk*, or spells which translate any language, allow one to breathe underwater, or create an extra-dimensional pocket to hide in.

I cast *mrikyelk* from the scroll and stepped toward the tree. Glitter began to ask me what I was doing, but I was snatched up by a noose-like vine before I could respond. Even with the spell's protection, I found it difficult to breathe as the fear I may have drastically miscalculated nearly overwhelmed me. The long red eyes seemed to gaze into my very soul, awakening every anxiety and regret. I heard my father sneer that he had no son, Vletraka died in my arms, Glitter erupted in flames, Ial'rafiost and Tsukatta faded away. I stood over my friends, raising my skeletal arms in victory, celebrating their deaths by my hand. I screamed in rage and the visions began to fade.

As my mind began to clear, I saw Hyxi race past the tree on Waltheri, their sword barely scratching the creature's bark while Glitter's mouth opened unnaturally wide and released a gout of acid, which melted away a sizable divot as well as one of the creature's eyes. Three spheres of lightning circled the trunk, lashing it with electricity for a moment before vanishing, Effay groaning from the effort.

When I was nearly over the tree's maw, I forced myself to concentrate and began casting *avularihbolmos*, and released it directly into its gullet. The iron sphere exploded, tearing through the trunk and shredding the bark from the inside. The vine holding me released its grip as the tree ceased its movements. I reached to grab it, only to have it slip through my fingers. I landed, sitting on a long, jagged wooden tooth which split my leg open as it went past. Hissing in pain, I reached down and cast *umakraazt* to stitch up the wound and saw the damage done to the tree was beginning to repair itself.

"The tree is regenerating." I shouted to my companions as my wound closed, the new scar bright and pulsing.

Brother Ironknuckle, Vondro, and Faldrein remained prone at the base of the arboreal nightmare, while Effay sat away, curled up and hugging her knees.

"How do we stop it?" cried Glitter, casting *ukurihboj*, the rings of rose quartz crashing into the trunk while Hyxi continued their hit-and-run tactics, slashing the tree and bolting before the vines could react. When Hyxi was clear, Effay cast *rihklivevuku* and pelted the tree with hailstones, while I launched a barrage of silver shards into the maw with *mroozikbiizuzul*.

The nightmare tree continued to regenerate.

Another vine wrapped around my neck and tugged me toward the internal cavity. I grabbed at a branch as my leg slid across the sharp wooden teeth and sliced back open. Glitter roared in frustration and released a blinding flash of sparks. The tree shuddered and stopped healing for a few moments.

"That worked. More light." This was not a fight I was prepared for, and I only had a myzling to temporarily blind an opponent, which used bright light.

Glitter raised her arms and threw her head back, shining ever more brightly through a cascade of colors. I turned away and looked for any purchase to climb from my horrid perch. Below me, Hyxi slashed away with grim determination, disappearing in the deepening shadow created by Glitter's burst.

With a groan and a series of cracks, the tree began to collapse beneath me, and I called on Ial'rafiost's spirit to guide me as I leapt away. Glitter screamed as I landed first on my feet, then fell forward onto my knees, sliding enough so my robe went taut and pulled my head down. I found myself on all fours, a ghostly wolf staring down at me. Waltheri licked me once and bounded back to Hyxi.

I stood and rushed around the tree to find Glitter on her knees, her head still arched back.

"Glitter?" I called, my voice tentative. "Are you all right?"

She raised her head and looked at me, her eyes glassy and prismatic, leaned forward, and vomited on the ground. Groans sounded around me as my other friends began to shake off the tree's influence.

I knelt beside Glitter and placed a hand between her shoulder blades to show support as I have seen others do. When I touched her, I could feel the damage she had done to her life force in channeling so much light, which reminded me of when I first learned to do something similar to harm undead.

"Weapon of last resort?" I asked with concern.

"Weapon of last resort," she confirmed, her voice hoarse. Her sparkles had dimmed to a dull grey, disappearing into the landscape, and I feared how much of her life she had burned away.

"Rest. I will see if Faldrein is recovered enough to help you." I looked over to my dazed friends. Hyxi had already pulled Faldrein over to Effay, who was slowly relaxing.

"What happened?" asked Vondro, rubbing his neck and surveying the situation.

"The tree was much more than it seemed," I responded, pointing to the branches and toothed maw. The nightmarish creature had toppled over and had turned a dark grey. "It grabbed and attempted to eat you. What is the last thing you remember?"

"I was chatting with Ashleth, telling her about Dureltown. Then without warning she told me to run as a red rope wrapped around her neck. Now I'm out here."

"Same happened to Tordek," added Brother Ironknuckle. "We were…"

"Naked," Hyxi finished for him.

Brother Ironknuckle reddened.

"Good for you. It's not always easy to find someone, especially in a place like this."

"It… it doesn't bother you?" He rubbed the scars on his chin.

"Why would it?" asked Glitter, using my shoulder to get back on her feet. "Is that why your beard is gone? They burned it off for that?" She was aghast.

I said nothing, as I thought his punishment was for killing a fellow grommold.

"In part, lass." He wept, tears following the contours of his burns. "Such behavior is not acceptable to my people." He turned to me. "The man I killed, that I left Yremvun[20] fer, was no stranger. Devvor couldn't live with our secret and wanted to explain himself to his family. We argued about it, 'cause at the very least we'd be exiled from grommoldi society." He rubbed the scars on his face again, looking at each of us in turn.

"I lost me temper and beat him to death. When I returned to face punishment, they let me live since Devvor was a *niphbax* like me and might 'ave been killed anyway.

---

[20] Literally translates to 'Iron Hole' in Umani.

That man represented everything I loved and hated about meself. Here, in the land of the dead of all places, I thought I'd found a piece of Devvor." He dropped to his knees and covered his burned face with his large craggy hands. "I'm sorry." He began to pale into the landscape.

Effay and Hyxi stepped up and wrapped their arms around him. "We're sorry you've had to carry this burden for so long," murmured Effay'ost'kao into his hair. "No one should be restricted in love."

Glitter took my hand and walked me over to them.

"Do not ever call yourself that again," I commanded Brother Ironknuckle. "I have been studying your language, and you are not an aberration. You are a good man, full of strength and wisdom, and I will not accept any deprecation from you or others to that fact."

Glitter squeezed my hand, and I could see her sparkles turn bright yellow.

"You are our friend," she added. "We forgave you suns ago after our respective meltdowns. Loving another is not a crime."

"You lost the one you love. I understand that pain as much as anybody," said Vondro, melancholy filling his voice. "But you destroyed it yourself and I can't imagine how hard that must be. I've raged against Cratillus, the world, and myself for Tsukatta's death—you must have carried that all within."

Ashleth appeared in our midst, along with the other people of the town, emerging into view one by one.

"Thank you for releasing us!" exclaimed the barmaid. Her sentiments were echoed by the crowd.

"We're sorry we had to keep you here, but that creature gave us little choice," spoke the painter pointing at the tree, which was crumbling like ash in a light breeze.

"I was one of the first ones it caught," said Zonos. "It would take us and torture us, only giving us respite if we helped to add souls to its collection. The more of us there were, the less often we would be dragged in to feed it."

Tordek handed Brother Ironknuckle his clothes and kissed him on the cheek. "Be well and thank you."

The townsfolk and town faded away, back into the flat landscape of the Greylands. We looked around at the bare terrain, having already forgotten about the dreary solitude of this world.

Faldrein stared at his shuffling feet. "Look, Brother Ironknuckle, I won't pretend to understand your relationship, but I can sympathize with your pain." He looked over at Hyxi and Effay. "Like you two."

"Four," Hyxi interrupted, their eyes darkening. "Gwenaz and Farandi are part of us."

"Okay, the four of you," he corrected. "I understand the friendship, but not the attraction. I don't disagree with it, but it doesn't make sense to me. True, I've never been in love, but when it happens, I can't imagine it being with another man."

"And that's okay too," smiled Effay as she walked over to Faldrein and hugged him. "Love in whatever way is right for you and accept the same for others. Love isn't about sharing bodies but sharing hearts. Everything else is just everything else."

"You're not upset with me?"

"You are trying to understand. That's enough for me." Effay squeezed him and stepped back. "Now, let's get moving before this place drains my sap again."

We began our march once again in that directionless land, knowing only our destination but not the path.

Chapter 14: The Grand Mausoleum

There is no calculating the size and scale of the Grand Mausoleum, as it grows with every death. It is designed to accommodate every soul that passes through the Bone Gate, itself a massive structure of wrought iron and bone some sixty feet high and at least as wide. The Bone Gate is set into a wall nearly as tall made of earth, stone, wood, and bones, which surrounds the Grand Mausoleum yet is not tall enough to hide it.

As the kazkul that Faldrein and I spoke with had said, the Bone Gate was closed. Spirits of those who had passed were lined up as far as one could see from the entrance, and further beyond that. The Greylands have no horizon, at least not a discernable one to separate earth from sky, but if it did, the line would stretch past that limit. I was surprised by the patience and civility of the assembled. There was no one pushing forward, no milling about, nor any other signs of exasperation with the lack of movement of the queue. When asked, the common answer from those waiting was that they had only been there for a short while regardless of their distance from the front of the line. Time seemed to have limited meaning for spirits.

Thessylia flew toward the top of the wall then veered away. *'I can go no further. There is a... presence that pushes me back.'* She wheeled over the crowd near the Bone Gate.

I felt her fear, but that was not the cause of her inability to enter the environs.

'This is not my place.' She flew off and disappeared within the vast grey which was not a sky.

I could still feel her. She was puzzled, yet sure of her direction. *'Where are you headed?'* I asked, transferring my senses to hers.

'To where I belong,' she answered, almost as a question. *'Where the others are.'*

Out of the Greylands emerged a forest, which formed a boundary against an open grassland. Thessylia barked and was answered by the hoots, chirps, and trills of hundreds of owls of various species. She increased her speed, spurred on by joy, and flew to the forest's edge. A cacophony of owl noises combined with humanoid languages called to greet her.

'They can speak, and understand each other? Are they all familiars?' I tried to focus my attention on a single owl, but there was too much activity and I could only catch pieces of conversations as each vied for the attention of the newcomer. *'Have fun with your parliament. I will call you when we are ready to return.'*

'I will know. I will be there.'

We had expected the Gate to be sealed, so Glitter, Faldrein, and I had prepared *uvaazaasl* to fly over the wall. We each carried a passenger, while Effay transformed into a vine and climbed up and over. Unlike castles from our Material realm, there were no guards or archers atop the wall as no one would dare to attack, though I am certain the goddess could summon reinforcements if needed. The courtyard was filled with souls standing idle, unaware of how much time had passed since their demise. Unlike at home, ghosts are tangible in the Greylands, as we quickly learned after bumping through the crowd.

After pushing through the mass of spirits, we made our way to the Gates of Acceptance. Only souls who have come to terms with the reality of their situation are allowed to pass and continue toward their final destination. As we were still alive, the Gates had no power to stop us from continuing on to the Alcove of Patience. Here are inscribed the names of all who stand outside the Grand Mausoleum, their names appearing elsewhere once they enter. This area too was filled with the disembodied.

The Mausoleum is constructed of tombstones—every room, hall, wall, and pillar—which bear the name of every individual who has died and passed through the Dark Lady's sanctum. If one lays a hand on a stone and calls out the name, an image of the deceased appears and gives basic biographical information, including date of birth and death, family names, and highlights of the life they led. The souls are not attached to these stones and they are by far the most useful example of illusion magic I have ever encountered.

The Grand Mausoleum is, normally, in a constant state of growth due to the perpetual influx of souls. There is likely a plan or pattern to the appearance of new stones, but I was not there long enough to discern it. Within is a section called the Catacombs of Centuries, where the ancient dead can be sought, so it may be that the stones move, are moved, or are reallocated over time.

At the far side of the chamber was an archway carved with dragonflies and skulls. We were careful to avoid disrupting the crowd, but those we made contact with seemed surprised we were even there and generally oblivious to their surroundings. I learned later that each individual believes themselves to be alone, guided by instinct as they wend through each chamber. The Dark Lady deals with each individual personally, but many simultaneously for the sake of efficiency. It is not widely known or appreciated that the goddess of death is also the goddess of time.

Beyond this archway, which seemed to get further away as the crowd grew, lies the Chamber of Judgement. This is as far as most souls go within the Grand Mausoleum. The Dark Lady's throne, a massive structure of stone and iron, sized for someone four times my height, sat at the top of a dais. It is decorated with dragonfly carvings along the top and arms, but not ostentatiously so. Neither is it padded as one would expect, either because She has no need for comfort or Her Office is not one in which one *should* be comfortable. Great pillars held up a ceiling of indeterminate height and alcoves with carved depictions of the other deities lined the walls. Otherwise, there are no other decorative elements.

Unexpectedly, it was not the Dark Lady sitting on the throne but Cratillus. He looked upset, yelling at the assembled souls, who hardly noticed his presence.

We ducked down along the back wall of the Chamber to hide behind the crowd of spirits.

"How in the Pits is *he* here? I think he is still alive," I whispered to my friends.

"Who is that?" asked Faldrein. "That is most certainly *not* the Dark Lady."

Vondro slid his sword from its sheath. "Cratillus," he growled. "The man who murdered Tsukatta."

I held up my hand to stop him from doing anything reckless.

"We need a plan. He will kill us all if we simply charge up to him. These souls could be endangered, and I do not know what will happen to the dead should they be slain in the Land of the Dead."

There are theories, of course. Most believe the soul is immortal, or, more technically, beyond mortality, and cannot be permanently harmed. Still others believe that over time a soul can be twisted and warped into another configuration. No mortal has been able to verify or study such theories, and extra-planar sources of this information are dubious at best.[21]

Eighteen spirits, their eyes and auras black, stood at the front of the dais and shoved the others away at his command.

"No," Cratillus shouted to the souls who moved in to replace the ones his guards had shoved aside, interrupting our whispered conversation. "You are not going anywhere; the other gods aren't coming for you. How many times must I repeat myself? Coruld is coming, and you all belong to Him now." He paused. "The rules have changed. You now have the honor of serving the Dread King." He was still for a moment as if listening to someone. "Look on the bright side. You will get to return to the land of the living and see your loved ones again. You'll still be dead, of course. On the other hand, you can make them join you."

"Stealth, then," offered Hyxi. "Surround him. Those who can attack from a distance do so while the rest of us will use that as our cue to hit him from all sides."

"Why is he even there?" asked Effay. "He says he's waiting for Coruld. Why has the Dark Lady allowed this?"

"Because even she can't stop me." Cratillus' voice boomed through the Chamber.

---

[21] Numerous texts on the subject exist. I recommend *The Life of the Soul* by Raithehuen, *Conversations with Miz'zrak the Scourgre* by Yivnia Foltzro, and *Metaphysical Immortality* by Spaqua'aloinu.

While we had been discussing our plans, his guards had silently surrounded us. We were grappled, held, and dragged to the dais before we could mount a counterattack.

Cratillus laughed at our struggles as the black spirits drained our strength.

"Did you think I would not notice you there? You're the only other living things in this room. Hiding behind these worthless souls—you may as well have stood in a misty rain carrying lanterns." His laughter continued.

"Mithron, Mithron, Mithron." He shook his head while throwing his arms out as if expecting an embrace. "You followed me all the way here. Did you finally come to your senses? Are you finally going to offer your life to me?"

I glared at him, my body too weak to form words.

"Still defiant? Well, there's still time. We'll talk later.

Anyone else want power and immortality?" he asked the rest of my friends. "I'm in a unique position to grant requests." He patted the throne which was far too large for him. "How about you, little one?" He pointed at Hyxi and forced Waltheri to tear from their heart and manifest, causing them both to yelp in pain. "I could make you both phantoms, travelling the world together eternally, never having to mourn each other."

Waltheri leapt at Cratillus, stopping in midair as bolts of pale orange energy cascaded through her before she dropped in front of the platform.

"None may approach the throne uninvited."

I hated that smirk.

"I want something," Vondro said with a groan.

"Ooh, one of you has finally gotten wise. What can I do for you?"

Vondro coughed. "I want your head on a pike," he laughed.

Brother Ironknuckle and I joined in.

Cratillus sighed. "I suppose I should have seen that coming. You are all a stubborn lot." His gaze shifted to his ebon spirits. "Bury them."

We were dragged off in different directions. Glitter and Faldrein screamed in terror while the others, aside from Effay, raged in defiance; she put up no resistance. I was furious but knew I had to calm myself if I was to have any chance of escape. After being dragged down a long hall, I watched as the stones in the wall pulled apart, revealing a hollow within. As the two spirits began to push me in, I released the burst of life energy I had been building, searing away most of the guards. The pair slipped away into the shadows as I dragged my weakened body up the wall to stand.

Likely, they are returning to Cratillus to report my escape. I need to find somewhere to hide, but I can barely walk and I have no idea where I am going.

Using the wall as a crutch, I pulled myself down the hall away from the usurping madman. There is a spell to hide oneself from the undead, altering the aura of the living to disguise their life energy, but I had not expected to need it, so I had not prepared it. However, I realized I was making the only sounds here with my grunting and foot dragging, so I cast *arihskauuom* to create a sphere of silence around myself. The guards had moved soundlessly, so I would not hear them sneaking up on me anyway should they return.

In a normal castle, there is endless activity. Servants run about on errands or completing chores while the nobles amble at their own pace. Here, however, there was literally not a soul to be found as I crept through the halls. The more I moved, the more my strength returned, and soon I was lurching along without needing the wall for support. Not long after, I was able to walk normally, by which time the silencing spell had worn off. I found no signs of my friends, though I assumed the wall would have sealed once I was ensconced. Perhaps my name would have appeared on one of the stones or there might have been another indicator. For all I knew, they had also already escaped and were looking for each other in this maze.

On further reflection, the halls of the Grand Mausoleum reminded me of the Mazeworks. They are an endless network of corridors, turning and splitting at random with no outlet. In the hopes that it might function similarly, I stopped, closed my eyes, and envisioned a door leading to someone who could help. But when I opened my eyes, nothing had changed.

I continued along my path until I spotted a carving of an open book beneath a name I did not recognize on the floor. I reached down, touched the stone, and called the name. Vletraka's image appeared before me. Tears ran down my face, and I was so torn between my feelings of loss and concern that her true name was on display that I paid almost no attention to her recited biography.

For a moment, the image wavered, as if two Vletrakas were attempting to share the same space. "Mithron? Why are you here alive?" she asked.

"M-Mistress?"

"Quickly, follow me." She floated down the hallway for about a minute then abruptly stopped and turned right. The stones on the wall shifted to reveal a heavy arched oak door, which opened of its own accord. I followed her in, and the door closed with a whisper. My attention was immediately drawn to shelves of books and scrolls stretching beyond the limits of my sight, both laterally and vertically. Hundreds of spirits flew among them, shelving and reading the infinite knowledge.

"You should be safe here. He hasn't found this place yet." She looked me over then flew in and embraced me.

I sobbed into her semi-solid shoulder. "I've missed you. I'm so glad that you're well."

She pulled back. "How long has it been? Tell me everything you've learned."

I told her how I had met my friends, tracked down Cratillus, and thought we had killed him until discovering him here; about Ormak and his tragic life, unlife, and death; about Glitter and I transitioning from rivals to friends to something more which I could not adequately define. There was so much I wanted to say, but I felt my time was limited.

"Why are you here?" I asked, waving my hand to the Living Library. "Actually, I think I am jealous. My friends were captured and placed somewhere in this maze. How are the kazkulim kept captive, and why has the Dark Lady not intervened in all of this?"

"As you know, I didn't follow the dictums of any god very closely, but when the Dark Lady offered me a place in the Living Library, I accepted without hesitation. How could I not?" She smiled. I had missed that smile. "Many of the greatest wizards are here, studying and cataloging the accumulated knowledge and life-experiences of the mortal world. Everyone who has ever existed, every lifetime, is written within these volumes. Every text ever written has a duplicate here. I have as much time as I want to read and study before taking a new life."

"That sounds wonderful. But if you take a new life, will you not forget all you have learned here? What would be the point?"

"The Dark Lady knows everything we do. Our studies inform Her, that She may better understand each individual as they pass into Her halls." I was about to interrupt when she spoke over me. "Time works differently here. I can read someone's entire history before they are even aware they are standing outside the Bone Gate. When they stand before Her, She is fully aware of who they are and where they are to go from there.

"As for forgetting, new life experiences are drawn best on a blank canvas. Some things, like the love of learning and talent for magic seep through, but we are not our previous incarnations. Here, I have access to those lifetimes, but I am Vletraka now. When I return, I will be another person with knowledge of Vletraka."

"That is a much grander perspective than I have ever conceived," I said without focus, my mind attempting to comprehend the infinity of life. "Does that happen for everyone, or only the Dark Lady's chosen? I suppose asking to see my previous lives would be too much. If time is different here, as you said, then I am not in such a hurry after all."

"I would not recommend that," she responded with a wan smile. "The living mind is limited in its capacity. Too much knowledge of the infinite can cause serious damage. I cannot speak for all the other gods, but there are volumes proving that reincarnation happens regularly. It may be an individual choice to return to the world—infinity can be dull without change."

"I have already learned the price of knowledge. I used the *mbikvlidyk* ritual to speak to Sylekhis and nearly lost myself. But it did lead us here. We need to free the kazkulim."

She closed her eyes for a few seconds. "Come." She floated through the Library until we reached her destination. "Wait here," she commanded before vanishing.

Assuming my Mistress led me here for a reason, I scanned the shelves for something interesting to peruse during her absence. My eyes fell on *Inner Light* by Zalgovathi. I paged through the volume, taking mental note of areas of particular interest before returning to the beginning and reading through. Zalgovathi's work seems to predate Falleoraeli Zolthliam's *Accentuating the Positive: A Study of Divine Channeling and Its Arcane Equivalent*, focusing on first using the enhanced life-energy, which he called "vrada", into the mind to strengthen the will and remove fear and doubt, then focusing the vrada to a point to inject it into undead creatures.

I was concerned about how long Vletraka was gone. I tried to leave the Library to look for my friends but could not find an exit, so I returned to practicing these techniques while reading, and long after finishing, before she returned. When I commented on her absence, she reminded me that time is more subjective within the Library, and from her perspective only a few minutes had passed while it had been months for me.

"The cage is maintained by eight wizards. Even if they were to be removed, the spell has built up enough magic to sustain it for some time. I don't know if I can break the spell, but I may be able to weaken it."

I looked around the Living Library. "How many wizards are in here? Surely some would be willing to help."

"I'll see who I can convince," she said with some doubt. "Most have been here so long they have all but forgotten life outside of the Library. Did you find anything to keep you busy while I was gone?"

I pointed to the book which another spirit was re-shelving. "Yes, yes I did. Thank you, Mistress."

She hugged me again and kissed my forehead. "Go find your friends. I will see what I can do about the kazkulim." Vletraka turned her head and a door appeared.

"I do not want to leave, but I must. Will I see you again?"

"Unless you choose a new path, I expect you will be working here at my side when your time comes. But please, take your time." She laughed. "You've made me proud. Now, go." She floated away to speak with her fellow librarians.

After leaving, I realized I still had no idea how to find where my friends might be held. I shifted my sight to look for signs of life and found nothing but an emptiness so vast that I could not maintain my altered vision for long. Treating these halls like the Mazeworks had worked before, so I calmed myself and asked for guidance again. I examined the names on the stones around me, seeking a familiar name to lead me forward.

No one of note came to my attention, and, after searching hundreds of names, I began to lose hope. How many have passed since the world's beginning? Is this solely from our world or are there others? Do the dead from other planes pass through the Grand Mausoleum or do their souls stay in the realms of their gods? How does even a primal goddess handle the constant cycle of birth and death of countless individuals?

As I pondered, I noticed the name Almeond Sunnythrush, the author of *Fluttering Tapestry: What Picture Does the Weave Portray?* It was the influence of her thoughts on the nature of the Weave which nearly started an argument with Ormak back in his tower. I placed my hand on her stone and called her name. Almeond was tillalian, her florescent orange skin contrasting sharply with her indigo hair and lilac eyes. She was born nearly two hundred suns ago in the city of Aurora, which was nestled in a mountain valley and went on at length detailing her family history as tillalli are wont to do.

After a time, her image wavered as Vletraka's did and she spoke to me directly. "Hello, hello. I can't remember the last time somebody listened to my stone. What can I do for… you're alive, aren't you? Well, braid my hair, what's a living human doing here in the Grand Mausoleum? You're not one of those looking for their loved ones to return, are you? I hear that's what most of them want. Or power? Wealth? Well, come on, speak. I don't have… actually, I do have forever."

I had to concentrate to keep up with her rapid speech.

"Actually, I am lost. Spirits are not leaving the Material Plane to come here, and the dying are taking far too long to pass, so my friends and I came here to help fix the problem. The kazkulim are trapped in a cage, a madman is sitting on the Dark Lady's throne, and my friends are missing. Can you help?"

"Well, there's not much I can do, being dead and all. Her Absoluteness took to Her study a while ago. Maybe She's still there? I don't remember seeing Her leave the Chamber of Solace, but I've been busy. So much pondering. The Weave keeps its secrets, yes it does. But like magic you must understand one thread at a time. The more threads, the bigger the picture, yes? But you're not interested." She frowned. "Busy with other things. Come, come."

I followed Almeond until she stopped and looked up at a random spot on the ceiling. As before, the stones moved to reveal a heavy door which dropped open. She floated up easily while I grabbed the pull ring and clambered onto the door. As my feet left the floor, gravity switched, and I fell through into the room. Spirits were huddled in small groups around chairs, cushions, and tables covered with ink, quills, and paper. Bookshelves were set at intervals with books transitioning between here and the Living Library as needed.

"The gods are merely a manifestation of our collective will," I overheard. "If so many did not believe in them, they would cease to exist."

"Nonsense. People exist *because* of the will of the gods," responded another voice. "They are real—it is *our* existence that is the illusion."

"The gods created us for the sole purpose of worshipping them," said a third. "It is our adoration which feeds and sustains them."

"If that were true, how did they survive without us in the beginning?" asked the first. All three spirits were humanoid and human-sized, but aside from the timbre of their voices, there was little to distinguish them from each other.

"They likely drew energy from their creation to use until they could create worshippers. It must have been a finite source," the second finished as the third tried to interrupt.

Almeond pulled me away before I could hear more. "Those three have been debating since before I arrived. None will concede that the others' opinions are valid, nor can they obtain any proof. It's not as though the gods are going to walk in here and tell us the truth as they know it. They probably don't know either. Theories, theories are all most of us have, but there is something behind it all, some way to make it all make sense. I think it's the Weave, but honestly, I don't know any more than anyone else. We'll never stop seeking. No. This is who we are.

"But this is not why you are here. No. The Dark Lady has Her own chamber there," she pointed to another door. "None of us ever dare to disturb Her. She has been there for longer than usual. If you bother Her, you might never leave," Almeond warned. "She insists on proper protocol, so be nice."

"Thank you for your help," I bowed. "I must speak with Her. The world needs to be put back into balance." As I advanced to the door, fear and trepidation welled up in me. *Am I really going to interrupt a goddess in Her chambers and make demands?* I stopped, took a deep breath, and centered myself. *We need Her. What happens to me is not important.* The door swung open surprisingly easy, and I slipped into the room.

She stood in the center of the chamber, some twenty feet in height in a veiled black dress. Through the veil I could see Her occluded face; skeletal and packed with enough grave dirt to form cheeks, lips, and a brow. It took every bit of my will to not die on the spot.

"Another mortal," She snarled, Her hollow voice seeming to come from Her general direction rather than Her mouth. "What does that pompous cretin want now?"

I could not answer as my jaw had locked tight.

"Have you come simply to stare? Speak!"

"Y-yes, my Lady," I stammered. "I-I mean, no, I have not come to stare. I came for your help."

"Your master has seen to it that I can help no one. Go away."

"Cratillus is not my *master*, nor shall he ever be." Her comment had given me enough anger to speak clearly. "I am here because there is too much suffering and are too many spirits who cannot find their way to Your realm, while countless others are queued up outside the Bone Gates. It is no small leap to assume Cratillus is to blame for the capture of the kazkulim. Why have You not done something about this?" I felt a boiling rage mixed with...embarrassment? I closed my eyes and breathed to center my emotions.

The Dark Lady looked away from me and over Her left shoulder. "That is why."

I stepped around her to see a large iron spike, at least two feet in length, driven into the floor behind Her.

"How?" I began to ask before She interrupted my query.

"An ancient artifact, one of the first tools made by Acclin. He designed it to hold His island workshop in place so that it would not drift with each blow of His hammer. He has not used that shop in millennia. Now, the spike is being used to hold Me," She huffed and growled.

"That explains a lot," I mumbled aloud. Obviously, She could not remove it Herself or She would have already done so. "Could You not summon assistance to pull the spike out?"

"None were strong enough, and those who tried were assaulted by shadows."

As She spoke, Her shadow shifted, rippling as a pond with an anxious frog, and a dozen shadowy forms emerged and floated toward me. I released some of the vrada I had stored up and burned them away with my life energy.

"I have to get you free."

"Why would you aid me, mortal? You are promised to my Husband."

I looked at her in shock, my eyes wide with horror. "Just because I am a necromancer does not mean I revere the Lord of the Undead. In fact, I chose my career in order to learn how to destroy such creatures."

"Then why do you carry his marks on your bones?" She asked with the accusatory air of one who has caught another in a lie.

"I do not understand what you mean," I replied, both confused and unnerved by her allegation.

She glared at me as if I were a child denying my guilt, but Her gaze softened when She spoke. "You truly do not know. Here." She pointed a long, bony finger at my chest and a number of runes glowed through my robes.

"I... I remember those being carved into my skin. You said they were etched into my bones? What do they mean?"

Before She could answer, another wave of unliving shadows poured out from behind Her. Once again, I focused my energy outward to burn them away, leaving me momentarily staggered.

"I do not know how many more times I can do that. I have to remove the spike."

"If you touch it, you may never leave my Realm," She warned. "Judging by your life force, you can release it three more times before exhausting yourself."

I stared first at the goddess, who could so easily determine my life energy, and then at the rune-covered spike.

"How did Cratillus drive it in, if he could not touch it?" I wondered aloud.

"He carried a hammer with similar markings. Perhaps it protected him." She crossed Her arms and let out a long sigh, Her frustration with either or both me and the situation evident.

"Curse you, old man," I muttered. "Your belligerence is going to save the world."

I reached into my shoulder bag with the extra-dimensional space and pulled out the tongs which I had neglected to give to my father. I hoped that being magical in nature, they would not only afford me the necessary leverage to pull the spike but protect me as well. I did not expect them to glow bright blue while the spike emanated a pale orange. *Perhaps that is why Ormak kept them in the chamber with the other powerful items. I* knew *there had to be a reason.*

I gripped the spike under the head and began rocking it side to side to loosen it from the ground. As I did, a dozen shadows began pulling at me, and I was forced to channel out another fraction of my stored life energy. The spike refused to be released, and more shadows came for me.

"You had best hurry. I cannot help you while I am trapped like this."

I glanced over to her while I burned the shadows away again. "I am fully aware of my limitations, thank you," I growled under my breath. It is not prudent to speak in such a fashion to a goddess, but fortunately She did not chide me for doing so, as I needed to concentrate on the task at hand.

If only I had Vondro's strength. No, I must use my own strengths, I scolded myself.

Taking a deep breath while letting my eyes shift, I took a closer look at the Weave, which wrapped more tightly around the pair of items than when Tsukatta swaddled me after my rescue from Cratillus. Sigils I could not see before shone sun-bright, compelling me to avoid staring at them directly. When I blinked, I could still see them in my mind's eye, their colors reversed but appearing more distinct without the background glow of the items. There were six runes around the top of the spike, and six more around the teeth of the tongs, but none looked quite right, as if they were…incomplete!

I slowly began turning sunwise around the spike, releasing the last bit of stored energy as another wave of shadows ascended from the ground where the spike had pierced it. My head spun, my knees buckled, and I nearly dropped the tongs, but I knew this was the final moment. I staggered two more steps to my left, and the runes connected, causing both items to flash even brighter, their combined energy throwing me back like a misused toy. When I regained my senses, I found I still held the tongs, and they in turn held the spike.

The searing pain came a moment later. My hands felt as though I had washed them in acid; upon inspection, they looked like it as well. My fingers were locked around the handles and I could not let them go. The odor of my cooked flesh reminded me once again of Glitter's near brush with death. The emotional pain coupled with the physical was too much to bear, and I screamed before passing out again.

"Few things surprise me," spoke a hollow voice somewhere in the distance, "but you have managed to do so consistently."

With a conscious effort, I managed to pry open my eyes to see a very unfocused Dark Lady standing over me.

"I expected the spike to extinguish the last spark of your life essence, yet you still live, though diminished."

"Where?" I began to ask before remembering. I pushed myself to a sitting position, immediately regretting the decision. My head swam, the nausea causing me to lose the remains of my last meal, but the scorching agony in my hands made that hardly noticeable. My hands were mostly dry bone below the wrist, with a few shards of flesh, mostly on the back, remaining. Curiosity over how the bones stayed connected in spite of missing ligaments, muscle, and skin battled with the shock of the realization of my current state. "How?"

"Your tool seems to have protected you, only partially killing you. I appreciate your sacrifice. I will summon you once I have dealt with the perpetrator of this affront." With that, She faded away.

I stared at my denuded fingers. One digit at a time, I flexed, the pain becoming more tolerable each time until it registered as merely a dull ache. The edges of my remaining flesh had been seared, and there was no feeling at all until I poked an inch away from the edge. My fingertips were sharper than I had expected, and I made small punctures in my skin on the first few attempts. Aside from the pain, there was no feeling in my exposed bones, and I had to look to be certain of where they were.

Fascinated though I was, I was more interested in what was currently happening in the Chamber of Judgement, especially what the Dark Lady might do with Cratillus. Wincing as I pushed myself up, I hurried out of the chamber to seek the goddess, stopping first to retrieve both the tongs and the spike, for it would not be wise to leave powerful artifacts lying around unattended.

I wound my way through the hallways which would keep teams of historians occupied for lifetimes and made my way to the Dark Lady's throne room, following the sounds of voices echoing through the halls. Cratillus sat upon Her seat of power, appearing to have not moved since I saw him last.

"This is no longer your realm," he sneered. "I sit here now until your Husband comes to claim it. You no longer rule here."

"You think my power rests in a chair?" She rebuked. "I AM this realm, and Coruld has no claim here anymore. That seat is indeed yours. I am sure you have noticed that by now."

Cratillus looked past her, noticing me for the first time. "You! Of *course* her freedom is your fault! How did you manage to survive? Oh, I see, you didn't," he chuckled pointing at my hands. "I told you to let me kill you. Now, you will suffer." He spoke a single word infused with magic.

I held my staff tightly so it would absorb the spell, but the sound was garbled, and I could not understand it properly.

"No," the Dark Lady said simply.

Cratillus looked upon her in shock then turned his gaze back on me. "I see you found someone else to fight for you.

Coward. You know you can't defeat me on your own. In fact, you know I have already won. No matter what, you belong to Coruld now."

"No, I do not," I growled. "I belong to Her," I nodded my head toward the Dark Lady. "You may have forced this condition upon my body, but your violations have not changed my mind or spirit. You chose the Dread King of your own volition and you will suffer eternally for it. I have not."

In a fit of rage, Cratillus cast his most powerful spells at the Dark Lady, to no avail. Mortal magic cannot affect the gods, and I must assume he acted out of desperation.

"You dare to attack me? To hold me in my own chambers?" roared the Dark Lady.

I admit, I took great pleasure in seeing Cratillus so helpless.

"These, too, you have stolen from me." She pointed at him and opened Her hand. Mist poured out from somewhere on Cratillus' person and coalesced before the Dark Lady, forming the likenesses of nearly a dozen people, two of which looked like Ial'rafiost and Tsukatta.

While the spirits looked around at their new surroundings, Cratillus cast a spell to take them back without effect.

The Dark Lady snapped Her hand shut and the Weave separated from him entirely. "I've indulged your fantasy of power long enough." She stepped forward but stopped as a figure stepped out of a shadowed alcove. It was cloaked in darkness, only the white skeletal hands, much like my own, and mandible visible against the absolute blackness.

Fear and wrath warred within me as I viewed the visitor.

"**THIS ONE IS MINE, WIFE. GIVE HIM TO ME**." His voice was cold and hollow like a leaden bell struck by a closed fist.

"This mortal dared to attack Me. It is My right to punish him," She answered without looking at Her estranged husband.

"**NONETHELESS, I AM HERE FOR THIS ONE. BY THE ANCIENT COMPACT, I CLAIM HIM. NOW**."

She turned to look upon Her former king. A wry smile appeared on Her face, grave soil cracking off her cheek. "If You insist." She grew taller as She stepped toward Cratillus, wrapped a clawed hand around his torso and pulled straight up. His hips and legs stayed firmly attached to the appropriated throne while the rest of him convulsed in her left hand ten feet above his waist. She tapped his chest and a murky wisp emerged from his mouth. The Dark Lady pinched the released spirit with the gentleness of a lioness lifting her cub, turned, and handed it over to Coruld. "His soul, by the accords of the Ancient Compact. You have no claim on his body."

A wave of anger washed over me from without. I turned away from the scene in fear of what I might see, doing my best to calm myself in the presence of two deities whose emotions easily overrode my own. My mind had only recently recovered and even the idea of peering into the depths of such divine darkness nearly brought me to tears.

"These, too, are yours," she added as eight new spirits were carried into our midst by Sylekhis himself. "Their imprisonment of my kazkulim is over. You may punish them for their failure to you however you wish."

"VERY WELL, MY WIFE," the Dread Lord snarled. **"I ACCEPT WHAT IS MINE."** He returned to the alcove and disappeared with the souls of Cratillus and his minions; Cratillus's physical remains rapidly crumbled to dust.

With the Dread King's departure, she turned to me. "You impress Me, mortal. To sacrifice yourself for One you do not even worship is unexpected." She reduced Her size and sat on Her throne, unimpeded by the pile of Cratillus'. Her grey eyes bore into my heart. "You have earned without seeking what so many have come here for."

Yoffa, Vletraka, Tsukatta, and Ial'rafiost appeared before me.

"One may return."

I looked up at the Dark Lady, joy and sorrow mixing in my heart. "Thank you. This is a great honor but also the hardest decision of my life."

"Where are we?" Raf and Tsukatta asked as one. Upon realizing the other was there, they turned and hugged.

"Don't worry about me, smith's son," Yoffa smiled. "I've lived a good life and I'm ready to retire to Ioddenri's bosom." She stepped up and hugged me. "You were my best student and I'm so pleased with the man you've become." Then she stepped back and vanished.

"I also couldn't have asked for a better student," said Vletraka. "I'm glad I get to say a proper farewell this time. Take care of our home and our friends. I miss you, but I'm happy here."

"Goodbye, Mistress Vletraka," I bowed. "Thank you for... everything. I am glad you are happy."

She turned and floated toward the Living Library.

"I…" my remaining two friends started together, then encouraged the other to go first. "I want to live," Raf began. "There is still so much to see and do." He turned to Tsukatta. "I don't want to be selfish, but I want to be selfish. I'm sorry."

"Me too." Tsukatta turned to me. "Vondro and I were starting to know one another. I want to see where our lives would lead together. It's an impossible choice for you."

"It is. I want you both to return, but that is not an option." I looked to the Dark Lady. "That will not work, will it? If they split their time, half-a-sun each, it would prove intolerable. We would watch them die every year as the other took their place." I looked back at my friends. "And you would each be forced to endure a constant cycle of death and rebirth, only to live half a life." I turned my gaze back to the Queen of this realm. "That is where the others failed, correct? They got greedy and asked for more or tried to bargain with you."

She smiled by way of an answer.

"Raf, you were a great friend, wise, funny, and more brilliant than you ever gave yourself credit. I appreciate the sacrifice you made to save us from Cratillus, and I have missed your ebullience and understanding.

"I promised Vondro I would bring back Tsukatta if I ever got the opportunity. He loves her deeply, and her death nearly broke him. I'm sorry." I turned to the Dark Lady. "I choose Tsukatta to return."

"It is done." With a blink, Tsukatta became solid flesh.

"No," Ial'rafiost cried. "I gave my life for you. I sent Cratillus through the portal like you told me. I saved everyone. I deserve to live."

"Yes, you do, and I am sorry I could not bring you both. Please forgive me," I begged.

"This isn't fair," he screamed. "You have to save me. I don't want to be dead. Please."

Tears welled up in my eyes. "There is nothing more I can do."

Raf dropped to his knees bawling. "Please," he pleaded.

The Dark Lady raised a hand and he faded away.

"Thank you," I said through unhindered tears, "for Tsukatta's life. If it is not too much to ask, will you allow Gwenaz to be healed? She was blinded by your challenges on our journey here. Faldrein tried before but was denied."

She held out Her hand.

A librarian appeared with an orange and white book, which she placed onto the Dark Lady's hand.

"That is between her and her patron. I have not disallowed it. My debt to you is paid. Now, I want you mortals out of my realm."

The world twisted, and we were all standing before a turquoise gateway, Thessylia appearing on my shoulder.

"Tsukatta?" Glitter and Vondro said simultaneously. Brother Ironknuckle stood speechless with mouth agape. Faldrein, Hyxi, and Effay were simply happy to be free.

"We need to leave," I told the group as Tsukatta was wrapped up by three bodies. "We can celebrate back in Beus' tower." I grabbed Glitter's arm and pulled her toward the portal.

"Ow, you pinched me," she exclaimed and grabbed my hand. "My gods, what happened to your hand?"

The others suddenly noticed my fleshless hands.

"I will explain later, we must leave now. The Dark Lady has grown irked by our presence." I stepped through the portal to stand beneath the draconic archway of Aerioma'sadae'iot.

I was soon joined by the others with Vondro carrying Tsukatta in his arms, kissing her the whole time. It was good to see him happy again. He set her down so we could hold hands with our teleportation charms in our palms and return to Master Beus.

Chapter 15: Stillness

Tsukatta nearly fainted from the teleportation. After all, she had only been alive again for a few minutes and this was a new experience for her. Vondro caught her and held her tight, claiming he would never let her go again. An arrogant, idle promise, but understandable given the circumstances.

Hyxi and Effay ran ahead to check on Gwenaz, while Faldrein and Glitter stopped my advancement.

"That really has to hurt," remarked Faldrein as he grabbed my wrist. "How did this happen and how are they still working?"

I related my experience within the Chamber of Solace, concluding with, "Likely the same magic which keeps a kulda together." I shifted my gaze to see orange and blue lines connecting the bones. "Or not. This is the same energy as Acclin's artifacts."

Glitter placed my skeletal hand in hers then quickly pulled away. "They're so cold. It's like being in the cryogalt chamber again."

"I do not feel anything different aside from a dull ache when I flex," I said while stretching my fingers. I cast a simple *uvaazumak* myzling to repair the minor damage to my clothing from our journey. "I can still cast, at least, and the pain stopped while doing so." I cast the spell again on Glitter's robe. "Interesting." I was suddenly enveloped from behind by thin arms.

"Thank you for bringing me back. I wish Raf could have come too," said Tsukatta, her voice muffled by my robe.

"As do we all," I said, careful not to touch her. "He deserved to return as well."

"Once I have reconnected with Kimitsu, I will tend to your hands."

"Thank you, but I fear this is beyond healing. You are welcome to try, but this is not the time to focus on me."

Vondro stepped in front of me, placed his hands on my shoulders, and pulled me into a strong hug. "You kept your word and brought her back."

I felt a wetness on my cheek, though I was not crying.

"I owe you everything. Anything, any time." He squeezed harder.

"You could release me," I said, and my voice strained. "Your armor is pressing into me uncomfortably." Once he stepped back, I continued, "At least we now know why we could not bring her back before. Cratillus had captured her soul."

"It was strange," Tsukatta said, circling me to take Vondro's arm. "It felt like I was in a small room, but everything was blue. There was nothing to do but wait. Thank you for releasing me so quickly."

Vondro turned her and gazed deep into her eyes, tears forming as he spoke. "It was two years. I thought you were gone forever."

"Two…? No, it can't be…" Tsukatta trailed off as the pair hugged again, crying into each other's shoulders.

"From what we have seen in the Greylands, time does not seem to pass for the disembodied," I told them. "As for the blue, you were likely trapped in a sapphire. A valuable gemstone, based on rarity and structure, is necessary for the *mraykliskawa* spell, which steals and traps the souls of the victim. I thought he had merely killed you with a *zukliihilsk*."

"You're back, and that's what's important," said Glitter as she grabbed my arm. "Let them have their space," she whispered in my ear.

"We'll be inside," Faldrein announced as he raised his hand. An amulet appeared and he handed it to Tsukatta. "The others have one already. It will keep you safe while you're here."

She nodded and kissed Vondro.

"This is the first time I have seen him happy in some time without a drink in his hand," I commented as we neared the door to Beus' tower. "I wish I could have brought Ial'rafiost back as well. I will tell the story once we are all together," I added, forestalling inquiries from my fellow wizards.

"Welcome back," shouted Beus as he pulled Faldrein into an embrace. "Everything went well, I take it? Aside from Gwenaz, that is."

Our fellow wizards were all there, curious and anxious to hear the results of our trials. Goldfire wrapped Glitter in an embrace as Faldrein began telling Beus of our journey to the Dark Lady's realm when Vondro and Tsukatta walked in. Each of us added our own details up to the point when we were separated by Cratillus. Then, each was buried in their own section until Effay transformed into a vine and broke free.

"You can only bury a seed for so long," she laughed. She had dusted us all with pollen at some point—I assume from all the hugging—and summoned bees to locate us. I could not be found due to my time in the Living Library, but she did manage to locate the others shortly before the Dark Lady returned us to Aerioma's portal.

My story diverged at that point, and I told them of my meeting with Vletraka and freeing the Dark Lady from Acclin's spike. "As this was caused by a god's artifact, I doubt anyone but Him can fix my hands. Similarly, the Dark Lady told me Gwenaz's blindness is not Her doing, but that of her patron. You will have to find out why yourself," I said to the sonchia.

Gwenaz began to speak, then was silent as Stella nuzzled her ear. "Okay. I will wait," she told her fox. When her friends pressed her for answers, she said she needed to be patient and gave no further explanation.

"As Sylekhis brought eight souls to the Dark Lady for the Dread Lord, I have to assume Vletraka gathered enough librarians to free the kazkulim," I continued.

"We could summon one and ask," Faldrein suggested.

"We should give them some time first," Beus countered. "They have much to do so all the appropriate souls are gathered. With the Dark Lady free from Her imprisonment, I am certain She will restore balance."

"How was Cratillus even there?" asked Brother Ironknuckle. "I thought he and Raf died together."

"When Raf placed the extradimensional space within the other, it opened a rift into the Shadow," I answered. "They should have been lost forever, though I expect Cratillus killed Raf immediately afterward. He told me once that his Gift is never getting lost, so perhaps that led him to the Greylands."

I then related my decision to bring back Tsukatta. "There was no good way to bring you both back."

"I know," said Tsukatta ruefully. "I listened to your arguments and was trying to think of another way myself. I miss him too, but I think She would have rescinded Her offer had you tried to bargain for more." She snuggled into Vondro, oblivious to his metal armor. "I'm so happy to be back."

"This certainly calls for a celebration, then," said Nari as mugs and glasses appeared before each of us. My cup contained hot peach juice seasoned with jinzibar and nutmeg, giving the sweet liquid a warm spicy aftertaste.

"You actually spoke with the Dark Lady?" asked Beus after pulling me aside from the rest of the gathering. "I can't say I'm not jealous. What was it like to be in Her presence?"

"Terrifying, as one would expect," I answered. "She is a primal goddess who was trapped by a mortal and had to rely on another for freedom. I am as grateful that She did not punish me for Cratillus' impudence as I am for Tsukatta's return. There is so much about the Grand Mausoleum which I must put in writing before it is forgotten and left to the storytellers to mishandle."

"We don't always 'mishandle' stories," Farandi interrupted. "We just make them more interesting." She laughed. "I will tell our tale regardless, so you better give me the details, so I don't have to make them up."

"I promise. After it is written, first."

Farandi began to plead when Effay grabbed her arm and pulled her into an embrace, giving me the opportunity to step aside toward Glitter.

"What did Nari conjure for you?" I asked Glitter, her eyes matching mine. It was one of the few times I remember them being a standard color for humans.

"Strawberry wine," she said, offering me a sip while sniffing my cup. "Don't worry, I'm pretty sure there's no alcohol in it. Spiced peach?"

I nodded as we tasted each other's drinks. Hers did taste mildly of spirits, but not enough to be offensive.

"So, what are we going to do about these?" Glitter asked as she grabbed my wrist.

"If they cannot be healed, then I might need to wear gloves, at least around others. If the local villagers distrust wizards already, this will ensure they never speak to me again," I said with a wry smile.

"And the rest of you feels alive?"

"I think so. I am breathing. I can feel my heart beating." I shifted my sight to see the living and unliving and shook my head. "My hands are that of the undead, but my life force glows through the rest of me." I looked around the room. "Aside from Beus and Faldrein, I seem to have the brightest shine. Those months studying lessons from *Inner Light* have certainly made a difference. No doubt Tsukatta will dazzle once she has had some time to meditate."

Glitter choked on her drink. "Months? How were you gone for months? Effay found us after a day or two at most."

"Time is different in the Living Library," I shrugged. "I am grateful for the time to study a tome I would not otherwise have access to, and I am glad I was not gone so long as to worry you. When Mistress Vletraka left and returned, she said she was only gone a few minutes. I do not know how time passed in the other chambers."

"How did you survive? I can't imagine the dead have food or drink."

I paused. "I do not recall eating, drinking, or even sleeping. The magic of the place must have sustained me."

"I wish I was there with you. You said every book ever written was stored there? It must have been difficult to leave."

"It was. I actually could not until Vletraka opened the door. I tried to search for everyone, but I was trapped in paradise without you, so I made the best use of my time."

Glitter wrapped me in a tight embrace, kissing my mouth.

I hugged her back without using my hands, returning her kiss—I think. We had kissed before, but never one so long and enduring. I never knew if I was doing it correctly. The images of her burning away were still there, as expected, but were not as affecting as they had been. *I am getting used to seeing her suffering. I do not know how to feel about that.*

"Are you certain this is what you want?" I asked her after she pulled back. "I love you, but my limitations continue to mount." I frowned, holding up my desiccated hand.

"You are a good, sweet man. Every time I push you away, you stand at my side with patient compassion. Anyone else would have given up on me by now. How could I not love you?"

"Is that enough? I still have to control my heart to avoid your pain, and now I cannot even hold your hand. I will always care for you and I will always desire your friendship, but I think it is a mistake to tie your heart with mine. You deserve more than I can give."

A tear formed in her ice-blue eye as she smiled. "You always have my best interests at heart. This is why I love you. We have some challenges to face, and I am not perfect either, but we are better together. I wouldn't want anyone else." She kissed me again and our joyful tears melded.

The rest of that evening passed in a blur. There were conversations and stories shared, which I paid little attention to as I could only think of Glitter. Aside from holding a drink or eating, I kept my hands tucked into my sleeves to avoid the stares of my colleagues and for fear of touching anyone. By night's end, I had managed to tear a number of holes in my robe before Nari manufactured thick leather gloves via *buvliboj* for me.

Wearied by the day's events, we went upstairs to Beus' guest rooms. When I kissed Glitter goodnight, she pulled me into her chambers before I could go to my room. We spent the night talking and cuddled on her bed, which was too small for two people to sleep comfortably without staying close. Such contentment would not occur often in my life, and I will forever think fondly of that night of peace and ease in pink and violet light.

Nor will I ever forget the next morning.

When I awakened, my arm had gone numb from Glitter's head pressing on my shoulder. I slid my arm out from under her with care so as not to wake her. I stood and shook my arm to get feeling back into my limb. While doing so, I saw my bare bony hand free from the glove. Apparently, the glove had rotted away during the night where it touched the bones, and fragments remained around my wrist.

I looked over to Glitter and saw her eyes were open in a look of shock. "Sorry, I tried not to wake you," I told her to no response. "Are you alright?" She did not even blink. "Glitter?" I asked again, a little more loudly without answer. I shifted my sight to make certain she still lived, and then informed her I would return with help.

I ran to find Beus. He answered after nearly half-a-minute of pounding on his door.

"What's wrong?" he asked, fixing the clasps on his robe. Nari was dressing behind him.

"Glitter is not moving. I need your assistance." I turned away and ran back to her room while he asked for details. I held up my denuded hand and waved him to follow.

"What's happening?" asked Effay, who had poked her head out of her room as I passed.

"I think Glitter is paralyzed," I said through clenched teeth while holding back tears of anger and frustration without slowing.

She followed after Beus with Nari close behind.

When I returned to Glitter's chamber, I saw to my regret that she still had not moved.

Beus entered and examined first her aura then mine. "I was afraid of this. She's safe. You can fix this."

"What do I need to do?" I asked, fear and relief vying for dominance in my voice.

"Center your life force into your hand, like when you are using it to damage the undead. Then touch her," he said with a calmness which helped me focus.

Having mastered the technique, it only took seconds for me to shift my vrada. Unexpectedly, my hand then ignited in purple flames. I screamed in both pain and surprise and the flames died out.

"Again," he commanded.

I gritted through the pain when my hand reignited and then placed it on Glitter's shoulder. She immediately jumped back away from me.

"Are you all right?" I asked her.

"I-I think so," she stammered, drops of fear filling her eyes.

I turned to Beus. "How did you know how to fix this?"

"Your auras were connected through your hand. I didn't know if it would work, and I know a spell which would if it came to it, but I thought if you could reverse it, then you needed to know how."

"I am so sorry," I said to Glitter while tucking my hands into my sleeves.

"That's okay." Her pale yellow and blue sparkles showed her fear, though she hid it in her voice. "You didn't know."

"Since you're up, let's get you some breakfast," said Effay. She gently pulled Glitter out of bed and directed her out the door, shooting a concerned look to me as they left.

I sat on the empty bed and stared at my hands.

"You are going to be nothing but trouble," I said to them. Anger and fear were blending into depression. "What am I going to do?" I asked Beus and Nari.

"Give us some time to work on it," suggested Nari. "This is new to all of us." They whispered as they closed the door, leaving me alone in Glitter's chamber. The only word I made out was 'jozalk'.

Appendix I

Book List

Abominations: Creating New Creatures from Old by Pumliov

Accentuating the Positive: A Study of Divine Channeling and Its Arcane Equivalent by Falleoraeli Zolthliam

Buried Secrets: A Compendium of Fabled Artifacts and their Disappearance from History by Rujin Steeplish

Conversations with Miz'zrak the Scourge by Yivnia Foltzro

The Dirges of Calnerion

Fluttering Tapestry: What Picture Does the Weave Portray? by Almeond Sunnythrush

A History of Enchanted Weapons and the Warriors Who Wielded Them by Voorsha "Songhammer" Thurssif

In Between: On the Transition from Life to Death to Life

In Pieces and In Whole by Brosqua

In Shadow's Embrace by Tinnetol Omyuf

Inner Light by Zalgovathi

The Life of the Soul by Raithehuen

Metaphysical Immortality by Spaqua'aloinu

Secondaries: A Guide to the Handmaidens and Generals of the Gods written by Yasky Huftici.

Skin Twisting: A Study of Distortion Through Flesh Manipulation of the Self and Others by Cogrist Ojo

Tongue of Stone by Urvanu

The Trials of Nuviellu by Troskin

Without A Whisper by Geimoll Ovicht

The Wizard's Cudgel: Creating Staves for Combat and Mystic Supplementation by Fotroc

Appendix II

Draconic

Although its influence is still strong in many modern languages, Draconic is generally lost as a spoken language, save for wizards, a few scholars, and of course, dragons themselves. All magical runes and words stem directly from Draconic, and it is theorized that both dragons and the Weave came into existence together, or that one led directly to the other. Even the eldest of dragons do not have the answer, or are unwilling to share this secret with lesser beings. As Draconic has been used extensively throughout this work, it seems prudent to give a short primer on the language.

Rules:

• The letters c, f, g, n, p, q, and x are not part of Draconic, as these sounds are either difficult for dragons to enunciate, or their sounds are represented by other letters or combinations of letters.

• 'y' is always pronounced as a hard consonant, as in 'you' and 'yet'.

• 'yt' at the end of a word denotes plurality.

• All letters are pronounced. There are no silent letters in Draconic, nor any dipthongs.

• A single vowel has the short sound (e.g. hat, bin); a double vowel is pronounced long (e.g. seen). The Draconic word for 'light' is *juut*, which is pronounced 'jute'.

• The only vowels to start a word are 'a' and 'u', except as follows:

o   'i' begins a word to show possession.

o   'em' at the beginning of a word indicates one who uses or does something. For example, *aji* is the word for magic, and *emaji* is the word for wizard.

o   'oo' at the beginning of a word denotes femininity, where applicable and necessary, while 'o' denotes masculinity. Otherwise, nouns are essentially neutral. For example, 'vrii' can be either a masculine or feminine god, 'oovrii' denotes a goddess, and 'ovriiyt' is a number of masculine gods.

o   Many creatures have existed since the time of dragons, and though the names have been altered over time, many are spelled and pronounced based on the ancient Draconic ones with Umani influences, typically the double-vowel to show plurality. For example, a single vulzu (vul-zŭ) and a pair of vulzuu (vul-zū), or a yomki (yom-kĭ) and many yomkii (yom-kī)

Draconic	**Umani**
aasl	fly
aaslska	float
aatok	claw
abyil	cloud
aji	magic
akt	water
aktwa	blood
alsk	ray
arih	globe/sphere
avrim	cavern
avul	iron
avulaatok	sword
avulhysayt	armor
bezyaam	great/major
bezyaamyuv	explosion
bezyam	large
biiz	silver
bimzilt	resistance
bokvi	bundle/group
bokwa	crowd/group
bolmos	burst
bul	rune/symbol
bulhysa	ward
buvli	conjure
daama	curse
dee	fake/false

dimt	pull
dmalv	bag/sack
dmuu	share
dmuuvad	kiss
dov	wood
dovkaz	house
dovlek	lance/spear
dovwa	tree
drase	quiet/silent
droob	body
dubom	prism
dubomyt	colors
dulaa	bone
dyk	plane
emaji	wizard
embul	read
emmrayk	thief
emtzizi	warrior
hi	ask
hilsk	line
hivli	summon
hraakiid	begin
hruk	servant
huuhb	poison
hyhy	defend
hysa	scale
ikaaskiil	messenger

jejleem	tentacle
juut	light
kaaskiil	message
kaek	cube
kaz	cave
khuuma	human
klivev	frost
koomba	reflect
lek	shard
lial	far/away
liska	hold/trap
looskim	darkness
mak	heal
mbik	talk
mevzem	area/space
mim-	non-/un-
mimzel	invisible
mlur	mind
mlarliska	charm/enchant
mlok	head
mrayk	steal
mrik	neck
raazt	injury/wound
rih	circle
rihboj	disk/ring
root	rope
roziit	comfort

seedu	shake/shiver
ska	stop
skamiiv	enough
skialosk	acid
sklid	lock
sree	joy
srukak	fire
tiimu	breath
tlum	stone
traa	appear
tre	feel
trezel	detect/perceive
tzi	attack
tzizi	fight
ubrel	aura
uku	crystal
uldrak	dragon
ulk	push
ulv	zyla
umak	repair
umslykt	compel/force
umslyktwa	kill
uose	horse
usu	fast
uuaa	excrement
uuom	thunder
uvaaz	minor
uvaazkaek	memory

uvaz	little
uvla	sleep
uzk	dirt/earth
uzul	tooth
vad	touch
vezivi	lightning
vli	elsewhere
vlivriiwa	dream
vlok	move
vlokwa	animate
vrii	god
vriijuut	sun
vriiwa	life
vrokt	fill
vul	eat
wa	soul/spirit
wulmiiv	block/barrier
yelk	wall
yuf	fear
yuv	break
yuvam	disrupt
yuvii	dispel
yuvjuut	shadow
zel	see
zukla	dead
zuklii	death
zumul	negative energy

zuuv   give/bestow

Appendix III

Glitter's Recipes

Glitter has done all she can to teach me how to prepare better foods, in part because she enjoys cooking and partially because she believes that I cannot care for myself. To be fair, she may be right in this regard. Such wisdom should not be kept hidden, so I have included her teachings so that others may enjoy her culinary talent.

<u>Author's Note</u> The following have been updated for modern cooking, as access to fantasy ingredients and wood-burning ovens are likely limited. For these recipes, an equal amount of sugar can replace the honey, though the latter adds a richer flavor than processed sugar.

Kohlrabi fries

Ingredients:

2 whole kohlrabies
1 tsp olive oil
½ tsp garlic powder
½ tsp paprika (or ancho chili powder if you want it spicier)
½ tsp salt
½ tsp pepper
1 Tbsp grated Parmesan cheese
1 Tbsp chopped parsley (dried is fine)

Preheat oven to 425°F.

Remove leaves and bottom of kohlrabies, then halve and core. Cut into thin wedges or strips and place in bowl. Drizzle with olive oil, and sprinkle garlic powder, chili powder (or paprika), salt, and pepper, mixing until coated.

Spread fried in an even layer on baking sheet and bake 25-30 minutes, turning halfway. Sprinkle with Parmesan and chopped parsley.

Buttered pork loin

Ingredients:

1 whole pork (or beef) tenderloin
2 sticks butter
3 Tbsp salt
3 Tbsp pepper
3 Tbsp rosemary
2 Tbsp honey

Place tenderloin in heavy foil roasting pan and coat with seasonings. Put butter in pan and place on grill, shifting the meat over the butter as it melts. Turn over every 8-10 minutes until meat browns and reaches at least 145°F internal temperature. If butter cooks away, add more.

Transfer tenderloin to cutting board and rest for 10 minutes before slicing. While meat is resting, add honey to melted butter and combine. For a thicker sauce, add two tablespoons of flour.

If using a beef tenderloin instead, remove meat from grill when temperature reaches 125-130°F.

Potatoes au gratin with fennel

Ingredients:

2 to 2-1/2 lbs. potatoes (preferably gold)
2 Tbsp butter
1 small onion, thinly sliced
2 small fennel bulbs
2 cloves garlic, minced
1 Tbsp fresh parsley, chopped
2 Tbsp flour
¼ tsp pepper
1-1/2 cups milk
1 cup shredded sharp cheddar cheese
Salt and pepper

Peel potatoes and thinly slice. Rinse and cover with water, then boil for two minutes. Drain and rinse with cold water to stop cooking.

Remove stalks from fennel and cut bulbs lengthwise. Remove cores and thinly slice crosswise. Melt butter in saucepan and add onions and fennel, sauté until tender, then add garlic, and parsley. Stir in flour and pepper until smooth. Gradually add milk, cooking and stirring over medium-low heat until thickened. Add cheese and stir until melted and sauce is smooth.

Heat oven to 350°F.

Arrange sliced potatoes in 2 to 2-1/2 quart casserole dish, sprinkling each layer with salt and pepper to taste. Pour sauce evenly over potatoes. Cover dish and cook for 40-50 minutes until potatoes are tender.

Lemon and nut sweet rolls

Brioche dough:

4-1/2 tsp active dry yeast (2 packets)
1/3 cup warm water (110-115°F)
1/3 cup warm whole milk
3-3/4 cup flour
2 tsp salt
3 large eggs, room temperature
¼ cup sugar or light honey
3 sticks unsalted butter, room temperature

Place yeast, water and milk in standing mixer bowl and stir with a wooden spoon until yest has dissolved. Add flour and salt, then mix with dough hook at low speed until flour begins to incorporate to avoid a mess. Increase speed to medium-low until flour is moistened into a shaggy mass.

Scrape sides and bottom of bowl with a rubber spatula. Set mixer to low and add eggs, then sugar/honey. Increase speed to medium and beat about three minutes until dough forms into a ball. Reduce speed to low and add butter in 2 Tbsp chunks, beating until nearly incorporated before adding next piece. The dough will be soft and batter-like. Increase speed to medium-high until dough pulls away from the sides of the bowl; about ten minutes. If dough clumps around hook, scrape with rubber spatula and continue until uniform.

Transfer dough to clean bowl, cover with plastic wrap, and leave at room temperature until doubled, about 40-60 minutes. Deflate by lifting dough around the edges and letting it fall back in.

Cover bowl again and refrigerate, slapping dough every thirty minutes until it stops rising, about two hours. Leave covered dough in refrigerator overnight.

Use half the dough for the sweet roll recipe. Either freeze remaining half, or make two cylinders of rolls, freezing the second for later. Do not be tempted to make a half-recipe of dough, as the larger recipe makes better dough.

For filling:
1/3 cup unsalted butter, melted and mostly cooled
½ cup fine honey
Juice and finely grated rind of two large lemons
Optional: 3/4 cup pecans, finely chopped, or other nuts if you prefer (almonds work well)
Stir the butter, honey, lemon juice, and lemon rind together. Generously butter a 9" X 13 X 2" glass casserole dish.
On a flour-dusted surface, roll chilled dough into a 16" square. Using fingers or pastry brush, spread filling over the dough, leaving a 1" strip bare on the side furthest from you. Sprinkle with nuts if using. Tightly roll dough into a cylinder away from you toward the bare dough. At this point, the dough can be wrapped and frozen for up to two months for future use. If frozen, defrost in refrigerator overnight.
Using a gentle sawing motion, trim away edges of cylinder if ragged and not well-filled. Start with a center cut and divide in halves until you have 16 1" thick buns. Fit them into the casserole dish, leaving space between them.

Lightly cover pan with waxed paper and set in warm place to allow buns to double in size, about 1 hour and 45 minutes. They should be soft, puffy, and likely touching.
When nearly fully risen, preheat oven to 375°F. Remove wax paper and bake on center rack for about 30 minutes or until puffed and golden.
While the rolls bake, make glaze.
Glaze:
1 cup sifted confectioner's sugar
1 Tablespoon milk
1 teaspoon pure vanilla extract
a tiny sprinkle of salt.

Combine in a small bowl and drizzle over warm rolls.

Cinnamon lime biscuits

Ingredients:

2 cups flour
1 Tbsp baking powder
2 tsp honey
½ tsp salt
¼ tsp ground cinnamon
¼ cup (half stick) cold butter
1 cup milk
1 lime
Melted butter (about 1 Tbsp)

Preheat oven to 450°F. Grease baking sheet.

In a bowl, combine dry ingredients, zest lime, and cut in butter until crumbly. Add honey, juice from half the lime (about 2 Tbsp), and milk. Drop balls of dough, about ¼ cup, onto baking sheet; moisten fingers for smoother biscuits. Brush with melted butter and sprinkle with more cinnamon. Bake for 12-14 minutes or until lightly browned. Serve warm.

Makes about 15 biscuits.

Meat pies

Pastry dough:

¾ tsp. kosher salt
1⅓ cups (180 g) all-purpose flour, plus more for surface
¾ cup (1½ sticks) chilled unsalted butter
4 Tbsp ice water

Combine flour and salt in medium bowl (you can also add 1-1/2 tsp sugar for a slightly sweeter dough). Cut butter into long rectangular pieces and toss with flour mixture. Pour out onto work surface and use rolling pin to flatten. Scrape off rolling pin and/or work surface as needed until you have long strips of dough.

Gather dough into a pile with scraper and drizzle water. Fold water into dough with hands and scraper until distributed, then gather into pile. Roll into long rectangle, then fold into thirds. Dough will be crumbly at first but will come together when worked. Turn 90° and repeat twice more. If dough does not hold together, then roll it out again. It should look creamy overall though still shaggy at the ends.

Wrap folded dough in plastic, press into 1" thick disk, then refrigerate for 30 minutes.

Meat filling:
2 lbs. beef chuck, diced
½ cup flour
3 Tbsp olive oil
2 onions, thinly sliced
2 cloves garlic, minced

½ tsp thyme
½ tsp dried mustard
¼ tsp ground cloves
¼ tsp black pepper
1 tsp salt
¼ tsp sage
4 Tbsp tomato paste
1 cup red wine
1 qt. beef stock
1 Tbsp Worcestershire
2 Tbsp corn starch
4 Tbsp water
1 egg

Toss beef in flour to coat. Heat oil in large pot, then add meat, cooking over high heat until browned. Remove meat, then add garlic, onion, and spices until onions are soft. Add beef, tomato paste, wine, stock, and Worcestershire.

Reduce heat to low and simmer for about two hours, stirring occasionally, until beef is tender. Whisk water and corn starch until smooth, then add to pot, blending until incorporated. Continue simmering until thickened.

Preheat oven to 400°F. Butter a 9" pie plate. Roll out slightly more than half the dough and put in plate, leaving extra to hang over the edge. Poke holes with a fork. Fill crust with meat mixture, leveling with knife or spatula. Roll out second half of dough. Moisten edges of pie crust, and top with remaining dough. Press down to remove air, then pinch edges together to seal. Whisk egg and brush over top, then slit top to allow steam to vent.

Bake for 10 minutes, then reduce heat to 350°F. Bake for additional 15 minutes or until crust is golden brown.

Griddle cakes

Ingredients:

3 cups flour
3 tsp baking powder
1-1/2 tsp baking soda
¾ tsp salt
3 cups buttermilk
3 Tbsp honey
½ cup milk
3 eggs
1/3 cup butter, melted

Combine dry ingredients in large bowl and wet in separate bowl. Heat griddle and butter lightly. Pour wet mixture over dry ingredients, blending with wooden spoon or fork until just combined. Pour or scoop ½ cup batter onto griddle for each pancake. Brown both sides.

Feel free to add small berries or chopped fruit to mix or sprinkled on cooking cakes.

Serve with butter, syrup, fresh fruit, or fruit compote.

Oat balls

Ingredients:

1 cup oats
1 cup dried fruit (raisins, cranberries, apricots, etc.)
½ cup peanut butter (or other nut butter, such as sunflower, cashew, or almond)
1/3 cup honey
Dash cinnamon, glove, and/or ginger

Chop larger dried fruits. Combine all ingredients in small bowl. Roll into balls.

Chilling for 30 minutes helps to firm mixture and is easier to roll.

David F. Balog was born, raised, and still lives in the Greater Cleveland area with his cat. He grew up in the libraries of Lakewood and Parma, and his babysitters were the creatures of the Cleveland Aquarium; he had a special fondness for the giant octopus. Ever inquisitive, he dove deeply into science, paranormal studies, mathematics, and mythology at an early age, and never let go of the idea that they, and other studies, were all tightly connected.

His fascination with fables and mythology led him first to Dungeons & Dragons, then other role-playing games. Here, he learned to hone his talent for character creation, world building, and storytelling, more so as individual games extended into long campaigns. Over time, basic concepts became fully realized, and months and years spent focused on a single character gave time for them to develop depth.

An avid reader, particularly, but certainly not limited to, science and science fiction, David always sought to learn more about the world. In his youth, he went to the Gifted Challenge Institute, essentially a summer camp for knowledge set on campus at local colleges, where he studied mathematics, biology, and physics far above his grade level. This had the unfortunate side-effect of putting him off traditional academia for a time, as regular classes were not available at his age to continue with his accelerated learning, causing his grades to slide from boredom.

Years later, he would attend Cuyahoga Community College, Ursuline College, and Cleveland State University, eventually earning a Bachelors' Degree in both History and Social Studies, and a Master's Degree in History. All through his studies, he continued to focus on the theology, mythology, and fables and how they connected societies throughout time and regions. Though the stories and characters change, the underlying truths always remain the same: primarily, the constant striving of individuals to become better people.

At long last, it fell on David to contribute his own stories and mythologies to the public consciousness. With the experience of developing characters and worlds combined with writing numerous research papers, David began work on his first novel: Necromancer's Lament, the first in a planned trilogy.

www.ingramcontent.com/pod-product-compliance
Lightning Source LLC
Chambersburg PA
CBHW030109310726
48970CB00004B/1205